R. Barri Flowers is an award-winning crime, thriller, mystery, and romance fiction featuring three-dimensional protagonists, riveting plots, unexpected twists and turns, and heart-pounding climaxes. With an expertise in true crime, serial killers, and characterising dangerous offenders, he is perfectly suited for the Mills & Boon Heroes series. Chemistry and conflict between the hero and heroine, attention to detail, and incorporating the very latest advances in criminal investigations are the cornerstones of his romantic suspense fiction. Discover more on popular social networks and Wikipedia.

Rachel Astor is equal parts country girl and city dweller who spends an alarming amount of time correcting the word 'the'. Rachel has had a lot of jobs (bookseller, real estate agent, 834 assorted admin roles), but none as, *ahem*, interesting as when she waitressed at a bar named after a dog. She is now a *USA Today* bestselling author who splits her time between the city, the lake, and as many made-up worlds as possible.

Also by R. Barri Flowers

The Lynleys of Law Enforcement
Special Agent Witness
Christmas Lights Killer

Hawaii CI
The Big Island Killer
Captured on Kauai
Honolulu Cold Homicide
Danger on Maui

Chasing the Violet Killer

Discover more at millsandboon.co.uk

MURDER IN THE BLUE RIDGE MOUNTAINS

R. BARRI FLOWERS

THE SUSPECT NEXT DOOR

RACHEL ASTOR

MILLS & BOON

First Published in Great Britain 2024
by Mills & Boon, an imprint of HarperCollins*Publishers* Ltd
1 London Bridge Street, London, SE1 9GF

www.harpercollins.co.uk

HarperCollins*Publishers*
Macken House, 39/40 Mayor Street Upper,
Dublin 1, D01 C9W8, Ireland

Murder in the Blue Ridge Mountains © 2024 R. Barri Flowers
The Suspect Next Door © 2024 Rachel Astor

ISBN: 978-0-263-32219-4

0224

This book contains FSC™ certified paper and other controlled sources to ensure responsible forest management.

For more information visit: www.harpercollins.co.uk/green

Printed and Bound in the UK using 100% Renewable Electricity at CPI Group (UK) Ltd, Croydon, CR0 4YY

MURDER IN
THE BLUE RIDGE
MOUNTAINS

R. BARRI FLOWERS

To H. Loraine, the love of my life and best friend, whose support has been unwavering through the many wonderful years together. To my dear mother, Marjah Aljean, who gave me the tools to pursue my passions in life, including writing fiction for publication; and for my loving sister, Jacquelyn, who helped me become the person I am today, along the way. To the loyal fans of my romance, mystery, suspense, and thriller fiction published over the years. Lastly, a nod goes out to my wonderful editors, Allison Lyons and Denise Zaza, for the great opportunity to lend my literary voice and creative spirit to the successful Heroes series.

Prologue

Jessica Sneed was a proud member of the Eastern Band of Cherokee Indians, a tribe based in North Carolina. But she was even prouder of being the mother to a rambunctious little dark-haired boy named Garrett. Being a single parent at age twenty-five was anything but easy. Had it been up to her, she would be happily wed with a strong marriage foundation and Garrett would have both parents to dote on him. That wasn't the case, though, as his father, Andrew Crowe, wasn't much interested in being a husband. Much less a dad. Besieged with alcohol-related issues and a self-centered attitude, he'd left the state two years ago, abandoning her, forcing Jessica to go it alone in taking care of her then three-year-old son. Well, maybe not entirely alone, as her parents, Trevor and Dinah Sneed, did their best to help out whenever they could.

Shamelessly, Jessica took full advantage of the precious little time she had to herself, such as this sunny afternoon when she got to hike in the Blue Ridge Mountains. She loved being in touch with nature and giving back to the land her forefathers had once roamed freely, through retracing their footsteps in paying her respects. She made sure that

Garrett, whom she'd given her family surname, was aware of his rich heritage as well. They spent some time in the mountains and forest together when he wasn't in school.

But today, it's just me, Jessica told herself as she ran a hand down the length of her waist-long black hair, worn in a bouffant ponytail. She was wearing tennis shoes along with a T-shirt and cuffed denim shorts on the warm August day as she trekked across the hiking trail on the Blue Ridge Parkway, the hundreds-of-miles-long scenic roadway that meandered through the mountains. She stopped for a moment to enjoy some shade beneath the Raven Rocks Overlook and took a bottle of water from her backpack.

After opening it, Jessica drank half the bottle and returned it to the backpack. She was about to get on her way when she heard a sound. She wondered if it might be coming from wildlife, such as a chipmunk or red squirrel. She had even noticed wild turkey and white-tailed deer roaming around. Humans had to adapt more than the other way around. Some did. Others chose not to.

She heard another noise coming from the woods, this one heavier. Suddenly feeling concerned that it could mean danger, Jessica headed back in the direction from which she'd come.

But the sounds grew louder, echoing all around her, and seemed to be getting closer and closer. Was it a wild animal that had targeted her? Perhaps rabid and ravenous? Should she make a run for it? Or stay still and pray that the threat would leave her alone? As she grappled with these thoughts, Jessica dared to glance over her shoulder at the potential menace. It was not an animal predator. But a human one. It was a man. He was dark haired, with ominous even-darker eyes and a scowl on his face. In one large hand was a long-bladed knife.

Her heart racing like crazy, Jessica turned away from him to run but pivoted so quickly that she lost her balance and the backpack slipped from her shoulders. She fell flat onto the dirt pathway, hitting her head hard against it. Seeing stars, she tried to clear her brain and, at the same time, get up. Before she could, she felt the knife plunge deep into her back. The pain was excruciating. But it got much worse as he stabbed her again and again, till the pain seemed to leave her body, along with the will to live. What hurt even more was not getting to say goodbye to her son. She silently asked Garrett for forgiveness in not being around for him before complete darkness and a strange peace hit Jessica all at once.

HE TOOK A moment to study the lifeless body on the ground before him. Killing her had been even more gratifying than he had imagined in his wildest dreams. He recalled his mother once telling him as a child that he was messed up in the head. The memory made him want to laugh. Yes, she'd been right. He had to agree that he wasn't all there where it concerned being good and bad, much more preferring the latter over the former. His sorry excuse of a mother had found out firsthand that getting on his bad side came with dire consequences. Too bad for her that he'd put her out of her misery and made sure no one ever caught on that he'd been responsible for her untimely death.

His eyes gazed upon the corpse again. How lucky for him that she'd happened upon his sight at just the right place and time when the desire to kill had struck his fancy.

It had been almost too perfect. A pretty lamb had come to him for her slaughter. He wondered what had been going through her head as she'd lain dying, a knife wedged deep inside her back. Maybe it had only been his imagination, but there had almost seemed to be a ray of light in her big brown eyes before they'd shut for good, as though she'd been seeing something or someone out of his reach.

He grabbed the knife with his gloved hand and flung it into the flowering shrubs. There were plenty more where that had come from. And he intended to make good use of them. Too bad for the next one to feel the sting of his sharp blade. But that wasn't his concern. A man had to do what a man had to do. And nothing and no one would stop him.

He grinned crookedly and walked away from the dead woman, soon disappearing into the woods, where he would slip back into his normal life. Before the time came for a repeat performance.

Chapter One

Thirty years later, Law Enforcement Ranger Madison Lynley drove her Chevrolet Tahoe Special Service Vehicle along the Blue Ridge Parkway in the Pisgah Ranger District of Pisgah National Forest, where she was stationed in North Carolina. It was a gorgeous span of nearly five hundred miles of scenery that ran through the Blue Ridge Mountains.

She had been employed as a law enforcement ranger with the National Park Service for the past eight years, or since she'd been twenty-seven, after completing four months of basic training. Along with receiving her bachelor's degree in natural resource ecology and management and a master's degree in environmental science from Oklahoma State University. In the process, she had chosen to go in a different direction than her brothers, Scott and Russell, who were both FBI special agents, as well as their adopted younger sister, Annette, who was a sheriff's department detective. All of them had followed in the footsteps of their parents, Taylor and Caroline Lynley, with long careers in law enforcement. Their father had been a chief of police with the Oklahoma City Police Department, while her mother had once been an Oklahoma County District Court criminal judge.

The fact that both were now deceased pained Madison, as they'd been the rocks of the family, leaving it to their children to carry on without them. All seemed more than committed to doing just that, remaining fairly close, in spite of each going their separate ways in adulthood as they navigated their lives, careers and other interests.

In full uniform on a slender five-eight frame, Madison continued to drive. She admired the forest—rich in chestnut oak, birch and buckeye trees—on this late summer day. As one of only a relatively small number of rangers patrolling the more than eighty thousand acres of land along the parkway, she never tired of this, loving the freedom and appreciation of nature and wildlife the job provided. Beyond patrolling the park in her vehicle, she had also ridden on bicycles, snowmobiles, ATVs, boats and even horses in the course of the job. She had participated in search-and-rescue missions, dealt with car accidents, wildfires and dangerous or wounded animals, you name it.

Then there was the criminal activity, such as illicit drug use, drug dealing and occasional crimes of violence that forced Madison into the law enforcement part of being a ranger. She was equipped with a Sig Sauer P320 semiautomatic pistol in her duty holster, should she need it when having to deal with hostile and dangerous park visitors.

Thank goodness I've never had to shoot anyone yet, she thought, while knowing there was always a first time for everything.

Madison's mind turned to her love life. Or lack thereof. She was now thirty-five years old, nearly thirty-six, and still very much single. She couldn't even remember the last time she had gone out on a real date. Actually, she could. It was two years ago when she'd been dating Garrett Sneed, a handsome Cherokee special agent with the National Park Service Investigative Services Branch. For a few months there, they'd been hot and heavy and had appeared headed for bigger and better things. And then, just like that, it had been over, as though it had never begun.

She couldn't really put a finger on why they'd broken up. Only that neither had seemed ready to make a real commitment to each other and the opportunity to fix things that had gone unsaid or undone had slipped through the cracks. Before she could even think about trying to get back together, Garrett had gotten a transfer to another region, as though he couldn't leave soon enough. They'd lost touch from that point on, leaving Madison to wonder about what might have been if they had tried harder.

When she got a call over the radio, Madison snapped out of the reverie and responded. It was her boss, Tom Hutchison.

"Hey," he spoke in a tense voice, "we just got a report of a dead woman discovered by a hiker along the Blue Ridge Parkway."

"Hmm…not a great way to start the day," Madison muttered, never wanting to hear that a life had been lost, whatever the circumstances. "Are we talking about an accident, suicide, animal attack or…?"

"Could be any of the above." Hutchison was vague. "Check it out and make your own assessment. We'll go from there."

"I'm on my way," she said tersely, after being given the location.

As was the case any time she had to deal with a death,

all types of things went through Madison's head. Who was the victim, and why had the person been at the park? Was this something that could have been prevented, such as the taking of one's own life? Or was it the result of actions beyond the control of the deceased, such as an encounter with a black bear? Or a human predator.

Bad news no matter what, Madison told herself frankly. She would soon get some clarity, as she parked her car and was met by an anxious-looking African American woman in her fifties, with curly black crochet braids and hiking attire.

"I'm Ranger Lynley," Madison said. "And you are?"

"Loretta Redmond."

"You found a body?"

"Yeah. While I was hiking, though I nearly missed seeing her where the body was located. I could tell she was dead." Loretta took a deep breath and shook her head in dismay. "I still can't believe it."

Madison understood, as seeing a corpse outside of a funeral setting was something that was hard to forget for most people. "Can you take me to her?"

She followed Loretta through a wooded area and down a steep embankment, asking, "Did you see anyone else coming or going?"

"No one," Loretta replied without hesitation.

"Okay." Madison was thoughtful as they reached a spot off a trail that was overgrown, where there lay the body of a tall and slim female. She was lying flat on her stomach, wearing a purple-colored sports bra, printed blue running shorts, and white tennis shoes. Blood spilled onto the dirt from several gashes in her back, neck and elsewhere that Madison speculated had come from a long knife. She glanced at the thirtysomething victim's short red hair in a pixie cut with tapering sideburns.

Only then did a sense of familiarity hit Madison like a hard smack in the face. Upon closer inspection of the person's discolored round face that was turned awkwardly to one side, her lids shut, Madison realized with shock that she was looking at her friend and neighbor Olivia Forlani, a brown-eyed attorney from the nearby town of Kiki's Ridge. Both loved to jog and just yesterday had met up on Madison's day off for a run on the popular trail at Pisgah National Forest.

As though sensing her troubled expression, Loretta said, "You look like you've seen a ghost."

Madison swallowed thickly in turning away from Olivia's body. "Worse than that," she remarked, maudlin. "There's nothing supernatural about what's happened here. It's very real. Someone killed her."

Which left Madison wondering who would have done such a horrible thing to her friend. It would be left largely up to the NPS Investigative Services Branch to figure that out. She would need to phone this in and have them get a criminal investigator out there right away, while wondering who would do the honors with Garrett now working on the other side of the country.

All things considered, she believed that was probably for the best as neither of them needed distractions, and her friend's death as a near certain victim of homicide would be the top priority of the ISB agent sent.

"A WOMAN HAS reportedly been stabbed to death on the Blue Ridge Parkway," Carly Tafoya, the recently appointed director of the South Atlantic-Gulf Region of the National Park Service Investigative Services Branch, said glumly.

ISB Special Agent Garrett Sneed cocked a thick brow as the shocking news registered while they stood in his midsize, sparsely furnished office in Region 2, in Atlanta, Georgia, where he was stationed. His sable eyes gazed at the petite green-eyed director who was ten years older than his age of thirty-six but looked younger. She had short brunette hair in an A-line cut and wore a brown pantsuit with black pumps.

"That's terrible," he uttered candidly.

"Tell me about it." She rolled her eyes. "This isn't the way we want to greet visitors to the park. Not by a long shot."

Garrett couldn't have agreed more, as he towered over her at six feet, two and a half inches on a muscular frame. "Who called it in?" he wondered, knowing this was ranger territory.

"Law Enforcement Ranger Madison Lynley," the director replied.

Garrett reacted to this revelation, though having guessed that his ex-girlfriend would be at the center of the investigation, whether he wanted it or not, with the strained history between them. Some things in life simply couldn't be helped.

"Ranger Lynley," he said equably. "We worked together when I was with the region previously."

"Makes sense." Carly nodded. "Apparently a hiker spotted the victim and reported it."

Garrett pinched his nose. "What about the perpetrator?"

"Still on the loose, unfortunately." She frowned. "I'm assigning you this case, Sneed," she told him without preface.

"Should be right up your alley. Especially after you recently cracked the Melissa Lafferty case."

He thought briefly about the missing person investigation at the Grand Canyon National Park in northern Arizona. Turned out that the missing twenty-two-year-old Lafferty had been abducted by an ex-boyfriend who'd held her prisoner for weeks in a room at his Phoenix house before she'd been rescued and the kidnapper arrested and charged with multiple offenses. Garrett was happy that though Melissa Lafferty had been put through the ringer, she'd survived, knowing that wasn't always the end result, with the current Blue Ridge Parkway case a sad but true example.

He winced while running a hand through his hair. Eyeing the director squarely, Garrett said painfully, "My mother was murdered in the Blue Ridge Mountains while hiking."

"What? That's awful. I'm sorry to hear that." Carly wrinkled her nose, thoughtful for a beat. "If this hits too close to home, Garrett, I can assign the case to another special agent."

"I've got this," he told her flatly. "It happened a long time ago." Moreover, Garrett knew that with fewer than forty ISB special agents in the entire country under the authority of the NPS, none had the luxury of picking and choosing assignments based on their history or personal circumstances. It was no different with him, even if he had more than one reason for not being enthusiastic to return to North Carolina. "I can be there in three hours," he told her, taking into account normal traffic and speed limits along the way.

"Good." Carly gave him a soft smile. "The sooner you can wrap this up, the sooner we can ease the legitimate concerns of park-goers."

"I agree." In Garrett's mind, it also meant the sooner he could get out of North Carolina and the bad memories he'd left behind, which did not include his prior involvement with Madison. It was perhaps the one bright spot, even if things had ended between them prematurely. At least it seemed that way to him, looking back.

Garrett drove his department-issued silver Chevrolet Tahoe Special Service Vehicle back to his two-bedroom, nicely furnished, nearly a-century-old condominium on Peachtree Street in downtown Atlanta. There, he packed a bag, placed his loaded Glock 23 40 S&W caliber semiautomatic pistol in a shoulder holster, and was out the door.

Soon, he was on I-85 North en route to the Blue Ridge Parkway. Garrett pursed his lips as he thought about the stabbing death of his mother, Jessica Sneed, who'd been part of the Eastern Band of Cherokee Indians, a federally recognized sovereign nation in Western North Carolina. He'd been just five years old at the time, when someone had taken her life that hot summer day thirty years ago. The case had never been solved, and Garrett was forced to live with that haunting reality, blaming himself for not accompanying his mother that day to protect her from a killer. Of course, he'd been too young to have been able to do much to thwart the brutal attack, but he only wished the opportunity had been there to try his hardest to make a difference. After her death, he had been taken in by his maternal grandparents, Trevor and Dinah Sneed, who lived in the Qualla Boundary, land owned by the EBCI and kept in trust by the US government.

When he'd reached adulthood, Garrett had left the Qualla, still stung by the memory of his mother's death. Having never known his father, it had been Garrett's grandparents who'd taught him how to be a proud Cherokee and to fend for himself. He'd attended North Carolina Central University, where he'd gotten his bachelor's degree in criminal justice, before becoming a park ranger and working his way to being an NPS ISB special agent.

Garrett's musings turned to Madison Lynley, an attractive ranger he had fallen hard for. He was pretty sure she'd been equally into him, the few short months they'd been an item. But somehow, the timing had seemed off and they'd broken up. Though it had been mutual and he believed they'd parted on good terms, if that were possible, rather than put pressure on either of them while working in the same space, he'd put in for a transfer to the National Park Service Investigative Services Branch Southwest Region and had been assigned to the Grand Canyon National Park field office. But three months ago, Garrett had been reassigned again to the South Atlantic-Gulf Region, opting to stay in Atlanta and not make things uncomfortable for Madison.

Now he wondered if that had been a mistake. Two years had gone by since he'd last seen her. No texts, emails, phone calls or video chats. Nothing. Had she truly forgotten everything that had existed between them? What about keeping in touch as they had pledged to do? Was he any less guilty of breaking that promise than she was? For his part, if honest about it, Garrett knew that not a day had passed when he hadn't thought about Madison on some level, wondering how she was getting on and if she had moved on with someone else. He had not. Some relationships were hard to substitute, even if they'd failed to progress into something truly meaningful and lasting.

When he arrived at the Blue Ridge Parkway a few hours

later, Garrett was admittedly as nervous about seeing Madison again as he was determined to solve the homicide on the parkway. *I'll just have to suck it up and treat this like any other investigation*, he told himself, getting out of the vehicle and approaching a group of law enforcement and personnel from the medical examiner's office. But from the moment he laid eyes on Madison, looking as gorgeous as ever, even in her law enforcement ranger uniform that hid that hot body and with her long and luscious blond hair tucked away in a bun, Garrett knew he had to throw that game plan right out the proverbial window. This would definitely be anything but "any other investigation" as long as she was part of it.

She separated herself from the others and met him halfway, those big pretty blue-green eyes widening quizzically beneath choppy bangs and above a petite nose and full lips on a heart-shaped face.

"I wasn't expecting the ISB special agent I requested to be you," Madison spoke in clear shock. He hadn't decided if it was a good or bad shock on her part.

Garrett grinned awkwardly. "Surprise." He thought about giving her a quick hug, if only for old times' sake. Being able to make body contact wouldn't be bad either. But he sensed it would be an inappropriate gesture at this time.

A hand rested on a hip of her slender frame as she questioned, "So, how long have you been back in this region?"

Uh-oh, he told himself. Was there any right way to answer her?

"Not long." Garrett took a middle of the road approach. "I was planning to call you," he lied. Though perhaps he would have gotten around to it sooner or later. Or was that just a convenient rationalization for not knowing whether or not it was smart to go there?

"Right." Her curly lashes fluttered cynically. "Anyway, this isn't about us," she stressed, with which he concurred. "Someone I know has been murdered, and we need to work together to solve the crime."

Garrett was caught off guard on the notion that she'd been acquainted with the dead woman, giving him even more incentive to complete the investigation as soon as possible— hopefully leading to an arrest or otherwise preventing the unsub from harming anyone else.

"Sorry to hear that you were connected to the victim, Madison," he voiced sincerely. "Why don't you take me to the body and fill me in on any details you have thus far, and we'll proceed from there."

"Fine," she told him tersely. "Olivia deserves no less than to have whoever did this to her off the streets and behind bars."

Garrett thought back to his mother and her untimely demise. He only wished she had gotten the justice she'd deserved. Maybe this time around it would be a different outcome. "We're in total agreement."

Chapter Two

I almost wish he wasn't still so handsome, Madison thought as she assessed Garrett Sneed, her ex-boyfriend. Had that been the case, it might not be as bad to see him walk back into her life after two years apart. But as it was, if anything, the ISB special agent was actually even more striking than she'd remembered. He had dark eyes, a Nubian nose, prominent cheekbones reflecting his Cherokee heritage and a square jawline on an oval face, with a light stubble beard. The thick dark hair, she realized, was different. Instead of the hipster style he'd worn before, it was now in a mid-fade haircut that suited him. Tall and well-built, he was wearing a short-sleeved green shirt, tan slacks, and a vest that had Police Federal Agent on the back, along with comfortable plain toe Oxfords.

Madison blushed when he caught her studying him, though she had noticed him doing the same in seeing how she'd been holding up since the last time they'd met. Knowing her food-and-exercise regimen, she was confident that she'd passed the test just fine. Assuming he was grading her.

"Follow me," she told him, trying to keep this professional.

"Lead the way," he said evenly.

She introduced him to sheriff's deputies from Transylvania, Buncombe and Watauga Counties and staff from the medical examiner's office before they headed down a well-worn path toward the crime scene.

"This is really hard," Madison commented. "Not exactly the way I expected to meet again."

"I know." Garrett followed close behind her through the grove of trees. "Losing anyone you're connected to is a hard pill to swallow. Not what I was expecting, either, in seeing you again, but duty called for it."

Along with the fact that you just happened to have returned to this region, which made such an unlikely reunion even possible, she thought, feeling his breath as it fell on her skin. She wondered just how long he had been in her neck of the woods and never bothered to get in touch, if only for old times' sake. Or was that really necessary, considering that things had ended for them and there was no going back?

She came upon the area that had been cordoned off with yellow tape and had crime scene investigators searching for and collecting evidence. Weaving her way through with Garrett, who flashed his identification as the lead investigator but unfamiliar to some at work, they headed down the steep embankment to where the decedent was located beneath dense brush.

Madison gulped. "There she is." It pained her to see what was once a living, breathing, healthy human being now a murder victim. On hand was Deputy Chief Medical Examiner Dawn Dominguez. The fortysomething doctor was small boned and had brunette hair in a stacked pixie.

"Long time no see, Special Agent Sneed," Dawn remarked as she planted brown eyes upon Garrett.

"It's been a minute, Doc," he allowed.

"Sorry you had to be brought back in under these circumstances."

"So am I. But it comes with the territory." Garrett favored Madison with an even look and returned to eyeing the victim. "What can you tell us?"

Dawn, who was wearing nitrile gloves while conducting a preliminary examination of the body, responded, "Well, my initial read is that the decedent was the victim of a multiple-stabbing attack, resulting in her death."

His brow furrowed. "Any defensive wounds?"

"None that I can see thus far. It appears as though the assailant caught her by surprise and from behind before going on the attack."

Madison anguished over the thought of her friend's painful victimization and agonizing end to her life. "What was the estimated time of death?"

Dawn took a moment or two to contemplate and answered, "I have to say she's probably been dead for anywhere from four to six hours. I'll know more when the autopsy is completed."

"Any indication of a sexual assault?" she had to ask, even if Olivia was fully clothed.

"Doesn't appear to be the case. Again, I can be more definitive after the autopsy."

"The sooner I can get that report, the better," Garrett stressed.

"Understood," the medical examiner said. "We all want to get to the bottom of this."

Madison nodded in concurrence, while hopeful that Olivia hadn't suffered the further indignity of a sexual victimization in the course of losing her life.

After the decedent was put in a body bag, placed onto a gurney and wheeled to the medical examiner's van, Garrett asked Madison, "Any sign of the murder weapon?"

"Our initial search has turned up nothing," she told him, wishing that weren't the case. "Hopefully, the CSIs will find the knife used in the attack." But truthfully, she wasn't holding her breath on that one. These days, any killer who watched true-crime documentaries, or even scripted procedurals, would likely leave with the murder weapon to avoid being tracked down through DNA or fingerprints tying them to the crime. There were always exceptions, of course, with those who were overconfident or not privy to modern-day police work.

Garrett scratched his chin. "What about the victim's personal belongings?"

"The key to her car was still in her pocket and collected as evidence," Madison pointed out. "But Olivia's cell phone, along with her driver's license, is apparently missing. As for other belongings, given that she appeared to be on the parkway for a run, she probably kept her wallet or handbag hidden in her car. That isn't to say Olivia didn't have cash on her when she started out. If so, it's missing now."

He seemed to make a mental note before saying, "We can assume that the unsub may have taken the cell phone and anything else of immediate value."

Madison lifted a brow. "You think this was a robbery gone horribly wrong?"

"Quite the contrary. The apparent viciousness of the attack tells me that it was personal. Or something to that effect. Taking her possessions, if any, was strictly after the fact."

This made sense to her, though Madison was unaware of any clear-cut enemies Olivia had. Though she had recently ended a relationship, it had appeared as though it had been mutual and without malice either way.

Much like how we parted ways, Madison thought.

"We'll be reaching out to the public for any photographs or videos that may have been taken this morning in and around the area," she said, "to assist in our investigation. Or if anything or anyone suspicious was seen during the livestream of the Blue Ridge Parkway's webcams."

"Good." Garrett nodded. "Let's see what comes up."

Madison sighed. "Whoever did this was brazen and is obviously very dangerous while still on the loose."

"Tell me about it."

He frowned, closing his eyes for a moment, and she sensed that Garrett might have been thinking about the stabbing death of his own mother on this very parkway some thirty years ago in what had turned out to be an unsolved homicide. Madison knew he had a chip on his shoulder because of it. Even going so far as to believe that, at five years of age, he might have been able to thwart the deadly attack had he only been present. Would these painful reminiscences hamper his ability to conduct this investigation?

"Do you know if the victim has any relatives in the area?" he asked, bringing Madison back to the present.

"Her dad lives in Kiki's Ridge," she said. "Not far from where Olivia stayed."

"I need to go see him." Garrett's voice was equable. "Apart from notifying the next of kin and you identifying the victim, we still need a family member for formal identification of her."

"I know." Madison understood how things worked from both her own experience as a law enforcement ranger and her siblings in the business who were also called upon to be the bearer of bad news from time to time. "I'd like to be there when you tell her dad, Steven Forlani. I owe Olivia that much as her friend and neighbor."

"Of course." He gazed at her. "This is your case as much as it is mine. We'll do this together."

"Thank you." She welcomed his cooperation and understanding. Moreover, she liked the notion of them working together on a case. Even if they had failed at working things out romantically.

Madison received word on her radio that a vehicle registered to Olivia Forlani had been located in a Blue Ridge Parkway Visitor Center parking lot. "We're on our way," she told dispatch.

"Maybe the car can tell us something," Garrett speculated.

"Maybe," she agreed, but she suspected that the attacker had not followed Olivia from her vehicle. Instead, it seemed more likely that the unsub had either been lying in wait for her off the trail or had come upon Olivia randomly, while still targeting her for the kill.

When they reached the parking lot, Madison recognized her friend's white Toyota Camry.

"It was undisturbed and all by its lonesome," Nicole Wallenberg, a park ranger, reported.

Madison examined the vehicle. There were no indications that something was amiss. It was locked, and nothing seemed unusual inside at first glance. She spotted an item of clothing on the back seat that appeared to be concealing something beneath it, such as Olivia's handbag.

She gazed at the twentysomething ranger, with a tousled dark bob parted on the side and blue eyes, and asked her to be sure, "You saw no one checking out the vehicle?"

"Nope."

Another park ranger, Leonard Martin, joined them. African American, tall, solid in build and in his thirties, with curly dark hair beneath his campaign hat and wearing shades, he backed Nicole up. "I took a look around and didn't see anyone who was acting suspicious."

"Why don't you see if the ranger in the visitor center can tell us if Ms. Forlani ever went inside," Garrett told them. "And if she had company or there was anyone who may have followed her."

Leonard nodded and Nicole said, "We'll check it out," before they walked off.

Madison took out her cell phone. "I'll try calling Olivia and make sure she didn't leave her phone inside the vehicle."

"Good idea," he said and looked in the car window. "Go ahead."

She made the call, and it rang through her end. Neither of them heard Olivia's phone coming from the car or otherwise gave any indication that it was in the car.

"It's not there," Madison surmised, which told her that, short of the phone being located by investigators, there was a good chance that it was in the possession of the unsub.

"We'll ping her number and see if we can pinpoint the cell phone's location."

She nodded. "Let's hope it's being used or was left on."

"In the meantime, Forensics can see if they can come up with anything material to the investigation when they go through the car," Garrett said.

"Given that her car key wasn't taken, I'm thinking that the unsub never had any interest in stealing the vehicle," she said.

"I think you're right." He studied the vehicle again. "Whoever murdered your friend, he or she had another agenda than auto theft."

Madison squirmed at the thought of who might have wanted Olivia dead. "We need to know exactly what that was."

He nodded. "First, the victim's next of kin needs to know what happened to her."

"Right." She gulped, dreading what had to be done.

GARRETT WAS ADMITTEDLY finding it hard to keep his concentration on the road as he drove down Highway 18 South with Madison alongside. He vividly remembered when they'd been all over each other before everything had fallen apart. Now they were simply supposed to forget their history and focus on what, the present investigation and nothing else?

"So, how have you been?" he asked, hoping it didn't come across as awkward as it sounded to him.

"I've been good," she responded coolly, without looking directly at him. "How about you?"

"Same. Just work and more work." He wondered if she was seeing anyone. Though he had gone on a date every now and then, the truth was she was a hard act to follow for any other woman.

Madison batted her eyes wryly. "Not even a little play?"

Garrett chuckled. Was this a test to see if he was sleeping around? "Only when I forced myself to step away from the demands of the job," he told her. "Maybe a little hiking, working out or whatever distractions came my way." *Did I just give her the wrong message?* he asked himself, though not exactly sure what that was.

"I see," she muttered thoughtfully. "Thank goodness for those distractions that life can offer."

"It's not what you think," he spoke defensively.

"Not thinking anything," Madison insisted. "What you do and who you do it with these days is your own business."

"True enough." He couldn't argue with the philosophy of her tart statement. Which was just as true in reverse. Their relationship had ended before he'd left. They weren't dating any longer. Therefore they didn't owe the other any explanations on their love lives. Or lack thereof. So why did he feel the need to clarify where things stood with him in that department? While also wondering what lucky guy, if any, had taken his place in her life.

"I am curious, though, about how you ended up back in the South Atlantic-Gulf Region," she said. "What, did they kick you out of the Southwest Region? Or maybe you grew homesick?"

Garrett was struck by the bluntness of her inquiries. Sounded like she'd missed him. Or was that more wishful thinking? "Well, I was actually making a real impact with the field office in the Grand Canyon," he responded confidently. Never mind the fact that maybe he had been a bit hasty in his departure from North Carolina. If he could backtrack, things might have gone a different way between them.

"So, what happened?" Her voice crooned with impatience.

"What happened is that Special Agent Robin Grayson unexpectedly retired and, since they were already short on qualified agents with my experience, I was brought back to this region to take her place." He wrinkled his brow. "Not like I had much of a choice."

"And if you had?" Madison regarded him challengingly.

Sensing it was a backed-into-a-corner-type question, Garrett gave an answer that maybe even surprised himself a little. "I think it would have been the same result." Not sure how he wanted her to read that, he lightened the response by saying, "It gets too damned hot in Arizona, and the wasps and bees were a pain in the neck, no pun intended."

She laughed. "I'll bet."

Garrett liked the sound of her chuckle. She hadn't done it enough the first time around. Now seemed like it might be a wise time to change the subject again. "So, how's your family?"

"Everyone's doing great." She paused. "We got together earlier this summer for my sister's wedding and had lots of fun."

"Nice. Congrats to the newlyweds." A twinge of envy and regret rolled through him. It would have been nice to have tagged along. Even if their own romance had fizzled.

Garrett gazed at the road. If truthful about it, when they'd been together, he had found himself slightly intimidated by Madison's family members, all in law enforcement professions. It had been almost as though he'd needed to prove himself. On the other hand, he felt more than up to the task of doing just that. Maybe the opportunity would present itself again.

"So, how long have you been friends with Olivia?"

She considered this. "Probably seven or eight months. Why?"

"Just wondering if there was anyone in her life who may have wanted her dead."

"She never said anything to me about being afraid of someone." Madison drew a breath. "Not that she would have necessarily, as not everyone is as comfortable talking about such things, sometimes believing it was something manageable. Till proven otherwise."

"What about a boyfriend?"

"Olivia had been seeing someone till about a month ago," Madison informed him. "A bank manager named Allen Webster. They supposedly ended things amicably, and I never heard her say anything about him being a problem after the fact."

"Hmm…" Garrett's voice was low, thoughtful. He understood that not all things were as they seemed. Especially when it came to dating and domestic violence and the ability of many to keep up appearances, for one reason or another. Was that the case here? "Do you know if she started seeing anyone else?"

"Olivia went out on dates every now and then, but she never indicated that anyone was stalking her."

"We'll see about that," he said, "assuming the investigation doesn't point in a different direction."

They reached Kiki's Ridge, and shortly thereafter he

pulled up to a ranch style home on Ferris Lane. Parked in the driveway was a silver Ford Escape. "Someone's home."

"That's Steven Forlani's car," Madison noted.

Garrett took a breath. "Better deliver the bad news."

She nodded, and he could see that this would be difficult for her but knew she would handle it as a pro. Just as he would in having to deal with this part of their occupations.

THEY HEADED UP to the house and heard a dog barking inside. The door opened just as they stepped onto the porch. Olivia's father was in his midsixties and kept his head shaved bald. Madison could see the French bulldog in the backdrop, itching to come out but trained enough not to do so.

"Hi, Steven," she said, ill at ease.

"Madison," he acknowledged tentatively, turning his gray eyes upon Garrett.

"This is National Park Service Special Agent Sneed," she introduced.

Steven nodded at him. "Agent Sneed." He turned back to her.

"We need to talk to you about Olivia."

"What's happened?" he asked nervously.

"Can we talk inside?" Garrett spoke up.

Steven allowed them in and peered at Madison. "What's going on?"

She glanced at the dog, who was studying her with curiosity as he sat beside a leather recliner, and then at Garrett, before eyeing Olivia's father steadily. "I'm afraid I have bad news," she began. "There's no easy way to say this. Olivia's dead."

Steven's knees buckled. "What? How?"

"She was killed on the Blue Ridge Parkway."

"By who?" he demanded.

"That's still under investigation," Garrett told him. "I'm sorry for your loss."

Steven ran a hand across his mouth. "Why would someone do this?"

"We're trying to figure that out." Madison looked at him compassionately.

Garrett said, "Sir, we need you to come to the morgue to positively identify the body."

Olivia's father lowered his chin in agreement, and Madison knew that his pain would get worse before it got better, as was the case for all secondary victims dealing with homicides.

While they waited for him outside, she told Garrett, "You know, his only true peace will come when we catch the unsub. And even then…"

Nodding, he said thoughtfully, "Sometimes that peace never comes." He sighed, and she mused about the grief that was obviously still in his heart over his mother's tragic death. Something that Madison could relate to on a different level in losing her own parents in a car accident. "But we can't let that stop us from giving it our best shot, right?"

"Right." Madison knew that while the victimization of Garrett's mother had moved into the cold-case category that might never be resolved, Olivia's case was still very much open and solvable as they moved forward in the investigation.

Chapter Three

After her shift ended, Madison drove her duty car down the Blue Ridge Parkway and onto Highway 21 North before soon reaching the area where she lived in Kiki's Ridge. Nestled in the Blue Ridge Mountains, the quaint town had fewer than two thousand residents—most of whom knew or had heard of each other and would therefore be affected to some extent once the news spread about the murder of Olivia Forlani.

Turning onto Laurelyn Lane, Madison came upon her two-story, two-bedroom mountain chalet. She had purchased it three years ago and loved everything about it, including the creek out back, a great deck and easy access to walking trails and the river. The only thing missing was someone to share it with.

Having grown up in a large family, she was anything but a loner. But the one person she'd thought there might be a future with had just upped and left, putting that fantasy to bed. Now he was back, reminding Madison of what they'd once had, even when she fully expected Garrett to return to Atlanta when the current case was over.

Parking and going inside, she took in the place with its

open concept, a floor-to-ceiling window wall with amazing views of the landscape, midcentury furnishings and hickory hardwood flooring. She headed up the winder stairs, removed her clothing and hopped into the shower of her en suite bathroom. Afterward, she wrapped her long hair in a towel and slipped into a more comfortable cotton camp shirt and jeans before heading back downstairs barefoot.

Madison went into the rustic kitchen, took a beer out of the stainless-steel fridge and went into the living room, where she grabbed her cell phone. Sitting on a retro button-tufted armchair, she called her sister, Annette, for a video chat to catch up.

After she accepted the request, Annette's attractive face came onto the screen. Biracial and a few years younger than Madison, her wavy brunette hair was long and parted in the middle with bangs that were chin length. Annette's brown-green eyes twinkled as she said, "Hey."

"Hey." She smiled back, while feeling envious that her sister had recently tied the knot with her dream guy and was experiencing the marital bliss that Madison could only dream of at this point.

"What's happening in the Blue Ridge Mountains these days?" Annette asked her.

"Since you asked, some bad and still-yet-to-be-determined things."

"Hmm… Why don't you start with the bad," her sister prompted.

"All right." Madison sat back. "A friend of mine was murdered today on the parkway."

"Oh, that's awful." Annette made a face. "I'm so sorry."

"Me too. Olivia was so full of life, and now that's been taken away from her."

"Do you have the killer in custody?"

"Not yet." Madison furrowed her brow. "It's still under investigation, but as long as the killer remains on the loose, it's not a good look for the National Park Service and park visitors in general, who want to feel it's a safe place to hang out."

"I'll bet. I'm sure you'll solve the case soon."

"Hope so."

Annette paused. "So, what's the still-yet-to-be-determined news?"

Madison took a sip of the beer and responded ambiguously, "You'll never guess who showed up from the NPS as the lead investigator in the case."

Her sister cocked a brow. "Garrett...?"

"Yeah." Madison was not at all surprised at her quick powers of deduction, given that Annette had held her proverbial hand when things had gone south between her and Garrett. "He was reassigned to this region and handed the case."

"How do you feel about that?"

"Truthfully, I'm still processing it," she answered.

"Maybe he is too," Annette threw out. "Have you had a chance to talk?"

"Not really, other than about the investigation and generalities."

"Well, my advice to you is just wait and see how things play out," Annette told her. "You never know, you two just might be meant for each other after all, bumps in the road notwithstanding."

Madison chuckled. "I wouldn't get too carried away with

this," she said. "Things between us ended for a reason. There is no magic wand that will change that. We both have a job to do and will do it. No expectations. No pressures."

"Whatever you say." Annette smiled. "Just know that I have your back, wherever life takes you."

"Thanks, sis. I have yours too."

After ending the conversation, Madison heated up some leftover chicken casserole to go with a freshly made tossed salad, ate and thought about losing a friend and possibly regaining a friendship all in the same day.

THE NEXT MORNING, Madison drove to the headquarters of the Pisgah Ranger District on Highway 276 to update her supervisor, Law Enforcement Ranger Tom Hutchinson, on the investigation into Olivia's death. It was hardly an everyday occurrence on the Pisgah Region of the Blue Ridge Mountains but was something that needed to be dealt with in as expeditious a manner as possible.

When she arrived, Madison went directly into Tom's small office, cluttered with computer equipment and papers. He was sitting at a wooden desk, talking on his cell phone. In his late forties, thickset, with thinning brown hair in a short, brushed back style and blue eyes, he was in uniform. Only a few months on the job, he had replaced the previous district ranger, Johnny Torres, who had been fired after getting arrested for soliciting an undercover cop whom he'd believed to be a sex worker.

Cutting his call short, Tom said, "Hey."

Madison said the same and then, "I wanted to drop by and talk about what happened on the parkway."

"Sit." He motioned toward a well-worn guest chair, which

she took. "I'm sorry about your friend," he said sincerely. "There are no words to express how shocked I am."

"I feel the same," she told him, but she wanted to express her feelings anyway. "Olivia loved running in the park. That someone would go after her is unconscionable."

"I agree." Tom sat back in his ergonomic office chair. "The fact this happened on my watch, and yours, makes it a priority that we work hand in hand with the special agent assigned to the case."

"I know." Madison gazed across the desk. "His name is Garrett Sneed. We've worked together before." She saw no reason to mention their prior romantic involvement, as that had ended two years ago and had no bearing on the current homicide investigation.

"That's good," Tom said. "Should make it easier to co-ordinate your efforts, along with other law enforcement, to solve this case."

"True." She had no problem working with Garrett, as he was obviously very good at his job, having been brought back to this region because of that. "I'll be sure to keep you updated on any developments along the way."

"Thanks, Madison." He smiled. "Let me know if there's anything you or Agent Sneed need in bringing this case to a close."

"I will."

After leaving the office, Madison drove to the Blue Ridge Parkway, wondering what Garrett was up to this morning. She pictured him starting the day with a workout of some sort before getting down to business. Apart from wanting to do his job successfully, she suspected that losing his mother in a similar manner had given Garrett even more motivation to solve Olivia's murder.

Madison's daydreaming was interrupted when she received a call over the radio from Nicole, who said, "I've got a potential witness regarding the murder who you may want to talk to."

Madison was attentive. "Who?"

"Maintenance Ranger Ward Wilcox."

After Nicole gave her the location, Madison said hurriedly, "I'm on my way." Before she passed this along to Garrett, she needed to see if the information was credible.

Upon going through a tunnel and farther into the Blue Ridge Mountains, driving alongside mountain ridges, she reached her destination. She parked and headed into a wooded area, not far from where Olivia's body had been found. Nicole and Leonard were standing there with Ward Wilcox.

Madison recognized him, having seen him around and spoken to him on occasion as a park employee. In his mid-sixties, Ward was tall and seemed in reasonably good shape for a man his age. He had dark eyes with heavy bags underneath on a weathered square face and wavy, gray locks in a shoulder-length bob. He wore a maintenance uniform and sturdy work shoes.

"Hey," Nicole said, wearing a campaign hat with her uniform.

"Hey." Madison glanced at the other ranger.

"Ward has something interesting to say," Leonard told her.

Madison gazed at the man. "Ward."

"Tell her what you told me," Nicole urged him.

"Okay." Ward sighed. "Yesterday, I saw a guy who was acting strange and holding on to a cell phone as if it contained the secrets to the universe. When I tried to talk to him, he ran off and disappeared into the woods."

"When was this?" Madison asked.

"I'd say around eight in the morning or so. Hadn't really given it much thought till I heard later about the young woman found dead on the parkway and started to put two and two together." Ward ran a hand through his hair. "Maybe it was nothing at all. Maybe it was something. Thought you needed to know, one way or the other."

"Glad you reported this," she told him, well aware that any possibilities in a murder case were worth pursuing, even if they led nowhere. She was curious, in particular, about the cell phone the man had been carrying. Olivia's phone was still missing and was believed to have been taken by the unsub. "Do you remember the color of the cell phone the man was holding?"

"Yeah," Ward said without prelude. "It was red."

Olivia's phone case was red, Madison told herself. Coincidence? The timeline for when Olivia might have been murdered fit too.

"You said this man was acting strange. How so?"

Ward scratched his chin. "I don't know. Just seemed like he was agitated. Something was definitely off about him."

"Can you describe him?" she asked intently.

"Yeah, I think so."

Madison listened as he gave the description of a slender, lanky, sandy-haired man with a scruffy beard in his early to midtwenties and wearing dirty jeans, a T-shirt that may have had something resembling blood on it and dark tennis shoes.

"What do you think?" Nicole pursed her lips in looking at Madison. "Could this be the killer?"

"Seems to fit," Leonard contended.

Though unwilling to take that leap, it was more than enough for Madison to look into the possibility seriously. "I think we need to find him and have a talk with him... and soon."

GARRETT WAS UP early in the two-bedroom log mountain cabin he had rented, located just off the Blue Ridge Parkway. It had contemporary furnishings, a full kitchen, Wi-Fi, white-oak hardwood floors, a private deck and enough space for him to operate. He had turned one of the bedrooms into his temporary office, using the oak table within as his desk. Admittedly, he hadn't slept very well, as Madison had been as much on his mind as the death of her friend. It was unfortunate that a homicide should bring them back together. At least in an investigative capacity. Though he wasn't necessarily opposed to rekindling what they'd had two years ago, Garrett doubted that Madison had much interest in going down memory lane. Could he blame her? What was done was done. No going back. Was there?

Having had a quick run on the property's hiking trail, he now sat in the small accent chair in front of his laptop, sipping on a mug of coffee, while reading the autopsy report on Olivia Forlani. According to the medical examiner, the victim had been stabbed eleven times in something akin to a horror movie, with deep stab wounds to the back, neck, shoulders and buttocks. Based on the injuries and patterns thereof, the still-missing murder weapon was described as likely a survival knife with a smooth eight-inch, single-edged blade. The cause of death was ruled a homicide, resulting from acute multiple sharp-force trauma inflicted upon the victim.

Garrett sucked in a deep breath, closing his eyes at the thought of the horrible death. He couldn't help but reminisce once again about the similar way that his mother's life had ended. Though he seriously doubted one had anything to do with the other, the two stabbing deaths still struck an eerie chord. Olivia Forlani's murder wouldn't go unpunished if he had any say in the matter.

His cell phone rang, and Garrett answered, "Sneed."

"Agent Sneed, this is Deputy Sheriff Pottenger."

Garrett recalled meeting Ray Pottenger of the Transylvania County Sheriff's Department yesterday when arriving at the Blue Ridge Parkway to take over the investigation. "Deputy," he said.

"Wanted to let you know that we pinged Olivia Forlani's cell phone and have tracked it to a campground not far from the parkway."

This told him that the unsub had turned on the phone and was likely using it. "Send me the info, and I'll get the ball rolling on a search warrant and meet you there."

"You've got it," Pottenger said.

After setting the wheels in motion for what he hoped would lead to Olivia's killer, Garrett phoned Madison to let her know what was going on. She answered after two rings. Before he could speak, she said, "There's a person of interest in Olivia's murder that you need to know about."

"Oh…" Garrett was all ears. "Go on."

"A maintenance ranger named Ward Wilcox reported seeing a man acting weird on the parkway yesterday at around the time Olivia may have been killed," Madison told him. "He was holding a cell phone that looked an awful lot like the one she owned. There may also have been blood on his T-shirt."

"Actually, I was calling you on that very subject," Garrett informed her, piqued by the news. "Deputy Sheriff Pottenger from the Transylvania County Sheriff's Department just phoned to say that Olivia's cell phone has been tracked to the Sparrow Campground on Bogue Lane."

"Really?" He could hear her voice perk up.

"Yeah. I'm on my way over there right now."

"I'll meet you there," she said eagerly.

"Okay." Garrett hoped they weren't in for a disappointment, knowing that this was personal for Madison. And if the truth be told, it was for him too. Her friend's death had managed to dredge up memories he would just as soon have kept buried. He was on his feet and got out the Glock 23 handgun he kept in a pistol case when not in use. Putting it in his shoulder holster, he headed out the door.

MADISON'S HEART WAS racing as she and the others approached the campsite. Her pistol was out and ready to use, if needed. She wanted to get a look at the unsub and possibly Olivia's killer. The fact that Ward Wilcox had seen what might have been her cell phone, coupled with it pinging in this location, seemed too much of a coincidence. When Garrett ordered the suspect out of the A-frame tent and there was no reply, deputies opened it. There was some clothing and other items for outdoor living haphazardly spread about. But no unsub.

Wearing latex gloves, Garrett went through the things in search of the cell phone. He came up empty but did pull out a T-shirt that appeared to have dried blood on it as well as what looked to be a hunting knife. "We need to get these analyzed and see if either has Olivia Forlani's DNA."

Deputy Sheriff Ray Pottenger, who was six-five and in his thirties with a dark crew cut beneath his campaign hat, gazed at him and said, "I'll get them straight over to the lab."

Madison took a peek inside the tent, and something caught her eye. "Looks like methamphetamine in the unsub's lair," she stated knowingly, "along with drug paraphernalia."

"I saw that," Garrett acknowledged. "Another reason to find out who this tent belongs to."

Putting away her gun, Madison got out her cell phone. "I'll try calling Olivia's number." She hoped that whoever had the phone and apparently cut it off before they could locate it had turned it back on.

To her surprise, she heard the phone ring. It was coming from the woods. She spotted a tall, slender man holding the phone. He promptly dropped it like it was a red-hot coal and bolted.

"Stop that man!" Madison's voice rose an octave. "He had Olivia's phone."

"We'll get him," Garrett promised, and they went after the unsub.

Following in pursuit, Madison took her gun back out while trying to keep pace. It didn't take long before they had the suspect cornered behind a beige Winnebago Revel RV. He was taken into custody without incident on suspicion of murder in the death of Olivia Forlani.

Chapter Four

The suspect was identified as Drew Mitchell. He was a twenty-six-year-old unemployed army vet, who'd served in Afghanistan before being discharged for misconduct. Garrett sat across from him in a wooden chair in an interrogation room at the Transylvania County Sheriff's Office in the city of Brevard on Public Safety Way. He gazed at the person of interest in Olivia Forlani's violent murder, while awaiting results from the DNA testing. Mitchell was around six feet tall, slender and blue eyed with dirty-blond hair in a long undercut and a messy beard. Apart from his current predicament, there was an outstanding warrant for Mitchell's arrest in South Carolina for burglary and drug possession.

"Why don't we just get right down to business," Garrett told him in no uncertain terms. "You're in a heap of trouble, Mr. Mitchell. But I'm sure you already know that."

"Okay, you got me." Mitchell's nostrils flared. "Yeah, busted for being an addict and stealing drugs. That's what happens when you run out of options."

"We're talking about more than drug addiction and possession." Garrett peered at him as he slid the cell phone that was inside an evidence bag across the table. "Care to tell me about this?" The suspect remained mute. "It belongs to a woman named Olivia Forlani. She was stabbed to death yesterday. Have anything to say about that?"

Mitchell squirmed. "I didn't kill anyone," he spat defiantly. "I swear."

Garrett rolled his eyes doubtingly. "You want to explain how you were caught with the victim's cell phone?"

"I found it." His voice thickened. "The phone was lying near some bushes. I needed a cell phone, so I took it. I had no idea the person the phone belonged to was dead."

"Is that why you ran when we came looking for you in your tent?" Garrett wasn't sure he was buying this. "Or why you took off when the maintenance ranger confronted you yesterday while you were in possession of the phone?"

"I ran when you guys showed up because I knew there was a warrant for my arrest. I freaked out." The suspect sucked in a deep breath. "I ran away when the maintenance dude came up to me because I thought he might try to take away the cell phone. I didn't want to give it up. So I fled."

Garrett remained less than convinced he was on the level and glanced up at the camera, knowing that Madison and other law enforcement were watching the live video. "Why was there blood on the T-shirt you wore yesterday?" he asked pointedly.

"I cut myself," Mitchell said tersely.

"What were you doing with a hunting knife inside the tent?" Garrett pressed the suspect. "Did you use it to cut someone?" Even in asking, in his mind, it didn't appear to be the same knife described in the autopsy report as the murder weapon in Olivia Forlani's death.

"I only used the knife for gutting an animal and have it for defending myself," Mitchell insisted. "I never cut anyone with it!"

Garrett went back and forth with him for a few more minutes, in which the suspect stuck to his story of innocence in the murder of Madison's friend. When they were interrupted by Deputy Pottenger, Garrett stood and walked over to the door.

"What do you have for me?" he asked him.

Pottenger sighed. "The tests on the T-shirt and knife have come back. It's Mitchell's blood on the T-shirt," the deputy said. "Blood found on the hunting knife came from an animal."

Garrett frowned. "So, no DNA found belonging to the victim?"

"Not as yet." Pottenger glanced at the suspect. "I think he's telling the truth about finding the cell phone."

Even though he wanted to believe otherwise, Garrett was inclined to side with the deputy. Drew Mitchell was going down on drug and theft charges—but apparently was not the killer of Olivia Forlani.

WITH DREW MITCHELL seemingly no longer the lead suspect in Olivia's death, it seemed logical to Madison that they go back to square one in the investigation. That meant interviewing the last known person Olivia had been involved with—Allen Webster. Though there were no obvious red flags to believe he'd had anything to do with her death, he needed to be checked out. Between her own years in law enforcement and stories she'd heard from her siblings and parents, Madison knew that a high percentage of female victims of homicides were killed by current or former significant others. Could that have happened in this instance?

I'll withhold judgment till we speak to Allen, Madison told herself as she drove with Garrett to Kiki's Ridge Bank on Vadon Street, where Allen Webster was the manager.

"Mitchell could have still killed Olivia and gotten rid of the murder weapon," Garrett suggested, behind the steering wheel.

Madison turned to his profile. "You really think so?"

"It's possible, though unlikely." He pulled into the bank's parking lot. "We have to keep all suspects on the table, so to speak. But as for now, Mitchell seems too messed up and sloppy to have pulled this off without a hitch."

"You're probably right," she agreed musingly. "We'll see what Olivia's ex has to say."

"Yeah." Garrett turned to her. "You okay?"

She met his eyes. "I'm fine. Like you, I just want answers, you know?"

"I do." He touched her hand, and she got a surprising jolt, as if struck by lightning. "We'll find them, wherever we need to look."

Madison nodded, feeling reassured somehow by his strength in words and conviction, along with the gentleness of his touch. They left the car and headed inside the bank. After Garrett flashed his identification to a burly and bald security guard, they made their way to Allen Webster's office. Sitting at a U-shaped desk, Madison recognized the man from a time she'd gone out for drinks with Olivia and him. In his late thirties and wearing a navy suit, Allen was muscular and gray-eyed with dark hair in a short fade.

"National Park Service Special Agent Sneed," Garrett told him.

"Agent Sneed." Allen shifted his gaze and said, "Madison...er, Ranger Lynley... I guess you're here to talk to me about Olivia?"

"That's correct." Garrett eyed him. "We need to ask you a few questions."

"Of course. Please sit." He proffered a long arm at the designer guest chairs in front of his desk, which they took. "I'm still trying to wrap my head around what happened to Olivia. Not sure how I can be of any help, but I'll do my best."

"Thank you," Madison said politely. "We're just covering the bases as we try to find out who killed her."

"I understand," he said evenly. "Olivia and I stopped seeing each other a few weeks ago. I have no knowledge about who might have murdered her. If there was something else you needed—"

"You can start off by telling us where you were yesterday between, say, seven and ten in the morning," Garrett said.

"Right here." Allen quickly lifted his cell phone and studied it. "Just wanted to take a look at my schedule to pinpoint exactly what was going on then." He paused. "Had a staff meeting to start the morning and then made a few phone calls and did some work on my laptop. All of this can be easily verified."

Madison had no reason to doubt that he was telling the truth, though they would check out his alibi. Still, she asked, "So why did you and Olivia break up anyway?"

Allen sat back with a frown on his face. "We stopped clicking, to put it bluntly. It just seemed like we were spinning our wheels trying to make it work, till deciding mutually that we were better off as friends. I certainly never wanted anything like this to happen to her."

Neither did I, Madison thought sadly, while also relating to the reality that some lovers were better off as friends. She wondered if that was true with her and Garrett. "Do you know if there was anyone who might have wanted to harm Olivia?" she asked Allen.

He chewed on this for a moment, then responded, "Not really. But if you asked me if there was anyone who might benefit from her death, I'd have to say the person who was Olivia's chief competitor at the law firm where she worked—Pauline Vasquez. They had both been trying to make partner, and someone would be left out in the cold, so to speak. I'm not suggesting in any way that Pauline would have gone so far as to kill for the job. That's for you to determine."

"We'll look into it," Garrett said.

"Hope you solve this case." Allen took a breath. "Our differences aside, Olivia was really a good person and she deserves some justice."

"I agree." Madison met his eyes. "We'll do our best to see that she gets it."

They stood, along with Allen, who walked with them and introduced them to other employees, who verified his presence the previous morning, seemingly eliminating him as a suspect.

"WHAT ARE YOUR thoughts on the so-called rivalry between Olivia and Pauline Vasquez?" Garrett asked as he drove away from the bank.

"I'd heard Olivia mention it from time to time but saw it as a spirited but friendly competition, more or less, to make partner at the firm," Madison admitted. "But who's to say it didn't go much further than that? Women are just as capable of committing acts of violence as men, even if there's a lower incidence of it in society. It wouldn't be the first time that jealousy and fierce competition led to murder."

"True. Or the last. The law firm's not far from here," he pointed out. "We might as well swing by and see how Vasquez reacts."

"We should." She was in total agreement. "All possibilities remain open at this point, right?"

"Right. I have to say, though, that after reading the autopsy report, the viciousness of the attack has me believing the culprit is more likely than not a male."

"We'll see about that," she said, glancing at him.

Garrett kept an open mind. The fact that the case against Drew Mitchell fell through meant that the hunt for Olivia's killer was wide open and the potential suspects were not gender specific.

They reached the Kiki Place Office Building on Twelfth Street and Bentmoore. After parking in an underground garage, they took the elevator up to the third-floor law offices of Eugenio, Debicki and Vasquez.

"Why don't you interview Ms. Vasquez," Garrett told Madison as they stepped inside the lobby. "I'll check out the rest of the firm and see if anyone might have had it in for Olivia."

"All right," she agreed, and they approached a reception desk.

MADISON ENTERED THE carpeted office of Pauline Vasquez, the newest partner in the law firm. *She didn't waste any time*, Madison thought as she was greeted by Olivia's former colleague. In her thirties, Pauline was small and attractive with long brunette feathered hair and green eyes. She wore a brown skirt suit and high heels.

"Law Enforcement Ranger Madison Lynley," she introduced herself.

"Pauline Vasquez." She offered her hand, and Madison shook it. "All of us here have taken Olivia's death very hard. She was a valued employee."

"And one you no longer have to worry about beating you out for partner," Madison said in pulling no punches.

Pauline expressed disapproval. "If you're suggesting that I had something to do with Olivia's death..."

"Did you?" Madison questioned sharply to see if this shook her up any. "You apparently had the most to gain by her death."

"I had nothing to do with that," she insisted, running a hand liberally through her hair. "Yes, we were both battling to make partner, however, I was actually given the news that I'd been the one chosen several days ago, but was told to keep it under wraps till the official announcement, which coincided with Olivia's tragedy." Pauline sighed. "In any event, I would not have resorted to murdering my rival for the privilege. I achieved this on my own merits as a hard worker. Nothing more."

Madison held her gaze. "In that case, I'm sure you have a rock-solid alibi for where you were yesterday morning between seven and eleven?"

Pauline sighed exaggeratedly. "As a matter of fact, I do.

I was in Raleigh, doing work for the firm. I arrived the night before and returned to Kiki's Ridge last night after eight o'clock. You can check the flights, the hotel I stayed at, two restaurants I went to and, of course, the meetings I attended."

"I'll do that." Madison took down her information to that effect. As it was, she sensed that they were climbing up the wrong beanstalk with Pauline as Olivia's killer. Should it be proven that she had hired someone else to do her dirty work, that would come out sooner or later.

She forced a smile at the attorney. "Thanks for your time. I'll show myself out."

GARRETT STOOD BY a floor-to-ceiling window in the office of Henry Eugenio, the fiftysomething CEO of the law firm. Henry, who was slender and wearing a designer suit, with wavy gray hair in a side-swept style, expressed remorse about the murder of Olivia Forlani. This seemed genuine enough to Garrett. As did the support for Pauline Vasquez, whom he insisted had been chosen to make partner before Olivia's untimely death and, as such, would not have had any reason to harm her.

This only fed into Garrett's belief that the unsub was a male perpetrator. "Did Olivia ever have any trouble with men in the firm?" he asked him.

Henry pushed the silver glasses up his long nose and blinked blue eyes. "Not that I knew of. Everyone got along great with her."

No one gets along perfectly with everyone, Garrett thought. "So, you never heard anything about unwanted advances or anything like that?"

Pausing, Henry gazed out the window and back. "I was once told that one of our newer junior associates made a pass at Olivia," he said. "But as we strongly discourage office romances, that was put to rest pretty quickly. Olivia never indicated it went any further than that."

But what if it had and escalated into something more ominous than nonviolent sexual harassment? Garrett asked himself. "I'd like to question this junior associate, if I can."

"No problem," Henry responded. "I'll buzz him to come in."

"Actually, if it's all the same to you, I'd rather speak with him alone," Garrett said, not wanting the suspect to be unnerved by an interrogation in front of his boss, perhaps causing him to lie.

"Whatever you say, Agent Sneed."

"What's his name?"

"Alex Halstead."

"Just point me in the right direction, and I'll find him," Garrett said after Henry had walked him out of the office.

"All right," he agreed, touching his glasses. "I'm sure you'll find that Alex was not involved in Olivia's death."

Garrett knew there was a tendency to see the best in people. Till proven otherwise. "Hope you're right about that."

A few doors down, he saw the nameplate and went into the office. In his late twenties, tall and fit, Alex was blue-eyed and had dark hair in a French crop style. He was standing and approached Garrett.

"Alex Halstead?"

"Yeah?" He tilted his face. "Did we have a meeting scheduled?"

"No," Garrett responded, realizing the man had him by

two inches. "I'm Special Agent Sneed from the Investigative Services Branch of the National Park Service. I'm investigating the murder of Olivia Forlani."

Alex wrinkled his nose. "Sorry to hear about Olivia," he claimed. "She was a great lawyer." He paused. "What do you need from me?"

"I understand that you hit on her," Garrett said, peering suspiciously.

"Yeah. It was a mistake."

"Some people don't know how to take no for an answer," Garrett stated.

"Not me," Alex insisted. "I apologized and never went there again."

"Can you account for your whereabouts yesterday morning?"

"I was at my apartment, sleeping through a hangover after getting wasted the night before," he responded quickly. "Didn't get up till noon. It was my day off."

Garrett eyed him. "Can anyone verify this?"

Alex cocked a brow. "If you're asking if I was with someone, the answer is no." He frowned. "If you're implying that I went after Olivia on the parkway because she didn't go out with me, you're way off base. I may not be perfect, but I'm definitely not a killer."

Aware that not all alibis included witnesses, Garrett was left to give him the benefit of the doubt, in the absence of evidence to the contrary. "I'll take your word for that."

"Thanks," he said smugly.

"By the way, you don't happen to own a survival knife, do you?" Garrett thought he would throw that out there, considering that the murder weapon was still unaccounted for.

Alex narrowed his eyes. "I'm not a hunter, outdoorsman, survivalist or anything like that," he contended. "So that would be no."

"Then I guess that will be all for now," Garrett told him. "If anything else comes up, I know where to find you."

He left the office, believing that Alex Halstead had not killed Olivia Forlani.

Chapter Five

"Do you want to grab a bite to eat?" Madison asked Garrett during the drive, after they had compared notes on Pauline Vasquez and Alex Halstead. Neither seemed likely as Olivia's killer, joining Drew Mitchell as former suspects as things stood. That meant they still had their work cut out for them if they were to catch the perpetrator before the case could start to run cold.

"I'm down with that," Garrett told her. "Actually, I'm starved."

For some reason, Madison felt relieved, as though she'd feared he would decline the dinner invite, which she'd only made because she too was hungry. Since they were still out, it seemed like a good idea, with no expectations beyond a good meal.

"I thought we could go to Janner's Steakhouse," she suggested, given that it was just around the corner. Never mind the fact that it had been a favorite place for them to dine when they'd been dating.

He smiled. "Sounds good."

Soon they were seated at a table by the window, where Madison ordered a boneless ribeye steak and heirloom tomato salad, then watched as Garrett went with familiar lamb chops and au gratin potatoes. *Apparently some things never change*, she thought, amused. They both chose a glass of Cabernet Sauvignon wine to sip on.

"So, what's next in the search for a killer?" Madison asked as a relatively comfortable conversation starter while she tasted the wine.

Garrett considered this. "Well, we need to go back over everything we have and don't have, including going through Olivia's belongings with the cooperation of her father, and see what we can gauge from this in deciphering possible clues on the unsub."

"I get that, but what do you think drove the perp into attacking Olivia in particular?" she posed to him curiously as the chief investigator. "Since it doesn't appear as yet that she was being stalked."

"That's the thing," he said, sitting back. "We don't know that is the case. Yes, it could well have been a random attack. But if Olivia was a regular jogger on the parkway, the unsub may have been aware of this pattern and waited for just the right time to strike."

Madison cringed. "Olivia and I liked to jog together sometimes on trails in the Pisgah Region," she noted. "Not to mention my own solo runs. Her killer could have been spying on me as well."

"That's always a possibility." Garrett furrowed his brow. "Did you ever see anyone who aroused your suspicions?"

"I honestly can't say that was the case," she replied contemplatively. "On the other hand, I always try to be on guard for any human or wildlife threats, but it's quite possible that an unassuming predator could have escaped my notice."

"Well, do me a favor—let's not have any more solo runs for the time being until we catch this person. I'd hate for you to be faced with the threat of a knife-wielding killer."

"All right." She felt that his concern for her safety was as much for what they'd had as his being a special agent. Not that she would have expected anything less, as his safety on and off the job was important to her too. "I won't make myself an easy target." Carrying her firearm when off duty, even for a run, was never a guarantee of safety these days. Especially if an assailant was armed too.

"Good." Garrett tasted his wine. "Of course, if you need a temporary running mate, I'm happy to volunteer for the job. Just let me know."

"I will." Madison had not forgotten that he ran too and that they had enjoyed jogging and hiking together. She wondered if doing so would be so simple, if he had no intention of sticking around just as she started to grow comfortable with him again.

GARRETT FELT QUEASY at the thought that Olivia's killer could have had Madison in his sights. As a male assailant was the most likely unsub at this moment in time, Garrett was going on that assumption in their search for the culprit. Though there was no reason to believe as yet that Madison was being targeted, he was glad to know she would not make herself an easy mark for anyone. Of course, as an active member of law enforcement for the NPS and with family in this line of work, he had no doubt she could handle herself in almost any situation. But that didn't stop him from being concerned for her safety. Especially as long as he was around to help keep an eye on her, and her seeming willingness to allow him to do so.

When the food arrived and they began eating, Garrett felt the urge to see where things stood in Madison's love life at the moment. He studied her as she ate, finding himself turned on even with this normal act. She was once again in uniform as a ranger and still kept that hair in a bun. Neither stopped him from appreciating what was right in front of him. "So, are you seeing anyone these days?"

Madison looked up as though startled by what seemed to him a reasonable question. She stopped eating and responded succinctly, "No, I'm not."

He tried to read into that. Was this because she had just broken up with someone? Had she been single since their own relationship ended? Or was she not interested in dating anyone right now? "Any decent prospects?"

She laughed. "No—not even any indecent ones."

He grinned crookedly while slicing into a lamb chop. "Has there been anyone in your life since we broke up? Or is that none of my business?"

"No, and yes," she told him. She forked a piece of steak. "To be honest, I haven't been asked out by anyone who captured my fancy enough. But that could change." Madison rested her gaze upon him. "As for it being your business, you gave up that right when you moved across the country."

"Fair enough," he conceded, even when it had seemed best at the time. "Sorry for getting into your business. My bad."

"What about you?" Madison asked. "My turn to be bad. Who are you dating right now?"

"Not a soul." Garrett held her gaze. "Tried dating once

in a while but, truthfully, it's been hard to get you out of my system. Not to say I've ever wanted to, even if we went our separate ways."

"Why did we anyway?" she posed in a casual manner.

"Excuse me?" He wasn't sure what she was getting at.

"Why did we go our separate ways?" Madison squared her shoulders. "I mean, it seemed like we had a good thing going. Then, just like that, it all went away." She sighed. "Or you did."

Garrett set down his scoop of au gratin potatoes. "As I recall, we both decided it was best that we end things between us. Or am I living in an alternate reality or something?" He regarded her questioningly, wondering if he somehow had it all wrong.

She took a deep breath. "You're not. It was what we both wanted. At least I thought so at the time. But we never really talked about this the way we probably should have. It was like burying our heads in the sand was easier than seeing if what we had was worth holding on to."

"I agree." He drank some water and grabbed his fork again reflectively. "It just seemed like neither of us was ready for a commitment, for whatever reasons. Maybe we were just trying to shield ourselves from being hurt. Or maybe the maturity or confidence level wasn't there to take that step in our relationship."

"We should have tried harder to see if there was more there." Madison pouted, while playing with her food. "I mean, didn't we owe ourselves that much? Or is it only me who can see that?"

"It's not just you." Garrett wasn't going to shy away from being equally culpable for their breakup. "I regret that we didn't hash through things more. Whatever we were running away from, we should have stopped and laid it all out and let the chips fall where they may. For better or worse."

Her mouth hung open. "You think?"

"Yeah," he admitted. "In hindsight, I wish I had stayed and worked harder to see where we went wrong. Or steered off course. But given the state of things, I thought that if I had stayed, it might be too weird being around each other and trying not to step on the other's toes while doing our jobs."

"You're right," she told him. "Probably would've been weird. Even if I wish we had done things differently."

"Me too." Garrett sat back, wondering where they went from here. Was there any chance at all for a redo? Was she open to this? Was he? "I never wanted us to stop being friends," he spoke truthfully. "But when I never heard from you again via text message, calls or whatever, I just assumed you had moved on and wanted no part of me in your life anymore."

Madison arched a thin brow. "I never meant for us to lose communication," she said in a heartfelt tone. "I wanted us to stay connected in some way. But after you left, I wasn't sure you felt the same way and didn't want to press it."

He nodded understandingly. "I did feel the same way," he promised her. "And didn't reach out to you more for the same reasons."

She smiled. "Looks like our communication skills really suck."

Garrett chuckled. "Yeah, probably could use some work."

"So, now that you're back in this region, can we at least be friends again?" Madison put forth hopefully. "We probably owe ourselves that much, regardless of how things ended between us."

In his mind, the *at least* part implied she might've been open to going beyond the friendship level. He felt that way too. Or at least exploring the possibilities. "Yes, I would like that," he told her.

She flashed him a toothy grin. "Cool."

He smiled back, already believing they had turned a corner and that the door was wide open for whatever might come next, over and beyond the investigation into Olivia Forlani's murder.

WHEN SHE GOT home that night, Madison was still thinking about the unexpected "airing things out" with Garrett. *It was overdue*, she told herself. She was unsure exactly what it meant in terms of going forward. Both had admitted to mistakes in the way they'd handled the situation two years ago. She wished they could go back and make things right. But there was no such thing as time travel, except in sci-fi, so they could only take what was handed to them and see what they wanted to do with it. They had agreed that a renewed friendship was a great place to start. Would it really be that simple though? Could either of them forget about what they'd once had and not want to have it again once the comfort level had kicked in?

Madison showered, brushed her teeth and went to bed. It was a country-style bed, like the other furnishings in the spacious room, and reminded her that it was where she and Garrett had first made love. A flicker of desire caused her temperature to rise before she brought it back down. She realized that in spite of the sexual chemistry that still existed between them, any attempts at recreating the passions they'd shared might do more harm than good. Even if he planned to stick around once the investigation had run its course, Atlanta, where Garrett lived, was still hours away. Did it really make sense to want to jump into what amounted to a long-distance relationship that could just as easily fizzle like the last time around?

Before an answer could pop into her head, Madison fell asleep. In her dreams, thoughts shifted to Olivia and the terrible way she died, along with needing to bring the killer to justice. No matter what it took.

OLIVIA FORLANI'S KILLER walked deep in the forest, surrounded by hemlock, hickory, birch and white pine trees. He was pensive as he approached Julian Price Lake along the Blue Ridge Parkway. The moon was starting to set beyond Grandfather Mountain, reflecting on the water's surface. He listened to the hoot of an eastern screech owl, then heard the crunch of his own cap-toe ankle boots on the dirt path. He was tempted to stop and take in his surroundings while breathing in the night air. But he forged on instead, eager to return to his campsite.

He thought about the one he had stabbed to death two days ago. It was something he had been thinking about for a long time, and when the opportunity had come his way, he hadn't hesitated to take it. Well, maybe he had paused for consideration, knowing that once he'd moved ahead, there would be no turning back. But the urge in him had been much too great to have second thoughts. Not when he had contemplated this moment in his head time and time again. But something had held him back, as if a voice from the grave was warning him against proceeding.

He'd suddenly become deaf to this as another voice had prodded him to continue what he had started long ago. This mighty call to kill had overtaken him the way illicitly manufactured fentanyl might get an addict in its grip.

So when Olivia Forlani had gone for her predictable run, he'd lain in wait to strike. And he had, over and over again. Till her blood-curdling screams had been no more, silenced by death. Making his getaway had been tricky, as others on the parkway could have spotted him and notified the authorities. But he was too smart to be caught, blending in as he had learned to do so well in his life. He had succeeded in taking away a life and rejuvenating his own in the process.

As he reached the campsite and the tent he called home these days, he could only crack a smile at the thought of his hiding from pursuers in plain view. Just as rewarding were the dark musings in his head that told him that the adrenaline rush he experienced in his homicidal urges was bound to come back again. Sooner than later. When that happened, he would find another to take the place of Olivia Forlani, in feeling the cold steel of his knife as he plunged it inside of her till death came mercifully.

He laughed in admitting that he was showing no mercy in his acts of violence. But then, none had been shown to him when he'd needed it most. Life worked out that way sometimes. He accepted this and wanted no sympathy. Nor would he give any.

Another wicked laugh escaped his lips, even as another call of an owl rang out, letting him know he was in preferable company as he retired for the night.

Chapter Six

The outdoor funeral service for Olivia Forlani was held at the Kiki's Ridge Cemetery. Garrett stood beside Madison to pay his respects to her friend. The fact that they had yet to make an arrest in her death bothered him. Someone was still out there, perhaps overconfident in the ability to avoid detection and apprehension. As he glanced at Olivia's father, Garrett couldn't help but think about his own mother and how the five-year-old version of himself had been overwrought at the notion that he would never see her again. Now Steven Forlani was in the same boat, more or less. The fact that he had gotten to see his daughter reach adulthood and achieve some of her professional objectives didn't make the pain of losing her prematurely to senseless violence any less.

Garrett gazed at Madison, remembering that she, too, had known such loss with the tragic death of her parents. No matter the manner of death, it was still a shock to the system and was something that would always be with you, whatever your lot in life.

"You okay?" he whispered to her.

Madison nodded. "Olivia's in a better place," she surmised.

"Yeah." Garrett wanted to believe this too for her friend, their parents and everyone who had moved on from this world.

He scanned the other mourners, seeing Olivia's colleagues huddled together. They seemed genuinely moved, and he wanted to believe none of them had anything to do with her death. Garrett eyed others in attendance, while wondering if Olivia's killer could be among them. As sick as it was, he was aware that some killers liked to come to funerals to gloat about their kills under the cloak of grievers. Was that the case here?

Garrett pondered this as he listened to the pastor sing the praises for Olivia, even as the perpetrator remained at large and the Blue Ridge Parkway a danger zone as a consequence. Till an unsub was made to answer for the homicide.

Two DAYS LATER, Madison was on duty, patrolling the parkway. Garrett was still investigating Olivia's death, but no arrests had been made thus far. Madison was certain that it was only a matter of time before the unsub was behind bars. As she well knew, these type cases were not always cut and dried. The perp could have gone after Olivia for any number of reasons and now be as far away as Timbuktu in an effort to escape justice.

Well, you can run, but you can't hide, she thought. At least not forever.

Her musings turned to Garrett. They had resumed a friendship, which she liked, while also seemingly gone out of their way to smother any flames that could erupt into something more, as though a bad thing. Was it really? Or should they let it happen and deal with whatever came after?

Madison snapped out of the thoughts as she received a report over the radio that a black bear had been spotted on the parkway. And, worse, that it was threatening a young couple. Or was it the other way around? Black bears were, in fact, omnivores. They took up residence along the Blue Ridge Parkway and weren't afraid to venture out of their habitat in search of food. But sometimes curiosity and fascination got the better of visitors, who got too close to a bear, placing themselves in danger. Was that the situation here?

Either way, Madison was duty bound to come to their assistance. "I'm on my way," she told the dispatcher.

Shortly, she turned off US 221 at Milepost 294 and entered the parkway near Moses H. Cone Memorial Park and Bass Lake. Passing by a grassy hill, Madison spotted Leonard and Ward in a parking area. They were flagging her down, as though she couldn't see them.

When she pulled up to and exited her vehicle, Leonard said ill at ease, "The feisty black bear went after a couple just trying to enjoy their lunch."

"Where's the couple now?" Madison was concerned. "Were they harmed by the bear?"

"They're holed up in a Jeep Grand Cherokee Laredo over there," Ward said. "Apparently when the bear got aggressive, they were able to fend it off long enough to get into the SUV, with only a few scratches."

"Well, that's good anyhow," she told them. "Any sign of the bear?"

"As a matter of fact, it looks like we've got its attention." Leonard's voice shook. He angled his eyes toward the woods. "And it's scaring the hell out of me."

Madison saw that the black bear had reemerged and sized

them up as potential prey, while snorting, popping its jaws and stomping its feet. With her heart skipping a beat, and not particularly interested in being the bear's meal, she raced back to her Tahoe and pulled out a 12-gauge shotgun. It was loaded with cracker shells which, when fired, would emit a loud booming sound in hopes of scaring off the animal.

As what looked to be a three-hundred-pound male took the measure of them while bellowing and standing on its hind legs, Madison ordered the two rangers to get behind her vehicle. Just as she was about to take cover too, the bear suddenly began to charge across the parking lot toward her. Tempted to panic but refusing to do so, she screamed at it and, remaining steady, placed the gun barrel at a forty-five-degree angle, firing the projectile in the bear's direction. It traveled some four hundred feet downrange before there was a flash and huge bang.

Repeating this seemed to do the trick as, spooked, the bear abruptly stopped in its tracks, pivoted and ran back off into the woods. Only then did Madison lower the shotgun and let out a deep breath. "Is everyone all right?" she asked, to be sure.

Leonard and Ward came out from behind the Tahoe. "We are now," Ward said. "Glad you showed up when you did, Ranger Lynley."

"Good shooting," Leonard quipped.

"You do what you have to do," she told them modestly, thankful things hadn't gotten out of control for her or the bear.

"You can come out now," Ward shouted to the young couple, still huddled inside their SUV. "I think the danger has passed."

Madison wasn't sure that the bear might not come back, when regaining his courage and desire for something to chow down on. She interviewed the couple, visiting from Hawaii, and could see that they were still shaken up from their ordeal. But otherwise not the worse for wear. Still, given the fact that the bear had attacked humans at all meant that rangers and wildlife biologists would need to locate it and act in accordance with the protocols of the North Carolina Wildlife Resources Commission.

With the present threat contained, Madison thought she might check out the woods close to the grassy area where the couple had been picnicking. She wanted to be sure that the black bear hadn't first gone after some other vacationers, who might be in trouble. The last thing she wanted was to see someone's dream turn into a nightmare, with no one the wiser till too late. Hopefully that bear had not caused more havoc to deal with.

Having walked along the trail and through the tall trees, with the sounds of nature all around her, Madison felt a sense of calm. She decided maybe all was well and she could get back in her patrol car. Later, she imagined that Garrett would probably tease her about the black-bear encounter. When something caught her periphery, Madison jerked her head in that direction. There was something lying between trees. Or someone.

Putting a hand to her mouth, she realized that it was Ranger Nicole Wallenberg who was lying flat on her back. At first glance, Madison thought that the black bear might have attacked her before going after the couple. But homing in on her fellow ranger, she believed otherwise.

Blood oozed from cuts through Nicole's uniform that appeared to have come from a knife. Her blue eyes were wide open but gave no signs of life.

Madison gulped. *It wasn't a bear attack*, she told herself. This wasn't the work of an animal but a homicide perpetrated by a human being. Much like that of Olivia. Someone was targeting women on the parkway.

GARRETT HELD MADISON as she rested her head on his shoulder. She wept a little over the murder of their colleague. Coming on the heels of Olivia's death, and apparently in the same manner, had undoubtedly shaken Madison. It grated on his nerves as well, as this told Garrett that they were likely looking at a serial killer who had chosen the Blue Ridge Parkway as the killing grounds.

Madison pulled away from him and uttered diffidently, "Sorry about that." She wiped her nose with the back of her hand. "Just kind of overwhelming that this would happen again."

"I know. And you don't have to apologize." Indeed, it felt quite natural to be comforting her, and he would happily do so anytime she needed this. "You have every right to feel unsettled with what happened."

"We both do," she pointed out. "Nicole was one of our own. Now she's dead."

"Yeah." Garrett turned to look at the dead ranger, lying just as Madison had found her. She had clearly been put through an ordeal before someone had taken her life. Who? Why had someone gone after the ranger? Did she have any connection with Olivia Forlani? Or were both women victims of opportunity?

The immediate area had been cordoned off, and the crime

scene technicians and sheriff's deputies were processing it for evidence. Garrett contemplated the scenario: Madison had staved off a black-bear attack, preventing herself and others from being a good bear meal. This had been, in and of itself, an act of bravery on her part, even though it was part of the job description. Then a routine and necessary check of the perimeter and she'd come upon Nicole. Could Madison have scared the killer off? Or was this act of violence a pattern of behavior that had been well planned and executed before the unsub had made a getaway?

"So, you didn't see anyone?" Garrett asked evenly.

"No," Madison replied. "But I'd just left two rangers, and another ranger joined us. Haven't had the chance to question them as to whether or not anyone saw anything."

"Okay." He gazed at the dead ranger's body. "What about the couple who said they were attacked by the black bear?"

"They apparently left the parkway afterward, upset by the incident."

"Did either ranger actually witness their encounter with the bear?"

"I believe the rangers arrived after the fact." She looked up at him. "You think they might have something to do with Nicole's murder?"

"Probably not," Garrett answered, rubbing his jaw. "On the other hand, if they had, the bear roaming around would have been a convenient diversion. Then there is the timeline. Assuming Nicole was victimized around the same time, this would have given the couple a perfect means for distraction and escape. At the very least, they may have seen something while on the grassy hill. Or someone."

"Between webcams along the Blue Ridge Parkway and

a good description of the vehicle driven by the couple," Madison said, "I'm pretty sure we can track them down."

"Good." Garrett turned to see that Dawn Dominguez had arrived to take over from here. "Dr. Dominguez," he acknowledged.

"Special Agent Sneed." Dawn looked to Madison. "Ranger Lynley."

Madison nodded. "The latest victim is a member of the National Park Service," she voiced sadly.

Dawn frowned. "So sorry about that." She glanced at Nicole. "I'll do my best to expedite matters in giving you what I can for your investigation."

"Thank you."

Garrett added, "We need to know how she died, signs of a struggle and approximately how long ago we're talking about when the incident occurred."

"Got it." Dawn met his eyes and slipped on nitrile gloves before immediately giving the decedent a preliminary examination.

After a few minutes, she told them, "From the looks of it, the victim was stabbed at least six times, maybe more. There does appear to be some defensive wounds, but no evidence thus far that she was able to get DNA from her attacker. No initial signs that this was a sexual assault."

"What about the time of death?" Garrett asked.

Dawn touched the decedent. "I'd say she was killed in the last hour or two."

Or in the same time span that the couple claimed they were attacked by a black bear, he thought. Looking at Madison, it was clear that she was thinking the same thing. They needed to find the pair, if only to eliminate them as suspects.

THIS WAS MADISON'S second time speaking on the phone with Tom since learning of Nicole Wallenberg's murder. Only this time it was on video chat and was no more of an easier pill to swallow than the first time. "The deputy medical examiner has more or less confirmed that Nicole was stabbed to death."

Tom's brow furrowed, and he muttered an expletive. "She had big dreams with the NPS," he said sourly. "They probably would have all come true."

"I think so too." Though Madison hadn't been that close to Nicole, they'd had the chance to speak on occasion outside of work. And the ranger had been enthusiastic in her job and where it might take her over a long career. Now any such plans had been put to rest.

"Where are things in the investigation?" Tom asked fixedly.

"We're interviewing anyone who may have information," she responded, knowing they had yet to locate the young couple who had been supposedly in fear of their lives from an aggressive black bear. Though she could attest to that much herself, Madison still had to consider them persons of interest in Nicole's death. Till they were ruled out.

"Do you and Special Agent Sneed believe this is related to the murder of Olivia Forlani?"

"It looks that way, at this point." Madison almost wished that weren't the case, hating to think that a serial killer was in their midst. But the similarities between the homicides couldn't be ignored. Including the fact that the murder weapon was yet to be found in either case.

Tom wrinkled his nose. "If true, we need to get to the bottom of it as soon as possible," he stressed. "We can't have a killer running amok on the parkway or anywhere in the Pisgah Ranger District."

"I understand," she told him. "We're utilizing all the resources at our disposal to come up with answers."

"Keep me posted."

"I will."

After disconnecting, Madison got out of her vehicle when she saw Law Enforcement Ranger Richard Edison drive up. He had been working on the parkway since transferring from the Commonwealth of Virginia, where he'd been a ranger at Shenandoah National Park, four months ago. Single and her age, he was flirtatious and wasn't bad looking but still not her type. He exited his car and approached her, tall and well built in his uniform. Beneath his campaign hat was a bleached-blond Caesar haircut. Sunglasses covered his blue eyes.

"Hey," he said in a level tone.

"Hey." She forced a smile.

"You okay?"

"No, not really," she confessed. "Our colleague was just murdered."

"Yeah, it sucks." His voice dropped an octave. "Nicole was a great ranger."

Madison smiled at the thought. "Yes, she was."

He paused. "You wanted to see me?"

She nodded, eyeing him. "Weren't you with Nicole earlier?"

"Yeah," he said readily. "We rode together for a bit, and then I let her out for foot patrol."

"Did you see anyone else hanging around at the time?"

"Yeah, lots of visitors and workers." Richard adjusted his

glasses. "If you're asking if I saw anything unusual going on, the answer is no."

"Did Nicole indicate she was planning to meet with someone?" Madison asked.

"Not that I can recall." He leaned on one long leg. "I think she may have been dating someone, but I'm not sure."

Madison regarded him. "Did you ever go out with her?"

Richard's mouth creased. "No way. We were friends, but she was too young for me to date."

I'll have to take your word on that for now, Madison thought. "If you think of anything that might help in the investigation, let me know."

"I will." He jutted his chin. "I want whoever did this to Nicole to be brought to justice just as much as you do."

"Okay." Madison had no reason to believe this wasn't true. "See you later."

Next, she met up with Leonard at Julian Price Memorial Park, neighboring Moses H. Cone Memorial Park, at Milepost 297. He had been out questioning parkway visitors, with nearby road closures during the investigation given there was a killer at large.

"Hey," she said. "Get anything?"

"Nothing suspicious as yet," he reported. "Other than some sightings of the black bear, most people I spoke to apparently didn't hear or see anything that got their attention."

"Hmm…" Madison figured that Nicole would have screamed or made other sounds while being attacked. Could the perp have knocked her out first to prevent this? "Did Nicole ever say anything to you about being stalked by someone?"

"No." Leonard tilted his campaign hat. "We were cool but

never talked about issues outside of working for the NPS and in the Blue Ridge Mountains."

"All right." She wondered if Nicole had known her attacker. Or if he'd known her. "Maybe someone will come forward with information."

"I'll let you know," he said.

As she headed back to her vehicle, Madison received a call from Ray Pottenger. "We've located the couple who first reported spotting the black bear," he informed her.

"That's great news," she told him.

"I'm sending you and Special Agent Sneed the address where you can find them."

"Okay." Madison reached her vehicle. Inside, she texted Garrett to let him know she was ready to follow up with the couple if he wanted her to interview them. Whatever it took to get the jump on Nicole's and, apparently, Olivia's killer.

Chapter Seven

Garrett drove to Linville Falls, in the Blue Ridge Mountains, at Milepost 316, where he located Maintenance Rangers Ward Wilcox and Ronnie Mantegna. They were picking up trash in the picnic area. Garrett hoped one or the other might have some useful information regarding the fatal attack on the parkway.

After bringing the men together, Garrett flashed his ID and said, "I'm investigating the murder of Park Ranger Nicole Wallenberg." He peered at Ronnie, who was in his midfifties, solid in build and had brownish-gray hair in a buzz cut and raven eyes. "When did you last see Ranger Wallenberg?"

"I saw her this morning," he responded. "She was with Ranger Edison, alive and well. Never saw either of them afterward."

Garrett took note of this. He turned to the other maintenance ranger. "What about you?"

Ward wiped sweat from his brow with the back of a work glove. "I saw Ranger Wallenberg on foot near where the black bear was located. She was alone. By the time Ranger Lynley arrived on the scene, Ranger Wallenberg had moved farther into the woods, away from the area." He paused. "That must have been when she was attacked."

Garrett recalled that he had run into Drew Mitchell on the parkway, who'd been in possession of Olivia Forlani's cell phone, before fleeing. "Did you see anyone else in the vicinity of Ranger Wallenberg?"

"Yeah, as a matter of fact," Ward answered surely. "The couple who reported being confronted by the black bear had been hanging around that area earlier."

Garrett nodded and then handed both men his card. "If either of you see or hear about anything else pertinent to this investigation, give me a call."

"We will," Ronnie said, stuffing the card into the pocket of his shirt.

"Yeah, count on it," Ward seconded.

Garrett was already back in his car when he listened to the voice mail from Ray Pottenger, informing him that they had found the persons of interest in the death of Nicole. He texted their address. Garrett saw the text as well from Madison. He called her and, when she answered, said, "Hey. Got the text. We should check out the couple together and see where it leads."

"Sounds good to me," she told him. "Where are you?"

Garrett told her, and they arranged a place to meet. He welcomed any opportunity to spend time with Madison, on and off the job. And if it could help them crack what was becoming a more and more unsettling case, all the better.

THEY DROVE TO the Rolling Hills Bed and Breakfast on Danner Road, where Madison immediately recognized Stan and Constance Franco. They were standing outside the two-story

Victorian. According to Deputy Pottenger, they were visiting from Honolulu. It was hard for Madison to imagine that they had decided in the middle of a vacation to the mainland to become killers along the way. But stranger things had happened.

"That's them," she told Garrett.

"Okay," he said. "Let's do this."

They exited the car and approached the couple. Both were in their late twenties, fit and good looking. Stan was tall, tanned, with slicked-back long hair in a man bun and brown eyes. Constance was nearly as tall and had big green eyes and fine blond hair in a short blunt cut, parted in the middle.

"Hi again," Madison said, after having spoken with them following the bear attack.

Constance smiled at her. "Hi."

"Ranger Lynley, right?" Stan said, eyeing her questioningly.

"Yes, and this is Special Agent Sneed," she told them. "We need to ask you a few questions."

"About the black bear?"

"Actually it's about a murder that took place on the Blue Ridge Parkway," Garrett said.

"Murder?" Constance grimaced. "Who?"

"A park ranger named Nicole Wallenberg," Madison informed them.

Garrett narrowed his eyes. "Someone stabbed Ranger Wallenberg to death during the time you were on the parkway."

Stan pursed his lips. "I'm sorry to hear that," he said. "But you don't think we had anything to do with it, do you?"

"We're questioning everyone who was there or may have

seen something," Madison answered evenly. She didn't want to frighten them unnecessarily. But there was never an easy way to confront potential suspects in crimes. "Ranger Wallenberg was killed not too far from the grassy area where you said you had a picnic. Did you hear or see anything?"

Constance's eyes darted to her husband's and back before responding, "Actually, around the time we spotted the black bear, there was what sounded like a woman crying out. But then the bear began making noises, and we thought that was what we heard."

Garrett regarded Stan keenly. "That true?"

"Yeah, it is," he insisted and turned to Madison. "When you showed up, along with the other rangers, to scare the bear off and nothing seemed to come of the other sounds, we assumed it was either our imagination or too much wine. Or the bear."

To Madison this seemed somewhat plausible, if convenient. "Did you see anyone leaving the area?" she asked, eyeing Constance.

"Yes." Her voice rose. "I saw a man running off in the woods."

"What did he look like?" Garrett asked.

She batted her lashes nervously. "I only noticed him at a glance, so I can't really tell you much about him. Honestly, I never gave it much thought one way or the other at the time. Sorry."

Madison turned to Stan. "Did you get a look at him?"

"Just the back of him as he was running into the forest," he told her. "I couldn't tell you anything else about him because he was too far away. And, to be honest, I don't know if he was trying to escape or just out for a jog."

"Neither do we," Garrett told him candidly. "But he's certainly someone we'd like to talk to."

"Afraid we can't help you there," he said.

Garrett looked at him. "How long will you be in town?"

"Till the end of the week."

"And you've been here for how long?"

"We arrived yesterday afternoon," Constance responded. Stan frowned. "Why do you ask?"

"No reason in particular," Garrett answered, though Madison knew it was to establish an alibi for their whereabouts when Olivia had been killed. If this was true, it would eliminate them as suspects, making it less likely they could have been involved with Nicole's death. "In case we have any more questions, we'd like to get your contact information."

"Sure, no problem," he agreed.

Madison gazed at Constance and said smilingly, "Hope the ordeal with the black bear hasn't scared you off."

"Honestly, I'm still a bit shaken from it," she said. "But it's even scarier to think that a murderer is apparently on the loose."

"Yeah," her husband grumbled. "Not exactly what we bargained for when deciding to vacation in North Carolina."

"None of us bargained for this—trust me," Garrett told him with an edge to his tone. "Unfortunately, things happen. Our job is to try to solve the case."

"Thanks for your time." Madison grinned at Stan. "We'll get out of your hair."

He nodded, and Constance said, "Thanks for coming to our rescue when the black bear didn't seem to want to leave us alone."

"Just doing my job," she said, diffident in accepting gratitude in this instance.

When they left, Garrett said, "What do you think?"

"I think they're innocent." Madison adjusted in the passenger seat. "Their alibi is easy enough to check out, if needed."

"True." He drove off. "If this man they saw running off is the real deal, then there's a good chance he was running away rather than toward something."

"Exactly." She faced him. "So, we really are looking at a likely serial killer?"

Garrett paused. "We'll see what the autopsy reveals on the cause and method of death," he voiced. "And what Forensics comes up with. But as of now, it seems like a distinct possibility."

"At least we have a solid lead to work with in trying to track down the perp," she pointed out.

"Yep. We just need a better description of the unsub in narrowing down the search."

Madison concurred. "Whoever he is, the unsub apparently knows his way around the Blue Ridge Parkway, if not the entire Pisgah National Forest," she speculated, what with his ability to avoid detection.

"I had that thought too." Garrett clutched the steering wheel. "Which makes him all the more dangerous."

Madison angled her face. "Are you thinking the unsub could be someone who works for the National Park Service?"

"Not necessarily. Apart from the many people employed by the NPS, there are plenty of regular visitors who are outdoorsmen, adventurers, hunters, survivalists, you name it, who choose to interact with nature in their life and times. Any one of them could have decided to become a killer along the way."

"Chilling," she uttered.

"Yeah." He drew a breath. "But we'll do whatever we have to in order to stop this from escalating," he told her.

Madison thought about her siblings investigating serial killers. She wondered how they managed to cope with the multiple lives lost at the hands of one or more killers. If they were suddenly dealing with this in her neck of the woods, she only hoped the unsub could be stopped in his tracks sooner rather than later. Having Garrett as lead investigator made her believe that this was a battle they would definitely win, no matter the obstacles before them.

When he pulled up behind her car, Garrett waited a beat, then turned toward Madison and leaned into her for a short kiss on the mouth. She felt her lips tingle, welcoming the kiss, but was still confused. "What was that for?"

"I just felt like kissing you," he responded point-blank. "Your lips are still as soft as I remember."

"Oh." She blushed but tried not to show it.

"Did I overstep?"

"No," she told him, realizing it was something that almost seemed inevitable, in spite of their attempts to place limitations on the nature of their relationship. But now was not the time to test those limits further. "I'll catch you later."

Garrett lowered his chin. "All right."

Madison exited his vehicle, sensing him watching until she had gotten into hers. He followed her briefly, till veering off in a different direction.

THOUGH IT HAD been quick and sweet, Garrett still had heart palpitations from kissing Madison when he walked inside his rented log cabin. He probably shouldn't have kissed her, aware that it could only lead them down a path they had mutually rejected before. But he didn't regret it. On the contrary, kissing her was maybe the best move he'd made since returning to Kiki's Ridge. He believed that Madison was amenable to it as well and that it was a step in the right direction toward reestablishing what had existed between them before. Even if he had no idea where they might be headed, one thing was clear to him: he didn't want to let fear of failure be his guide. What was meant to be would happen, one way or the other. He preferred to control his own destiny, while hoping it could align with hers.

After grabbing a beer from the refrigerator, Garrett broke away from thoughts about his personal life in favor of the criminal investigation that had shifted in a different direction somewhat with the discovery of a second murder victim, Nicole Wallenberg. She had been isolated just long enough for a killer to come after her. This was a similar pattern to the stabbing murder of Olivia Forlani. Why had the unsub targeted them? Or could they be separate incidences with two different killers?

Either way he looked at it, Garrett knew that public confidence was bound to be eroded in the comfort level and security surrounding the Blue Ridge Parkway for as long as safety was an issue. It was up to him as the main investigator in this region to solve these unsettling homicides. Or save the day. While hardly a superhero, this was his forte as an ISB special agent, and he didn't intend to let down those who depended on him. That included Madison, who had known one victim and discovered another in the course of her own duties as a law enforcement ranger. She needed to feel safe in her own workspace without having to constantly look over her shoulder for fear that a killer might be lying in wait.

IN THE MORNING, Garrett stuck with his routine of a jog and a workout to get the blood flowing. He hoped to get to do this with Madison soon, knowing that he had asked her to refrain from going out alone on the parkway trails as long as one or more killers were at large. He couldn't help but think about the ultimate workout they could have together in bed. Madison was a great lover, and it was one of the things he missed most about being with her. Would they get to experience the pleasure of one another's intimate company again? Or had that opportunity passed, in spite of a new understanding between them?

By the time he had gotten back to the cabin, showered and changed clothes, Dawn Dominguez had sent Garrett the autopsy report on Nicole Wallenberg. He read it on his laptop. The medical examiner confirmed that Nicole had been the victim of a vicious stabbing attack. She'd been stabbed ten times, including in the chest, stomach, back and arms, resulting in death as a homicide. He took note that, similar to Olivia's death, the undiscovered murder weapon was an eight-inch, single-edged blade knife characteristic of a survival knife.

I have to assume these homicides were perpetrated by the same offender, Garrett told himself while he drank his coffee. They were indeed facing a serial killer on the parkway. And the unsub had no qualms about stabbing his victims in a brazen daytime attack. This evoked thoughts once again to Garrett about his mother's murder in the same Blue Ridge Mountains thirty years ago. Who had gone after her and gotten away with it? He didn't want to think about history repeating itself with a new killer in the forest and mountains. Handpicking or having stalked his victims and never having to answer for it.

On his laptop, Garrett contacted his boss, Carly Tafoya, for a video chat to update her about the investigation. When she came on, he got right to the point. "There's been new developments to the case."

"Tell me," Carly voiced anxiously.

Having phoned her yesterday about the sad news of Nicole's murder and the speculation of its link to the murder of Olivia Forlani, Garrett said firmly, "We do think we have a serial killer on our hands. The autopsy report indicated that Nicole was stabbed to death in a way that mirrors Forlani's death, by and large. The murder weapon in both homicides is believed to be a survival knife."

Carly muttered an expletive while making a face. "That's not good."

"Not at all." Garrett frowned. "There's more. Witnesses reported seeing a man who may have been running from the scene of Nicole's murder. Though we haven't nailed down a solid description as yet, it fits with the strong suspicions on my part that the killer of Nicole and Olivia is male."

Carly sighed. "Use everything you have at your disposal, Sneed, to stop this man."

"I intend to," Garrett assured her.

"Whatever support you need, just ask."

"I will." As of now, what he needed most was to alert

local and other federal law enforcement and communities in and around the Blue Ridge Parkway to be on guard for a likely serial killer on the loose. If they were able to at least rattle the cage somewhat of the unsub, it might be enough to force him to go underground and away from potential targets. Till they could nail him. And Garrett wouldn't rest till the deed was done.

Chapter Eight

Madison sat on the U-shaped bench in the breakfast nook, looking at the autopsy report that Garrett had sent her on her laptop. It was painful to read about the nature of and verdict on Nicole Wallenberg's death. Like Olivia, she'd been murdered by stabbing. A survival knife was thought to be the weapon of choice by the unsub. By all accounts, it seemed that they were looking at a serial killer and one who was elusive and violent enough to send a chill through Madison.

We can't let this monster get away with this, she told herself. Even then, the fear was that the longer it took to find the perp, the more likely it was that he would strike again.

She closed out the report and went onto Zoom for a video conference with her brothers, Scott and Russell Lynley. Both worked for the FBI as special agents, albeit in different capacities and locations. Scott was older and separated from his wife, Paula. Madison hoped they would be able to patch things up. Russell, who was younger, was married and about to bring a new Lynley into the world.

When they appeared on the screen, Madison broke into a grin, feeling comfort in talking with her brothers. Both were incredibly handsome and gray-eyed, much like their father. Scott had a square face and thick coal-black hair in a comb-over, low-fade style, while Russell had more of an oblong face to go with black hair in a high and tight cut.

"Hey, you two."

"Hey," they spoke in unison and paused before Scott said solemnly, "Heard you lost an NPS ranger."

"Yes, we did." Madison was not surprised that the news would reach them before she could pass it along. "Nicole was stabbed to death off the Blue Ridge Parkway," she said painfully.

"Sorry about that," Russell voiced, his thick brows knitted.

She twisted her lips. "Worse is that it comes on the heels of a similar death on the parkway of a friend of mine."

"Yeah, Annette mentioned that to me the other day. I reached out to you."

Madison acknowledged this and said, "It's certainly unsettling."

"So, what, we're talking about a serial killer lurking around in the Blue Ridge Mountains?" Scott put forth.

"Seems that way," she responded. "Between the location, manner of attack, type of injuries and the kind of knife believed to have been used to murder them, yes, I'd say a serial killer is at large."

Russell scratched his nose. "Who's heading the investigation?"

"Garrett Sneed," Madison answered equably.

Scott frowned. "Not the same ISB special agent who bailed on you?"

"One and the same," she admitted, though knowing it wasn't quite as simple as that.

"I thought he went to Arizona," Russell said. "Or was it New Mexico?"

"Did Sneed come back to give you more headaches?" Scott asked.

"Enough, already." Madison realized that they were just doing what overprotective brothers did in trying to look out for her best interests in their own ways. "Garrett and I are good." *Or at least no longer bad in terms of miscommunication,* she thought. "Anyway, this isn't about my love life. Or lack thereof. It's about Garrett coming in to do his job in investigating one, now two, homicides in the Pisgah Ranger District."

"You're absolutely right about that." Russell tilted his face. "He's obviously good at his job, as are you. Whatever you need to work out on a personal level, I'm sure you will."

She grinned. "Thanks for saying that."

He nodded. "We always have your back, sis."

In trying to lighten the mood, Scott said, "Still, if you ever need us to gang up on Sneed, we will."

Madison chuckled. "I don't think that will be necessary. He's one of the good guys."

"Okay." He sat back. "What can we do to help in the investigation?"

"Right now, I just need your support and an occasional virtual shoulder to cry on."

"You've got both," he said, and it was seconded by Russell.

Madison was grateful for such, knowing it worked both ways, as well as with Annette. When the chips were down, as Lynleys, they were there for each other, something she never took for granted.

After the chat ended, Madison got ready for work and headed for the parkway. Upon arrival, she parked and got out on foot and headed to the area where she'd found Nicole's body. The crime scene tape had been removed, allowing for free access. Though it was eerie to be back there, Madison thought she might check around for anything the crime scene techs and other rangers might have missed. It also occurred to her that the unsub might morbidly return to the scene of the crime. And even come after her.

Were the latter the case, she would be ready for him. Madison instinctively placed a hand on the firearm in her magnetic leather holster. In the meantime, if there was anything she could do to move the investigation along in trying to nab her fellow ranger's killer, she was up for the challenge.

Just as Madison was studying the dirt path Nicole would have taken to reach that point and happened to notice a fallen tree branch that she imagined could have been used to cover tracks, she heard what sounded like footsteps coming up fast behind her. Sucking in a deep breath to suppress the fear that gripped her heart, Madison yanked out her pistol and flung herself around at the intruder, with no plans to ask questions first.

To her surprise, a hard question was posed to her instead, as the familiar deep voice barked, "What are you doing here?"

It took Madison only an instant to come to terms with the so-called intruder as actually Garrett. Releasing a sigh, she responded sardonically, "I work here, remember?"

"I remember." He put up his hands in mock surrender. "Don't shoot!"

Realizing she was still pointing the gun in his direction, she put it back in her holster. "Sorry about that. I thought you might be—"

"The killer?" Garrett deduced. "I gathered that much." He lowered his arms. "So you came to this spot in hopes of luring him out, or what?"

"No, I came in search of evidence," she told him matter-of-factly. "Seemed like a good place to start. After all, as you've reminded me more than once, this is my investigation too." Was she acting a bit too defensive? Was that really necessary?

"It is *our* investigation," he reiterated. "In fact, I made my way over here for the same reason. I was just surprised to find you here ahead of me."

Madison relaxed, feeling that she'd overreacted. "Guess great minds think alike," she quipped.

He grinned. "Did you find anything interesting?"

She took a few steps toward the tree branch, pulled a latex glove out of her pocket and put it on, then picked up the branch. Turning it over, she saw a faint discoloration on one part. She held it up to him. "That could be human blood."

Garrett studied it. "Possibly."

"If so, it could belong to Nicole or the unsub," Madison said. "Forensics can tell us. If it is the killer's DNA, then CODIS might be able to identify the unknown DNA profile."

"You're right." He ran a hand along his jawline. "We'll get this to the state crime lab in Hendersonville," he said and looked at Madison curiously. "Did you find anything else?"

"Only that the area, largely hidden from the grassy hill and parking lot, suggests that the unsub made a conscious choice to either lure Nicole here or was lying in wait for anyone who happened to come to this spot to go after." Madison looked in a direction where the cluster of trees made for the perfect getaway. "He had to have gone that way to avoid detection for as long as possible."

"I think you're right." Garrett gave her the once-over, and she found herself coloring as she imagined he was undressing her with his very eyes—something she had admittedly found herself prone to doing with him from time to time since he'd returned. "We're checking dumpsters, trails, mountains and the water for the murder weapon and any bloody clothes the unsub may have ditched."

"Good." Madison hoped something would come up that pointed toward the perpetrator. She thought about Scott and Russell ribbing her about Garrett. In spite of their relationship being thrown off course for two years, Madison felt they were back on track now, even if it was unclear what train they were taking. Or, for that matter, what their next stop was.

When his cell phone rang, Garrett removed it from the back pocket of his chinos, looked at it and said, "I'd better get this." He answered, "Sneed," before saying, "Sheriff Silva. Yes, it has been a while. What can I do for you?"

Madison knew that Jacob Silva was the sheriff of Buncombe County, which bordered the Blue Ridge Parkway. She listened as Garrett lifted a brow and continued with, "Really?" Then, after a long pause, "Okay. Right. Good. Keep me posted."

When Garrett disconnected, he eyed her and said, "There's been a development…"

"What?" Her voice rose with interest.

His mouth tightened. "A woman was stabbed to death this morning in Buncombe County. The suspect, identified as Norman Kruger, carjacked another woman's vehicle and is currently on the move in her blue Hyundai Elantra." Garrett waited a beat and said tonelessly, "Silva thinks that Kruger could be the unsub, who the local press is now referring to as the Blue Ridge Parkway Killer."

GARRETT STOOD TOE-TO-TOE with Sheriff Jacob Silva, whom he'd known since his previous stint as a Region 2 ISB special agent. They were the same height, but Silva was a little heavier. In his midforties, he had brown eyes and short brown hair with a sprinkling of gray and a horseshoe mustache.

"What can you tell me about the suspect?" Garrett asked as they stood outside an interrogation room at the sheriff's office in Asheville, where thirty-four-year-old Norman Kruger was waiting to be interviewed. An hour ago, he had been taken into custody without incident after a high-speed chase had come to an end when he'd lost control of the car. Though shaken up, the carjacking victim, seventy-three-year-old Diane Fullerton, had been unharmed.

"Kruger is a real piece of work," Silva told him. "He's been in and out of jail for most of his life for crimes ranging from larceny-theft to aggravated assault to kidnapping and drug possession. He's currently being charged with first-degree murder in the death of thirty-two-year-old Frances Reynolds, thought to be the girlfriend of the suspect. She was stabbed multiple times and left for dead in her apartment. He's also facing charges of armed carjacking, unlawful use of a weapon and resisting arrest. Other charges are pending. And, obviously, there could be more, after your interrogation of the suspect."

"What about the murder weapon?"

"We collected as evidence a survival knife that we believe was the weapon he used to stab to death Frances Reynolds. It's being processed right now."

"Good," Garrett said, thoughtful. "I'll take it from here."

Silva nodded. "He's all yours."

When he stepped inside the room, Garrett knew that Madison would be watching the interrogation on live video in a different room with interest, hoping, like him, that they had the man responsible for the cold-blooded murders of Olivia Forlani and Nicole Wallenberg. He turned his attention back to the suspect, who was seated at a square metal table and handcuffed, and told him, "I'm Special Agent Sneed of the National Park Service's Investigative Services Branch."

Norman Kruger was lean, wearing a dirty T-shirt and jeans. He had dark hair in a skin-fade cut with the top textured. Snarling at Garrett, he retorted, "So what do you want with me?"

Garrett sat in a metal chair across from him and glared at the suspect. "Why don't we start by discussing why you're here," he began coolly. "You're facing a murder rap in the stabbing death of Frances Reynolds, among other charges."

"Tell me something I don't know." He jutted his chin. "That bitch had it coming to her after two-timing on me with another dude."

"What about the elderly woman who nearly had a heart attack when you ordered her out of her vehicle at gunpoint?" Garrett peered at him. "Did she have it coming too?"

"I needed some wheels," Kruger hissed. "She was just in the way."

I'll bet, he mused cynically. "Didn't get you very far for where you're going from here. Did it?"

Kruger twisted his lips. "Whatever."

He sighed, knowing it was time to confront the smug suspect over the homicides that had occurred on the parkway. "Why don't we talk about the two women murdered recently on the Blue Ridge Parkway," he said casually, noting the suspect had not asked for an attorney.

Kruger stared at him with a furrowed brow. "Not sure what you mean?"

"I'll try to clarify," Garrett snapped. "You're being investigated as a person of interest in the murders of Olivia Forlani and Nicole Wallenberg. Both were stabbed to death in separate incidents along trails off the parkway, reminiscent of your attack on Frances Reynolds."

"Hey, I had nothing to do with those."

Garrett bristled with skepticism. "Someone fitting your description was seen running off after murdering Park Ranger Nicole Wallenberg yesterday morning," he pointed out. In reality, Garrett knew that the description of the unsub was pretty vague at best. But Kruger didn't need to know that at the moment. Especially if this helped lead to a confession when he was backed into a proverbial corner.

"Wasn't me," Kruger maintained. He wrinkled his crooked nose. "I wasn't anywhere near the parkway yesterday."

Garrett dismissed this with a wave of his hand. "So where were you?"

"I was in Charlotte," he argued.

"Doing what?"

"Playing at a dive bar called the Parties Pad," Kruger said. "I play guitar with a band that travels around the state and elsewhere. Did three sets and played pool afterward. I have witnesses. Didn't get back here till early this morning, after hitching a ride with another member of the band— Chuck Garcia. So no, you can't pin the ranger's death on me."

Garrett looked at the camera, wondering what Madison's take was on the suspect. Was this another dead end? He regarded Kruger. "We'll check out your story." He paused and then asked for his whereabouts during the time of Olivia Forlani's murder, not ruling out that there might still have been more than one killer at work.

Kruger again claimed he'd been on the road with his band, giving dates and places they'd performed. It would be easy enough to verify. Garrett still had his suspicions, though, and asked Kruger if he would be willing to take a lie detector test. "It'll help us rule you out for the parkway murders," he told the suspect.

"Yeah, whatever." Kruger shrugged. "But you're wasting your time. As I said, I never killed anyone on the Blue Ridge Parkway."

Garrett leaned forward. "That remains to be seen."

He left the interrogation room and arranged with Sheriff Silva to have the test administered by a polygraph examiner before going to confer with Madison in a viewing room.

"So, what do you think about Kruger?" he asked her.

"He's definitely a creep," she stated flatly. "But I'm not sure he's guilty of being the Blue Ridge Parkway Killer. He seemed too arrogant and clear in his denials."

Garrett was inclined to agree. "We'll see if he passes the lie detector test and if the knife he used to kill his girlfriend yields anything."

Madison folded her arms. "If nothing else, at least they got him for what he did to her."

"Yeah."

Sheriff Silva entered the room and said with a frown on his face, "The polygraph examiner is on her way. In the meantime, we can add attempted murder to the growing list of charges Kruger faces. Just received word that he practically beat to death a man named Peter McLachlan. Kruger's girlfriend was apparently having an affair with McLachlan. Looks like he'll pull through, but he's got a long haul ahead of him."

Madison grimaced. "Kruger was clearly a loose cannon with others paying the price."

Garrett shook his head in despair. "He definitely went off the deep end in his homicidal vengeance."

"And he's going to pay for it," Silva said with certainty. "The only question left is whether or not we can pin the parkway crimes on him."

"There is that," Garrett conceded, but he only wanted things to go in that direction if Kruger was actually guilty of the serial murders.

Two hours later, they were informed that Norman Kruger had passed the polygraph and that his alibis checked out. Forensic testing of the survival knife used to kill Frances Reynolds had found no DNA or blood evidence to tie the weapon to Olivia or Nicole. Moreover, the blade of Kruger's knife measured just four inches, compared to the eight-inch knife the killer had used against Forlani and Wallenberg.

This was more than enough for Garrett to move away from Norman Kruger as a suspect, even as the book was thrown at him for the murder of his girlfriend and other offenses.

Chapter Nine

"What do you say we split a pizza?" Garrett offered that evening as he rode with Madison.

"Sure," she responded, her stomach growling after missing lunch. "Takeout?"

"Yeah. Unless you'd rather eat at the restaurant?"

"Takeout is fine."

"All right. Takeout it is."

Madison took the Blue Ridge Parkway to Beaubianna Drive, where she pulled into the Dottie's Pizza parking lot.

"So, what would you like on your half?" Garrett asked, unbuckling his seat belt.

Had he forgotten that she loved pepperoni, anchovies and cheese pizza? She grinned at him. "Surprise me."

"I can do that." He returned the smile. "Back in a few."

While she waited, Madison wondered if there could still be a future for them. Or had that ship sailed and there was no need to think in terms beyond camaraderie and working together on a case?

She was still mulling this over when Garrett returned. "All set?"

"Yeah. I think you'll be pleased with the selection of toppings for your half."

"Can't wait to taste it." The inviting aroma of the pizza made her stomach growl again.

"So, your place or mine?" he asked casually.

"Hmm…" Madison contemplated this. "Mine. There's beer and wine in the fridge to help wash down the pizza." Never mind that the place was her own comfort zone.

Garrett grinned. "Sounds fine to me."

They were mostly silent during the drive, except the occasional comment on the landscape or something new that Garrett noted along the way from when he'd lived in the area previously.

When they reached her house and went inside, he hit the lights, scanned the place and said, "Looks pretty much like I remember."

Madison batted her eyes. "Did you think it would have changed?"

"Not really. Sometimes people do like to redecorate or whatever, just for the hell of it. In this case, the house is perfect just as it is."

"Thanks." *He always had a way with words*, she thought, smiling. Madison took the pizza box from him and said, "I'll set everything out. Make yourself at home."

"I'd like to help," he insisted, following her into the kitchen.

"Okay," she relented, handing him back the pizza. "We can eat at the dining room table. Napkins are in that drawer—" she pointed "—in case you've forgotten."

"I remember." After washing and drying his hands, he grabbed a batch of napkins and headed into the dining room.

Madison washed up. "Did you want beer or red wine?" she asked, taking a couple of plates out of the rustic cabinet.

"Beer."

She'd suspected as much. After setting the plates on the mahogany square table, she got out two bottles from the refrigerator. Handing him one, she sat across from him in an upholstered gray side chair. Madison noted that the pizza box was still closed.

She gazed at Garrett, who was grinning sideways as he said to her, "I'll let you do the honors."

When she lifted the lid, Madison broke into a smile as she saw that the entire pizza was covered with pepperoni, anchovies and cheese. He'd remembered. "Cute," she uttered, blushing.

He laughed. "Hey, some memories never go away."

And others? She wondered just how much he recalled about their previous time spent as a couple. "Good to know."

They began to eat and drink while talking about the investigation. "Too bad Norman Kruger didn't pan out as our killer," Garrett bemoaned.

"I know." Madison dug into a slice of pizza. His disappointment matched her own. "At least Kruger is off the streets for his own horrific crimes."

"Yeah, you're right about that." Garrett sipped his beer. "As for the Blue Ridge Parkway Killer, as they're calling him, with the technology we have working for us, he's not about to slip through the cracks."

"Something tells me he doesn't want to," she surmised. "At least not totally. If the unsub was willing to kill two women on the parkway, there's no telling how many more he's capable of killing, if the opportunity is there. Clearly, he's able and willing."

"And we're just as able to come between him and his dastardly plans," Garrett insisted. "We're onto him now, and he knows it. Homing in on other vulnerable women just got much more difficult for him, if he hopes to remain in the shadows instead of behind bars."

"I want that to be true." She took another bite of pizza. "This can't go on for much longer. Not if we want to restore sanity to the Blue Ridge Parkway. And the rest of the Pisgah National Forest, for that matter."

"It won't." Garrett's voice deepened with conviction. He suddenly reached across the table and ran a finger down the corner of her mouth. "Some cheese had managed to get away from you. Thought I'd help out there."

Her face flushed with embarrassment. Or was it more of a turn-on to feel the touch of his finger? "A napkin would have sufficed, thank you."

He cut a grin. "Maybe. But what fun would that have been?"

"I thought we were here to eat. Not have fun."

"Why not do both?" Garrett bit into his own pizza slice and seemed to deliberately allow a web of cheese to hang down his chin. "Think I could use a little help here," he said, a catch to his voice.

"Oh, really?" Madison played along and used her own finger to wind around the cheese before removing it. "Satisfied?"

He stood up and took her hand, pulling her up. "Actually, I'm not quite satisfied, not yet."

They were close enough that she could feel the heat emanating from him. "And what else did you have in mind?"

"This…" Garrett held Madison's cheeks and planted his mouth on her lips for a solid kiss. It felt good and neither seemed in any hurry to stop kissing one another.

When she finally unlocked their mouths, Madison looked him in the eye and saw the desire, which she felt too. "Are you sure this is a good idea?" she asked, wondering if he would be the voice of reason before things went too far to pull back.

"I'm sure it's an idea that's long overdue," he indicated. "Yes, I want to kiss you some more and then make love to you, Madison."

"I think I want that too," she admitted, quivering at the thought. "Yes, I do want it," Madison felt the need to make clear.

"So, let's do this." He regarded her keenly and took her hand. "I think I remember how to get to the bedroom."

"I'm sure you do." She smiled as her heart skipped a beat. "Lead the way."

Once they stepped inside the room, Garrett stopped and said, "There's something else I've been dying to do since I laid eyes on you again…"

She held his gaze with anticipation. "Oh? What's that?"

"This," he said as he unraveled her hair from the bun it was in, allowing it to fall freely upon her shoulders. He tousled the hair. "I love your long locks."

Madison knew this, but they had not been in the right situation for her to wear it down. Till now. "Kiss me," she demanded, grabbing his shirt.

"With pleasure."

They stood there, kissing one another like old lovers, which Madison knew they were. This both frightened and excited her. More the latter, as the intensity of the kiss grew as their bodies molded together while they wrapped their arms around each other. She was all in for the ride, even if the future remained uncertain.

After they shed their clothes with lightning speed, removing any barriers between them, Madison felt just a tad self-conscious in baring all to a man for the first time since their relationship had ended.

But this quickly went away with the sheer appreciation she saw in his stare that he followed with, "You're still gorgeous."

Drinking in the sight of his hard body and six-pack, causing a stir in her, she couldn't help but say in response, "So are you, Garrett."

"I'll take that, coming from you." He stepped closer and lifted up her chin. "And give this in return." Another mouth-watering kiss was laid on her, making Madison feel as though she were floating on air. When it came time for them to take this to bed, she removed a condom packet from the nightstand that had not yet expired.

Handing it to him, she smiled and said, "From the last time you were here."

Garrett chuckled. "Glad you saved it."

"So am I." Madison gazed at him desirously. "Better not let it go to waste."

"Oh, it won't," he promised, tossing the packet onto the bed to come back to later. "First things first."

Her lashes fluttered with anticipation. "What might that be?"

Garrett kissed her forehead. "A little of this…" He kissed both cheeks. "A little of that…" He ran his hands through her hair while kissing her on the mouth. "Maybe some of that and this…" He touched one nipple, then the other, causing waves of delight to shoot through Madison. It caused her desire to be with him to kick up another fervent notch.

"I get the picture," she cooed impatiently, taking his hand and leading him to the bed. "Let's move on…please."

"Got it." His voice rang with conviction as they got on the sateen duvet cover. He draped one leg across hers. "Before we get down to business, I'd like us to reacquaint ourselves with one another."

"Oh, would you now?" Madison kissed him, moving her hand down his body teasingly as he stiffened. "I'm sensing some familiarity here."

"So am I." Garrett had a sharp intake of breath as his nimble fingers went to work on her, finding all the right intimate spots. "And I'm liking what I'm feeling."

"Umm…me too," she voiced dulcetly, body suddenly ablaze as an orgasm roared through her. When she couldn't take the pure torture of a partial victory anymore, Madison demanded, "I'd like to feel even more of you inside me. Now!"

"As you wish," he said, kissing her mouth again before ripping open the packet and putting on the condom.

But even as she longed for further fulfillment, Garrett once again showed enormous patience for his own needs as he stimulated her more before finally moving atop and working his way between her legs. Ready as ever, Madison was definitely hot and bothered when he entered her. She absorbed his quick and powerful thrusts the way the skin did the sun's rays, meeting him halfway each time.

Their mouths were locked passionately as their bodies moved in perpetual harmony. In short order, Madison climaxed again, at the same time as Garrett. She could feel the erratic beating of his heart, matching her own as the moment came and left them catching their breaths afterward.

"Wow." Garrett laughed as he lay on his back beside her. "That—you—were amazing."

"So were you," Madison admitted, resting her head on his shoulder.

"Some things in life are worth waiting for—again."

She chuckled. "You think so?"

"I know so." He kissed her hair. "This was definitely worth a two-year wait. Every scintillating second."

Though she didn't disagree, Madison was left to wonder what came next. Did he even know? Should it be an issue?

"WHAT ARE WE DOING?" Madison asked him as she propped up on an elbow, giving Garrett a nice view of her nude body.

He pretended he didn't get her drift as he took in her perfectly sized breasts, shapely form and long lean legs, while quipping, "I should think it would be obvious. It's called jumping each other's bones."

She laughed and hit him playfully on the shoulder. "You know what I mean."

He did and, as such, turned serious when facing her, while considering how best to respond without overpromising or understating where they were. "Well, I think we're simply reconnecting in one way in which we were crazy for one another," he spoke honestly. "Seems like it worked out pretty well. Don't you think?"

"Hmm..." Madison met his eyes thoughtfully. "What happened to just being friends?"

Garrett held her gaze when he responded dubiously, "Friendship comes in many forms."

"And what form would you call this?" she asked. "Friendship with benefits?"

He laughed. "I think I'd be more comfortable with friendship and the enormous possibilities it presents for a brighter future between us, in one way or another."

Okay, I came out with where I'd like to see this go, sort of, Garrett told himself. He hoped they were on the same page.

Madison raised a brow. "That doesn't scare you?"

"It might have once," he confessed. "But not now. I'm open to whatever comes next. You?"

She waited a beat and then said evenly, "Yeah, I think I am."

"Cool." He beamed and, taking in her scent, suddenly felt himself aroused again. Running a hand across her back, he asked, "Are there any more of those packets in the nightstand?"

"There might be one or two more. Why?"

"Oh, I was thinking it might be fun to go a second round."

Her eyes lit. "Really?"

He grinned. "Well, things did go a bit more quickly than I would have liked," he admitted.

"I see." She touched his chest. "Sure you can handle another round?"

He chuckled. "Without a doubt. Being with you gives me all the energy I need."

"Then I say let's go for it," she said enthusiastically.

This was music to Garrett's ears as he started to kiss her, slipping his tongue in Madison's mouth. He absolutely loved the taste and feel of her, making him want her even more. By the time they had worked each other up into a near frenzy, he had managed to slip out of bed just long enough to put on the protection before picking up where they'd left off. Their bodies were entangled in the heat of passion and exploration.

Madison moaned as he hit her sweet spot time and time again, then called out his name when she reached orgasm while on top. Having held back just long enough to wait for that to happen, Garrett played with her hair and brought their faces together for a toe-curling kiss before letting go in achieving his own pinnacle of sexual gratification. Only then did they settle down and ride the rapids of contentment.

"Was it just as good the second time?" Madison asked with a giggle. "Not counting our previous lovemaking sessions."

Garrett grinned slyly beside her. "What do you think?"

"Umm… I think so, judging by how wonderful it was for me."

"Good deduction." His voice deepened. "You never fail to amaze me just how incredible you are in bed."

Her eyes narrowed. "Just in bed?"

He chuckled, realizing how what he'd said might have come across. "In and out of bed," he promised. "Breaking up had nothing to do with how great you are as a person." He hoped she knew that.

"I could say the same about you," she told him while running her fingers over his chest.

"Yeah?"

"Of course. You've always been able to capture my fancy, Special Agent Sneed, even when we were no longer together."

"I'll take capturing your fancy anytime," he said lightheartedly but meant every word.

"Oh, really?" Madison brushed her lips against his. "If you think you can handle a third go at it, I'm game."

He laughed. "You're insatiable, you know that?"

"And you're not?"

"Guilty as charged." Garrett couldn't keep a big smile off his face. He loved being able to take his time in pleasuring Madison and being pleasured by her. It was the one sure area where they clicked on all levels. The fact that it felt so natural, as if not missing a beat, didn't surprise him. Hell, he'd never felt for one instant that their lovemaking wouldn't be everything it had been before. But he'd been wrong. The sex was better than ever between them. This told him that she'd been the one thing missing in his life for two years that had left him feeling a void. Now that they had rekindled things, he wasn't about to let what they had slip through his fingers again.

The fact that they were still dealing with an unsub serial killer on the parkway was troubling for sure. But Garrett was as equally committed to having a second shot with Madison as he was to stopping the murders on the Blue Ridge Parkway. Something he had never been able to do to save his mother from falling prey to a bad man.

Chapter Ten

"Are you up for a run this morning?" Madison asked, wanting to take advantage of Garrett's presence after halting her runs temporarily while a killer was on the loose. Of course, she knew he was in her bed, naked, and hadn't brought any jogging attire after spending the night. Whereas she had been up for half an hour, made coffee and, after putting her hair into a high ponytail, had thrown on a sports bra, running shorts and sneakers.

Rubbing his eyes of sleepiness, Garrett replied, "Yeah, sure. We can pop over to my cabin, and I'll get dressed for a run. There's a great trail there. Then we can have breakfast there, back here or wherever you like."

"Sounds good." Madison smiled at him, feeling a fresh surge of desire after getting little sleep. But she kept it in check, not wanting to read too much into what had happened between them—in spite of the indication by both of them that it was a building block for a renewed relationship, rather than an exciting trip down memory lane. The last thing she wanted was to end up disappointed once more. "I'll wait for you downstairs," she said, not trusting herself in getting too cozy again.

"Okay," he said simply, sitting up. "I won't be long."

Twenty minutes later, they were running along a trail meandering between bigtooth aspen, tulip and magnolia trees. Madison managed to keep pace with Garrett, who had changed into a blue T-shirt and running shorts—with his muscular arms and legs in full display—and training sneakers. She studied him. He seemed caught up in his own world, in spite of having regained a place in hers.

"You don't talk much about your mother," Madison tossed at him for some reason. In their previous relationship, she'd only been given a general accounting of what had happened to her and him thereafter. Madison wanted more but didn't feel it was her place to ask.

Garrett gazed at her thoughtfully and said, "Kind of a hard thing to talk about, you know?"

"Yeah, I get that." She acknowledged that it wasn't so easy to think about her own parents' tragic death, much less air out her feelings about losing them too soon in life. But given the way his mother had died and his own shattered childhood as a result, it was still different. "Might help, though, to share what it is you're feeling. I know it's been a long time having to carry the memory of her death."

"You're right." He took a breath. "I want to let you in on what I've been carrying around for thirty years." Another sigh. "With no father in the picture, my mother, as a single parent, meant the world to me. She taught me everything she could to a five-year-old about the Cherokee culture but not nearly what she would have, had she lived longer."

Madison flashed him a sympathetic look. "I can only imagine how much it took out of you to have been deprived of this."

"Though she's been gone a long time, I still find myself trying to come to terms with the lost opportunity," he stated musingly. "The fact that her killer was never found only makes it worse."

"Which I know is only exacerbated by the current case we're working on," she voiced sadly.

Garrett nodded, wiping his brow with the back of his hand. "Yeah. But I can't go back and undo what was done to my mother. Hard as it is, I have to live for today. That includes my job. And getting to spend time with you again."

Madison took solace in his words and was encouraged by them. "I feel the same way."

He gave her a thin smile and said, "Better head back now."

"Okay." She took the lead and stayed just ahead of him as they navigated the trail and were silent while listening to the sounds of nature all around them.

GARRETT FELT BETTER in sharing his thoughts about his mother with Madison and having been raised by his grandparents. As someone he wanted to play an important part in his life, he understood that this included being open about his history and their own potential future beyond a serial-murder investigation. In turn, he needed just as much from her if they were to have a chance in making this work.

That morning, they met up with Leonard along the parkway. His brow creased as he said, "A couple of the maintenance rangers found a blood-soaked shirt and a survival knife buried in a dumpster."

Madison reacted with interest. "Really?"

"Yeah. They were apparently in a black plastic bag and underneath other trash, as if by design."

"And where was the dumpster located?" Garrett asked curiously.

"Not far from the Blue Ridge National Heritage Area," Leonard answered.

"Hmm…" He pondered this. "If this proves to be what we think it is, that would mean the unsub went the extra mile, so to speak, to try to hide evidence of one or more murders."

"Yeah, looks that way to me," Leonard concurred.

"Where are these items now?" Madison asked the ranger.

"Turned them over to the crime lab for processing."

"Good," Garrett told him. "We need to know, like yesterday, if this is a solid lead or not."

Leonard nodded. "I hear you."

"Makes sense that the unsub in one or both murders would try to unload the evidence of the crimes," Madison said. "Especially as the investigation heats up."

"We'll see," Garrett said, preferring to reserve judgment for now, while remaining optimistic that this was a potential breakthrough development.

Two hours later, he and Madison drove to the Western Regional Crime Laboratory in Hendersonville on Saint Pauls Road. There, they met with Jewel Yasumori, a slender, thirtysomething forensic analyst, for the results on testing of the items recovered. Earlier, she had been sent the tree branch that Madison had found near the spot where Nicole had been murdered.

Garrett was impatient as he looked at Jewel, whose short black hair was in a pixie bob with tapered sideburns. He asked point-blank, "What did you learn from analyzing the shirt and survival knife?"

Jewel blinked dark brown eyes and said, "Let's start with the shirt." She turned on her monitor that had an image of a man's casual button-down blue shirt. It was stained with blood. "We tested the blood for DNA and found that it was a match for Ranger Nicole Wallenberg's DNA."

Garrett watched Madison's jaw drop with the confirmation before she asked, "Did you find anyone else's DNA on the shirt?"

"Afraid not," Jewel said. "However, we were able to gather some fibers from the shirt as trace evidence. They were consistent with fibers found on Ranger Wallenberg's clothing, which can further be used to make a case against the unsub."

Garrett took note of that and asked her with interest, "What about the knife?"

Jewel's brow creased as she pulled up an image of a survival knife on her display. It had a rubber handle. "We found blood stains on the stainless-steel survival knife with a single-edged blade that measured eight inches. They matched the DNA profiles of Nicole Wallenberg and Olivia Forlani," she told them. "As such, this was almost certainly the weapon used to kill both of them."

Madison wrinkled her nose in disgust. "The perp was so brazen as to keep the same knife to go after Olivia, then Nicole."

"But smart enough to get rid of it rather than take a chance that the weapon might be discovered on his person or property," Garrett surmised. What concerned him was the unsub getting another survival knife to carry on his killings. "Were you able to pull any prints off the knife?"

"Actually, we do have some positive news on that front." Jewel perked up. "We were able to recover a latent palm print from a right hand off the knife," she reported enthusiastically. "It was entered into the FBI's Next Generation Identification system biometric database with its Advanced Fingerprint Identification Technology and the State Bureau of Investigation's Computerized Criminal History file." She sighed. "Unfortunately, we haven't been able to get a hit as yet on the unsub, if he's in the system."

Garrett frowned. He had to consider that the perp might somehow have been able to avoid arrest or incarceration, keeping his prints from being on file. "So, no DNA potentially belonging to the unsub?" he had to ask.

"We're still probing for this." Jewel licked her lips. "It's possible that we might be able to obtain a partial DNA profile of the unsub from the palm print or the part of the knife where it was left. This will depend on the number of cells we can gather from the latent print." She paused. "Of course, if we can retrieve an unknown DNA profile, we'll be able to upload it to CODIS and see if there's a match to an arrestee or offender or DNA profile."

"That's a lot of ifs," Madison pointed out skeptically. "But at least it gives us something to work with in going after the unsub."

"My sentiments exactly," Garrett said, believing that either way he looked at it, they were a step or two closer to identifying the Blue Ridge Parkway Killer. "For instance, we've now confirmed, more or less, that a single perpetrator was responsible for the stabbing deaths of Olivia Forlani and Nicole Wallenberg. And that he's running scared in trying to bury the evidence of his crimes."

Jewel nodded and said, "Forensics has a way of allowing us to catch up to unsubs, no matter their efforts to the contrary."

"Amen to that," Madison uttered, eyeing Garrett.

"Yeah, we're thankful for that," he concurred before they headed back to the parkway, having made progress in their endeavors of solving two homicides.

MADISON AGREED THAT forensic evidence linking the murders of Olivia and Nicole to one assailant was a breakthrough in the case. Whether this would be enough to identify the unsub remained to be seen. But at least they seemed to be headed in the right direction, even if it was still frustrating that the serial killer remained at large for the time being.

We just need to find him before he goes after someone else, she told herself while riding back to the parkway with Garrett. Like her, he was caught up in his own thoughts. Madison imagined that these meandered back and forth between his own past family tragedy and determination to prevent the present-day killer from becoming tomorrow's cold case. As for their own evolving relationship, she was willing to take it one day at a time and see where it went, while trying her best not to presume their history would repeat itself and leave them both unsatisfied.

That cloudy afternoon, a memorial service was held for Nicole Wallenberg at Julian Price Memorial Park. Attendees included park rangers and other NPS employees and volunteers. All had come to pay their respects for whom

Madison believed had been a dedicated worker who'd given her all to the job.

Garrett and her boss approached Madison as she stood alongside Leonard and other rangers. "How are you holding up?" Tom asked her in a sympathetic tone.

"Just trying to get through this," Madison confessed, something that had never become routine to her.

"You will," he said, his voice filled with confidence. "In the meantime, we'll do all we can to bring Nicole justice."

"To that effect," Garrett said, brushing against Madison's shoulder, "my boss has approved offering a twenty-five-thousand-dollar reward for any info that leads to the arrest and conviction of Nicole's killer. Which obviously will give us justice as well for Olivia Forlani."

Madison's eyes lit. "That's good to know. Hopefully this will motivate someone to do the right thing, even if it takes a cash reward to make that happen."

"It's been a proven means of loosening lips," he told her.

"You never know how these things will go," Tom spoke realistically. "But between Carly and myself, we're committed to leaving no stone unturned in solving this case. Rewards are often a last resort, but we want to jump on the momentum we have going for us. That includes showing images of the shirt worn by the unsub in the hope that someone in the public will recognize it, along with a vague description of the man seen running into the woods."

Leonard added, "We're also interviewing people who may have seen someone hanging out by the dumpster around the time shortly after Nicole was murdered."

Madison nodded. "Looks like we have the bases covered in trying to nab the unsub. Now it only needs to happen."

"We just have to let the system play itself out," Garrett told her evenly.

"Right." She met his eyes, tempering her eagerness to give Nicole the peace in death that she deserved.

"I wouldn't be surprised if we're inundated with leads shortly," he contended. "It only takes one to blow this thing wide open."

Madison concurred, and then turned her attention to some rangers who stood at a podium to say a few words on behalf of Nicole. One was Ward Wilcox, the maintenance ranger who'd been present when Madison had gotten the black bear to run off into the woods and leave parkway visitors alone. She was surprised at his heartfelt words about Nicole, whom he described as someone who could have been his daughter. These sentiments were echoed by maintenance worker Ronnie Mantegna, who said, "Nicole struck me as someone who only wanted to make a difference. For some bastard to take that away from her is reprehensible. Whoever did it needs to be held accountable."

I couldn't agree more, a voice in Madison's head told her. They all had a responsibility to come together on behalf of Nicole and Olivia in not letting the unsub get away with cold-blooded murder. It appeared as if they were doing just that. She gazed at Garrett, who seemed to be reading her mind and gave her a look of resolve in seeing this through.

After Leonard spoke to the gathering, it was Madison's turn to step to the podium. She took a moment or two to collect her thoughts before honoring Nicole's life and what she'd stood for as a park ranger. Though they hadn't exactly been friends as far as hanging out together, with Madison being older, but she'd been on friendly terms with Nicole and had occasionally offered her career advice, and they'd shared some anecdotes about ranger life. In Madison's book, that counted for something that she would carry with her for the rest of her life. Just as she would the brief time she'd gotten to know Olivia before her life had also been cut short by a ruthless killer.

Chapter Eleven

That evening, Madison did some house cleaning, feeling the need to keep her mind preoccupied. It was her proven strategy for dealing with the difficult parts of being a law enforcement ranger and not become overwhelmed by it. *I can take it, but I'm still human too*, she told herself. Something she always tried to keep in a proper perspective when having alone time.

As for Garrett, neither of them had rushed into a repeat performance from last night. Passionate and pleasurable as it was to make love, she didn't want to overdo it at the expense of having something real that went well beyond the bedroom. She sensed that Garrett felt the same way, respecting him for that. If they were to make it work this time, great sex would only be part of the equation, with a happy balance between personal and career lives essential to success.

When she got a call from Annette, Madison stopped dusting and took the video chat while standing in the kitchen.

"Hey," her sister greeted her.

"Hi." Madison smiled. "Thanks for rescuing me from my chores."

Annette laughed. "Actually, I could say the same about you. I needed an excuse to take a break."

She chuckled. "I'll gladly give you that."

"So, what's happening with you and Garrett? Or shouldn't I ask?"

"You may." Madison grinned. "Let's just say that we're working on getting back together."

"Hmm..." Annette's eyes widened. "Does that mean you're putting in plenty of overtime 'reacclimating yourselves to one another'?"

She colored. "We're taking one step at a time," she told her diplomatically.

"Okay." Her sister sat back. "What's the latest on your investigation?"

Madison brought her up to speed on where things stood, then finished with, "All hands are on deck, Annette, as we try to put the squeeze on the unsub."

"You'll get him," she spoke with confidence. "Having been there, done that last year, it's not something I'd wish on my worst law enforcement enemy. Much less my big sister. But between you and Garrett, along with the support staff, I have no doubt that an arrest of the culprit is imminent."

Madison flashed her teeth. "Since when did you become so much like Mom and Dad?" she teased her, still remembering when Annette had first become part of their family when brought home from the adoption agency, and had been instantly adored, proving that she belonged.

"Look who's talking." She laughed. "I think our parents left an indelible mark on all of us."

"I agree." They talked a little about Annette's married life and their brothers before they said their goodbyes.

Madison returned to cleaning the house and then took a nice relaxing bubble bath. There, she couldn't help but recall the times when she and Garrett had played footsie and explored one another in the tub during their previous relationship and then made their way to bed for some great sex. Suddenly feeling aroused, she quickly shut off those thoughts and considered what tomorrow would bring in their investigation of a deadly unsub.

THE FOLLOWING DAY, while looking over data on the case at his log cabin, Garrett got word about a disturbing text the ISB tip line had received in relation to the Blue Ridge Parkway killings. The National Park Service routinely received hundreds, if not thousands, of tips from the public annually on various crimes and otherwise suspicious activities that took place in national parks. Every one of these was taken seriously and, when appropriate, investigated. Normally, he would have passed this off to local park rangers. But upon being sent and reading the text, it obviously merited his own attention, in light of the investigation underway.

I'm the man you're looking for. I killed those women with my trusty survival knife, then dumped it. If you want to talk, I'm ready. —Blue Ridge Parkway Killer

Garrett felt a chill at the casualness of the text message from a purported killer. Was this truly their unsub? Had guilt eaten at him like an insidious cancer so he was ready to turn himself in and atone for his crimes through the judicial system? Identifying himself as Special Agent Sneed, he texted the person back, asking for more details. The suspect responded with another text.

All I can tell you right now is I stabbed them multiple times after catching them off guard. The park ranger put up more of a fight but still ultimately succumbed to my blade like the first victim before I ran off into the woods. I'm being straight with you.

Garrett sipped on coffee thoughtfully. *Sounds like someone who was actually involved in the homicides and needed to get this off his chest*, he mused, while still remaining skeptical. Was this simply an attention-seeker who was merely repeating public information or the real deal? If this was indeed their unsub, he was likely using a burner phone to avoid being traced back to his location. They needed to bring him in to further check out or dismiss his story. Garrett asked the man for his name.

You can call me Sean.

Garrett suspected it wasn't his real name, but it was a start in establishing a dialogue. He texted Sean for a face-to-face meeting, expecting him to reject this out of hand. Instead, Garrett was shocked at what came next.

I'm ready to turn myself in, Agent Sneed. Just tell me when and where.

Not willing to look a gift horse in the mouth, in case this was their serial killer, Garrett put him to the test by asking that he report to the Transylvania County Sheriff's Office at noon. When Sean agreed, Garrett immediately phoned Ray Pottenger and informed him that the person of interest in the case was reportedly set to arrive his way in an hour.

Pottenger made arrangements to that effect, accordingly. "We'll see if he shows."

"I'll be there, if he does," Garrett assured him.

He then called Madison. "Hey."

"Hey." He could tell that she was driving and had him on speaker phone.

"Got some news." Garrett told her about Sean using the tip line and the noon meeting at the Transylvania County Sheriff's Office.

"Hmm. You really think this guy is legit?"

"We'll find out soon enough," he responded noncommittally. "He seems to know things."

"Such as?"

"Basic info on the killings that may or may not be a first-hand account."

"I'd like to be there for the interrogation, if it happens," Madison said.

"I want that too," Garrett told her, believing she deserved that much, if they were to make an arrest.

"Good."

"I'll see you then."

"Okay," she replied and left it at that.

After disconnecting, Garrett was pensive. Part of him regretted not spending last night with her. It had been a judgment call. As much as they clicked in bed, he didn't want to overplay his hand in putting more emphasis on the mind-blowing sex than the overall strength of what they had going for them. If things went as they should, there would be plenty of times ahead for much more intimacy between them. Right now, they needed to see if the unsub in the investigation had come to them, rather than the other way around.

THE SUSPECT IDENTIFIED himself as Vincent Sean Deidrick. Madison, who sat beside Garrett, studied the man sitting across from them in the interrogation room. Wearing loose casual attire, he was in his midthirties, slender and around six feet, she guessed. His medium-length black hair was in a bro-flow cut, and he had a chinstrap beard on a long face with a jutting chin. He stared back at her so fiercely with dark eyes, it caused her to turn away briefly before meeting his gaze head-on.

Garrett, who was recording the interview, had the suspect reiterate his name and state his age of thirty-four before asking him straightforwardly, "So, to be sure, Mr. Deidrick, you're confessing to the murders of Olivia Forlani and Nicole Wallenberg?"

"Yeah, I am." His voice did not waver as he lifted the glass of water before him with his right hand and took a sip. "I stabbed them both to death and had no problem doing it."

Garrett drew a breath. "Let's talk about that." He leaned forward. "What exactly did you use to stab the victims?"

"A survival knife," he claimed.

"Can you describe the knife?"

Deidrick shrugged. "Yeah. The blade was eight inches long. Bought it at a hardware store some time ago."

"What type of handle did it have?" Madison thought to ask.

"Just a handle," he said flippantly.

"Well, was it wooden, rubber, what?" she questioned.

He paused. "Rubber, I think."

You think? Or was that a lucky guess? Madison wondered, glancing at Garrett. "So you used the same knife to kill both women?"

"Yeah, it saved me the trouble of having to use different knives." Deidrick gave her a smug look.

Garrett peered at him. "What did you do with the knife?"

"Got rid of it," he replied, taking a drink of the water.

"Got rid of it where?"

"I tossed it in a dumpster."

"Where was that?" Garrett's voice hardened.

"On the parkway somewhere," Deidrick said tonelessly. "In trying to get away, I didn't exactly take the time to keep track of my every move."

"Maybe you should have, now that you're confessing to the murders," Madison stated, her lips pursed with doubts.

He sneered. "Guess I screwed up, huh?"

Garrett angled his face at him. "What about the clothing you were wearing during the murders? I assume you got rid of them, too, since they had to have been covered with your victims' blood."

Deidrick hedged. "Yeah, I did."

"You tossed those in the dumpster too?" Garrett asked.

Deidrick waited a beat and said, "Actually, I washed the clothes. No reason to throw away something I could still wear, right?"

Caught him in at least one lie, Madison thought. How many more lies were there in his story? "Speaking of clothes, do you happen to remember what the victims were wearing when you killed them?" she asked him.

Deidrick squirmed in the chair. "To tell you the truth, I wasn't paying much attention to their clothes." He paused. "The ranger had on a ranger uniform."

Good deduction, Madison mused sardonically. It didn't sound like the voice of direct experience to her. "Tell us again how you went about killing the women and when each killing occurred." She was intent on breaking down his confession even more.

The suspect recounted what he had already said and was able to provide the correct dates and general time frame in which the murders took place. Madison was still not convinced that he was their killer. She exchanged looks with Garrett, who asked him bluntly, "Why did you kill them?"

Deidrick sat back and responded shakily, "A voice in my head told me to do it. Can't really explain, other than to say it was just something I felt compelled to do."

"Why those women in particular?" Madison asked him straightforwardly, wondering if he'd been stalking them beforehand, were he the true culprit.

"They just happened to be in the vicinity when the desire to kill hit me." He regarded her darkly. "Wish it had been you that I came upon instead, Ranger Lynley," he said icily.

Garrett looked as if he was ready to go after him right then and there. "That wouldn't have gone well for you, Deidrick," he stated. "She would have made you work even harder to get what you wanted out of it."

Madison touched Garrett's forearm to let him know that she wasn't flustered by the suspect's attempt at intimidation. "But it wasn't me," she snapped. "I'm here right now, and if you did what you claim to have done, you'll never hurt another woman again."

Deidrick furrowed his brow. "I did it," he insisted. "Killed them both."

"So you say," Garrett muttered. "Why confess now?"

"Why not?" His voice lowered an octave. "I felt I needed to before the urge to go after someone else overcame me."

"I see." Garrett gave him a quizzical gaze.

"Are you going to arrest me, or what?" he demanded.

Garrett considered the question and said equably, "First, we'd like to collect a sample of your DNA, as well as get your fingerprints, as part of the process."

Deidrick stared at him, nonplussed, and said flatly, "That won't happen till I'm charged with the murders."

As Madison exchanged glances with Garrett in assessing the situation, she took note of Deidrick finishing off his glass of water in practically a show of defiance. She looked up as the door opened and Deputy Pottenger popped his head in. He indicated a need to speak with them outside the room.

"Will you excuse us?" she told Deidrick politely as she stood with Garrett and left him at the table. She wondered what the deputy had for them.

In THE HALL, Garrett was curious as to what Ray Pottenger had learned after checking out the suspect's background. It was obvious there were some major gaps in Deidrick's account of the killings, which Madison had clearly picked up on as well. That left a lot to be desired in believing him to be the actual Blue Ridge Parkway Killer.

Pottenger scratched his pate and said sourly, "Looks like

Vincent Sean Deidrick has had mental health issues most of his life. He's been in and out of institutions and is apparently prone to delusions, among other conditions." The deputy sighed. "Deidrick also happens to be a true-crime addict. Combine these with the fact that most of the accurate information he gave was readily available through the media and online and his story starts to fall apart."

"Why am I not surprised?" Madison frowned. "Deidrick acted like a wannabe serial killer, and now we know why."

"He must have been following the story as it happened," Garrett decided, "and figured this was a good time to make his move for fifteen seconds of notoriety."

Pottenger nodded. "Seems to be the size of it."

"Still, he knew just enough to keep him on the radar," Garrett said. "At least till we're certain that his palm print isn't a match for the one Forensics pulled off the survival knife used in the killings."

"We'll assign a deputy to keep an eye on Deidrick for the time being," Pottenger said.

On that note, Garrett stepped back inside the interrogation room and said disingenuously, "We appreciate you coming in with the confession, Sean. We'll take everything you said under consideration. For now, you're free to go."

Deidrick's nostrils flared. "So, that's it?" he voiced with disappointment. "You're not taking me into custody?"

"Not yet." Garrett jutted his chin. "We can't just go on a confession alone, convincing as it is. There's a process we need to go through. But we have your address and cell phone number. As soon as everything is in order, we'll bring you back in and go from there. In the meantime, a deputy will show you out."

Reluctantly, Deidrick got to his feet, and Pottenger came in and walked him from the room and to the front door of the sheriff's office. Garrett watched briefly before going back into the interrogation room, where he put on a nitrile glove and carefully lifted the glass Deidrick had drank out of. There was a clear palm print that he'd left. Garrett put the glass into an evidence bag. They would get this over to the Western Regional Crime Laboratory pronto and see if they had a match.

In Garrett's mind, he doubted that would be the case. As much as he wanted Vincent Sean Deidrick to have handed them the guilty party on a silver platter, it was looking like another red herring in the effort to bring the cagey Blue Ridge Parkway Killer to justice.

Chapter Twelve

An hour later, Madison was in her patrol car on the Blue Ridge Parkway, pondering what to make of Vincent Sean Deidrick's confession. She found it hard to imagine that anyone could be so fixated on violent behavior so as to wish to become a serial killer for the vicarious thrill of it. On the other hand, if by some miracle Deidrick did turn out to be the parkway killer, then he had done them a solid by turning himself in.

At least we'd have no trouble tracking him down and bringing him back in with a deputy shadowing his every move, Madison mused.

When her cell phone rang, she put it on speaker after seeing that the caller was Garrett. He had left the sheriff's office to go directly to the crime lab to have the glass Deidrick had drunk from tested for his palm print.

"Hey," she uttered. "What did you find out?"

"That Deidrick's right-hand palm print was not a match for the print left on the survival knife murder weapon," Garrett replied matter-of-factly. "Jewel Yasumori dismissed any notion that Deidrick might still somehow be our serial killer."

"Figures," she said acceptingly.

"That's the way it works out sometimes in this business. You're going to get people who want to involve themselves in criminal activity, whether real or not. Mix that in with mental issues and you get a Vincent Sean Deidrick."

"I suppose." Madison paused. "Someone knows something," she declared. "Maybe the tip line can still work in terms of providing solid info."

"That may be the case," Garrett said. "Especially with the reward being offered."

"We'll see about that," she told him, though not holding her breath. Cash incentive could only go so far in motivating people to do the right thing. Then there was the real possibility that the killer was hidden in plain view, completely fooling those around him into believing him to be a law-abiding citizen.

"I'm on my way back to the parkway," he told her. "Should be there in about fifteen minutes. Can you meet me at the Raven Rocks Overlook?"

"Yes. Why?" she wondered.

"You'll see…" He left her hanging with his mysterious words, while arousing her curiosity.

"I'll meet you there," Madison told him simply. She drove to the overlook that was popular for its sunsets and rock climbers. After pulling into the parking area, she got out of her car and waited for Garrett's arrival, while enjoying the amazing views of the landscape.

I never tire of this part of working in the Blue Ridge Mountains, she told herself, while knowing that someone was attempting to mar its beauty with ugly acts of criminality.

When Garrett drove up, parking alongside her, Madison

headed to meet him. She wondered if he had news pertaining to the investigation. "Hey," she said.

"Hey." He flashed a quick smile, replaced by a serious look. "Thanks for coming."

She blinked and considered that this could be a romantic move on his part. Or not. "What's up?"

"I wanted to show you something." He took her hand and led her to the wooden fence at the edge of the Raven Rocks Overlook. "This is where my mother was murdered," Garrett muttered, maudlin.

Clutching his hand tighter, Madison expressed sympathy as though it had just happened. "I'm so sorry."

"It was down there, where she ventured off a hiking trail." He drew a breath. "Someone was waiting for her or followed her to that spot."

Madison was speechless, unsure what to say. Reliving the memory of his mother's death, still an unsolved mystery, had to be gut-wrenching. Even after all these years. She knew that this had been triggered by the current parkway murders.

I need to try to ease his painful memories, she thought. "Your mother must have been a remarkable woman to have raised you alone, by and large, and still found the time to do something she loved."

"Yeah, she was." Garrett was still holding Madison's hand while staring out at the scenery. Suddenly, he faced her and said, "How do you feel about making our way down there?"

She glanced down. Though it looked a bit tricky, she was sure she could do it without making a fool of herself. Especially if it could help give him some closure. "I'm game if you are." She looked at him. "You sure you want to do this?"

"I'm sure," he said resolutely. "I need to."

They climbed over the fence and headed down the slope across rocks and dirt. At one point, Madison nearly slipped. Catching her in his sturdy arms, Garrett said coolly, "Watch your step."

With a giggle, while regaining her footing, she responded lightheartedly, "Now you tell me."

He chuckled. "You're doing fine."

There were no more hiccups before they reached the lower level that had grass, a dirt path with a wooded area and a thirteen-acre family farm nearby. Madison followed Garrett into the woods and watched as he surveyed the area, as if looking for clues of a three-decades-old homicide.

"She never had a chance once ambushed," he remarked. "Just like Olivia and Nicole."

Madison gazed at him. "You don't think the murders could somehow be connected, do you?"

Garrett pursed his lips thoughtfully. "Anything's possible." He added, "Right now, my mother's murder is still a cold case. The recent murders are heating up, in spite of the setbacks in identifying the unsub."

Madison pondered the possibility that the same killer could have spanned thirty years. Her brother Scott was a cold-case investigator and had cracked some previously unsolved homicides. But in most of these, the killer had laid low through the years. Could this be different?

Garrett got her attention. "After my grandparents' deaths, I kind of turned away from my people in the Eastern Band of Cherokee Indians," he remarked, a tone of guilt in his voice. "Part of me blamed them for not doing more to protect my mother—like getting someone to hike with her in the Blue Ridge Mountains instead of her going alone."

"Do you really think that was fair?" Madison questioned. "Maybe back then it wasn't any more unusual than now for a woman to hike by herself. Especially in this area that's usually considered a safe environment. I'm sure your mom had taken the trek alone other times with no problems."

"She had," he acknowledged, "and you're right." Garrett looked down. "I need to go back to the Qualla, where I still have a few distant relatives and the overall support of the Cherokee community, and make peace with the past and present."

Madison smiled. "That's a great idea."

"How do you feel about taking a ride with me to Cherokee?" he asked.

She knew that this was the tribal capital of the Eastern Band of Cherokee Indians, federally recognized as such, and located at the southern boundary of the Blue Ridge Parkway, around an hour-and-a-half drive. This would be the first time she had accompanied Garrett to his native land, as he'd been in no hurry to do so when they'd dated previously—and now she knew why. Madison had no problem taking the afternoon off and didn't think her boss would object, with other rangers on hand.

"I'd love to go to Cherokee with you," she told Garrett.

"Great."

With a grin on his face, he pulled her up to him, and they kissed. Madison welcomed this show of affection, the nearness of him causing her heart to flutter. She hoped that visiting the Qualla would be just what they needed to bring them closer together.

GARRETT FOLLOWED MADISON back to her place, where she changed into leisure clothes and put her hair into a high ponytail and joined him for the drive. There was silence mostly as they headed down the Great Smoky Mountains Expressway toward Cherokee in Jackson County where, along with Haywood and Swain Counties, the greatest contiguous part of the Qualla Boundary existed. Purchased by the Native American tribe in the 1870s and held in trust by the federal government as a sovereign nation that included forests, rivers and mountains, with the Great Smoky Mountains National Park nearby, it was a place that would always be near and dear to Garrett's heart. Having spent his youth there and embracing the heritage handed down to him by his mother and grandparents, it had never been his intention to turn his back on the Qualla. But it had taken him this long to overcome the self-guilt and blame that had kept him away. He knew now that it had been wrong to put his mother's murder on anyone but the unsub, who had used his own free will to butcher her to death and had gotten away with it.

"So, who are these distant relatives of yours living in the Qualla?" Madison broke the silence from the passenger seat. "And have you kept in touch at all?"

Garrett loosened his grip on the steering wheel as he responded contemplatively, "I've stayed in touch with a second cousin, Noah Owl, and his wife, Breanna. And one of the elders who knew my mother and grandparents, Jeremiah Youngdeer. But that's about it."

"Well, hopefully, this will give you the opportunity to reconnect and start a new chapter in your life as a member of the EBCI," she said.

Garrett grinned. "I'm counting on that." But he was

counting even more on strengthening their own reconnection, which could ultimately extend to his greater ties to the Qualla as well as her family.

When they arrived in Cherokee, Garrett drove to a residence on Black Rock Road. A red GMC Yukon was parked outside the rustic log cabin. Before they reached the door, it opened. A yellow Labrador retriever scooted out past them, followed by a tall and firm man in his late thirties with long dark hair parted on the side and deep brown eyes.

He broke into a grin and said, "Hey, stranger."

"Noah." Garrett met his gaze warmly. "Good to see you."

"You too." They embraced, and Noah shifted his eyes. "And who did you bring with you?"

"This is Madison Lynley," Garrett introduced her. "My cousin Noah Owl, who also happens to be the interim chief of the Cherokee Indian Police Department for the EBCI."

"Nice to meet you," Madison said with a smile and extended her hand.

"You too." Noah ignored her hand and gave her a brief hug. "Handshakes are strictly forbidden in these parts."

She laughed. "I'll try to remember that."

He called to the dog, "Bo, get over here!" The yellow Lab immediately bounded over to them on command, and Noah said, "Say hello to our guests."

The dog barked, and Garrett played with him a bit and said, "Good to see you again too," before Bo moved over to Madison, warming up to her instantly.

"Hi, Bo," she said spiritedly.

"What's all the ruckus out here?" a female voice asked.

Garrett turned to see Noah's wife, Breanna, step out. In her midthirties, petite and attractive with big gray-brown eyes and long and layered brunette hair with highlights, she was noticeably pregnant with what would be the couple's first child. Garrett was envious of them and looked forward to the day when he would become a father, along with a husband. "Hey, Breanna."

"Hey, Garrett." She flashed her teeth, hugged him and went to Madison, hugging her before saying, "You must be Madison, the ranger Garrett has been raving about reconnecting with."

Madison blushed, glancing at him and back. "Yep, that would be me."

"Nice to finally meet you."

"Same here."

Garrett regretted not having brought Madison there for a visit when they'd been seeing each other two years ago. But the timing had been off and he hadn't been in much of a hurry back then to return to Cherokee. He was glad to have her there now as part of his way of mending fences.

"Come inside," Noah told them.

Half an hour later, they were all sitting in rocker chairs on a wraparound deck with an amazing view of the Blue Ridge Parkway and the mountains. They talked about the parkway killings, life on the Qualla, which had seen an increase in drug activity in recent memory, and spending more time together. Garrett was certainly amenable to getting in touch with his roots again, with Madison being an essential part of that in bridging the gap, while looking ahead.

"So, how close are you to discovering who's behind the murders on the parkway?" Breanna asked, sipping lemonade.

Garrett furrowed his brow and glanced at Bo, who was

lying there lazily, taking it all in. "Not close enough to say that an arrest is imminent," he admitted. "But we're doing everything we can to track down the culprit."

Madison concurred. "It's a work in progress," she asserted positively, "frustrating as it's been."

Breanna sighed. "Just keep at it, and you'll get some justice."

"That's the plan," he said, his voice intent.

Noah drank some beer and said, "This has to hit pretty close to home, losing your mother in a similar fashion?"

"It does," Garrett acknowledged. This was one reason for his return, to try to reconcile what had happened to her with the current murders. "I kind of feel that she's pushing me to get to the bottom of the current investigation as a way to make amends for the past."

"None of what happened thirty years ago was your fault," Noah told him. "You get that, right?"

"Yeah," he said tonelessly, taking a swig of beer. "But there's still a side of me that wishes I had gone with her that day to the Blue Ridge Mountains. Maybe if I had, we would've taken a different route and she wouldn't have run into harm's way."

"Coulda, woulda, shoulda," Noah voiced in rejecting the idea. "We all go when our time's up, like it or not. That wasn't your time, Garrett, and you weren't in a position then to change fate. Don't beat yourself up in reliving a tragedy that was beyond your control."

"I feel the same way," Madison expressed gently, sipping beer. "Losing loved ones is the hardest thing. Worse would be to tarnish their memories by dwelling too much on the what-ifs."

"You're right." Garrett nodded in agreement, happy to have her in his corner. But even with that understanding, there was still something that wasn't sitting right with him between his mother's murder and the current ones attributed to the Blue Ridge Parkway Killer. Was it even possible after all these years that the killer could be one and the same?

BEFORE THEY LEFT, Garrett paid a courtesy call to Jeremiah Youngdeer, who was on the Tribal Council. At eighty, he was still rock solid in build and had short silver hair and black eyes deeply creased at the corners. As a Cherokee elder, he carried the respect afforded to him among the Eastern Band of Cherokee Indians.

"Nice to be back here," Garrett told him as they walked through the Oconaluftee Indian Village, an authentic replica of a 1760s Cherokee village, on Drama Road.

"You're always welcome, Garrett," Jeremiah told him, walking with a limp from arthritis in his knee. "This is your home too, no matter where you go in life."

Garrett smiled respectfully. "I appreciate that."

Jeremiah regarded him. "I want you to know that not a day goes by that I don't think about your mother, Jessica," he said, maudlin. "As one of our own, we all felt incredible pain over the unfortunate loss of life for her at such a young age."

Garrett waited a beat before asking in a low voice, "Do you remember my father, Andrew Crowe?"

"I do." Jeremiah's weathered face sagged. "Andrew was a hard worker. Sadly, he also developed a predilection for the bottle. It caused him to forget a big part of his heritage and commitment to family." He took a deep breath. "Your mother wanted to stay with him, become his wife. But by then, Andrew was too far gone, and he left her—and his people—high and dry. And that was it. He never returned to the Qualla."

Garrett got a lump in his throat at the thought of being cheated out of having a real father. Especially in light of his mother's early death. But since Andrew Crowe had made his choice, it was something Garrett would have to live with, as he had all these years, while maintaining strength through his mother's memory.

He eyed Jeremiah, knowing what would come next was delicate but necessary. "Is it possible that someone from the Qualla could have followed my mother to the mountains and killed her?" Given that his father had abandoned them two years prior for parts unknown, Garrett had no reason to believe that he had perpetrated the attack as domestic violence.

The elder creased his brow. After a long moment, he responded levelly, "Anything is possible. But with my ear to the ground then and the strong sense of community, I'm all but certain that it was someone from the outside who randomly crossed paths with Jessica and decided to harm her."

Garrett nodded. This was his sense too. Which gave him peace of mind on the one hand. And on the other, a renewed sense that his mother's killer might not only still be alive and well but could have picked up where he'd left off years ago in hunting young women in the Blue Ridge Mountains.

MADISON WAS HAPPY that Garrett had invited her to accompany him to the Qualla Boundary and get to know his relatives and the richness of the environment itself. They were able to step away from the pressures of the criminal investigation by hanging out at Harrah's Cherokee Casino and going to a fun Cherokee bonfire, where they listened to amazing stories by Cherokees told to the sound of drums.

When they got back, Madison spent the night at Garrett's log cabin. Putting aside any hesitancy to fall back into enjoyable old and recent habits, they made love, enjoying each other's company while extending their passions well into the wee hours of the morning. Afterward, thoroughly exhausted, they lay cuddled together in his log bed, where Madison could have sworn that Garrett said he loved her before drifting off to sleep. She wondered if this had been a slip of the tongue in the aftermath of good sex. Or had he meant it?

Given that her own feelings for the man had risen to the "starting to fall in love" category since they had become involved again, Madison could only hope that this was indeed reciprocal as they navigated the waters of a renewed romance that came with the same risks and rewards as before. Only this time would hurt far worse should things fizzle out and they ended up going their separate ways. She fell asleep on that note, while resolved to remain positive where Garrett Sneed was concerned.

Chapter Thirteen

"I'd like to take a look at the cold-case file on my mother's unsolved murder," Garrett told his boss in a video chat the following day at the cabin.

"Really?" Carly Tafoya raised a brow in surprise. "Do you think it has something to do with the parkway murders?"

He considered the question carefully, knowing full well that this was a long shot at best and a waste of precious time at worst. Nevertheless, it was a shot that he needed to pursue. "There are some similarities that simply can't be ignored," Garrett reasoned. "For one, they occurred in the Blue Ridge Mountains, albeit thirty years apart. The female victims were all stabbed to death," he pointed out uneasily. "With none of the various suspects for the two recent murders panning out, I decided I needed to expand the range of possible unsubs to include those old enough to have murdered my mother."

Carly gave an understanding nod. "Okay, I'll send you what we have on the case."

Garrett smiled. "Thanks."

"You might also check with the Buncombe County Sheriff's Office," she suggested. "They would have been the local law enforcement agency to head the investigation in working in conjunction with us."

"I'll do that." He was sure he would get cooperation from Sheriff Jacob Silva. "Can you look up the name of the special agent who handled my mother's case?"

"Yes. Give me a sec." Carly stepped away for a moment. She said when returning, "It was Special Agent Dexter Broderick. He retired about fifteen years ago and is still alive."

That's good to know, Garrett thought. "I don't suppose you know his whereabouts?"

"As a matter of fact, he lives in Buncombe County," she told him. "At least that was his last known address."

"Send me his contact info. Hopefully I can track him down."

"Will do." Carly paused. "Honestly, Sneed, linking these cases seems like a stretch, as the culprit in your mother's murder would have to be pretty old today and likely not as able-bodied as a younger man to commit two brazen murders on the parkway and make a clean getaway in the woods in a snap. I'm just saying. Don't want to see you get too keen on the prospect of solving your mother's murder, only to be left disappointed."

This was fair to point out to Garrett, leaving him little room for push back. Especially as these were legitimate points in his own mind too, all things considered. But his gut told him that, even against the odds, he might be onto something. "I appreciate your concern," he voiced evenly. "If at any time it seems like I'm barking up the wrong tree, I won't reopen a cold case that doesn't appear to be connected to my present investigation," he promised. "I'm totally committed to solving the deaths of Nicole Wallenberg and Olivia Forlani, no matter what it takes."

"Okay," Carly said acceptingly.

After signing off, for an instant, Garrett had second thoughts about going down this road. Did he really want to dredge up old and painful memories at a time when he had just started to get back in touch with his roots? Then he realized it was for that very reason that he needed to see this through, for better or worse.

Even Madison seemed to support the possible connection. He had run it by her in the middle of the night, somewhere between the sounds of intimacy and uttering his love for her. She had responded positively on both fronts, giving him reason to believe they were on the same page in terms of the investigation and wanting to be together as a couple when this was all over.

Half an hour later, Garrett was giving the material on his mother's death a cursory glance on his laptop. Jessica Rachel Sneed, age twenty-five, had been found dead below Raven Rocks Overlook on the Blue Ridge Parkway. Fully clothed in a green T-shirt, denim shorts and tennis shoes, she'd been stabbed to death. Next to the body had been a pink lightweight backpack that had contained the victim's water bottle and a few other personal effects. Garrett winced when he read from the autopsy report that his mother had had eight stab wounds to her body. The murder weapon, a survival knife, was shown and described as having a smooth eight-inch, single-edged blade. It had been found by some kids playing in the bushes.

Garrett couldn't help but think that the knife bore a strong resemblance to the one found in a dumpster and positively linked to the murders of Olivia Forlani and Nicole Wallenberg. Was this coincidence? Or an indication that a decades-old killer had a preference for a long-bladed survival knife?

DNA had been collected at the crime scene, including an unknown DNA profile belonging to the unsub that had never been positively identified. Garrett gazed at a photograph of his mother that had been taken earlier that year she'd died. He remembered it being shot by his grandfather outside their house in the Qualla. *She looks so young*, Garrett thought, with her high cheekbones on a diamond-shaped face and bold brown eyes, surrounded by long black hair worn in braids. The resemblance to himself was unmistakable.

He had to check himself at the thought that they had never been given the chance to get to know one another as adults. Hell, his mother hadn't even been around during his teenage years. Or when he'd left the nest in becoming a man and a special agent with the National Park Service. But maybe they could bridge the gap across the spiritual divide should he be able to solve her murder at long last.

Garrett turned to the info on retired Special Agent Dexter Broderick. Now seventy-five, he was apparently residing at a nursing home in Asheville on Mountainly Lane.

Let's see what blanks he can fill in, Garrett thought, and he was out the door.

MADISON RECEIVED A report of a possible armed robbery by Milepost 374.4, close to the Rattlesnake Lodge Trailhead. She headed there to rendezvous with Law Enforcement Ranger Richard Edison.

Back to business as usual...somewhat, she thought, with the Blue Ridge Parkway Killer still on her mind.

Garrett had just called to say that he was en route to see the retired ISB special agent who'd worked on the original Jessica Sneed investigation. Seemed as though Garrett was now of the belief that his mother's death might be tied to the current serial murders on the parkway. The notion gave Madison a fright. But it was also something she could see as a possibility, remote as it seemed given the wide time frame.

If Jessica's killer is still at large today, he deserves to be apprehended and sent to prison, Madison told herself. And if the unsub and the present-day perp were one and the same, all the better to solve it in one fell swoop.

Pulling off the parkway behind Richard's vehicle, Madison got out and approached him as he spoke to a thirty-something Asian man standing beside his car, a blue BMW Gran Coupe.

Richard turned to her. "Hey."

"What happened?" she asked, looking from one to the other.

"This is Pierre Yang," Richard said. "Why don't you tell Ranger Lynley what you told me?"

Madison gazed at the brown-eyed man, who was medium in build with short dark hair in a spiky cut, as he told her, "I pulled off to the side here to take some pics, and another car stopped. A guy got out, carrying a gun, and demanded my cell phone, camera and wallet, which had cash and credit cards in it." His voice shook. "Of course, I gave them to him. He got back in his vehicle and took off. I had a second phone in my car that I used to call you guys."

She frowned. "Sorry you had to go through that, sir."

"Me too." He scratched his pate. "Guess I shouldn't have stopped here."

"You have every right to." Madison believed that the culprit had likely followed the mark and waited for an opportunity to strike, as was the case for these types of crimes. She faced Richard. "Did you get a description of the suspect?"

"Yeah." He glanced at a notepad. "White male in his teens. Slender, blue-eyed with blondish-brown hair in a fringe cut and wearing a white T-shirt, jeans and black sneakers." Richard looked at the victim. "Is that right?"

"Yes," Pierre replied with a nod.

"What type of car was he driving?" Madison asked. She listened as he described it as a dark-colored sedan similar to a Mitsubishi Eclipse. When asked about the weapon the unsub was brandishing, Pierre believed it to be a .22 caliber pistol. "We'll do what we can to help you retrieve some of your stolen items," she told him. "I would strongly suggest you cancel the credit cards right away, to limit your liability."

"I'll do that," he assured her.

"Good." Madison turned to Richard and said, "After you finish taking Mr. Yang's statement, notify the local authorities and see if they have reports of any similar crimes of late. Could be this is part of a theft ring, seizing upon any opportunities that come their way on the parkway or greater area."

"Okay." Richard adjusted his campaign hat and looked at Pierre. "Let's go over everything that happened."

Madison left them, knowing that her fellow law enforcement ranger could take it from here. She headed back to her patrol vehicle, wondering why so many teenagers seemed to be going off the rails these days. She supposed there could be many explanations, not the least of which was a misguided belief that they were owed something for nothing. If she were so fortunate to have children of her own someday, she would certainly do her best to ensure they were well grounded with strong values. Madison couldn't help but think that if their father happened to be Garrett, he would be of the same mind.

GARRETT PULLED INTO the parking area of the Seniors at Blue Ridge Retirement Village. He got out and went inside the Victorian-style facility. At the front desk, he flashed his identification and asked to see Dexter Broderick. A moment later, a fortysomething female with a platinum bouffant approached him in the lobby and said, "I'm Wendy Schneider, the nursing home manager and health services coordinator."

"Special Agent Sneed," he told her.

"You wanted to speak with Mr. Broderick?"

"Yes. I'm looking into a cold case he investigated when he was with the National Park Service."

Wendy arched a brow. "Not sure he can be much help to you, Agent Sneed," she indicated sadly. "Mr. Broderick is currently suffering from moderate dementia as a result of Alzheimer's disease. His memory loss is pretty significant, and he's easily confused."

"Sorry to hear that." Garrett had come across people with Alzheimer's in his personal and professional life and wouldn't wish this progressive disease on anyone.

"But there are times when he's lucid," she said. "Moreover, Mr. Broderick rarely gets any visitors these days. He's currently out in the garden getting some fresh air. You're welcome to speak with him for a few minutes, if you like."

"I would like to do that, thanks," Garrett said, believing it was worth a try.

He was led through the facility and out a door to a large area with a well-manicured lawn, a variety of plants and flowers, a wilderness path and a pond. They approached an elderly, thin man who was sitting on an Adirondack rocking chair in a shaded area.

"Mr. Broderick," Wendy got his attention. "There's someone here to see you."

"Really?" Dexter's blue eyes lit beneath thinning white hair in a Boston style with a widow's peak.

"I'm Special Agent Garrett Sneed," Garrett said and stuck out his hand. Reluctantly, Dexter shook it with his own frail hand. "You worked on a case for the National Park Service thirty years ago."

"Did I?" He scratched his pate in straining to remember.

"It was a murder investigation on the Blue Ridge Parkway." Garrett took a breath. "The victim, Jessica Sneed, was my mother."

"Jessica Sneed?" Dexter's chin sagged. "Your mother?"

"That's right. I've reopened the case in trying to solve the crime," Garrett told him. "She was stabbed to death." He glanced at Wendy, who had stepped farther away to give them a little privacy but was clearly listening to every word, based on her expression.

"I'm sorry," the older man said sincerely. "I tried to find out who did it."

"I know you did." Garrett was thankful for his service and that his memory was still there on this occasion. "Do you recall anything that might be able to help me find her killer?"

Dexter sucked in a deep breath, peered at him and said, "Who did you say you are?"

"Special Agent Sneed of the National Park Service."

Dexter's eyes narrowed suspiciously. "Do I know you?"

"We just met." Garrett could see that he was losing him. "We were talking about the murder of Jessica Sneed on the Blue Ridge Parkway."

"We were?" Dexter widened his eyes, but they looked blank. "Sorry, but my memory isn't what it used to be. What is this about? And who did you say you are?"

Guess this is about as far as I'm going to get, Garrett thought, eyeing Wendy as her cue that the interview was over. He turned back to the former special agent and said, "Just a friend who came to check on you."

Dexter looked confused, then broke into a grin. "Nice of you. Thanks."

"Anytime." Garrett forced a smile. "Take care of yourself, Dexter."

"I will."

Wendy walked up to them and said to Garrett, "Hope you don't feel this was a waste of your time."

"I don't," he stressed. "NPS special agents always have a bond, no matter what. I'll show myself out."

MAYBE I'LL HAVE better luck at the Buncombe County Sheriff's Office, Garrett told himself as he took the short drive there. That was assuming this wasn't a wild goose chase in trying to open a cold case by tying it to a current investigation.

When he arrived, Sheriff Jacob Silva greeted him and said, "I had one of my deputies pull up what we had on the

Jessica Sneed case and lay it out in an evidence room for you to take a look at."

"Appreciate that," Garrett told him.

"No problem." Silva furrowed his brow. "I warn you, though, it may be difficult to look at."

"I get that." Garrett met his eyes steadily. "I'm up to the task."

"All right." Silva lifted the brim of his hat. "If we can do anything else to help solve your mother's murder, we're more than willing to do so."

"Thanks. I'll let you know."

Silva gave him a thoughtful look. "You're thinking that the same killer could now be targeting women on the parkway?"

Garrett waited a beat before responding contemplatively, "All options are on the table at this point."

"They should be." The sheriff bobbed his head. "Some of the worst serial killers started early in life and stayed at it or picked back up in their later years."

Garrett kept that thought in mind as he walked into the evidence room. On the metal rectangular table was a pair of nitrile gloves and evidence collected from the crime scene on the parkway thirty years ago. In plastic bags were his mother's clothing, shoes and backpack. Also bagged was the murder weapon. He put on the gloves and opened the bag, examining the survival knife while holding it by the wooden handle. This differentiated from the rubber handle used in the stabbing deaths of Olivia Forlani and Nicole Wallenberg. He didn't put much stock in that, as different times, different handles.

Garrett swallowed hard as he put the knife back into the

bag, pained at what it had done to his mother. Had the same unsub used another knife to resume murdering women? Or was the case unrelated, if not just as sickening? Once he had perused the evidence and gone over some witness statements and incidental notes by investigators, Garrett had seen enough to warrant continuing to investigate what could well have been a one-off in the killing of his mother.

Outside the room, he spoke with Sheriff Silva, who pledged continued cooperation and added, "By the way, the sheriff thirty years ago, Lou Buckley, is now retired and living the good life in Kiki's Ridge. You might want to speak with him. I'm sure he'd be happy to tell you what he remembers about the case."

"I'll do that," Garrett said, more than willing to follow up on this with the former sheriff in the pursuit of long overdue justice.

Chapter Fourteen

That afternoon, Madison accompanied Garrett to Price Lake at Milepost 297, where they found the man they were looking for, she believed. Retired Buncombe County Sheriff Lou Buckley was standing on the pier, trout fishing. It saddened her to learn that his former colleague in law enforcement, retired ISB Special Agent Dexter Broderick, was suffering from Alzheimer's disease. Madison recalled that her grandfather had been in the early stages of dementia before eventually dying from a heart attack.

"Since Buckley's office had jurisdiction on the homicide at that time, hopefully he can provide some insight into the case," Garrett told her as they walked down the long pier.

"We'll see," she said, still wrapping her mind around the notion that a cold case could be the key to solving a current one. She wondered if the unsub was the same or if they were connected to one another in some way.

Garrett cut into her reverie, remarking, "Glad to hear that your teenage armed robber ran out of steam quickly."

"That's what happens when you're dumb enough to try to use a stolen credit card less than an hour after stealing it." She rolled her eyes at the stupidity of the young criminal. "Duh."

He laughed. "Well, thieves aren't always the brightest bulbs in the chandelier."

"I'm just happy for the victim that his items were recovered with minimal loss," she said, while knowing Pierre Yang's story could have ended much more tragically since he was robbed at gunpoint.

"Yeah." They approached the seventysomething man, who was heavyset and wearing a fishing trucker hat with tufts of white hair beneath it. Garrett asked, "Sheriff Lou Buckley?"

He turned to face them with blue eyes behind browline glasses. "Haven't been called that in a very long time."

"Once a sheriff, always a sheriff," Garrett uttered respectfully.

Lou chuckled. "True enough."

"I'm ISB Special Agent Garrett Sneed, and this is Law Enforcement Ranger Madison Lynley."

"Nice to meet you both." He was holding a lightweight trout rod in the water. "In fact, Sheriff Silva gave me a heads up that you wanted to talk to me about a cold case—the murder of Jessica Sneed...your mother."

Garrett nodded. "That's right. I'm reopening the investigation. Anything you can tell us about the case would be helpful."

"First of all, I'm sorry she was killed that way," Lou expressed. "I seem to recall that you were, what, about five at the time?"

"Yes," he acknowledged, tilting his face to one side.

Lou glanced out at the lake and back. "Losing your

mother at such a young age...you both deserved better." He paused reflectively. "I had just been the sheriff of Buncombe County for a couple of years when the crime occurred on the Blue Ridge Parkway. It threw us all for a loop, as the parkway had been relatively peaceful in those days. Initially, our office battled it out with the National Park Service on who should take the lead in the investigation. Guess I had a stronger will and won out."

Madison asked him curiously, "What takeaways did you get from the case?"

Lou considered this before responding, "The biggest takeaway, I suppose, was that the killer had to have been someone who knew the parkway inside and out. This would have given him a way in and out quickly."

"You mean like a park employee?" Garrett wondered.

"Possibly, though we were able to eliminate as suspects everyone on duty that day. Even off duty workers, for that matter. Unfortunately, we didn't have the same access and inroads to visitors on the parkway or national forest. As such, it was likely someone among this group who killed your mother."

Garrett's jaw set. "Were there any similar murders during that time frame?" He thought about the evidence he'd reviewed in the case.

Lou sighed musingly. "As a matter of fact, a year later, a young woman was stabbed to death in a similar fashion near the Yadkin Valley Overlook on the parkway."

"Was the killer ever caught?" Madison asked.

"Yeah, an arrest was made a couple of days later. Man named Blake O'Donnell confessed to the crime, while insisting he played no part in the murder of Jessica Sneed.

Seemed like we had an open-and-shut case." Lou paused, frowning. "Then O'Donnell recanted his confession, claiming it had been coerced. The jury never bought it. Neither did I. He was tried, convicted and sent to prison."

"Was he ever released?" Garrett questioned.

Lou shook his head. "He was killed behind bars, five years into his sentence. Ironically, he was stabbed to death by a fellow inmate after getting into a fight."

Could the jury have gotten it wrong and sent a man to prison for a crime he hadn't committed? Madison couldn't help but ask herself. Might the Blue Ridge Parkway Killer have more murders under his belt than met the eye?

She took a step closer and asked the former sheriff intently, "Do you think it's possible that Jessica's killer could be at it again, killing women on the parkway?" She assumed he was aware of what was happening and the similarities between the cases.

Lou looked out at the lake, where his rod remained in search of fresh trout. "The unsub would likely be in his fifties and up," he muttered. "As I'm sure you know, most serial killers are younger than that. But the comparisons are hard to ignore. Even for an old geezer like me." He took a breath. "Anything's possible. If this is the direction you're going in, you're welcome to all my files on the original case, which I have in some boxes in my basement. If you'd like, I can send them over to the sheriff's office. Or to the Pisgah Ranger District headquarters. Your call."

"We'd like that," Garrett readily agreed. "The ranger district office would be good."

"Consider it done," he said. "Again, I regret that when I

was the Buncombe County Sheriff, we were unable to crack the case of your mother's death. It's one that got away."

"Don't beat yourself up, Sheriff. Not all cases go as we'd like them to." Garrett looked at him sympathetically. "I've had my fair share of investigations that dried up and there was nothing I could do about it."

"Same here," Madison pitched in, wanting to ease his burden, while knowing that law enforcement was anything but a perfect science where all the bad people were held accountable for their actions. Still, she could only hope that the unsub or unsubs who'd left Jessica Sneed, Olivia Forlani and Nicole Wallenberg dead well before their times would one day have to face justice.

"Well, we'll let you get back to your fishing," Garrett told Lou, adding, "I heard that rainbow and brook trout are out in force right now."

"Yeah, they are," he concurred, "along with brown trout and smallmouth bass. If you ever want to join me, be my guests."

Garrett grinned. "We'll keep that in mind."

They walked away from him, and Madison looked at Garrett and said, "I didn't know you were into fishing."

"I grew up fishing in the Qualla," he told her. "Not really my thing these days. But maybe once I'm retired from federal law enforcement, I can take it up again."

"Cool." She tried to picture him in retirement mode. Or herself, for that matter. If they could grow old together, all the better. Was this something he pictured as well? Or were they living in more of a fantasy world right now in being involved romantically again, with reality setting in once the cases before them were put to rest?

As promised, Lou Buckley had his files on the Jessica Sneed cold case delivered late that afternoon to the head office of the Pisgah Ranger District. That evening, Garrett went through them with Madison at her house. They sat at the dining room table poring over the materials while sipping wine, looking for anything that stood out as relevant to the current murders. Admittedly, Garrett wondered if they were searching for a needle in a haystack, given the thirty-year spread since his mother's murder. Had her killer really resurfaced and, as such, was out there for Garrett to find and bring to justice? Or was he deluding himself on a false premise?

I can't shake the feeling that there's something to my intuition, Garrett told himself as he tasted the wine. Maybe her killer had murdered another woman the following year and had been lucky enough to have someone else take the rap, giving the unsub a free pass to kill other women in the years to follow.

He looked at the sketch of an unidentified male that had been reported by witnesses as being on the parkway around the time of his mother's murder. The man was described as being anywhere from his midtwenties to midthirties and sturdily built with dark eyes and a long nose, while possibly wearing outdoor work clothes. The authorities had never been able to locate the unsub. Garrett recalled Sheriff Buckley stating that park workers had been accounted for and eliminated as suspects. Meaning the unsub had likely worked elsewhere but could still have been a local who'd known the lay of the land. So, who was he and what had become of him? Was this the killer or a false lead?

Garrett gazed at Madison, who was still in uniform but

oh so sexy. And, frankly, distracting. She was the one definite positive that had come from his returning to this region
to work. Wherever they went from here, he wanted it to be
as a couple and all that came with it. When she looked up
at him, he considered looking away but couldn't.

She batted her lashes curiously. "What?"

"Nothing," he said, as if she believed him, while he sup-
pressed a grin.

"Right." Madison glanced at the paperwork spread before her and back. "Since I've got your attention, in looking this over and the lists of identified suspects, it seems
like the one name that keeps popping up in the notes is Neil
Novak. And with good reason. Take a look."

Garrett gazed at a file she handed him and saw the name.
Neil Novak, age thirty-four at the time, had been an unemployed wrangler. A partial fingerprint belonging to Novak
had been found on the survival knife that'd been used to
kill Jessica Sneed. When confronted with this, Novak had
claimed that the knife had been stolen a week earlier. As
there had been no other physical evidence connecting him
to the crime and Novak had had a rock-solid alibi after finding work when the murder had occurred, authorities had had
no choice but to eliminate him as a suspect.

"So, maybe Novak never really had his knife stolen and
faked the alibi," Madison contended, "and was able to get
away with the murder of your mother."

"Hmm…" Garrett chewed on that notion. Alibis could
certainly be falsified. It happened more often than people
realized. The investigators on the case could only play the
hand dealt them. Sometimes they got it wrong. Even when
the evidence, or lack thereof, suggested otherwise. "You're

right—maybe we do need to take another hard look at Neil Novak, assuming he's still alive."

"I think so," she agreed. "And if Novak is among the living, is he local?"

"He'd be sixty-four now," Garrett pointed out. "Old enough to be out of the killing business, based on official data for the age range of typical killers—but still young enough, per se, to be able to perpetrate murders currently as the Blue Ridge Parkway Killer," he reasoned.

Madison perked up. "It's a lead anyway." She sipped her wine.

"Yeah." He gave her an agreeable look. "I think we need to learn everything we can about Neil Novak and what he may or may not have been up to."

"We will," she said steadfastly. "Wherever the leads take us, right?"

"Right." Garrett held up the sketch of an unsub. "And there's also this person to consider."

Madison grabbed the sketch, studying it. "True. Or he could have been someone's imagination or a male suspect that was totally unrelated to the death of your mother."

"That's possible," Garrett was inclined to agree, while still having to regard him as a person of interest. He drank wine as a thought suddenly entered his head. "Doesn't your brother Scott specialize in cold cases?"

"Yeah." Madison gazed at him. "Why do you ask?"

"Well, given that we've opened one, I thought you could get him on the phone to see if he could give us some input on cold cases in general."

"Really?" She flashed a look of surprise.

He chuckled. "Why not? Might help the cause." *At the*

very least, it could help me make further inroads in win-
ning points with your family, Garrett told himself. He assumed that Scott and her other siblings knew by now that
they were seeing each other again.

"Okay." Madison got to her feet and grabbed her laptop.
She put it on the table and sat next to him. "Sure you want
to do this?"

"Of course." He grinned. "I'm not too proud to ask for
help."

"Just checking." She smiled and called her brother for a
video chat. When Scott accepted it, Madison said cheer-
fully, "Hey."

Scott smiled. "Hey, sis."

"You remember Garrett?"

"Of course," he said. "Special Agent Sneed. How are
you?"

"I'm good." Garrett could read the surprise on his face in
wondering what this was all about in reacquainting themselves with one another.

"So, what's up?" Scott asked.

Madison leaned forward and said, "We're looking into
the murder of Garrett's mom thirty years ago."

Scott raised a brow. "Oh…?"

"We think it could be tied to a current case we're investigating," Garrett told him equably.

"The Blue Ridge Parkway killings?"

"You've got it," he verified. "Between the similar pattern and a dangerous unsub still at large, it seemed worth
exploring the possibility that my mother's killer could be
back and targeting other young women on the parkway.

Since you specialize in cold cases, we thought you might have some general thoughts about this…"

Before Scott could respond, Madison added, "And according to the sheriff at the time, there was a similar murder that occurred in the county a year later, in which a man confessed and recanted the confession but was still convicted of the crime. There is at least a possibility that he didn't commit the crime and the unsub who killed Jessica Sneed was the real killer, which would still make it a cold case, apart from the present serial killer on the loose."

"Wow," Scott uttered. "That's a lot to unpack."

"Take your time," she quipped.

He chuckled. "Without knowing the details of your mother's case, Garrett, I can tell you that cold cases can be tricky but still resolvable, even without the benefit of the culprit resuming his activities much later down the line."

Garrett listened attentively as Scott ran off some of the dynamics of cold cases that were typically violent and/or gained national attention, citing tunnel vision and advances in forensics as key variables that merited a second look for many such open-ended cases. Having worked on some cold cases in his career, Garrett had been privy to this but was happy to get Scott's take, if only to bridge the familial gap between them for the sake of smoothing the way toward a bright future with Madison.

"Jack the Ripper is obviously one notorious example of a very cold-case killer, who got away with murdering at least five prostitutes in Whitechapel in London's East End in 1888," Scott said. "While the infamous serial killer might never be identified conclusively, other cases and your mother's death could still be solved by identifying the unsub."

"You think?" Garrett asked in all seriousness.

"Yeah. May take some time though," he cautioned. "Not to tell you how to do your job, but you'll need to reexamine evidence, reinterview witnesses, seek out new evidence, etcetera."

"We get the picture," Madison ribbed him.

"You wanted my advice." Scott chuckled. "Anything I can do to help."

"Appreciate that," Garrett said sincerely. "I never turn down any free advice." *Especially coming from one of Madison's siblings*, he mused.

"Neither do I," Scott said and waited a beat. "So, what else is going on with you two? Anything I should know about?"

Garrett deferred to Madison on that one, not wanting to put words in her mouth in sharing his own thoughts on the matter.

Blushing, she told her brother simply, "We're good."

"Fair enough," Scott responded.

"Maybe better than good," Garrett spoke up. "But what do I know?"

Madison laughed and pushed him so he nearly fell off the chair. "Trust your instincts."

Scott laughed. "You heard my sister. Never argue with her. You'll lose every time."

He had to chuckle, though not wanting to ever test that theory any more than he had previously. "I'll keep that in mind."

After they ended the video chat, Madison said curiously, "Still think that was a good idea?"

"Absolutely." Garrett gave her a devilish grin. "Scott helped in more ways than one."

"Really?"

"Yes. He's convinced me that being on your good side always has its benefits."

She showed her teeth tantalizingly. "What might those be?"

"This for one…" Garrett kissed her and, at least for the time being, put aside the cold case he suddenly felt obsessed with thawing.

Chapter Fifteen

The next morning, Garrett gathered all he could on Neil Novak. Turned out that Novak was very much alive and living in Transylvania County. He had also spent time in prison for drug possession early in his life. Though there was no record of him being violence-prone, as far as Garrett was concerned Novak topped the list as a person of interest in his mother's murder.

"Think he'll talk with us?" Madison asked during the drive to visit the suspect.

Garrett sat back behind the steering wheel. "We're not going to give him much of a choice," he declared firmly. "If Novak had anything to do with my mother's murder, he's going to pay for it." Tightening his fingers around the wheel, Garrett added, "Same is true if he's the unsub in the Blue Ridge Parkway homicides."

They arrived at the Novak Ranch, a sprawling property with horses grazing on rolling hills, winding trails and mountain views on Chesterdale Lane in Owen Creek.

"Looks like Novak has done well for himself over the years," Madison commented after they stepped out of the car.

"Looks can be deceiving," Garrett muttered. "Beyond that, it's hard to escape from one's past if there's something there to escape from."

"True enough."

They bypassed the large Craftsman-style home and headed straight for the stables, where they heard voices. Inside, Garrett spotted a tall and slender thirtysomething woman with flaming long and wavy red hair at a stall feeding a quarter horse. Beside her was a sixtysomething man who was taller and heavier, wearing a white wide-brimmed cowboy hat with curly gray hair beneath and sporting a gray ducktail beard.

Garrett overheard the woman refer to the man as "Dad," and she appeared to be concerned about his working too hard. When they heard footsteps approaching, the two turned and stopped talking.

"Are you Neil Novak?" Garrett addressed the man.

"Yep, that's me." He peered at him through dark eyes. "Who's asking?"

"Special Agent Sneed, from the National Park Service's Investigative Services Branch." Garrett flashed his identification. "And this is Law Enforcement Ranger Lynley."

"Hi," Madison spoke evenly to both of them.

Novak jutted his chin. "What's this all about?"

"A cold-case homicide," Garrett responded succinctly.

The woman cocked a brow. "Dad...?"

"I've got this, Dominique." Novak tensed. "I'll see you in the house."

She looked as though she wanted to object, as green eyes darted from Garrett to Madison, before landing back on her father, after which she relented, "All right."

Garrett watched as she walked away, putting some distance between them. He gazed at Novak and said bluntly, "We've reopened the investigation into the murder of Jessica Sneed on the Blue Ridge Parkway." He drew a breath. "She was my mother."

"The parkway killing." Novak scratched his beard nervously. "Sorry that happened to your mother, but that was a long time ago. What does it have to do with me?"

"A survival knife that had your partial fingerprint on it was found to be the murder weapon, Mr. Novak," Madison told him. "I'd say it has everything to do with you."

"As I told the investigators back then, the knife was stolen from my pickup truck. I have no idea who took it and no knowledge of what it was used for by the thief." Novak breathed heavily out his nose. "In any event, I was cleared of any wrongdoing."

"About that," Garrett said. "It seems like your name continued to come up in the investigation in spite of the alibi. Why do you suppose that is?"

"You tell me." Novak's brow creased. "Maybe the cops and rangers thought I was somehow capable of being in two places at once. Well, I wasn't. On the day your mother was killed, I was working on a ranch thirty miles from the parkway and had plenty of others there who could vouch for it. Including the ranch's owner. Now I have my own ranch and have tried to put that dark time behind me for good. Obviously, that isn't so easy for you. Sorry you wasted your time coming here, but I can't help you solve the case."

"Can't?" Garrett glared at him. "Or won't?"

Novak stroked the quarter horse's neck. "Can't," he insisted, his voice steady. "Look, I'm older now and have nothing to hide. If that's all, I have a ranch to run."

Madison lifted her eyes up. "We think that whoever murdered Jessica Sneed may be back at it again," she stated.

His head snapped back. "What are you saying?"

"Two women have been stabbed to death recently on the parkway. The similarities to Ms. Sneed's murder, type of weapon used and location have given us reason to believe that they may have been committed by the same man."

Novak leaned against the stall thoughtfully, tilting the brim of his hat. "Same person thirty years later? Is that even possible?"

"Yes, it's quite possible," Garrett told him. "We think that my mother's killer may have stabbed to death another woman a year later but another man took the rap for it. So yes, that same killer could have remained dormant for years before returning to the parkway to go after other vulnerable women."

"Wow." Novak uttered an expletive. "Hard to believe the same killer from thirty years ago would be around to target others today and think he could get away with it."

"Why wouldn't he think that?" Garrett challenged him while wondering if Novak himself could be involved somehow with the recent killings. "After all, he got away with it before. Maybe more than once."

Novak wrinkled his nose. "If that's the case, I hope you get the bastard. But I'm afraid I still can't help you. As I said, I lost the knife, so…"

"Did you lose it, or was the knife stolen, as you claimed thirty years ago?" Madison pressed him.

"Stolen," Novak insisted. "*Lost* was just a poor choice of words."

Garrett wondered if that was the case. Or could it mean he was lying about both options and had, in fact, handed the knife off to someone?

Removing the sketch from the pocket of his khaki pants, Garrett said, "This person was seen in the vicinity of the area on the Blue Ridge Parkway where my mother was murdered. Does he look familiar?"

Novak took the sketch and studied it for a long moment before replying unevenly, "Can't say that he does…sorry."

"Take another look," Garrett insisted, sensing that he could be holding back for some reason.

Novak again stared at the drawing stoically. "Nope." He handed the sketch back to Garrett. "It's been thirty years, so my memory could be failing me. Not to mention it's just a sketch that may or may not even be an accurate portrayal of the person it's supposed to. Either way, it doesn't ring a bell. I wish I could say otherwise, but I can't."

Garrett glanced at Madison, whose expression matched his own in believing they might have reached a dead end here. If Novak did know something, he was unwilling to say so. And they were in no position to apply more pressure. "By the way," Garrett put out, "just for the record, I'll need you to account for your whereabouts when the two recent murders occurred on the parkway."

Novak gave him the dates and time frame. He claimed he'd been on his ranch those mornings in question and had ranch hands who could verify this. When they heard footsteps, Garrett turned to see Novak's daughter walking toward them in her tailored ankle booties.

"You're still here?" she questioned, eyeing them suspiciously.

"We were just leaving," Garrett told her, knowing where to find her father, should they need to interview him further. He took out his ISB business card and handed it to Novak. "If you happen to remember anything pertinent to our investigation, you can reach me on my cell phone."

Novak nodded. "I'll keep that in mind."

"Thanks for your time," Madison told him in a sociable tone of voice. She gazed at Dominique. "Have a nice day."

On that note, Garrett signaled to Madison that it was time to go. They walked away, leaving the father and daughter standing there staring, undoubtedly.

Once out of ear range, he commented, "I'm not totally convinced that Neil Novak is as oblivious as he claims to be regarding the supposedly stolen knife. Or lack of recognition of the unsub in the sketch, for that matter."

"Neither am I," she said. "But between his insistence that the knife was stolen and his alibi then and apparent one now, we can only take a wait-and-see approach while continuing the investigation."

"Yeah, I suppose," Garrett muttered.

They walked back to his vehicle as his thoughts turned to wondering if he had missed something in the overall scheme of things in pursuing one or more killers with a common theme and deadly intentions.

HOURS LATER, Madison was still weighing whether or not Neil Novak was on the level in his assertions of playing no part in the death of Jessica Sneed or, in fact, had succeeded in pulling the wool over the eyes of investigators for decades, when she was notified over the radio that another dead woman had been found on the parkway.

Madison's heart lurched against her chest as she phoned Garrett with the distressing news. "We have a new problem," she almost hated to say, with his mother's cold case having resurfaced in the investigation.

He took a moment to digest the latest death and, after giving him the location, Garrett said soberly, "I can get there in fifteen minutes or less."

"See you then." Madison hung up and headed to the scene she was closer to, fearful of what this meant in the bigger picture as her workplace was once again the center of unwanted attention.

She drove down the Blue Ridge Parkway to Milepost 364 and parked before heading on foot to the Craggy Gardens Trail that was lined with wild blueberries and numerous wildflowers and offered a stunning view of the Black Mountains.

Richard Edison approached her with a dour look on his face. "It's not good," the law enforcement ranger moaned as Madison caught sight of the body lying off the trail near gnarled sweet birch trees. "The victim has been identified as Heidi Ushijima, a twenty-five-year-old seasonal interpretive ranger for the National Park Service. She was discovered by a park visitor, Nadine Dobrev, who reported it." Richard's thick brows knitted. "Looks like she was stabbed to death."

"I was afraid of that," Madison muttered. She took a couple of steps forward for a closer look at the deceased park guide, whom she'd never had the pleasure of meeting when Heidi was still alive. Heidi had short brunette hair in a shag bob and was curled into a fetal position, while wearing a ranger's beige T-shirt, brown cargo pants and tennis shoes. Blood seeped through her clothing from multiple punctures to her torso and legs.

Madison looked away, believing that the Blue Ridge Parkway Killer had likely struck again. She wondered if this brazen attack in a well-traveled but challenging area to navigate suggested that the unsub was a different, younger perp than Jessica Sneed's killer. Or could they still be one and the same?

She eyed Richard. "Any sign of the murder weapon?"

"Not yet." His lips pursed as he scanned the trail. "I'm guessing the unsub took it with him. Either to toss elsewhere like before or hold onto to use again if an opportunity arises."

"That's what bothers me," Madison said. She had little reason to believe that the unsub wouldn't continue to attack isolated females on the parkway. Not unless they were finally able to stop him cold. She looked up and saw Dawn Dominguez arrive.

"Not another one?" she asked.

"I think so," Madison had to say sadly.

Dawn frowned, making her way to the corpse. "Let's have a look."

"Someone really went to work on her," Richard said bleakly.

"Same as the others," she concurred. Wearing nitrile gloves, she gave the body an initial examination. "At the risk of sounding like a broken record, I'd say she was stabbed seven or eight times with a long-blade knife, killing her in the process."

Madison cringed as she glanced at Richard and back. "How long ago would you estimate this happened?"

Dawn felt the skin and replied, "Still relatively warm. I say she was attacked within the past two or three hours."

This corresponded with what Madison was thinking, as it was unlikely that the victim could have been in this location all morning without being noticed. She had no reason to believe the killer had moved the body to Craggy Gardens as opposed to catching Heidi Ushijima off guard or following her in the course of her hiking there. Either way, all the signs pointed toward this being the work of the Blue Ridge Parkway Killer. But just how long had he been at this?

GARRETT ARRIVED AT the crime scene at the same time as Tom Hutchison. The strain on the face of Madison's boss was indicative of the gravity of the situation with a crazed and violent serial killer in the midst, as seemed to be the case. The fact that the same person could have been responsible for his mother's murder made it all the more unsettling for Garrett.

"Hey," he spoke lowly to Madison.

"It's him again," she stated surely.

Garrett swallowed. "Talk to me."

She brought him up to speed on the death of Heidi Ushijima in a manner that measured up to the recent murders on the parkway. It was disturbing to Garrett, to say the least, on more levels than one.

"Same old story," Madison complained. "See for yourself."

Garrett looked at the latest victim, more or less validating his greatest fears that this case had taken another deadly turn. "Seems that way."

"What is going on?" Tom's tone was boisterous with disbelief as he homed in on the body and glared at the deputy chief medical examiner.

"We're definitely looking at a homicide due to stabbing repeatedly," she declared.

Tom pressed down on his hat. "This is starting to get out of hand," he griped.

"Not just 'starting to,'" Garrett begged to differ. "Someone has taken it upon himself to use the parkway as his personal hunting ground. We can't let him get away with it."

"Seems to me he's doing just that." Tom sighed. "Do we need more manpower to track him down?"

Without answering this, Garrett said, "What we need most is to keep from panicking and realize that, in spite of his track record, the perp is only human and, whether he knows it or not, is running out of steam."

At least I want to believe that, Garrett told himself. There were only so many ways the perp could go to commit his heinous crimes and try to hide from it in a despicable cowardly manner. Whether or not they were searching for his mother's killer, the need to restore some sense of safety on the parkway and the general area itself had never been greater.

"I agree," Richard said, furrowing his brow. "Whoever's doing this seems to be acting in desperation right now. This tells me that, apart from being a loose cannon, he's also leaving the door open for us to catch him."

"We just need to find that door, which happens to be

somewhere in the vast Pisgah Ranger District," Madison pitched in, "making it that much more challenging."

"Please hurry up," Dawn said, a seriousness to her tone as she removed her gloves. "Believe it or not, I do have other dead bodies that need tending to."

"We get it," Garrett said, recognizing that they were all on the same page in the search for justice. He turned to Madison and Richard. "Find out all you can on the movements today of Heidi Ushijima, leading up to her death. Where she went. Where she lived. Why she chose to go to the Craggy Gardens. If she came here alone. You know the score."

Madison nodded. "Understood."

"Shouldn't be too difficult," Richard said. "Most of the seasonal workers hang out together and probably know one another's secrets, if there are any."

Garrett hoped that provided some answers. He said, "In the meantime, let's get the crime scene investigators out here and see what they can come up with in forensic evidence that might lead to a killer."

"On their way," Madison informed him, not too surprisingly.

"Good." They would coordinate their efforts with the local law enforcement in securing the perimeter, closing some roads leading to this part of the parkway and seeing if there were witnesses to track down and surveillance video to access. Garrett had to wonder if the unsub had left behind enough clues that hadn't been compromised by the terrain in which the corpse had been left, that could line up with other evidence gathered along the way with the clock ticking.

Chapter Sixteen

Once the body had been carted off to the morgue and the reality sank in of another murder on the Blue Ridge Parkway, Madison and Richard set out separately to see what clues they could find in the lead-up to Heidi Ushijima's death. By all accounts, the Japanese American Duke University graduate student had been well liked and had embraced her job as a seasonal interpretive ranger for the National Park Service. Madison was told by other park workers that Heidi had been in her element in teaching visitors about the parkway and Pisgah National Forest's history and cultural significance.

It was in this context of information gathering that she had apparently hiked to the Craggy Gardens, along with fellow seasonal interpretive ranger Quentin Enriques, whom Heidi had been said to be dating. But only he'd emerged alive. When Richard radioed her to say that he had located Quentin on the Cumberland Knob Trail at Milepost 217.5, Madison responded, "I'm just a few minutes away."

"He's not going anywhere," the ranger assured her.

As she drove to the location, Madison's immediate thought was could Quentin Enriques have been callous and confident enough to stab Heidi to death and then go about his business as though nothing had happened? If so, she imagined he would have needed to dispose of his bloody clothing somewhere along the way. Along with the murder weapon. Was this feasible? Or had Heidi encountered someone else at Craggy Gardens?

I have to keep all options on the table, Madison reminded herself. Just as Garrett was doing, in spite of his being drawn to the specter of his mother's murder in relation to the current happenings.

Madison reached the Cumberland Knob in Alleghany County, near the North Carolina-Virginia border, and parked. The site, which combined woodlands with open spaces, was popular for viewing different birds and wildlife. She spotted Richard talking with a tall and stocky twenty-something male with brown hair in a half-bun ponytail. He had separated the suspect from a group of tourists.

"This is Ranger Lynley," Richard told him and said to her, "I've just informed Quentin about the murder of Heidi Ushijima. He claims she was alive and well when they split up."

"This is crazy." Quentin's lower lip quivered. "Heidi's dead?"

Madison saw the distress in his face and brown eyes that seemed genuine enough. She still had to ask, "When did you last see Heidi?"

"About three hours ago, when we were together at Craggy Gardens."

"Why did you leave?"

"I needed to move on to my next assignment," he pointed out, "exploring the Cumberland Knob area with visitors."

Sounds plausible, Madison thought. She glanced at the tourists, who were taking pictures of the surroundings and seemed only mildly curious. "Did you see anyone else on the Craggy Gardens Trail?"

Quentin shrugged. "I passed by some people here or there, but no one who was traveling alone," he claimed. "Or otherwise seemed suspicious at the time."

Richard peered at him. "I understand that you and Heidi were dating?"

"Yeah, we hung out," Quentin admitted. "It wasn't anything serious. We were both just here for the summer."

"So, you didn't have a fight or anything at Craggy Gardens?" Richard questioned.

"No," he insisted. "We were cool."

"Did Heidi ever indicate to you that she wasn't cool with someone else?" Madison posed to him. "Either within the NPS or outside of it?"

Quentin shook his head. "If she was having a problem with anyone, Heidi never shared it with me."

Madison gazed at him while thinking that, given his age, at the very least he didn't square with a person old enough to have murdered Jessica Sneed. But might there have been some other connection between the killer then and now?

"Sorry we had to put you through this," she voiced sympathetically, giving him the benefit of the doubt that he was another innocent secondary victim of murder.

"You're just doing your job," he muttered.

"We may need to talk to you again," Richard cautioned him. "But for now, you're free to rejoin your group, if you like."

"Or take some time off to grieve," Madison told Quentin.

They had no reason to hold him further, she realized. It wouldn't make dealing with Heidi's death any easier for him or them. When Quentin walked away with his head down,

Madison surmised, "He didn't kill her. No signs of being cut himself. Or being able to dispose of the evidence and return to his duties without missing a beat."

"I was thinking the same thing," Richard said, frowning. "We'll keep at it."

Madison nodded. Once back in her car, she phoned Garrett with an update. "So far, we've hit a brick wall among Heidi's colleagues and the guy she was dating. He's only in his twenties, by the way," she threw out, conflicting with the cold to new cases homicide theory.

"Heidi was likely killed by someone outside her workplace or social circles," Garrett argued. "As to the age disparity in connecting the serial killer to my mother's murder, there's always the possibility of a copycat killer."

She agreed. "There is that."

"If this proves to be true or the Blue Ridge Parkway Killer of today is unconnected to a thirty-year-old homicide that stays a cold case, I'll have to accept that."

So would she. But for now, Madison still trusted his instincts and had to believe the link was there in some way, shape or fashion. "As long as the co-investigations persist, we'll just have to see where they take us."

"All right."

When they disconnected, Madison found herself looking ahead and knowing that they made a great team. Love did that to people who connected on a deep level. It was something that she hoped would blossom into an even greater appreciation of one another.

"IN LIGHT OF the latest homicide on the Blue Ridge Parkway, I've gotten the go-ahead from my boss, Wilma Seatriz, in

Washington, DC, to raise the reward to fifty thousand dollars for any meaningful information that leads to the arrest and prosecution of the unsub," Carly told Garrett an hour after he had updated her on the murder of Heidi Ushijima.

He was at his temporary cabin, video chatting on his laptop with the South Atlantic-Gulf regional director. Carly had managed to convince Seatriz, the NPS associate director for visitor and resource protection, who oversaw the Division of Law Enforcement, Security, and Emergency Services that Garrett worked for, of the importance in upping the ante to catch a killer. Though Garrett hated the thought of paying money for a solid lead, he hated even more the reality that the unsub had managed to elude them thus far. As such, with three women recently stabbed to death on the parkway and at least one murdered decades ago by perhaps the same killer, it was imperative that they use every means at their disposal to get justice. Whether or not doubling the reward would do the trick was anyone's guess.

I'm definitely on board with giving this a shot, Garrett told himself. "That's good," he said. "The public can still play an important role in solving this case."

"Maybe it won't need to come to that," Carly argued, wrinkling her nose. "I mean, we have the finest federal investigators in the business, starting with yourself. If anyone can crack this case the good old-fashioned way, it's you, Sneed."

Garrett resisted a grin, flattered by the suggestion while feeling the pressure of being put on a sneaky pedestal. He also read between the lines. She would rather they keep the cash in the federal coffers, if at all possible, to have handy for another day. "I'll see what I can do" was the best he could promise, while knowing she fully expected that and then some.

Carly waited a beat, then asked, "Are you still angling the parkway serial killer as being connected with the death of your mother?"

Garrett sat back, thoughtful. "I have no proof of that," he admitted, "but looking at it squarely, I believe it to be a real possibility that the unsub has crossed decades in taking lives and has either simply gotten lucky or maybe was incarcerated for committing other crimes, only to resume targeting women in the Blue Ridge Mountains once freed."

"Well, I trust your instincts," she said assuredly. "On that note, I've asked a criminologist that the NPS has worked with in the past to speak with you about the investigation."

"Oh…?"

"Her name is Katrina Sherwood. She specializes in serial killer cases, has written three books and may be able to give you some added perspective in trying to track down the Blue Ridge Parkway Killer."

As if he could refuse what amounted to a directive from his superior, not that he would turn down assistance from an expert on serial killers, Garrett responded, "I'd be happy to speak with Ms. Sherwood."

Carly smiled. "I'll text you her number, and you can give her a call."

"I'll do that," he promised.

"Keep me posted on the investigation."

Garrett nodded. "I will."

After ending the conversation, he left his makeshift office and grabbed a beer from the refrigerator. He thought about Madison and how much they had managed to recapture since starting over. He relished being able to take this and run with it, no matter the distance, in wanting to find that dream of a life together at the end of the rainbow.

Walking back into the living room, Garrett lifted up his cell phone and saw the number Carly had texted for Katrina Sherwood.

No time like the present, he thought, in giving her a call.

She answered after two rings with, "Katrina."

"Hi. I'm Special Agent Garrett Sneed," he told her. "Carly Tafoya asked me to contact you regarding a case I'm working on."

"Right. The Blue Ridge Parkway murder investigation," she acknowledged. "Carly brought me up to speed on where things stand and the possible cold-case connection."

"Okay." Garrett felt this was a step in right direction.

"Why don't we switch to video," Katrina requested. "It's better for a real dialogue. Don't you think?"

"Absolutely." He sat down on a wingback accent chair and tapped the Video icon on the phone. Katrina Sherwood appeared. African American and attractive, she was in her forties with bold brown eyes and curly blond hair in a Deva cut.

She flashed her teeth. "Nice to meet you, Agent Sneed."

"You too," he said evenly.

"Why don't we get down to business," she told him. "You're dealing with a serial killer in your midst who's stabbing to death women on the parkway, right?"

"Yes. He's apparently picking his victims at random but may also have been stalking them before things took a deadly turn."

"Typical," Katrina asserted matter-of-factly. "That is to say, it's typical that many serial killers seek out victims randomly, but just as many others may have stalked their victims for a while and then killed them when the best opportunity presented itself to do so. There are no absolutes when it comes to serial homicide and the heterogeneous nature and characteristics of the offenders," she stressed, "apart from the fact that a serial killer by definition kills two or more people in separate incidents, which I'm sure you understand."

"I do," Garrett conceded, "all too well. I am curious, though, as to your take on why stab the victims instead of, say, shooting or strangling them, given the messiness of a stabbing attack."

"Frankly, most stabbing serial killers give little thought to the messy nature of such assaults. Think Jack the Ripper, John Eichinger or Kenneth Granviel, to name a few." She twisted her lips musingly. "Some serial killers simply choose stabbing over other ways to kill because they get some kind of perverse thrill in the violence and suffering that goes along with it. Other serial killers may choose a knife as a more accessible weapon or easier to use to kill than say, trying to strangle the victim. Yet other serial killers may view inflicting pain upon another as a power grab."

Garrett grimaced as he pictured his mother being victimized this way. Though he had some idea, he asked, "Why start killing, only to stop for years or even decades before starting back up again?"

Katrina narrowed her eyes. "You're thinking about the murder of your mother, thirty years ago?"

"Yeah," Garrett confirmed and took a sip of his beer. "And the possibility that her killer may have killed another woman a year later, then laid low for decades, only to re-discover stabbing to death vulnerable females."

"I see." She took a breath. "Well, killers stop killing for all types of reasons," she explained. "These include fear of being caught, illness, romance, imprisonment for another crime or just deciding enough was enough. In the case of The Ripper, for example, the unsub apparently ended his killing ways abruptly after 1888, by some accounts, and never resuming. On the other hand, Lonnie David Frank-lin Jr., a serial killer also known as the Grim Sleeper, took a fourteen-year hiatus between killings. Similarly, serial killer Dennis Rader, aka the BTK Strangler, went over a decade since his last kill before being captured.

"My point is that if the man who killed your mother has resurfaced after all these years to target other women, as-suming he hadn't kept it going elsewhere in the country, it could be for any number of reasons. These include bore-dom, death in the family, an impulsive desire to get back in the game, opportunistic circumstances or an aura of in-vincibility, having been successful the first time around without getting caught."

Garrett gave an understanding nod. "I get where you're coming from," he told her bleakly. It also gave him food for uneasy thoughts to gnaw on. Had his mother's killer come back to terrorize the Blue Ridge Mountains and Pis-gah Ranger District once again? Or had another staked his claim in following suit as the Blue Ridge Parkway Killer?

THE KILLER HIKED in the mountainous forest and meadows. He enjoyed the solitude on the Blue Ridge Parkway, though at times encountering elk, peregrine falcons, white-tailed deer, wild turkeys and even a black bear every now and then. It was nature at its finest, and he was part of it. The fact that he had killed more than once and planned to do so again was who he was at his core. As was the case for any animal predator he ran into.

He continued to make his way through hollows and coves, mountain ash and yellow birch trees, and black huckleberry shrubs en route to his destination. Whistling, he broke the silence, save for the sporadic sounds of indigo buntings and red-winged blackbirds meandering through the trees. His thoughts moved to Heidi Ushijima, his latest victim. A flicker of guilt ripped through him that he'd taken her life. It disappeared in an instant, realizing that it was something that'd had to be done.

He had known beforehand that Heidi had had to die. The only question had been when. She'd provided him the answer when he'd overheard her talking about heading to the Craggy Gardens Trail. Accompanying her had been another seasonal interpretive ranger, Quentin Enriques. He had watched the two kissing from time to time, making it clear that they'd been sweet on one another.

Given that the desire to kill Heidi had nearly overcome all reason, he might have had to take out Quentin too. Only after a while, he'd left Craggy Gardens alone to go elsewhere. Then some others had come along, and Heidi exchanged pleasantries with them before they, too, had moved on. That was when it had been time to make his move. While Heidi had been preoccupied with wildflowers, he'd taken her totally by surprise. At first, recognizing him, she'd actually believed he'd simply been out and about.

Only when she'd seen the new eight-inch serrated knife

he'd produced, after ditching the last one, had the small talk come to a screeching halt. When she'd tried to make a run for it, he'd anticipated her move and surprised her by being quicker. He'd caught up to her and gone to work with the knife. Ignoring her cries, he'd finished the job in short order. He'd thought he'd heard someone coming and made his planned escape, using his knowledge of the parkway to hide from sight. When the coast had been clear, he'd continued to put distance between himself and his latest victim.

He reached his tent and felt as though it offered him the sanctuary he needed—till it was time to move on to greener pastures, where he could start fresh in appeasing his deadly appetite. But not before he could turn his attention to the pretty law enforcement ranger, Madison Lynley, who in time would soon come to feel her life being drained away when he struck time and time again with his blade.

Chapter Seventeen

"Agent Sneed," the raspy voice said. "This is Neil Novak."

Garrett was driving that morning when the call came. "How can I help you, Mr. Novak?" he asked coolly, though more than curious in hearing from the rancher.

"We need to talk," Novak said tersely.

So talk, Garrett thought, wondering if this would be a confession. "I'm listening."

"In person," he insisted.

"All right," Garrett told him. "I can be at your ranch in twenty minutes."

"Actually, I'd like to speak at my attorney's office."

With that, Garrett assumed what he had to say might constitute legal jeopardy and piqued his own interest all the more. "Not a problem."

"Her name's Pauline Vasquez," Novak said. "She's with the Eugenio, Debicki and Vasquez law firm in the Kiki Place Office Building on Twelfth Street and Bentmoore."

"I know where it is," Garrett said. He remembered Madison interviewing Pauline Vasquez about murder victim Olivia Forlani when they visited the law firm a few days ago. Was Vasquez's representation of Novak coincidental? Or something more unsettling in the scheme of things? "I'll be there," Garrett told him, agreeing to meet in half an hour.

"By the way," Novak said, a catch to his voice, "bring that sketch with you."

"Uh, okay." Garrett tried to read into that. Was he actually ready to come clean about the unsub in the composite drawing?

After disconnecting, Garrett glanced at the cowhide leather messenger bag on the passenger seat. It contained the sketch of the unsub and other case materials.

He phoned Madison on the parkway and said, "You won't believe who I just got a call from."

"Who?" she asked.

"Neil Novak."

"Really?"

"He has something to say," Garrett told her. "But will only do so in the presence of his lawyer, who happens to be Pauline Vasquez."

"No kidding?"

"I kid you not." He paused. "Novak has asked to take another look at the sketch of the unsub."

"Interesting," Madison hummed. "When is this meeting taking place?"

He told her and said keenly, "You should be there."

"Wouldn't miss it," she assured him. "If Neil Novak has something to get off his chest with legal representation, it must be something huge."

"Yeah, that's what I was thinking." Garrett gazed at the road ahead. "Let me know where you are, and we can drive there together." She gave him her location, and he went for her, knowing that Madison's curiosity was piqued as much as his in what this was all about. He longed for the day when they could spend even more time together on their own terms.

MADISON SAT IN an accent chair beside Garrett on one side of a white rectangular meeting table in a conference room with a wide floor-to-ceiling window. On the other side was Neil Novak; his daughter, Dominique Novak; and their attorney, Pauline Vasquez. One could hear a pin drop, making Madison wonder just where this was going in relation to their criminal investigation.

After a tense moment or two, Pauline pasted a thin smile on her lips and said, "Thanks for coming, Special Agent Sneed and Ranger Lynley."

Garrett leaned forward. "So, exactly why are we here?" he cut to the chase. For her part, Madison couldn't help but think that it could have been her friend Olivia representing the firm in this matter, had the partnership not been handed to Pauline prior to Olivia's death, without her ever being the wiser.

"My client, Mr. Novak, has information he believes to be relevant to your investigation into a cold case," the attorney responded. "But to be clear, the info is strictly voluntarily given and implies no guilt or knowledge beforehand."

"Got it," Garrett told her laconically and gazed at Novak. "What would you like to say to us?"

Novak scratched his beard. "Did you bring the sketch?"

"Yeah." Garrett produced it and slid it across the table.

Novak picked it up and studied it for a beat before setting the sketch back down. He sucked in a deep breath and uttered, "I've seen him before."

"Where?" Madison asked. "When?"

"Asheville," he asserted. "Thirty years ago."

"Did you know him?" Garrett asked straightforwardly.

"Yeah, I knew who he was, but we weren't friends or anything."

"Do you recall his name?" Madison asked, peering at him.

"Deschanel, I believe…" Novak said after a moment or two. "Yeah, it was Bryan Deschanel."

Taking his word on this for now, Madison watched Garrett make a note to that effect; then he asked him bluntly, "Did you give Bryan Deschanel the knife that was used to kill Jessica Sneed?"

"No, definitely not!" Novak insisted. "I can't even say if he was the one who took my knife. I do remember seeing him hanging around my truck but never made the connection between that and the stolen knife." He drew a breath. "Not till you showed me the sketch yesterday."

Garrett frowned. "So, you lied to a federal law enforcement officer when questioned about the sketch? Not a smart move."

"I didn't want to get involved," he claimed. "Apart from that, I couldn't be sure at the time without seeing the sketch again that it was the same guy I thought it might be."

"Are you saying you never saw the sketch before we showed it to you?" Madison asked, knowing that it had been part of the official investigation back in the day. How could he, as a person of interest and suspect, not have been shown the sketch?

"Never!" Novak asserted. "Don't ask me why, but the police never showed up at my door with this and I never saw it in the newspaper. Otherwise, I would've said something."

"My dad's telling you the truth," Dominique spoke up, tucking hair behind her ear. "It was me who talked him into coming forward and saying what he knew. Or thought he did. He would never have tried to impede a murder investigation. Or cover up for a killer."

"That should be obvious, just by us being here right now," Pauline argued. "My client is doing his civic duty by telling you what he knows. What you do with it is up to you, but as Mr. Novak was cleared of any involvement three decades ago, this is where his obligation as a citizen ends."

Garrett relaxed his rigid jawline. "We have no desire to go after your client, Ms. Vasquez," he told her.

She smiled. "Good."

"But we do have a few more questions for him," Garrett said.

Novak met his gaze. "Go ahead."

"Have you seen Bryan Deschanel lately?"

"Haven't seen him in thirty years," Novak alleged. "If I saw him on the street, I doubt I'd even recognize him today. Beyond that, as I recall him being a troublemaker who others thought was messed up in the head, he's not someone I'd want in my life or my daughter's."

"What kind of trouble?" Garrett asked him.

"He had anger issues and was prone to violence and vandalism."

Madison couldn't help but think about the viciousness of the attack on Jessica Sneed as well as the three recent victims of fatal stabbings. Could Bryan Deschanel have been responsible for all of these?

She eyed Novak and said, "It's possible that Deschanel is still around and is now targeting women on the Blue Ridge Parkway. Including a third woman stabbed to death since we last spoke to you."

"Yeah, heard about that." Novak lowered his chin. "Made me wonder if there could be a connection of some sort with what happened thirty years ago."

"I wondered too," Dominique said. "When my father told me about the possibility that the same person who murdered your mother, Agent Sneed, could be doing it again, I managed to convince him that he needed to do the right thing and speak up. And we are."

Garrett nodded. "I appreciate your coming forward," he told them.

"If it can help you solve your case, it will have been well worth my trouble," Novak said.

Pauline rested her arm on her leather briefcase and said, "I understand that there's a fifty-thousand-dollar reward on the table for information leading to the arrest and conviction of the so-called Blue Ridge Parkway Killer?"

Madison frowned. "So, this is all about money?" *Blood money*, she thought.

"It's not what you think," she responded quickly and turned to the Novaks.

Dominique sat up straight. "We don't care about the money," she stressed. "But if for whatever reason we qualify for receiving it, we intend to donate every cent to organizations that focus on violence against women." She sucked in a deep breath. "Five years ago, I lost my mother to such a senseless act."

As Dominique's words sank in, Madison stood corrected

on her initial assumptions and said sincerely, "I'm sorry to hear about your mother."

She nodded, and Novak said, "So, as you see, Agent Sneed, we have more in common than you thought."

"Guess we do," Garrett conceded.

"Anyway, any such reward would all be facilitated through Ms. Vasquez," Dominique stated.

"We would certainly see to it that their wishes were carried out to the letter," Pauline assured them.

Garrett responded, "Whether or not the information given to us results in anything is still up in the air. Right now, our goal in representing the National Park Service is to try to locate Bryan Deschanel and see what he's been up to. Or may have been running from for the past three decades."

Pauline smoothed a brow. "I understand."

"We'll be in touch," Madison said as the meeting adjourned and she left with Garrett, equipped with intel on a person of interest in both a cold case and one that seemed to be getting hotter with each passing day.

"YOU THINK BRYAN DESCHANEL is alive and well, lurking around the Blue Ridge Parkway, killing women?" Madison asked point-blank as Garrett drove down Hayten Road.

It was a good question, he knew, and one they both needed an answer to, one way or the other. "My gut tells me that Deschanel is still among the living," Garrett said flatly. "And that he may be closer than we think."

"And your mother's killer?"

"Yes." There was no sugarcoating this. Garrett cringed at the thought. "When you put the pieces together, beginning with the unsub's sketch ID'd by Neil Novak—I think that

Deschanel stole the knife from Novak's pickup, used it on my mother and likely attacked another woman the following year. I believe he's been lying low ever since. At least till recently, when deciding to resurface on the parkway and use his guiles to murder more women, while operating with impunity in plain sight. I'm betting that the latent palm print Jewel pulled from the survival knife used to kill Olivia Forlani and Nicole Wallenberg belongs to Deschanel and no other."

"I think you may be spot on," Madison stated. "We need to find Deschanel, wherever he's hiding, and hold him accountable for his crimes."

"Right." Garrett turned onto Overlook Road and approached the Blue Ridge Parkway. "I'll run a criminal background check on Bryan Deschanel and see what else I can learn about the man and his whereabouts. In the meantime, be extra careful on the parkway while he's still on the loose and dangerous as ever."

"I will," she promised, placing a hand on his shoulder. "You too. I have a feeling that Deschanel, evidently used to having his way, is a threat to anyone who comes into contact with him."

"I agree." Garrett grinned at her. "I can take whatever he dishes out and give back thrice as hard."

Madison smiled warmly. "I'm sure you can."

He knew she was capable of handling herself too and was armed, while having backup among other rangers. But till they had the dangerous suspect in custody, Garrett doubted he'd be able to relax and feel confident that she was out of harm's way. That was something he couldn't afford to take for granted.

Chapter Eighteen

Garrett went back to his cabin and, on the laptop, dug into Bryan Deschanel's criminal background and any other information that was accessible. Running his name through local law enforcement databases, the National Crime Information Center, the North Carolina DMV, the FBI's Next Generation Identification system, and various social media sites, Garrett found that Deschanel had no criminal record, per se, or outstanding warrants. Nor did his name show up in a Google search, on Facebook, Instagram or Twitter.

But Bryan Deschanel had been a person of interest in the death of his mother, Garrett noted, when digging deeper into police reports, and newspaper accounts in a search on Google. Helena Deschanel had died in a mysterious house fire when Deschanel had been in his late teens. Though suspected of causing the fire, police had lacked the evidence to prove it, and he'd been let off the hook. In his twenties, Deschanel had had other skirmishes with the law but had never been charged with a crime. He'd once been accused of domestic violence, but the victim had inexplicably withdrawn her complaint.

Garrett cocked a brow when he discovered that Bryan

Deschanel had been an early suspect in the stabbing death of twenty-nine-year-old Vicki Flanagan, who'd been killed on the Blue Ridge Parkway by the Yadkin Valley Overlook a year after the murder of Garrett's mother. Blake O'Donnell, who'd confessed to the crime and then recanted, had been ultimately convicted for it. *What if Deschanel was the true culprit and O'Donnell innocent after all?* Garrett wondered.

He went through the files again that ex-Sheriff Lou Buckley had lent them in the investigation, looking for any mention of Bryan Deschanel. Garrett found it. Deschanel had been questioned briefly as a potential witness by a deputy, but somehow no connection had been made between him and the sketch of the unsub. It made Garrett wonder if he was off base in suspecting Bryan Deschanel of being a three-decades-long serial killer.

Not when I look at this squarely, he told himself. The circumstantial evidence was there. Some physical evidence too, that might link the suspect to at least two of the murders. Along with too many facts that, when put together, had to be more than merely coincidental. Still, Garrett was troubled that Deschanel was not showing up on the radar. And hadn't apparently in years. Could he be dead, with someone else stepping into his shoes as a serial killer?

Garrett went even further in searching for evidence that Bryan Deschanel was no longer alive. Nothing came up in a Google search or other data. It was almost as though the man had dropped off the face of the earth. *I'm not buying it,* Garrett thought. He cross-checked Deschanel's name for any possible aliases that might be known to authorities. Nothing registered, frustrating him.

Still, the idea that Bryan Deschanel had either engaged in

identity theft or simply created from scratch or know-how a moniker he was going by to more easily operate without his past catching up to him was gaining steam with Garrett. He was all but certain that the murder suspect was not only alive and well but living or working within the vicinity of the Blue Ridge Parkway.

Garrett grabbed the sketch and studied it. But that was from thirty years ago. If Deschanel was still alive, what did he look like today? With that thought in mind and no known actual photograph of the suspect, Garrett believed that an age-progression sketch of Deschanel would give him a more accurate image to work with and circulate to other law enforcement.

He got on his cell phone and requested a video chat with Caitlin Rundle, a forensic artist at the North Carolina State Bureau of Investigation that the National Park Service had used in other criminal investigations. Thirtysomething, she was following in the footsteps of her father, Karl Rundle, a retired renowned crime-scene sketch artist. Caitlin accepted the call after three rings.

"Agent Sneed," she said, gazing back at him through blue eyes, with short blond hair framing her face.

"Hey, Caitlin." Garrett straightened his shoulders. "I need a big favor."

"Sure. How can I help?"

"I'm investigating a thirty-year-old cold-case homicide," he explained. "All I have right now on my chief suspect is a hand-drawn sketch that was done of him at the time. I need a better representation of what he might look like today."

Caitlin smiled. "I think I can assist you with that," she said with confidence. "Just send me what you have, and I'll do my best to give you a digitally enhanced image that is age appropriate for the unsub today."

"Wonderful." Garrett's eyes crinkled at the corners.

"How soon do you need it?"

"Would yesterday be soon enough?" he responded dryly.

She gave a little chuckle. "I'll get on it right away."

"Great." He gave her the relevant information he had on the serial killer suspect, including a digital picture of the composite drawing of him.

While Garrett waited to hear back from Caitlin, he again studied the clues that led him to believe that Bryan Deschanel was still alive, responsible for at least four murders by stabbing and posed a serious threat to even more women on the Blue Ridge Parkway.

MADISON WAS SITTING in her car, reading the chilling autopsy report on the latest female to die on the parkway. According to the deputy chief medical examiner, Heidi had been the victim of numerous stabbings—had been attacked with a knife seven times—to her back, buttocks and legs, resulting in death by homicide. The murder weapon was described as a sharp serrated-edge knife with an eight-inch blade.

What a monster, Madison told herself, hating that another fellow ranger had been brutally murdered in an unprovoked, callous assault. The fact that such a picturesque and usually hospitable setting as the Blue Ridge Mountains and Pisgah National Forest had been turned into a killing field made it all the harder to digest. Worse was that there was a good chance the perpetrator had also murdered Garrett's mother and managed to get away with it.

Till now. With Bryan Deschanel being fingered as the man in the thirty-year-old sketch, at the very least, this told them that he was likely Jessica's killer. And had quite possibly murdered another woman the following year. Though much older now, the stars lined up to the notion that he might have come back to carry on his homicidal tendencies today. If so, now that they had drawn a bead on him, it was just a matter of time before his reign of terror was over. Until then, Madison hoped that no other woman would see her life cut short by a madman.

When she got a call over the radio, Madison heard Leonard say with a sense of urgency, "We just got a report of a woman injured below the Raven Rocks Overlook."

The spot immediately struck a chord with Madison. It was the very area where Jessica Sneed had been killed. Had her killer done a repeat performance thirty years later?

"I'm on my way," Madison told Leonard.

Afterward, she relayed this to Richard and Tom, calling for backup while hoping they could quickly seal off any escape routes.

Madison drove to the parking area for the Raven Rocks Overlook. She spotted a gray metallic Land Rover parked there. Getting out of her car, Madison approached the vehicle cautiously. It was unoccupied but had tourist brochures spread out on the front passenger seat. Did this car belong to the injured woman?

Peeking below the overlook, Madison saw nothing unusual. She wondered if this could be someone's idea of a practical joke. It had been known to happen sometimes on the parkway. Usually the work of mischievous teenagers. But given the recent happenings on the parkway, Madison had to believe that a woman might truly be in distress and needed her help.

She made her way down the incline and headed toward the woods, where she thought she heard a sound. Was it an animal? Or human? Removing her pistol from the duty holster, Madison saw Ward Wilcox, the maintenance ranger, approaching her.

"Stop," she ordered instinctively, knowing this was outside his normal work area.

He obeyed, standing rigidly. "Ranger Lynley."

"What are you doing here, Ward?" Madison eyed him suspiciously aiming the pistol at him.

"I was told I was needed," he said simply. "What are you doing here? And why are you pointing your gun at me?"

"We received a report of an injured woman below the Raven Rocks Overlook," she told him. "Then I run into you… In light of the recent murders on the parkway, maybe I have good reason for holding you at gunpoint." Peering at the maintenance ranger, Madison wondered if she was looking at the Blue Ridge Parkway Killer. And Jessica Sneed's killer?

"Hey, I'm just as confused as you are," Ward insisted. "And I swear to you, I didn't hurt anyone. I certainly had nothing to do with the parkway deaths of those women." He took a step toward her.

"Don't come any closer!" Madison aimed the gun at Ward's chest as he stopped. "Put your hands up where I can see them, Ward. I mean it."

He complied, while saying tonelessly, "You're making a mistake. I'm innocent."

"We'll see about that." She took a couple of steps backward to put a little more distance between them and, while keeping the gun on him with one hand, removed her radio with the other to report the mysterious situation and that she was holding Ward Wilcox as a possible suspect in one or more crimes. She knew that erring on the side of caution was her smartest bet. No sooner had she gotten off the radio with help on the way that Madison heard what sounded like heavy shoes hitting the dirt behind her.

Before she could turn, Ward shrieked, "What the hell do you think you're doing?"

Suddenly, Madison felt a fist slam into the side of her head. Blurry-eyed, she caught sight of a familiar man and thought he said something wicked to her before she went down like a rock and everything went dark.

WHEN GARRETT HEARD back from Caitlin, she said coolly, "Agent Sneed, I've finished an age-progression digital sketch of Bryan Deschanel and what he might look like today, taking into consideration some standard characteristics that typically accompany aging into one's fifties and sixties."

"Let's see what you've got," Garrett responded eagerly on the speakerphone while in his car and heading toward the Blue Ridge Parkway, where he had been trying to reach Madison, to no avail.

"I'm sending it to your cell phone right now," Caitlin told him. "Keep in mind that I did this on short notice and not from an old actual photograph. But it should give you some perspective on your person of interest."

Garrett pulled over, grabbed the phone and gazed at the age-progression composite drawing of Bryan Deschanel, causing his heart to skip a beat in shock. It was a dead ringer for someone he had met before. Ronnie Mantegna, an NPS maintenance worker. And someone who had easy access in and out of the Blue Ridge Parkway without drawing undue suspicion, while being familiar with the landscape accordingly.

"What do you think?" Caitlin asked anxiously.

"I think you did a great job," Garrett told her. "Thanks for the quick work."

"Anytime." She paused. "If you need me to further enhance the sketch for greater clarity, let me know."

"I will." He disconnected and tried to contact Madison again. Still no pickup, concerning him. Getting back on the road, he called her boss, Tom. When he answered, Garrett said, "I can't seem to reach Madison."

"She went out on a call after a woman was reported injured," he said.

"What woman?"

"We're still trying to sort it out."

Garrett tensed. "What can you tell me about Maintenance Ranger Ronnie Mantegna?"

"He's been working for us for the last six months," Tom replied. "Let me take a quick look at his file... He's fifty-six, never married, has wilderness experience and been good at his job. Why do you ask?"

"I think that Ronnie Mantegna is an alias for Bryan Deschanel," Garrett said without prelude. "The man I believe to be responsible for my mother's murder thirty years ago and the Blue Ridge Parkway killings today."

Tom grunted and said, "Tell me more..."

Garrett gave a rundown of his solid case against Mantegna and sent Tom the age-progression digital image. "He's been right before our eyes the entire time I've been back here," Garrett stated knowingly. "And may be the one targeting another woman on the parkway now."

Tom mouthed an expletive. "We need to warn Ranger Lynley." He sighed exasperatedly. "Except I haven't been able to reach her either."

"Where did she go to respond to the injured female?"

"Raven Rocks Overlook." Tom made a sound, as if to himself. "According to the GPS tracker on her vehicle, that's where Madison still is, at Milepost 289.5."

"I'm almost there," Garrett told him, ending the conversation as he put on some speed, hoping to reach the destination in time.

Bryan Deschanel must have lured Madison to Raven Rocks Overlook, he figured, where Deschanel had stabbed to death his mother so long ago. Now in some sort of warped homicidal impulse, under the cover of his moniker Ronnie Mantegna or not, Deschanel planned to let history repeat itself by taking Madison's life in the same manner, Garrett couldn't help but sense.

I have to stop that bastard from killing the true love of my life—destroying any chance at a long-term future together. The thought that Mantegna could succeed in taking away another person so near and dear to him, decades apart, was unbearable to Garrett. He reached Milepost 289.5 and raced to the Raven Rocks Overlook.

MADISON OPENED HER eyes to a splitting headache, feeling as though she had been someone's punching bag. It took a long moment of trying to regain her equilibrium before she remembered what had happened. She'd been facing Ward Wilcox, believing he might have harmed a woman near the Raven Rocks Overlook and done even worse things, when someone had clocked Madison from behind. Her first thought was that maybe Ward had been partnered in crime with another person. But then she recalled right before being sucker punched that Ward had seemed just as unprepared for the moment and to be trying to warn her of impending danger. Before it had been too late.

"I see you're awake," she heard the familiar voice.

Realizing she was on the ground in a wooded area, Madison ignored the pounding in her head and turned her face slightly to the right. Hovering above her was Ronnie Mantegna, a maintenance ranger.

"Ronnie…" she managed as the wheels began to churn in the perilous moment she faced. Especially while taking note of the long-bladed serrated knife he was holding.

"Actually, my real name's Bryan Deschanel," he said smugly. "I'm guessing you've already come to the realization that I'm the one who knocked you out."

Madison knew she needed to play dumb while trying to figure out how she could still get out of this alive. "Why did you hit me?" she asked innocently. "And where's Ward?"

"You're entitled to know those answers. First question. I hit you because I needed to relieve you of your firearm without the risk of getting shot in the process. Plus, it was easier for my other plans for you." Deschanel glanced at the gun stuck inside his pants at the waist. "I'm the one you and Special Agent Sneed have been looking for."

"The Blue Ridge Parkway Killer?" Her mouth hung open as though in total shock. In reality, the pieces of the puzzle had already begun to fall into place the moment she'd gotten a grip on the circumstances she'd found herself in.

"You got it!" His eyes lit with triumph. "I killed them, and you're next, Ranger Lynley. For the record, though, I've been at this for a long time. My first kill was my own mother. She pissed me off one too many times, and I'd had enough. Made it so the fire seemed like an accident due to faulty electrical wiring, which I knew a thing or two about. Got what she deserved." He laughed, thoughtful. "Next was Agent Sneed's mother, believe it or not, who was hiking in this very spot before we ran into each other, catching her completely by surprise, and I did what I needed to do."

Madison's head had cleared enough that she was able to sit up without feeling dizzy. But he was still brandishing the knife and had her gun. Again, she sought to be genuinely taken aback by his revelation. "You really killed Jessica Sneed?"

"Is it that hard to believe?" He laughed. "I'm only halfway into my fifties. Meaning I was just in my midtwenties back then. Same was true the following year, when I stabbed to death another unsuspecting woman on the parkway. Got away with it too, thanks partly to some other idiot volunteering to take the fall before he tried to backpedal. But it was too late."

So, he admits to killing his mother, Jessica and a third female from three decades ago and earlier, Madison told herself. But why the long pause between then and now? "If you got away with it, why would you risk everything by starting to kill women again?"

"Yeah, about that… It's something inside me that I can't seem to control," he argued, rubbing his jawline. "Well, in trying to fit in as a law-abiding citizen, guess I was able to control my dark impulses for a while through drugs, therapy and whatnot." Deschanel pursed his lips. "But I grew tired of playing Mr. Nice Guy and ditched the drugs and therapy. I was happy to be myself again."

So that explains the long gap between serial killings, Madison thought. Too bad his inner demons had taken over again. It did little, though, to get her out of a predicament that placed her entire future in jeopardy. One she hoped to have with Garrett. Or had that page been turned forever?

"Anyway, I lured you here by falsely reporting that a woman was in distress," the killer explained calmly. "I was counting on them sending you in particular, as this is your neck of the woods, so to speak, to patrol."

Madison sought to buy more time as she studied the woods for escape routes. "Just let me go, Ronnie or Bryan," she said. "I'll give you a head start, and you can go anywhere you'd like."

"Yeah, right." His head snapped back as he chortled. "Since you've been cozying up with Agent Sneed, something tells me you wouldn't hesitate to blab to him about what I did to his mother the moment I allowed you to live. Sorry, no can do."

"You never said what happened to Ward Wilcox," Madison questioned. She scanned the area for any signs of him but saw none. "Did you kill him too?"

"Actually, Ranger Lynley, you did," Deschanel responded with a wry chuckle. He glanced at her pistol. "After roping him into showing up here to remove debris, I forced Ward to run into the woods, then fatally shot him with your gun. That was what you managed to do just before he cut you up with his knife that I intend to place in his hands once I'm through stabbing you to death. Then I'm outta here to look for a new place to settle down and cause trouble, while getting away scot-free with the parkway murders—again."

Madison scrambled to her feet, realizing that the serial slayer had her at a disadvantage. She considered going for the gun. Perhaps the element of surprise would cause him to let down his guard long enough to take it and shoot him before he could react. But with him holding the sharp knife firmly and having shown prowess as an attacker, she wasn't comfortable with those odds.

Deschanel bristled while moving toward her. "Sorry it's come to this, but it is what it is."

Or not, Madison thought. Her first instinct was to run. Though he was obviously in good enough shape to kill and evade detection and capture, she was sure she could out-run him as a jogger. But what if she were wrong? What if he proved to be just as quick on his feet, if not quicker, and caught her from behind? Wasn't that what had likely oc-curred with some of his other victims who'd had the same miscalculation?

Madison had never had any formal martial arts train-ing. But she had learned some hand-to-hand combat and defensive tactics during basic training. Moreover, her law enforcement family members had taught her a thing or two about survival skills. If she didn't make use of them now, when would she ever?

"Since you're going to kill me anyway," Madison said to the Blue Ridge Parkway Killer as he got closer, "can you at least find a way to pass along to my family that I loved them with all my heart?"

Deschanel seemed taken aback by the odd request but replied, "Yeah, sure, I'll do that for you, Ranger Lynley."

In the split second of time she was afforded, Madison noted that he had lowered the knife just enough to give her a window of opportunity to strike him before he could cut her. Balling her fist, she drew her arm back as far as she could before thrusting it forward with all her might. The fist landed squarely in the middle of his nose. The sound of bone cracking was quickly drowned out by the howl of pain that erupted from his mouth like an injured wolf.

During this distraction from his deadly intentions, Madison tried to grab her pistol from Deschanel's waist. But he was somehow able to recover enough to slice the knife across her wrist and throw her hard to the ground in one swift motion.

"You'll pay for breaking my nose," he spat, wiping away blood streaming down his face and neck. "You're going to die a horrific death, Ranger!"

Madison bit back the discomfort from her cut wrist and sucked in a deep breath as she wondered if his frightening forecast of her impending death was about to come true as he raised the knife threateningly with every intention of adding her to his three-decades-long list of victims.

Chapter Nineteen

When he'd spotted Madison's Tahoe in the parking lot of the Raven Rocks Overlook, alongside a Land Rover, Garrett didn't wait for the results of the run on the license plate of the Land Rover. By the time he had reached the area beneath the overlook and gathered with rangers and sheriff's deputies, Garrett had verified over his cell phone that the vehicle was registered to Ronnie Mantegna, the alias for serial killer Bryan Deschanel. It was clear to Garrett that Deschanel was intent on repeating history, dating back three decades, with Madison to be his latest victim.

I can't let that happen, Garrett had told himself with determination, as he removed the service pistol from his shoulder holster. He'd ordered everyone to spread out in search of Madison and the murder suspect in the woods. When Maintenance Ranger Ward Wilcox was found barely conscious but alive, having been shot in the chest, he fingered Ronnie Mantegna as his shooter and confirmed that he had taken Madison.

At least she was still alive, Garrett felt, as he'd zeroed in on the area he suspected Deschanel planned to make his move. It was the spot where the murderer had taken the life of Garrett's mother so many years ago. When rangers and law enforcement converged on the wooded location, Garrett gulped as he saw Deschanel holding a knife to Madison.

Just as it seemed like the perp would stab her before they could stop him, Madison delivered a head-snapping fist to Deschanel's nose. She attempted to reach for her gun that he had taken, but Deschanel appeared to slice her wrist and throw Madison down to the ground. As Garrett approached the culprit, who was holding the serrated knife in an offensive posture, he literally shot the weapon right out of Deschanel's hand, taking away a finger at the same time.

When Deschanel went for Madison's gun, Garrett tackled him, and the firearm fell harmlessly to the ground. Atop the criminal, he slugged him once in the jaw and another hard shot to his bloodied nose, causing the man to whine like a baby.

"You're under arrest, Bryan Deschanel," Garrett voiced sternly, "for the murder of Jessica Sneed, the attempted murder of Law Enforcement Ranger Madison Lynley, and a number of other crimes you'll have to answer to."

Resisting the strong urge to pummel his mother's murderer as payback, Garrett instead remembered that he was an NPS ISB special agent, bound by the law above all else, and climbed off. He turned him over to the Buncombe County Sheriff for processing, and Deschanel was promptly placed under arrest.

Garrett immediately raced to Madison, who was on her feet, her wrist bleeding. "Paramedics are on their way," he told her, having taken preemptive steps in requesting medical assistance during the drive to the parkway, in case needed.

"It's not that bad, really," she insisted.

"Bad enough to need stitches."

She grinned and glanced at Deschanel as he was being escorted away. "You should see the other guy."

"I already did." Garrett laughed. "Glad you were able to soften him up a bit for me to finish the job."

She chuckled, masking her discomfort. "Hey, that's what teamwork is all about, right?"

"Right." He hugged her, careful not to press against her wrist, while feeling grateful that she hadn't been killed. "Other than the cut, did he hurt you?"

Madison touched the side of her head. "Come to think of it, Ronnie Mantegna—er, Bryan Deschanel—did knock me unconscious when I wasn't looking to bring me to this spot."

Garrett shuddered. "All the more reason to get you to the hospital to be checked out."

"I suppose."

He was handed a piece of cloth by a park ranger to tie around her wrist to stop the bleeding. "That should do the trick," he said, knowing it couldn't take the place of stitches. Or painkillers.

"Thanks." She looked at Garrett sadly. "Deschanel confessed to killing your mother in this area."

Garrett's brow creased, feeling maudlin. "I guessed that was why he brought you here. Some sick kind of history repeating itself."

"Speaking of which, Deschanel also confessed to killing his own mother and getting away with it," Madison told him as they headed out of the woods, "along with stabbing to death Vicki Flanagan the following year, near the Yadkin

Valley Overlook. He was practically giddy at the idea that Blake O'Donnell had taken the rap for the murder."

"Not surprised by any of that," Garrett muttered, having already come to the conclusion that Deschanel had been responsible for both murders. "His depravity apparently knows no bounds."

"I agree." Madison made a face. "He also took full credit as the Blue Ridge Parkway Killer. Plus one, with the murder of Ward Wilcox." Her mouth twisted mournfully.

"We can subtract one." Garrett watched her carefully for any signs of a concussion from the blow to Madison's head. Or loss of blood. "Wilcox is still alive. He was shot in the chest but is expected to pull through."

"Thank goodness." She sighed. "Ward was an innocent pawn in Deschanel's scheming and tried to warn me, but it was too late."

"Actually, Wilcox was right on time," Garrett told her. "Before losing consciousness, he confirmed that you were still alive when he last saw you and that you were with Deschanel."

She nodded appreciatively.

They reached the Raven Rocks Overlook just as the paramedics arrived. "You were right to believe that one unsub was responsible for serial murders over three decades," Madison pointed out.

"Yeah, bittersweet." Garrett frowned. He took no great joy in making the right call of solving a cold and current case at once. It still wouldn't bring back his mother. Or the other four women to die by Bryan Deschanel's hand, for that matter. But it would allow all the surviving family and friends of the victims some closure. Himself included.

Right now, he was just happy to know that Madison had lived to see another day. Hopefully many days. Days they could spend together. But first was for Madison to be given a clean bill of health as she got in the ambulance after her ordeal with a ruthless serial killer.

THAT EVENING, Madison was at her mountain chalet resting, her wrist sewn and wrapped, headache barely noticeable, and relieved that she was alive and the nightmare over. Once he recovered from a broken nose, jaw and one less finger, serial killer Bryan Deschanel would be headed to jail. But as much as she wanted to focus on the satisfaction of knowing that the death of Jessica Sneed had at long last been solved and her son could put this cold case to rest on a personal and professional level, Madison's current thoughts centered on what their own future held. Garrett, as attentive as he had been all day, catering to her every need to make sure she was comfortable, had been strangely silent as to where his head was. Was he deliberately trying to drive her mad? Make her question that she was reading what they had correctly? Or was he still indecisive as to what he wanted and with whom? Only to decide that it might be time to put in for another transfer, rather than deal with tender matters of the heart?

As they sat on her midcentury sofa watching television, Madison decided it was time to lay her cards—or heart—on the proverbial table. She grabbed the remote from the glass top of the coffee table, cut off the television, and turned to Garrett before asking, "So, did you mean it?"

He faced her. "Mean it?"

"That you loved me?" She held his gaze. "You said that when…"

"I know when I said it." Garrett flashed a thoughtful grin, pausing. "I meant it, every word."

Her heart fluttered. "You never followed up on those deep words of affection."

"That's because I was waiting for the right time to do so," he claimed.

She batted her lashes. "You mean when I had to pry it out of you?"

He chuckled. "Not exactly."

Madison was confused. "Care to explain?"

"Okay." Garrett turned his body to face hers. "After our last attempt at a relationship went south, I was determined to make sure that this time around we wouldn't find a way to pull away from each other. That included allowing the relationship to grow at its own pace. Without the pressures that came with premature declarations of love. The last thing I wanted was to scare you off."

"That would never have happened," she insisted.

"Never say never," he stated wisely. "Except when it comes to knowing that I don't want to spend the rest of my life with anyone but you, Madison."

Her eyes lit. "You mean that?"

"With all my heart." He took her uninjured hand, which happened to be the one with the wedding-ring finger. "The truth is it scared the hell of out me when I thought for even an instant that Bryan Deschanel might have taken you away from me. I knew then that I never wanted to let you get away again. This evening was about giving you some time to heal and reflect, without having you believe that my asking for your hand in marriage was borne out of some sense of duty because of what Deschanel nearly got away with. Or as a doing right by my mother homage of some sort as the type of woman I imagine she would have loved for me to marry and be a mother-in-law to. While that last part is true, I want you as my bride strictly because I'm madly in love with you and want us to make the most of the years ahead, as husband and wife." He sucked in a calming breath. "So, with all that being said, Madison Lynley, will you marry me and make this special agent the happiest man on this planet?"

"Hmm…" She hesitated. "And where would we live as a married couple?"

"Wherever you'd like," he answered smoothly. "The great thing about working for the National Park Service and having the experience to back it up, with over four hundred individual national park units spread across the country and US territories, we can pretty much live anywhere we choose to."

"Good point," she had to admit.

"As for a ring, it's been on the back of my mind, but I hadn't really homed in on it," Garrett said and leaned his face to one side. "Been a bit preoccupied of late, you know?"

Madison laughed. "Excuses, excuses."

He gave her a serious look. "So, is that a yes?"

She pretended to think about it for a moment or two, then answered unequivocally, "Of course it's a yes! Yes, I'll marry you, Garrett Sneed."

He beamed. "Yeah?"

"Yes, with pleasure." She flashed her teeth. "Oh, and just for the record, I would have gladly married you wherever we lived and even without a ring, if that's what it took to get you down the aisle." Madison regarded him in earnest.

"I love you, Garrett, and want to get to know more about your culture, and you can learn whatever you don't already know about my family."

"We'll have a lifetime to accomplish that and much more, Madison," he promised. "Why don't we seal the deal with a kiss?"

"Say no more," she answered him, lifting her chin up and moving toward his lips for a long, deal-sealing kiss to warm the heart and soul.

Epilogue

A week later, Garrett happily placed a three-stone 18-karat rose-gold engagement ring on Madison's finger, thrilled to see her light up with this reflection of his love and commitment to her. He looked forward to a repeat performance when it was time to place the wedding band on her finger next year.

The following spring, they went jogging on the Boone Fork Trail off the Blue Ridge Parkway on a warm day. The five-and-a-half-mile loop trek was a habit Garrett had gotten used to during their off time from their National Park Service duties, after deciding to make their home together in the Blue Ridge Mountains. They meandered their way through the woods, abundant with rhododendrons and lush meadows, and spied Carolina ducks swimming in Boone Fork Creek.

"Bryan Deschanel was transferred to Central Prison," Garrett mentioned of the close-custody male prison in Raleigh.

Madison looked at him. "Really?"

"Yeah. Guess he got into some kind of skirmish at Piedmont Correctional Institution and was moved elsewhere from Salisbury for his own safety."

"Hmm…" She drew a breath. "As long as they keep him locked up for good."

"You can be sure of that," Garrett told her. He thought about the evidence that had helped bring Bryan Deschanel down. In retesting the survival knife that had killed Jessica Sneed, a forensic unknown DNA profile had been discovered that had proved to be a match for Bryan Deschanel's DNA. He'd been linked as well to the murders of Olivia Forlani and Nicole Wallenberg through his right-hand palm print that had matched the latent palm print from the survival knife used to stab to death the women. Lastly, DNA from murder victim Heidi Ushijima had been found on the same serrated knife that Deschanel had used to cut Madison, tying him to at least four murders and one attempted murder. He'd separately tried to kill Ward Wilcox with Madison's Sig Sauer pistol.

With the solid case against him, Deschanel had pled guilty to avoid the death penalty and had been given a life sentence without the possibility of parole. The $50,000 reward that had led to the serial killer's arrest and conviction had been awarded to Neil Novak. He and his daughter, Dominique, had been true to their word in donating the entire sum to female victims of violent crime groups.

Madison grabbed Garrett's hand and brought them to a stop. "Your mother would be proud of you."

"You're probably right." He was thoughtful, wishing she had been around to see him now. "That would have to begin with being smart enough to fall in love with the right person."

"Is that so?" She blushed, lashes fluttering wildly. "Just how smart are you?"

Garrett took her shoulders and said sweetly to Madison, "Sometimes, actions speak louder than words." With that, he gave her a searing kiss and knew their love was pure genius.

* * * * *

THE SUSPECT
NEXT DOOR

RACHEL ASTOR

Chapter One

Top 10 Worst Opening Lines for a Book

1. *It was a dark and stormy night...*
2. *Gazing into the mirror, I stared into my deep brown eyes...*
3. *In the end, it was all a dream.*
4. *My eyes refused to open as I flung my alarm clock across the room.*
5. *The phone rang.*
6. *The date was March 12, 1988...*
7. *I couldn't believe how big my butt had gotten.*
8. *Kaboom!*
9. *Storm clouds roiled above menacingly...* (aka an even worse riff on *dark and stormy night*)
10. *Once upon a time...*

I was fantastically screwed.

I'd legitimately typed—and subsequently deleted—each one of the awful lines onto the screen that kept staring at me, annoyingly blank. My muse had apparently gone for a smoke break.

Eight hours ago.

I sighed. I knew exactly *who* I wanted to write about—Amelia Jones, inspired by amalgamations of real-life kick-ass women, like Amelia Earhart, and famous fictional kick-ass women like Jessica Jones. In short, she was going to be very, well…kick-ass. She would be a fighter (and not in the "oh she's so strong emotionally" way, but more the "I'll take down a burly heathen whilst in evening wear and emerge unscathed save for a charming, dewy glow" way), be so clever she could take down any vainglorious *Princess Bride* weirdo in a battle of wits, and be gorgeous to boot, but in an accessible way, of course—no supermodel dimensions here.

Except… I couldn't think of anything for her to do. Like not a damned thing. Which was weird, because I used to be able to write and write and write about nothing in particular and then sometimes—when those elusive literary deities poured their sparkle juice into my keyboard—it turned into something great.

Or at least pretty good.

At the moment, anything other than incredible suckitude would be great. I ran my hands along my hair and held it up in a sort of mock ponytail, watching the cursor blink.

You. BLINK. Are. BLINK. A failure. BLINK.

How condescending.

Before I launched my laptop off the balcony and admired its beautiful spiral of doom—the sun glittering beatifically off its silvery edges before sailing to its final, magnificent shattering—there were a few things I needed to try.

I jumped up and went to my dresser, pulling out my favorite costume jewelry—a dazzling bracelet and a few massive ornate rings—topping them off with my pink feather boa. Maybe if I looked the part of a glamorous author, the words would start to flow.

I sat back at my desk, spitting out a stray feather and scratching the tickle from my nose. Man, those feathers really got everywhere. I set my fingers gently on the keyboard and started to…

…do absolutely nothing.

Damn.

Why? I wailed in my head. I used to believe writer's block didn't exist. That it was just some pathetic excuse for someone who was too lazy to sit down and do the work.

What a prime ass past me was.

I mean, sure there was a little more pressure to come up with something good now that I'd written a book that was published and actually sold well, but that was silly. That should mean I was even more confident about the magic I could weave with words, right?

Um. Apparently not.

I spit out another feather, fished an additional plume from my cleavage and shook my head. This was ridiculous.

Tossing the boa aside, I packed up my laptop and grabbed my coat. Perhaps a change of scenery would do it, and I could really use a cinnamon caramel latte while I was at it. Nothing soothed the writerly soul like the decadent scents of a coffee shop.

I stepped into Cuppa Joe on the ground floor of my apartment building, and instantly felt at home. I'd spent hours there writing my last book, and that had gotten me almost to the top of the *New York Times* bestseller list. My stomach did a little flip just thinking about it. Cuppa Joe was the reason I'd moved in once I'd been able to afford an apartment in the building.

I smiled as I took in the spicy sweet scents, the low murmur of voices, the clicking of spoons on dishes. Yes, this was the ticket. Surely the words would flow once I got my coffee and found a nice quiet corner and…*damn*. The place was packed.

Since when were there so many people who could just come to a coffee shop and write in the middle of the day? Didn't people have jobs anymore? Not that I had one, really. Well, not anything structured, like in an office or anything. Although if I didn't get some words going soon, I might have to find one. Which, from what I could recall, was decidedly not a lifestyle I would prefer to go back to. No shade to those who love being cooped up in a cubicle/ practice coffin begging for time off to go to the gyno or whatever, but those were not the things that brought me a whole lot of passion, personally.

Unfortunately, writing really hadn't brought much in the last while either.

Still, I knew this was my life's calling, so I needed to find a way to emblazon some words onto that screen.

Sitting at a table in the middle of the room, I felt like I was in some kind of performance piece, even if it was exceptionally mundane. I preferred to stick along the edges so no one could look over my shoulder. It wasn't like I was writing some super confidential plot twist (as if I had any semblance of a plot twist), but sometimes, when writing some of the more…romantic scenes, things could get a little steamy. And someone sneaking a peek out of context might wonder—or, you know, faint dead away or something. I put my coffee down and set up my workspace—laptop open, notebook handy to my right and phone to my left. Perfect.

Then obviously I had to check social media—just for a second—to see if anyone replied to that comment I made this morning. And while I was at it, I may as well play a game or two of Candy Crush, just to get nice and relaxed and in the mood for typing.

Finally, I set my phone down and really got ready, leaning back in my seat.

All the other people were typing away. Some of them incredibly fast, almost frantic—like they were so filled with ideas, they couldn't get them down fast enough. One girl in the corner, who was gorgeous and had the shiniest black hair I'd ever seen, had the biggest, beaming smile plastered on her face over whatever it was she was typing so passionately about. I briefly wondered what would happen if I got up, calmly wandered over and slapped her right across the face. Which of course I would never do, but it was tempting to think about getting rid of that radiant smile.

I tried to remember a time when something I wrote gave me that much excitement. There must have been a moment at some point, but I couldn't readily recall it. I mean, maybe she was just messaging with some guy or something, which led to thoughts about how I decidedly had no guy of my own to message, but I quickly banished that from my mind.

I could not go down that rabbit hole again.

Even the man in the corner, who was very serious about whatever it was he was working on with his stern look and harsh glasses, typed faster than, frankly, I'd ever seen a guy his age type.

I glanced around. These people were all so…productive.

I closed my eyes for a second.

Okay, time to stop worrying about what everyone else was doing and get to it. I stretched my neck to either side then readied myself at the keyboard once more. Here we go. Just write something.

Anything.

I blinked. The cursor blinked. I took a sip of coffee. The cursor blinked some more.

My phone dinged. *Thank god.*

How's the writing going?

Victoria. Who should know better than to bother me when I was working. Of course, she probably knew as well as I did that there was not a lot of actual work going on. She'd been an up-close-and personal witness to my writer's block for months.

It was so bad the writer's block had taken on its own persona. I called her Mabel.

Funny, I wrote back.

Well, kid. I don't know what to tell you. You've got to get out of this slump.

Tell me something I don't know.

Okay, one question. WWND?

???

What would Nancy do?

I smiled. Vic was well aware of my juvenile obsession with girl-detective books.

She'd go find a mystery for inspiration, of course, I typed.

Then you know what you have to do.

I set down my phone. Could she be right? I mean, maybe it *was* the whole "trying to think up a mystery out of thin air" that was holding me back. Surely other writers must look for inspiration in real life, right?

There was only one problem. How did one go about finding a mystery in the middle of a random Tuesday?

An hour later, my coffee was gone and my screen was as blank as ever. The raven-haired girl had left, leaving a sense of despair in her wake. Not her own, of course. She looked perfectly fine when she left. Happy even.

The despair was all mine.

I packed up my laptop and headed out to the street— there was no direct access from inside the building to the coffee shop, which I thought was a massive oversight until the barista, Frank, had explained that it was for the safety of the residents. "You wouldn't want people off the street to be able to access the building through one of the businesses, would you?" Fair point, Frank. Fair point.

Other than Frank, I hadn't made much headway getting to know many of the people in my building. Except Annie.

Annie was quickly becoming my favorite human. I'd basically already decided I wanted to be her when I grew up. And the *gossip*, my god, but somehow it was the complete opposite of snark and more just a way to talk about her favorite people, which was to say, everyone in the building. She talked shamelessly about all of us, and yet, we loved her. There had to be a name for that. Affectionmonger? Praisecaster?

In any case, Annie was my insider. For instance, the couple in Apartment 406 was a teacher and an office manager, which at first sounds like a perfectly tame combination. Until you find out the office manager, Samantha, was in charge of the nation's largest chain of adult toy stores. I had to admit, I was pretty glad I didn't have the apartment underneath those two.

And then there was Mrs. Appleton in Apartment 105. Until I'd moved in, I'd never even heard of a woman who'd had eight husbands. How does one even go about finding men that fast? I hadn't even had a date since Johnny and I broke up four months ago.

Anyway, Annie really was adorable, and that day was no exception as I unlocked the front door to the building and saw that she was, as she tended to be, sitting in one of the comfy lounge chairs in the lobby. Her outfit was pretty surprising though. Normally the woman looked like a unicorn had exploded on her, all rainbows and sparkles, but today she was pretty tame in a black sheath dress and black ankle boots. If it weren't for the leggings featuring cartoon characters and the electric blue wig, I would have thought something terrible had happened.

"Petra!" Annie squealed. "My gorgeous! How can you even be so spectacular with all that hair?"

I smiled, trying my best not to make a face. In the words of my favorite Nancy, compliments were not my chum.

"And this figure… You are to die for, honey. Those curves!" she said, fanning herself.

Frankly, I didn't love when people mentioned my curves. They were somewhat new—hello, slowing metabolism—and I hadn't quite gotten used to them yet. Seriously, I'd bought six different bras and they all fit just slightly wrong, though each in dissimilar, and increasingly mystifying, ways.

"Thanks, Annie," I said. "Your wig is stellar."

"Aw, thanks," she said, primping it a little. "I wasn't really feeling any of my outfits this morning, but the wig put me right in the spirit."

I wasn't sure what spirit she was talking about—maybe the spirit of RuPaul or something—but she always put me in a better mood instantly. Annie had a way of making everyone feel just a little bit better about their day.

"Come sit with me. Tell me everything."

So of course, I sat, though I wasn't really sure what she wanted me to tell her. There hadn't been a whole lot of "everything" since we'd danced this routine yesterday.

"I don't know what to tell you, Annie. There just isn't a whole lot going on these days."

Annie tilted her head, a sort of nondescript look on her face. It wasn't quite pity or disappointment or a "things'll get better" look, but it was maybe a combination of the three. In any case, it made me feel like I had to elaborate.

"Maybe I need to take a class or something."

Annie chuckled. "You certainly like your classes, don't you, kitten?"

I smiled. "What? It's been like, two weeks since Tae Kwon Do for Beginners ended."

"And before that it was?"

"La Dolce Vita: An Exploration of Italian Pastries."

"And before that?"

"An Introduction to American Sign Language."

"Uh-huh. Exactly how many classes have you taken this year?"

I shrugged. "I'm not sure. Maybe…six?"

"Petra," she said, taking my hands. "It's only April. That's more than one a month."

"Well, some of them overlapped. ASL can't be learned overnight, you know," I explained, not sure why I felt like I had to. Because seriously, I loved taking classes. What's not to love? Learn new things. Meet new people. Sometimes there was exercise…that intermediate pole dancing class was no joke, let me tell you.

"Is any of it helping with your writing?"

Did I mention Annie had a way of squeezing information out of people? We'd already extensively covered the subject of Mabel the writer's block, ages ago.

I shrugged. "I don't know. Learning new things has to be helpful, right? And I've been meeting a lot of people, so that's good for creating characterization."

"And how much have you written because of it?"

"Um, not…much?"

"Well, if you ask me, all these classes of yours are great, as long as they're not a distraction from your real work, and I hate to be the bearer of bad news, but I feel like they might be."

She was right, of course, and I was about to tell her so, except another distraction entered the lobby at that precise moment. And heavens to Nancy, what a distraction it was.

Ryan.

He was quite possibly the most gorgeous man I had ever laid eyes on. Tall, with a smirk that said he understood things about the world. Things you were sure would come in handy in every aspect of life, including the bedroom.

Annie jumped up at the sight of him. "Ryan, honey. Have you met Petra yet?"

Which kind of made me want to duck behind the chair since I hadn't gotten particularly dressed up to, you know, go down to the coffee shop.

He came over, looking like he wanted nothing more than to escape, but Annie was not the kind of person that was easy to escape from.

"Oh yeah, hey. I've seen you around the building," he said. "I'm Ryan."

I stood and he shook my hand.

I hadn't mustered the ability to do anything but blink quite yet, but Annie was kind enough to give me a little kick in the ankle.

"Uh, hi. Petra Jackson," was the best I could cobble together.

"Nice to meet you," he said, and smirked an even more adorable smirk than before. And yeah, a smirk is not always a good thing, but on Ryan it was like he was in on some sort of secret or something. And it was utterly captivating.

As was the view as he walked toward the elevators.

After the doors had safely closed and he was out of earshot, Annie perked right up. Which was to say she went from a level three on the perkiness scale—Charmingly Bubbly—to a level eight: Enthusiastically Vivacious. "So, I see you have a little spark of interest in our floor-mate."

My stomach squeezed. "He lives on our floor?" I asked, my gaze whipping from the elevator doors to her.

"2202. Right across the hall from you, my dear. I'm surprised you haven't seen him coming or going yet."

"Huh," I said, pretending like it was the most normal thing in the world that the most magical representation of the male species I'd ever seen in real life lived right across the hall from me.

I frantically thought back through all the noises I'd ever made since I'd moved in. Had I ever farted in the hallway? Thankfully, nothing came to mind. There certainly hadn't been any raucous sex noises or anything.

It took everything in me not to beg Annie to spill every morsel she knew about the guy, but even I knew that would arouse at least as much pity as the time I got that perm in fifth grade.

Then again…maybe this was exactly what I'd been looking for—*The Mystery of the Handsome Neighbor*, I mused silently, as I fought the urge to raise an inquisitive eyebrow as one might do in a good sleuthing novel.

Chapter Two

"Why don't you just go over there and knock on his door?" Brandt asked.

Ah, Brandt, what a wacky baboon. Somehow Brandt and Vic and I had become an inseparable crew when we were roommates in our early twenties, even though none of us really had much in common anymore. Still, I couldn't really imagine my days without them. Or their arguing.

Victoria looked at him as if another arm had just sprouted out through his luscious hair.

"What is it with guys?" Vic said.

"What?" Brandt said, as if he hadn't just proposed the most absurd thing in the history of the world. "Guys like it when a hot chick comes on to them."

I gave him a face. "As sure as I am that it's the *fantasy* of guys that hot chicks come on to them, have you ever seen it work in real life?"

"All the time," he said, straightening up, ready to defend his stance.

"And it resulted in a relationship, not just some hookup?"

"Oh," he said, looking dejected. "I didn't know you meant a relationship."

Vic scoffed. "You idiot. First of all, when have you ever known Petra to just want a hookup? And second of all, I can promise you that most women don't ever just want that unless they are either trying to get over someone else or have a serious need for some male attention. Neither of which guys probably really want to get involved with."

Brandt shrugs. "If a guy's getting laid, he probably doesn't care."

"Sure," I said, "until she catches feelings and starts contacting him, then it's all a big disappearing act."

"What? No one ever promised a relationship."

"Of course not," Vic says, putting her hands on her hips. "Guys don't do relationships anymore. Or if they do, they get bored after a month and pretend they were never into it in the first place. Typical."

Poor Brandt was looking a bit like one of those nocturnal little monkey creatures with the huge eyes.

I sighed. Dating had become more complicated than my uncle Marv trying to explain to a room full of women why he didn't think sexism was a real thing.

I sighed. Maybe it was just that Vic and I had reached the age where we were looking for more than just fun. Although frankly, I couldn't really remember a time when I was only looking for a hookup. I couldn't help feeling like the whole culture of dating had changed, effectively making me feel like an old plastic zip bag, discarded hastily at the first sign of its tenant—the dreaded fuzzy cheese. Or maybe I was the cheese.

"These days guys just want to 'hang out,'" Vic said. "Whatever happened to dating? Like real dating?"

"You sure want a lot," Brandt said, seemingly bewildered. "I had no idea. I just thought all girls liked hooking up."

I stared daggers into his soul. Or at least I would have if he'd noticed I was even looking at him.

"Unfortunately, no matter how much I'd like to, we are not going to solve the world's dating problems by hashing it out among ourselves," Vic said.

Brandt was still staring into space like he was deep in thought. As deep in thought as a guy with his mouth hanging open could look, anyway. "But I mean, they always *say* they just want to hang out."

"Are you stupid?" Vic asked. "Would you ever start dating someone who was all like, 'I really, desperately just want a relationship'?"

"Probably not," he said.

"See, it is the guys' fault," Vic said. "There is literally no other choice but to pretend we all just want to hang out." She looked like she had just eaten a sardine lollipop.

"Can we change the subject for a second, please?" I asked, hoping they were finished their immature, though often morbidly delightful, squabbling.

There was never a dull moment with two best friends who pretty much hated each other. And even though it was somewhat entertaining, why did I always have to be the glue that held them together? Especially now, when my life was akin to a sad plate of nachos, which had all the components to be a glorious, synergistic taco except it really didn't have itself together.

Thankfully, Vic was desperate to change the subject. Less thankfully, she chose everyone's least favorite subject, Mabel. "So you didn't get any writing done today?"

I sighed. "No."

"I don't really get why you even care about writing another book," Brandt said, finally snapping out of his weird thinking trance.

It really did seem to take a lot of concentration for my poor associate to think certain things through. He was super sophisticated in some ways—into art and culture and friggin' loved the bloody opera, but he definitely took up residence in Clueless Town over other things. It was like I had my own little Renaissance Caveman™.

"You have plenty of money. I mean, look at this apartment. Most people would kill to have a place like this."

"Well sure, but the very fact that I bought this means that if I don't keep writing, I'll be in big trouble. Money doesn't last forever."

"Yeah, but didn't you make like, a bazillion dollars on your book?"

I gave him another look. "I made enough," I said, "but that doesn't discount the fact that my publisher bought a two-book deal and if I don't deliver on a second book, I could end up having to pay some back."

"Look, dumbass," Vic interrupted, turning to Brandt, "money isn't everything, you know. Writing is Petra's passion, her calling. Haven't you ever had something you just felt compelled to do?"

"Makeup artistry *is* my passion."

Vic snorted. "I still don't know why you would pick *that* as a profession. You're like six-four and two hundred and fifty pounds."

"Um, hello…models," he said as if it really should have been obvious.

But the comment did little to make his case. Vic just stood there staring at him like he had neatly made *her* point.

"Whatever," he finally said. "It's not like you have some great calling."

"What does that mean? I'm an architect. I design buildings for a living. My firm created this very building you are sitting in. I make a difference."

Brandt chuckled. "Um, your bosses create buildings."

"Well, someday I'll be the one getting the credit. But you should know, the junior architects do most of the actual designing."

"Whatever you say," Brandt said, putting his hands up in mock surrender then smirking.

"Guys, seriously, change the subject."

"Do you want to talk more about your writing?" Vic asked carefully, as if she already knew the answer.

"No," I replied, my tone conveying I was as serious as my fourth-grade teacher's obsession with spelling tests—and believe me, I am not exaggerating when I say Mrs. Potts had an alarming affection for the English language.

"Tell us more about this dude," Brandt said, shoveling chips into his mouth.

It wasn't that I didn't want to spend a little time on my new favorite subject, but the truth was I literally knew nothing about Ryan. "I wish I could, but I've got nothing for you. I've already told you what he looks like, and that's pretty much all I've got."

"Did you check online? Like Facebook and stuff?" Vic asked.

"I have nothing to check. All I have is the name Ryan. I

don't even know if it's his first or last name. Or like, if he just goes by Ryan, you know, like Cher."

Vic opened her mouth as if to add another idea, then closed it again.

"So… I think I'm going to head out," Brandt said, as if it was a perfectly normal time to announce he was leaving and not right in the middle of a conversation. "Duty calls." He smiled, reading a message on his phone. "Or should I say, booty calls?" He laughed hysterically at his own joke.

Somehow Vic and I didn't find it quite as funny.

"What? I don't care what you guys think—none of my girls are complaining," he said, grabbing his coat and heading out the door with a bit of a skip to his step.

"That guy," Vic said, watching him leave.

I smiled. "Even *you* gotta admit, there's something likable about him."

She shrugged. "I suppose there's a certain…fascination that he draws, though I can't decide if it's allure, or more like a science experiment gone wrong."

I rolled my eyes.

"And that makes him all the more dangerous. It's those charmers you have to watch out for."

AFTER VIC LEFT, I pondered whether I should pull out my laptop. But then I realized I'd rather force a white-hot needle softly into my ocular cavity, so instead, I very productively wandered around my apartment trying to think of something to do. I mean, there was stuff I could do. There were still unpacked boxes in the spare room, certainly some cleaning that could be done, maybe a quick workout (insert laughing-with-tears emoji). But none of those things seemed to give me much of a spark. In fact, it seemed I'd been entirely spark-less for a while.

As I wandered past my front door for the third time, debating whether I might find something interesting to do outside the confines of my apartment, I heard some shuffling noises out in the hall that sounded like they might be coming from the direction of Apartment 2202, aka Home of the God. I sucked in a breath and crept to the peephole.

Ryan was most certainly coming out of his apartment. But…what was he doing heading out so late? I mean, I suppose it wasn't that late. I had, after all, just been debating going out myself. Still, I was intrigued by what might be causing Ryan to head out at an *almost*-late hour. I daydreamed for a moment that maybe he was just bored like me and wanted to grab some food or something. Yes! Maybe I should just happen to be leaving at the same time and he might ask me to join him.

I rolled my eyes. The chance that he was just heading out to do nothing was a pretty big stretch. Most people had a little more going on in their lives than the write, delete, lather, repeat that I did.

As if by some force outside myself, I reached for my coat and slipped into shoes as I continued to stare out the peephole, dropping my keys gently into my pocket. I pulled on a ball cap and tucked my hair up underneath as I cracked the door, listening for the elevator. (And yes, I did ask myself if sneaking out into the night to follow my perfect-looking neighbor was a bit, you know…stalkery, but I reminded myself that I was totally doing it for a good cause. Just a little research— That. Was. All! Seriously, you're so judgy). When the elevator doors started closing, I felt like Nancy as I scrambled out of my apartment, knowing timing would be everything. I obviously couldn't go down in the same elevator as Ryan, but I couldn't be too far behind, or I'd never see which direction he was headed. I hit the button to call the second elevator, which, thankfully, didn't take too long to get there.

The ride down felt like it took half a year, stopping on the eighth floor to pick up another passenger, an older gentleman I'd seen around the building a bit. What was with all these people heading out so late at night? I couldn't really be too mad though, since he smiled and tipped his hat at me like some jaunty fellow straight out of the fifties, which was quite adorable.

The doors finally opened on the ground floor to an empty lobby.

I raced out of the building, frantically scanning the area. Then I spotted him. He was already half a block away, but he was on foot, which gave me a chance to follow. A while back I'd taken this class on surveillance—it was part of the So You Wanna Be a Spy course. Not for the purposes of pursuing it as a job or anything, but more to lend my stories an air of credibility, and this seemed like as good a time as any to see if the techniques were any good.

Ryan slipped around the corner at the end of the block and I half ran, half walked to try to catch up. I didn't want to get too close, but I had to keep him in sight, or all would be lost. (Okay, that was maybe a little dramatic, but my curiosity certainly wouldn't have been quenched. Um, I mean, my research wouldn't have been complete.).

I followed pretty well if I do say so myself. Kept right up, corner after corner, block after block until I didn't really know where I was anymore. Still, I didn't panic. I figured I was intelligent enough to find my way home from a strange neighborhood. Plus, you know, app maps were a thing. Technology really was a godsend to those suddenly finding themselves in a strange place in the middle of the night when they were…just out for a stroll.

When Ryan walked for long stretches going straight, I kept a safe distance. There was no way he'd see me as far back as I was. Then when he turned, I'd make my run for it to catch where he turned again. I kept this up for what felt like an hour, though with all the adrenaline and excitement rushing through me, a more precise estimate would have been anywhere from twenty minutes to the end of life as we know it.

I was trying to figure out why he didn't catch a bus or a cab or something, when…suddenly, he disappeared.

Seriously, just disappeared. Vanished right into the delicate veil of the atmosphere. Wait, was he magic? Had I been following this gorgeous creature through the city only to find I was actually researching the beginnings of a paranormal novel?! The idea got my heart beating faster (hello, genre-jumping!) until I realized that perhaps…just maybe, I had been doing a bit too much reading lately and was losing my grip on the fragile boundaries of reality.

I stood and listened for a minute, hoping I'd hear his footsteps or something, but the area was eerily silent. I'd been super perplexed about so many people going out so late at night just a little while ago, but now my thoughts were more in the vicinity of, where the hell was everybody?

I wandered for a few blocks, hoping luck might be on my side, but I had apparently pissed off the ethereal beings in charge of serendipitous events (or maybe that old grip on reality was just loosening again). I spotted a man a block away and rushed to catch up, but it turned out not to be Ryan.

I felt completely ridiculous. The whole thing had been so silly. What did I think I was going to find anyway? He was probably out meeting a woman, and honestly, that was not something I was particularly keen to uncover.

I headed to the nearest corner. I'd been so busy trying to follow that I hadn't read a street sign for blocks. But it was time to give up the charade. I needed to figure out where I was and get my phone to draw me a map home. Easy peasy. I mean, I was a little disappointed, but it's not like I'd had anything else to do, and besides, I'd gotten a walk in for good measure.

Although, I wasn't sure I'd want to take another walk quite like this anytime soon. I couldn't get over how quiet the streets were. It was late, sure, but this seemed a little ominous, and frankly, I wanted out. I spotted a quick shortcut down an alley that would get me to the corner and back to my bearings. I was tired and frustrated, and apparently thinking with the clarity of a shallow pond at the end of summer after the weeds had overtaken the water and it sported that thin film of smelly, floating slime.

I scurried down the alley, my mind lost in thoughts of Ryan, wondering what he was up to at that exact moment. To be fair, I was lost in those swirling thoughts while also digging in my bag for my phone—which didn't seem to want to make an appearance, buried way down at the bottom somewhere—but still, I probably should have noticed the obvious and rather dastardly-looking illegal activity I was waltzing directly into.

Under a single light above the back door of some store or warehouse or something, several men had gathered. Which, of course, I would have noticed if I had been aware of my surroundings even a little bit—but unfortunately my brain was off gallivanting somewhere between what Ryan might look like with his shirt off and what I might wear if I was ever nominated for a big literary award. My mind only whipped back to the present after a rather ominous-sounding click, which was followed by several more. This was the moment I finally glanced up and became aware of the various guns pointed toward the approximate vicinity of my head, and I couldn't help but wonder if I might have gotten a wee bit more involved in a mystery than I had originally planned.

Chapter Three

It's strange what goes through your head when several scary-looking dudes have guns pointed at your face. Like, for instance, how bright that light above the door seemed to suddenly be and how bold these guys must be for doing whatever they were doing right there in the middle of it.

Honestly, thoughts can be very unhelpful sometimes.

I quickly became aware of a few things. One, the boldness of the under-the-light transaction was a good indication that very few people were apt to show up in that particular spot. Two, I couldn't hear any street traffic, which meant the area was probably on the industrial side, thus lowering the likelihood of spectators even more. And three, the dude on the left had some intense wheezing going on, which, even though he had a gun pointed at me and a look on his face that said he could easily use me as a snack, I still had the urge to tell him to be quiet already. Didn't he realize everyone could hear him? I mean, not that he could probably help it, I supposed.

I also really needed to adjust my underwear, which chose that exact moment to ride into an uncomfortable position, but I decided it might be best to wait on that issue. Unfortunately, this only reminded me of which underwear I was currently wearing—the larger grannyish ones (don't judge, laundry day was a bit overdue). I tried not to think of how embarrassing it would be if these were the undies I'd be found dead in.

"Um, hi, fellas," I said, my voice sounding intensely loud, echoing off the building. "I was just out for a bit of a midnight walk and didn't realize I'd, um, run into anyone. I was just heading back to the, um, street." I pointed up the alley.

You know, in case they had no idea how streets worked or something.

Nobody moved. They all just kind of looked at each other, clearly not knowing what to do. Opposed to what you might think from the movies, people did not, apparently, stumble into secret bad-guy deals very often.

I decided I may as well try to take advantage of the lack of action. I just sort of started to walk away, continuing in the direction I was already going, hoping the street was closer this way, although I had a bad feeling I was about exactly halfway.

A sturdy-looking man stepped out in front of me. Unlike many of the others, he had a shotgun, which he held at hip level and seemed more comfortable with—if only a little—than the others.

"Hold on there, lady," he said. "I don't think you'll be going anywhere."

My head began to get itchy, but I did not make a move to scratch anything. I felt like Nancy D. must have surely been in situations like this a time or two in all those mysteries I'd read, but I was having one of my CRAFT moments (i.e., Can't Remember A Flipping Thing). No doubt Ned or

Bess or George had come to the rescue or something, and I suddenly felt like a supreme jackass for not letting anyone know where I was or what I was doing. Although I'm honestly not sure how that conversation might have gone. *So yeah, I'm just out following my sexy neighbor around shady parts of town. No worries. Just, I dunno, see if you can come find me if I don't make it back in a couple hours. Whatevs.*

Unfortunately, I got the distinct impression I might not have a couple hours. And honest to god, how could the rest of these guys just stand there and listen to that wheezing?

I widened my stance ever so slightly, hoping that none of the guys would notice I was even moving. Then I slowly... very slowly...started to shift my weight, bending my legs slightly to ready my stance. My fingers began to curl.

And then BAM!

Two of them went down beside me. Straight to the ground, so fast I had absolutely no idea how in the hell they'd gotten there. But I decided it might be better to process the hows later, so I sprang into action, kicking the shotgun away from my torso and punching the sturdy guy in the face. He was startled but was far from going down. Thankfully, I'd expected that and was already on my way toward the arm holding the shotgun, spinning around and heaving my full weight and momentum into the guy, knocking both him and me off our feet while at the same time taking aim as I curled into him.

A tiny inkling that a gunshot would seem somewhat loud in this quiet place and probably alert people flashed through my mind, and for some reason against all logic, that felt like a bad idea, but obviously I was in a bit of a bind. So I squeezed the trigger anyway, aiming for the leg of the other man headed my way. There was no way in hell I actually wanted to kill anyone—figuring that couldn't be too good for the old karma, not to mention mental health—so the leg it was.

He yelped and went down, clutching at his thigh. The man underneath me was already trying to get his arms around me, seizing control of the shotgun again. He was so strong I knew I'd never have a chance to get another shot, so while he was focused on the gun, I rolled away from him, already searching for a place to take cover.

Inexplicably, something jumped out of the shadows from above me, taking out the shotgun guy with a flying kick to the head. The dude folded over like a piece of tissue paper. Two guys were still on their feet and the one I'd shot in the leg was beginning to get his bearings again. He reached for the gun he dropped on his way to the ground, but the shadow guy—even more inexplicably, wearing a ski mask—had his attention focused on the two who were still in good working condition.

The ski mask guy had a piece of pipe, already swinging it with incredible speed at one of the bad guy's heads. I didn't see how it went since I was already diving for the gun the bleeding man was headed for, but judging from the sickening thwack above me, I guessed that he'd made the desired contact.

I got to the gun half an instant before the injured guy, sliding feetfirst for the last stretch as if I were sliding into home, my hands grabbing the gun as my foot careened toward the dude's head. From the several martial arts and self-defense classes I had taken—jiujitsu, kickboxing, karate and a few others—I'd learned the places to strike to take down an opponent with the least amount of effort. Not that I'd ever tried to really knock somebody unconscious, but in theory I possessed the info.

Turned out, the theory held up. Dude flopped backward like a rag doll.

Just as I was about to spring up and assess the situation, another sick thud filled the air and the night went silent.

I sat for a minute, daintily catching my breath (aka panting like a damned dog in heat) and perusing the scene. Six men lay unconscious in a circle around me. Besides the one I'd shot in the leg, none of them seemed to be injured in any way other than the bumps and bruises they would wake up with.

The man in the mask was tending to the leg of the guy I'd just kicked in the face—and, you know, also shot—tying it off with a makeshift tourniquet.

I realized then, that even though I'd helped distract the guy whose shotgun I'd fired, I had only actually taken down one of these six men. Ski Mask had done the rest. Frankly, I felt a little like my fighting skills could use some brushing up. But I didn't really have a whole lot of time to lament my poor performance before Ski Mask strolled up and put his hand out to help me up.

So there I was, on the ground surrounded by unconscious men, trying to decide if I should allow myself to be helped up by a guy wearing a ski mask and holding out a hand covered in someone else's blood.

But he had also just saved my life. And to be fair, the blood was kinda my fault.

Needless to say, I took the hand.

He lifted me up as if I weighed nothing more than a small child. This guy was strong. This guy was also tall, I noted.

And...this guy was about to speak.

"So," he said, lifting his hand toward the mask. "Apartment 2201, right?"

Chapter Four

My stomach seized like the assets of a Ponzi scheme fraudster.

I blinked, my eyelids apparently the only thing on my body that would move, since my brain was using all its functioning power to try to process exactly what was happening. I couldn't figure out if I wanted the ground to open up and swallow me whole, or if I wanted to pretend to faint, landing conveniently in his arms.

"Oh, um. Hi, Ryan."

Was it bad that a little jolt of relief shot through me that he wasn't with some gorgeous woman?

He stood staring at me, one eyebrow raised as if to ask what in the fiery depths of hell I thought I was doing in a place like this in the middle of the night. I thought briefly of lifting my eyebrow right back in an attempt to convey the same thing, but quickly realized he was absolutely not in the wrong in this particular situation.

No, this was all me.

I was about to start squirming and wishing I had been the one shot, and maybe not just a flesh wound, when he suddenly seemed to come to a realization.

"Listen," he said—and holy hell, his voice sounded sexy.

"We need to get out of here. Someone might have heard that shot and called the police."

"Will we be in trouble?"

"It's not trouble from the cops I'm worried about. I really can't have anybody seeing me here."

"Just what, exactly, *are* you doing here?" I asked, dying to know what sort of situation I had just made much more complicated.

"Really? *You're* asking *me* that right now?"

I glanced at my feet, suddenly unable to look into those beautiful hazel eyes.

"These guys aren't going to be out forever. We've got to go."

As if on cue, a groan emerged from one of the first guys who had dropped. Ryan grabbed my arm and started walking me back the way I'd come, away from the street.

I decided not to argue, assuming he knew the way home much better than I did since, you know, he probably knew where we were. We walked at a startlingly brisk pace for several blocks and I could only hope we were getting closer to home. My choice of wedge sandals was decidedly not the best decision I had made all week, but it wasn't like I'd had time to plan or anything. And they did seem to work pretty well for kicking that guy in the face, actually. But my feet were killing me now, and I was having quite a hard time keeping up with Ryan.

Not that I was about to complain to him about it.

Still, I wasn't particularly known for keeping my mouth shut, even under the most awkward of circumstances. In fact, that's when the old talk hole seemed to want to flap the most. "So, um. What is it you do, exactly? I mean, you

saved me, so you must be a good guy but I'm just not entirely sure why you had the mask on—"

The look on his face made the words stop spewing from
my mouth.

"Not that it's really your business, but I'm a private detective."

My breath caught in my throat. Already my dream guy,
with the dreamy looks, but to cap it all off he had my dream
job too!

"Really?! That's amazing," I said, and started in on my
usual babble that seemed to burst forth every time I was
talking to a guy I was interested in. "I love detective work
so much. I mean, ever since I was a little kid and read all
the Nancy Drew and Hardy Boys books, you know." I rolled
my eyes at myself. Only I could sound that naive. "I mean, I
get that in real life the mysteries are way harder to solve and
stuff and the clues don't just happen to pop up in front of you
magically at the right time and everything, but man, those
books got my imagination going when I was a kid. Like,
totally set me on the path to my detective-work obsession."

Ryan looked over at me like I'd just vomited up a chicken.
Not that I could blame him, exactly. I had, after all, just admitted to an obsession with detectives immediately after
stalking him. God, he had to be super pleased that I lived
right across the hall from him.

"Yeah," he said, making a face like there was a bad smell
in the air. "You're right—it's not really like that."

I nodded, thanking my lucky stars we were still walking at the pace of super speed, which gave us something to
do besides me berating myself for being such a moron and

him wondering how the hell a moron like me even existed, let alone lived in the same building as him.

We walk-ran in silence for approximately thirty-eight years until he broke the silence. "So, Petra? What exactly were *you* doing out here?"

Oh. Dear. God.

"Um…"

I couldn't believe I'd had all this walk-running time to try to think of some kind of excuse for what I was doing and I had been too dense to do so. I had absolutely no sense of self-preservation whatsoever.

"Uh, well… I was kind of…following you?" I squeaked, picking up the pace even more.

Unfortunately, being amazingly tall, Ryan had absolutely no trouble keeping up.

"And uh, why, may I ask, were you doing that?"

Shit. There was definitely no right answer to that.

"Okay, so this is probably going to sound stupid, but I'm kind of a detective too. I mean, I'm not, but I took a couple classes on the subject as sort of research for what I do for a living and I guess I was a little bored so I was kind of just…practicing."

He raised his eyebrows. "Practicing being a detective?"

"Um, yeah. Sort of." I let out a sigh. "Look, it's not as stupid as it sounds. I mean it is, but I'm a novelist and I've kind of been having trouble with writer's block lately, and I write mysteries, you know? Well, sort of rom-com mysteries. So yeah, that's what I was doing."

"Following me."

I nodded. "I guess so."

"Why, of all the people in all the world, did you choose

me to follow in your little—what did you call it—rom-com mystery game?"

I tried not to be offended by his dismissal of my career research as a little game and tried to focus on some sort of sane answer. It probably wouldn't be the smartest to lead with *Well, I'm incredibly intrigued by you because you're the most beautiful thing in the world and I really wanted to know everything about you*, so instead I played it a bit more...vague.

"I don't know. I just heard you leaving because you're right there across the hall, and I didn't really think about it all that much and just went for it, I guess."

He shook his head. "Well, congrats. I gotta hand it to you. For an amateur, you really have done an outstanding job."

I smirked. "You had no idea I was following you, did you?"

He glared sideways at me, still walking at his break-neck pace.

"No. I certainly didn't, so good for you." He smiled a "you must be so proud of yourself" smile. "But that's not what I was talking about. What I meant was that it was quite spectacular that you were able to monumentally screw up the case I'm working on. So, congratulations."

Somehow I didn't feel all that pumped over my "victory."

We walked a while longer in silence. My feet were ready to fall off and all I wanted to do was cry, but I was not about to show weakness. At least...not any more than I already had.

I could finally see our apartment building a few blocks up. My feet were screaming and I was so emotionally spent I just wanted to go home and curl up in a ball. I usually didn't get so worked up, but this night had been something for the record books.

We entered our building in silence and rode the elevator to the twenty-second floor together. As we made our way to our end of the hall, he spoke. "So how did you learn to round-kick like that, anyway?"

I shrugged. "I took a class."

"Another class. You sure do like your classes."

I couldn't tell if he was making fun of me or not, so I shrugged. "I like to learn new things. Meet new people. Classes are a good way to do that."

"Uh-huh," he said, nodding. "Well, you did pretty well out there considering you were caught completely off guard. A lot of people would have just fallen apart."

"I never thought I'd have to find out what I'd do in a situation like that. I guess that's the good news," I said, smiling half-heartedly.

I still felt like a giant elephant anus for ruining Ryan's case.

"Well, now I guess you know you can kick some butt when necessary."

"I guess," I said, unable to look him in the eye. "So… what now?"

He looked at me for a moment and took a deep breath, letting it out through his nose in a long, slow whoosh. "Well… now I figure out what my next move is with the case, and you go inside and hope you never see any of those guys ever again."

I nodded, then turned to slip my key into the lock.

"And, Petra?"

I turned back to him. "Yeah?"

"Please, do me a favor and stop with the sleuthing," he said, his forehead creasing to drive home the point.

Too bad it just made him look more adorable than ever.

Chapter Five

"Do anything exciting last night?" Vic asked at brunch the next morning.

That's right, we did brunch on Sundays, and it would take a helluva crisis for us to miss it. I don't care what anybody says, brunch is not just for soccer moms and grandmothers. There is little in life that is quite as perfect as a Sunday brunch—the eggs, the pancakes, the "perfect amount of crispness" hash browns…the mimosas. All of it spectacular. Not to mention I got to hang out with my friends for an extra three hours a week, you know, 'cause almost every other day wasn't enough.

I sipped on my pre-mimosa coffee, stalling. I wasn't quite sure how to answer what was seemingly a routine question when I definitely did not have a routine answer. Obviously, I wanted to spill everything, but I had no idea if any of what had gone down last night was like, confidential or something. Eventually, I decided I hadn't taken any oaths, and Ryan hadn't told me not to say anything, so I figured it couldn't hurt to tell my best friends. Right?

"Well, um, I sorta followed Ryan."

Vic's eyes got wide, and Brandt even turned his attention

away from his menu—and believe me, not much could dis-tract Brandt from food, unless it was a woman. Even then, she had to be pretty spectacular.

Vic leaned in. "Oh my god, tell me everything. Did he go see a woman? No," she gasped. "A man."

"No, neither of those things."

"Perfect, so he's single."

"Vic, just because he didn't go see a significant other on one particular night doesn't mean he doesn't have one."

"So he does?" she asked, disappointed.

"I have no idea. I just know he didn't go see anyone last night."

I'd already lost Brandt to his menu again and Vic just looked at me like she was wondering why I was even both-ering to tell the story if I didn't have any juicy news about his personal life.

"Yeah, so anyway... I was tailing him, you know, like in that class I took."

Brandt didn't even try to stifle his chuckle. I could never figure out why everybody was always hating on my classes. I'd made some really good connections through them, and learned a lot of interesting stuff.

"And he walked forever and then I lost him."

Brandt glanced up at me like I was the saddest thing on earth. To be honest, at the time that I'd lost track of Ryan I had pretty much felt exactly that, but he could give me a *little* credit. Besides, it wasn't like I was wasting his time. I mean, what else were we going to talk about that was more interesting?

"If you're about to say, 'so then I turned around and went

back home,' I'm going to throw this sugar packet at you," Vic said.

Cripes, even Vic was getting bored with me.

"If you just let me talk, I'll get to the good part," I said, shooting them my best scolding look. Which probably wasn't really all that scolding so much as it was me trying to hide the excitement of what I was about to reveal.

Vic leaned back in her seat and crossed her arms. Brandt was nose-deep in the menu.

"So then, I started trying to get my bearings and figure out how to get home when I decided to take a shortcut up an alley and sorta ran right into a bunch of dudes in the middle of some shady transaction. You know, the whole works…a bunch of guns pointed at my head and everything."

"What?" Vic yelled.

Brandt simply folded up the menu, set it down and sat up as straight as I'd ever seen the man sit.

I nodded nonchalantly. "Yeah, so it was pretty scary and everything and I had no idea how the hell I was going to get out of that mess, when this masked guy jumped out of the shadows and started taking the dudes down one by one. And you know how I've taken a few martial arts classes, right?"

They were finally both hanging on my every word. Brandt with his mouth drooping open—he really had to work on that—and Vic with her eyes wider than I'd ever seen them.

"So, I jumped in and knocked one guy over, then shot another dude with that guy's gun, and the masked guy kept taking guys down, then I kicked the guy I shot right in the head and yeah, that's about it." I let out a breath.

"What the hell?" Brandt said. At least that's what I

thought he said. It was kind of hard to tell what with Vic freaking out at the same time.

"You shot somebody? Like actually shot them? With a bullet?" Her voice was getting rather loud for brunch, nevermind that the subject matter might not be entirely appropriate either.

"Yes," I said, in that strained way you do when you're trying to get someone to quiet the hell down.

"Oh my god. Oh my god," was all she seemed to be able to say.

"Okay, wait a second," Brandt jumped in, his eyes searching to piece the story together.

I couldn't help but feel a little smug at the fact that suddenly they were oh so interested in my evening.

"I would have had you pegged for a flighter, not a fighter."

Since Vic was on the same side of the table as he was, I let her go ahead and punch him in the arm instead of doing it myself.

"Ow! What?" he moaned.

"Holy crap, okay," Vic said. "So, you're there and all these guys are like knocked out or friggin' shot or whatever…" She raised her eyebrows to get me to continue with the story.

"Oh yeah, this is the good part. And then the masked guy came over and was all like, 'Apartment 2201, right?'" I finished in my best man-voice.

Vic gasped. Brandt scratched his head, not quite following as quickly. "Holy shit, it was Ryan," Vic said.

Brandt looked at her like she'd said the most absurd thing he'd ever heard.

But I nodded. "Oh yeah, he ripped off that mask and I

nearly fainted. And not just because I'd forgotten just how gorgeous he was."

"Oh my god, he's your hero," Vic said, excited.

Brandt rolled his eyes.

"Well, yeah, I guess," I said, "but it was kind of more like me being a big pain in the ass because I had totally ruined his whole spy operation."

"Dude's a spy?" Brandt asked, shifting excitedly in his seat.

"Well, no, but he's a private detective. He was working on a case and well, I sorta got in the middle of it. Literally."

Brandt cringed. "Seriously. That is so bad. And what the hell is he getting himself involved in, exactly? A bunch of guys with guns is not your typical investigation shit, you know."

I nodded, the sinking feeling in my stomach coming back now that I'd revealed the whole story. I really had gotten myself into a seriously dangerous situation.

Vic was apparently thinking the same thing. "What the hell did you think you were doing? What if you'd been shot? Or worse?" She was starting to get worked up into a bit of a panic now. Well, as much of a panic as Vic ever got into, anyway. Which, thankfully, wasn't particularly panicky.

"Well, I guess I was thinking I'd follow this cute guy around for a while to see what he did on a Saturday night. I thought he'd go to a movie or meet up with friends. I admit, I hadn't really thought through every possible scenario. Such as him being on a stakeout, watching a bunch of dudes with guns."

"Okay, start from the start again. I feel like I'm missing something," Brandt said.

"Well, maybe if you had listened the first time instead of obsessing over the damned menu," Vic said in her voice that seemed to be reserved solely for giving Brandt shit, "you would have understood a little better."

"Come on, you guys, just give it a rest for today, okay? I'm not in the mood to play referee."

They both opened their mouths to say something, but thankfully thought better of it. I finally gave my own menu some attention, deciding on the French toast. Carbs felt like the right thing on a day like today.

I set my menu aside and Vic moved to put hers on top of mine. "Oh shit," she said, glancing past my shoulder.

"What?" I asked.

"You don't want to know."

"Ugh," Brandt said. "Not this douche nugget."

I turned, totally confused as to who my two friends, who were usually very accepting of everyone besides each other, could possibly be so upset to see.

And my heart jumped into my throat, the same reaction I had every time I saw those doe-brown eyes.

Johnny.

Talk about a serious *Case of the Old Flame*.

"Petra! I have been looking everywhere for you. How come nobody will tell me where you moved to?" He got that sad, puppy dog look in his eye, which unfortunately undid me almost as much in that moment as when I used to believe he was genuine and sincere.

"Uh, hi, Johnny."

"Hi, guys." Johnny beamed to Vic and Brandt as he began to sit down in the free chair beside me, totally oblivious to the eye daggers they were hurling his way.

Vic and Brandt didn't agree on much, but when it came to Johnny their feelings were mutual.

Johnny leaned over and kissed my cheek. "Good to see you, Beautiful. So, tell me, why all the secrecy? Why aren't you answering my calls?" he asked, pouting again. Somehow, he was one of those guys who could get away with it. All charm and, as I had recently found out, very little substance.

"Um, maybe because you cheated on her, you irritating excuse for a human being," Vic said, kind enough to answer on my behalf.

Which was probably a good thing, since I was never quite able to actually say what I wanted to Johnny. He always found a way of making me want to take care of him. Which was exactly what I had been doing for the past two years, I was embarrassed to admit.

Johnny looked pained, like he couldn't believe he should possibly be held accountable for his actions. He was an artist (except he said it *artiste*, like a jackass), after all. He lived life by his emotions, and it was hardly his fault that the blonde waitress from the coffee shop in our old neighborhood made him horny and then she somehow accidentally landed on his penis.

While he was living with me.

Or more accurately, while I was supporting him and his "artistic endeavors." Which, incidentally, never seemed to pan out. Come to think of it, he really didn't even spend a whole lot of time creating art.

"Now, Petra," he said in that sexy voice of his, causing me to cringe over how much it still made me swoon. "I'm hurt. I can't believe you just took off like that and left me to fend for myself."

His face was so close to mine that I was having a hard time breathing over the scent of his cologne, and unfortunately, it was not in a bad way. More of an "I remember every single orgasm I had while smelling that cologne" way.

"You make it sound like I just ran off. I paid two months' rent in advance so you'd have plenty of time to find a place to live."

"But you just left without a trace."

"I left you a letter explaining everything."

"I know, but I never got a chance to properly say good-bye." He glanced down at my body, which should have made me want to slap him, but somehow got my blood moving at a slightly elevated pace.

Frankly, the only way I had been able gather enough strength to leave him was to slip out without saying good-bye. Johnny was nothing if not persuasive.

Or perhaps more accurately, manipulative.

"Okay, that's it. Just get the hell out of here, dude," Brandt said.

I'd like to say he was defending my honor, but I think it was more the fact that having another guy at the table who might have more swagger than he did made him entirely uncomfortable.

"What?" Johnny said, putting up his arms. "What did I ever do?"

"You know, that's your problem," Vic said. "You never think you do anything wrong. You're the universe's gift to humanity, right?"

Johnny smiled, deciding to take that as a compliment.

"You think the whole damned world owes you a favor, but

you know what? Your run is over, man. At least with anyone at this table. We are onto you, you freeloading dirtbag."

Johnny's smile faded quickly, and he decided he was
done paying attention to Brandt and Vic, turning his full
focus toward me. Which, I'm sad to say, was the worst thing
that could happen. For whatever reason, I was powerless
against Johnny.

"Come on, Petra," he cooed, running a finger up my forearm, which unfortunately sent shivers through me. "Just let
me see your new place. We can still be friends, at least, right?"

It occurred to me that there was probably something very
wrong with me that I actually thought it would be easier
to be back in that alley kicking the crap out of those guys
than what I was about to do. It literally took every ounce
of strength in my entire body to open my mouth and say
the words.

I cleared my throat. "No, Johnny. No, I don't think we
can be friends." I hated myself for the "think" part, but at
least I'd gotten it out.

Even Brandt and Vic looked a little stunned. And kinda
proud of me.

Johnny's mouth dropped open. He was apparently not
expecting to hear those words coming from me.

"But…"

"Oh no, you don't," Vic said. "Do not say another word.
Petra was very clear. She does not want to be friends. It's
time for you to leave."

Johnny turned to Vic, obviously only half listening.

The problem was, while Vic had the balls to say anything
to anybody, she was pretty much one of the tiniest humans
on earth, clocking in at about four foot eleven and maybe
ninety-five pounds. Brandt, on the other hand, was a giant

of a man, but was not really one to make waves about anything. If I could morph the two of them together, I'd have one hell of a badass best friend.

"Look, Petra," Johnny said, turning to me again.

My stomach dropped. Was he really going to make me say it again?

"The lady said now," Brandt uttered, calm as could be, then stood to his full height, maybe even stretching a bit for good measure. His chair screeching across the floor added to the intensity of the moment.

I could feel Johnny physically recoil beside me. "Um, yeah, sure thing, man. I was just on my way."

Johnny got up quickly and gathered his things. Unfortunately, he was one of those people that just took up space, not only with his body but with the stuff he was always setting down everywhere. He scrambled to gather his scarf, sunglasses, phone and wallet, clutching everything awkwardly to his chest when he normally would have made a big scene of putting things in their place before he left. If there was one thing about Johnny, it was that he always made a big entrance and an even bigger exit.

"And don't even think about bothering Petra again," Vic added as Johnny backed away a few steps.

"Petra," Johnny said, making one last plea. "Just…just call me, okay?" he said. And somehow the way he said it nearly broke my heart all over again.

Brandt slowly sat and picked his menu up again. "Now, can we finally eat?"

"I hear that," Vic said, and I realized I really didn't need one perfect badass friend when the two I had sitting here were both very much badass in their own perfect ways.

Chapter Six

I was decidedly shaken after the little run-in with Johnny, but Brandt and Vic snapped me out of it pretty quickly with approximately four hundred and thirty-seven more questions about what had gone down the night before. Which was exactly what I needed. Once I recounted the fight again, it reminded me that I was, in fact, a little bit badass myself.

And I was definitely stronger than Johnny could ever hope to be.

The real problem was that Vic and Brandt had this theory that Johnny was the root of all evil…and the root of my writer's block. It was an idea that I absolutely did not believe because when I wrote my first book, I hadn't been in a relationship at all—in fact, I wouldn't even meet Johnny until months after I'd signed my contract with my publisher. And yeah, he was around for some of the editing process, but honestly, he'd been more of a distraction than helpful in any way.

Of course, I hadn't felt like such a loser in love back then either. I'd dated my fair share before Johnny came around and never had any issues. Although, come to think of it, as incompatible as some of those other guys had been, none of them had made me feel as insecure as I'd felt when I finally realized that I'd fallen for Johnny's games and had to get out.

But he was just so good at what he did. Helping him felt like the right thing to do—it was that satisfaction of having someone to take care of, knowing that I was responsible for something outside of myself. I was proud of the fact that I had the means to take care of us both.

Unfortunately, I realized way too late—and only at the consistent prodding from my friends for much longer than I was quite comfortable admitting—that this was Johnny's schtick. He was the kind of person who made it seem like he was helping you by letting you help him. He had a special gift for off-loading the responsibilities of his life onto others without making it even seem like it was a chore.

Until, of course, he inevitably strayed from the hand that fed him.

So really, I suppose he had two special talents: a sophisticated grasp on the art of manipulation and a magnificent lack of conscience when it came to his extracurricular activities with potential future manipulees.

And he was so magnificent at it that just having him nearby made my pulse pitter-patter, and wanna get at 'er.

Honestly, what the hell was wrong with me? And yeah, I tried not to beat myself up about it—women fall for the wrong guys all the time—but still. It was just so pathetic of me to even give the guy the time of day.

Of course, now that I was crushing on someone new, I had to admit it was a little easier to stop thinking about ol' freeloader Johnny. Ugh, I did not want to be one of those girls that has to jump from guy to guy—I loved being on my own! And in my defense, it had been over four months since Johnny and I were over—and I'd barely thought about him in weeks until he sauntered on over to our table. I just had to keep him out of sight and out of mind.

And as I headed back to my building after finishing brunch in our leisurely three-hour manner, Ryan was squarely in the forefront of my mind and Johnny almost forgotten. Which was exactly where he belonged.

Annie was at her usual spot in the lobby when I got back to my building, lounging in a low-cut tangerine pantsuit that looked incredible on her, her silvery hair sleek and shiny.

"Hey, love, out for brunch?"

"Yeah," I said, sitting down to chat while wondering if I should be worried that she had my routine down already.

Was I that predictable? I mean, all the self-defense courses I'd taken talked about switching up your routine, which I always thought was a good idea. I just never thought I was important enough to be someone to have to worry about such a thing.

The lobby was surprisingly quiet, so I took my chance, glancing around to make sure a certain hot PI wasn't standing right behind me.

"So, Annie, I'm just curious…about Ryan."

Annie gave me a knowing smirk. My cheeks immediately warmed, and I suddenly felt like I was in seventh grade again.

"Ah, yes… Ryan."

"Well, I mean, I was just curious. Since he lives right across the hall and everything."

"Don't worry, hon, that man has caught the eye of you and every other female in this building, married or not. He is one fantastic example of maleness—there is no debate about that."

I smiled, hoping the redness wasn't as noticeable as it felt creeping up the back of my neck. "I'm sure he has."

She chuckled. "Well, believe me, I wish I had some juicy gossip on him, but he keeps pretty much to himself. He's friendly enough and puts up with my flirtations," she said, winking, "but never really gets into his personal life. I do know that he's some sort of a detective." She glanced at me with one eyebrow raised and I could tell she was thinking she was revealing some big secret.

"Right, I actually knew that already. We did have one little chat." I decided not to tell her how utterly uncomfortable it was and how it had lasted about forty blocks or so.

Not that distance counted really, since a lot of that time we had walked in silence. Tumultuous, soul-squashing silence.

Annie mock-gasped. "You've been holding out on me, Petra!" She smacked my hand good-naturedly.

I laughed. "Not really. I definitely don't know any more than you do." I left out the part where I might know a few details about a case he was working on and how dangerous his work might actually be.

"Well, that's pretty much all I know too," Annie said. "He's quiet. A good neighbor."

"Does he normally have a lot of…company?" I cringed even saying it.

"I'm going to assume you mean company of a female nature," Annie said brightly. "I've only noticed him bring home women a few times." And for some reason she stopped there. Like that was any way to end a sentence.

I looked at her expectantly.

"And well, the women those few times were quite…sophisticated looking?" She ended with an inflection like she was asking a question.

I guess that's the information I'd hoped for. I wasn't even sure. I'd just wanted more details, but now that I heard the word *sophisticated*, I knew for sure what I'd already suspected. He was way out of my league.

SUNDAYS WERE USUALLY a bit dull after brunch, and the guilt of not being able to write was getting to me.

When I first started writing I had this idea of what being a writer was going to look like.

Afternoon creativity walks.

Posh parties at sumptuous locations.

Words flowing from my fingertips as if sent from a higher power.

Mingling with fans at signings and getting recognized on the street for selfies.

What I hadn't bargained for was the constant guilt. Not being able to find the words, the hours of solitude feeling useless, the idea that I was letting so many people down. I had to figure out a way through this writer's block or start seriously thinking about what else I could do with my future.

And thing was, I loved writing…or at least I used to, before I had to write something better than the last book. Not that I didn't appreciate the success of my first book—I definitely did—it was just that surging to success sometimes meant there was nowhere to go but down.

It was enough to strike terror in me faster than a dimly

lit parking lot and a dog in an eight-legged spider suit jumping on me as I exited an elevator (seriously, have you seen that stuff on the internet?).

I opened my laptop and clicked on my word processing program, opening a new file. The lovely fresh, white page popped up before me, the cursor blinking innocently right there at the top.

I formatted my document as I would any work in progress, with my last name and page number at the top. I'd learned this in one of my beginner's writing classes years ago and the habit had stuck. It was like getting something... anything on the page was at least a start.

I typed "*UNTITLED*, by Petra Jackson" as a title page, then filled in "Chapter 1" on page two.

Which is precisely where I came to an abrupt halt.

I mean, it wasn't as though this was my first rodeo. I'd started plenty of stories without much of a plot or characters in mind, and everything had always been fine. You type away to figure that stuff out, right? It had always worked before.

I sat, looking thoughtfully into space. Then tried glancing around the room. For a while I stared at that blinking cursor, daring it to mock me.

Which of course it absolutely did.

I surfed the internet for a couple hours (avoiding all things with dogs and/or spiders) and was surprised to look up and realize night had fallen, the darkness creeping into my apartment without me even realizing. I'd been super enthralled in learning about travel capsule wardrobes—you know, just in case the character in my new novel had to do any packing for a trip, I guess. *Sigh.*

After dinner, I decided to relax and listen to some music, and a nice bubble bath might be in order later.

But then I heard it. Someone coming out of the apartment across the hall.

Ryan was on the prowl again.

My heart sped and my first instinct was to grab my coat and go racing after him. But his last words echoed in my ears: *Do me a favor and stop with the sleuthing.*

Although come to think of it, I never really had been one to do what people told me to for no good reason. And I mean, he probably thought he had a good reason, to keep me safe and all, but I was a big girl. I could take care of myself. Hadn't I helped take down all those men, after all?

My eyes darted around the apartment for a quick disguise. Thankfully Brandt was always bringing stuff around from photo shoots and stuff, so I grabbed a pair of teal prescription-less glasses and flung a floppy wool hat on along with a long, shapeless coat. I was looking rather hipster/I'm-too-cool-to-care, if I did say so myself.

Against my better judgment—which, frankly, I'm not sure I really had anyway—I stepped out of my apartment on a mission to follow once more. I mean, let's be honest, no one really thought my sleuthing would ever come to an end, and if they did then they didn't know me very well.

The elevator opened on the ground floor just in time for me to see Ryan heading in the opposite direction he'd gone the night before. I followed at about the same distance, but I had learned from my mistakes. I paid closer attention to where I was this time, even taking cursory glances at street signs here and there, and I was much more cautious when coming around corners. I promised myself if I did lose Ryan again, I'd head straight back home and use only the main streets, staying in the lighted areas.

But for now, I kept to the shadows.

We didn't go nearly as far this time, and my feet had never been so grateful. I'd grabbed much more sensible shoes, some slip-on sneakers, but still, the grotesquely peeled skin and jellylike pockets of fluid on my feet definitely had not had time to heal.

Ryan made his way up an alley, and I admit I paused before I followed. But I wasn't about to come this far just to turn around and go home. The classes said the good stuff always happened right when you were about to give up, and patience was rated the highest skill to practice above all else. I stayed well back and only moved into the alley once I knew Ryan had gone pretty far in.

I moved slowly, my heart beating so hard it drowned out any noise. If I was going to keep doing things like this, I was going to have to figure out how to get a grip on my fear...and my adrenaline.

I shook my head. *If I was going to keep doing things like this?* Sometimes I wondered if I was, in fact, losing my mind.

A noise loud enough to drown out my ridiculous heartbeat came from about halfway down the alley. A ladder on a fire escape being pulled. I stopped and flattened myself against the wall of the brick building beside me, trying to control my breath, though I was pretty sure I sounded like a German shepherd after a four-mile run.

Someone up ahead, presumably Ryan, held the ladder down for a full minute or two. I assume he was waiting to see if anyone had heard the noise and was coming to investigate. I channeled my inner Nancy (seriously, that girl had one giant horseshoe up her butt), hoping to River Heights that no one was curious. Other than flattening myself against the building, I had no place to hide and was pretty sure if someone came walking past me, I'd be more than a little noticeable.

No one came a-sniffing and soon I could see Ryan's silhouette climbing the ladder to the first-floor fire escape. Then he let the ladder back up slowly, so slowly it barely made any noise this time. When it quietly shifted into place, Ryan glanced around once more, then settled into a seated position. If I hadn't seen him climb up with my own eyes, I would have thought there was just a bag of garbage sitting out there.

Now that he was settled though, I suddenly realized I was trapped. He had the perfect perch for an excellent view up both ends of the alley, and no doubt any movement, especially movement that suddenly burst out of the shadows, would have him on high alert. And the last thing I needed was Ryan to know I was following him again.

You know, after he explicitly begged me not to.

Thoughts suddenly swirled. What if I had to sneeze? Or like, got snackish? Or, what if a bunch of murderous guys were about to walk directly past me? Or worse…what if I had to pee?!

Soon Ryan pulled out a camera with a massive telephoto lens, like something someone in the paparazzi might have. I couldn't fathom where the heck he'd been hiding that ginormous piece of equipment (that's what she said), since I hadn't noticed him carrying anything. My attention to detail could apparently use some work. Strike two on the old detective work for the evening. And no, I wasn't going to let myself think about how many strikes I'd gotten last night, thank you very much.

Ryan continued to snap pictures of the goings-on inside an apartment on the opposite side of the alley. Every once in a while, I caught a glimpse of someone walking past the window and Ryan's camera would start clicking away.

The evening moved on.

And on.

My legs were getting tired from standing in the same position for so long and the need to pee was becoming less of a theory and more of a reality. I really wanted to check my phone to see what the time was, but I was pretty sure a phone screen suddenly lighting up in the middle of the alley might be a tad noticeable.

Jesus. It wasn't until that moment that I realized I hadn't turned my ringer off. I guess that was strike three.

Most of the time I enjoyed when my friends remembered I existed, but in that moment, I prayed I had drifted as far from their consciousness as a fart released in a hurricane. But then I started worrying that by thinking about someone calling me, I might accidentally be sending vibes out for them to call. Gah! I tried to clear my thoughts. Which basically resulted in me never being able to think of anything *but* that ever again.

What felt like at least another hour later, Ryan finally moved. He'd made slight movements all along, taking pictures now and again, and sometimes it looked like he was writing something in a notebook, which made me want to take out my phone and make a few notes of my own, but again, the whole screen thing. I finally understood why some people still carried a pen around in their purse. But this time he was on the move for real, and I only had one chance to get out of there unnoticed.

As he carefully lowered the ladder, trying not to make noise, I began to inch my way up the alley, my eyes never leaving his figure both because it was a very nice figure to look at, and to make sure he had no idea I was there.

When he eventually turned his back to me to climb down the ladder, I started speed walking, placing my feet carefully so I wouldn't make any noise, then turned up the street the opposite way we'd originally come.

I'd never be able to stay off his radar if I was in front of him, so I needed to hide out and wait until he got well ahead of me again. Thankfully there was a recessed entranceway for a store fairly close by that I could duck into unseen.

Ryan was startlingly quick coming out of the alley but didn't seem to catch on that anyone had been with him most of the night. He headed back in the direction of our apartment building, and this time I gave him a lot of space. I had not come this far just to get caught now.

And while the night had been exceedingly dull, and frankly the main thing on my mind was getting to a bathroom, once I got home and did my business, I made quite a few notes while addresses and descriptions were still fresh in my mind. As I finished up with the notes, a quiet knock came on my door.

I tilted my head, wondering who the hell it could be. People didn't generally just knock on my door if I didn't know they were coming—especially considering this was a secure building where you had to be buzzed in.

I debated for a moment whether to answer it—my first

thought being that Johnny had somehow found me. But the knock came again, and I found myself moving toward the door, opening it a crack just as Ryan was raising his arm to knock a third time.

"Oh, hello," was all I could bring myself to say.

I was totally relieved that it wasn't Johnny, but at the same time, I had a feeling Ryan wasn't there to borrow a cup of sugar.

"Hi," he said.

I looked at him expectantly.

"So…did you have a good time?"

"I'm sorry?" I asked, my mind swirling.

"I know you were tailing me again," he said.

My stomach dropped to my knees.

Chapter Seven

I sighed and opened the door for him, having a feeling I might have a long conversation ahead of me. He looked around my apartment like any good detective would, I suppose. I cringed at the takeout container on the coffee table and the laundry basket heaped high in the corner, but mercifully, the place wasn't too much of a disaster.

"So, since asking nicely apparently isn't going to stop you from putting yourself in danger, not to mention invading my privacy and potentially screwing up my investigation…how about you tell me what will?"

I wish I could say his voice was kind, but frankly he sounded a tad pissed off. I mean, I guess I couldn't really blame him, but it wasn't like my intentions were bad, so it didn't seem fair.

"Ryan, I just want to help."

He scoffed.

"Look, I've got skills. I've got training. You saw what I could do out there when we were fighting those guys."

"You would have been killed on the spot if I hadn't risked my own life—and my investigation—trying to save you."

He had a point, but did he really have to put it like that?

"I know," I said, "but if I had known what was going on, I would never have stumbled into that situation."

"Of *course* you wouldn't know what was going on," he said, his eyes widening slightly. "Because you were secretly stalking me!"

Ouch. That stung. "I was *not* stalking you," I said, my face feeling as though it might be getting a little pink. Or, you know, burgundy. "I was just bored, and I needed something to do."

"Well, here's the thing. Following someone like that *is* actually stalking. Invading their privacy. And I get that you didn't know I was a detective or that I was on the job and things could get seriously dangerous, but even without all that, it's pretty damned reckless to just go following someone around."

"I was trying to practice my skills. It was research."

He snorted. "Yeah, research. And what makes you think I'm interested in being fodder for some ridiculous novel?"

I frowned. "My novel isn't ridiculous."

"It's a novel. And therefore fiction. And therefore ridiculous."

"You think books are ridiculous?" I was certainly seeing a side of Ryan I had not expected. He had seemed so intelligent, so interesting.

"No, books are good. The ones that actually teach you something or present you with new and interesting ideas. Fiction, on the other hand," he said as if he suddenly had a bad taste in his mouth, "is basic entertainment. Just made-up fairy tales."

My mouth dropped open. I wanted to defend fairy tales more than anything—fairy tales were the stuff of dreams—

but I figured I had a bigger issue on my hands. "Fiction is not just made-up stories," I said. "Fiction tells the emotional truth of real life. It gets us out of our heads when we need a pick-me-up. It takes us to places both real and imagined and allows us to live incredible adventures we would never otherwise get a chance to live."

He shook his head. "Whatever. It's not my thing. I get that it's yours and that's fine, but in no world, real or imagined, will I ever be interested in being some character in a ridiculous book. Aren't you supposed to figure that stuff out on your own anyway, not just follow someone around and tell their life story?"

"I certainly do not tell other people's life stories. It just helps make characters and situations more real if you have something solid to base them on. A realistic sense of a character is incredibly difficult to just make up out of nowhere."

He put his hands up to his head in frustration. "Look, I did not come here to debate the merits of literature. I just want you to stay the hell away from my case."

The last words felt like a slap in the face. Frankly, he was a little full of himself, if you asked me. It wasn't like I was following *him* per se; he just happened to be the person who was there. You know, purely random. Mostly. Give a girl a break. It just makes sense to follow someone who actually piques your interest.

"I don't really see what the problem is. Don't all detectives have partners, or sidekicks, or whatever? You've seen what I can do. The martial arts. The reconnaissance. I'm also really good with disguises and as you already know I've read all the Nancy Dr— Uh, detective stories, and I've also watched a million episodes of *CSI* and *Criminal Minds* and *Bones* and stuff. Not to mention it's my actual job to create mysteries. Plus, you know, I'd work for free." I gave him my most hopeful look.

He sighed. "I'm sorry to tell you, but none of that makes you a detective."

I squinted at him. "What does then?"

Somehow Ryan didn't seem like the type of guy who'd gotten into the private detective business because he used to be a cop, and if he hadn't been a cop, I was certainly interested to know what his credentials were. Not that I thought it was a huge deal, I just couldn't understand the difference between what I was saying and what he was saying.

"On-the-job experience is what makes a good detective," he said.

"Oh, so did you shadow someone for a while, you know, to get your experience, or like, have a mentor or something?"

He looked a bit confused. And a lot adorable, unfortunately. "No."

"Did you take a bunch of classes?"

He tilted his head. "Of course not."

"So, we can safely say that I have more knowledge and experience than you did when you first started this job."

He opened his mouth to say something, then promptly closed it again.

"So we agree, I can help with the case?"

"Petra, no. You're being ridiculous. It's way too dangerous, and I do not need a partner. Or a sidekick." He rolled his eyes.

"What if I can prove how valuable I can be?"

"No. How would you even do that?" he asked.

"Um, I don't exactly know yet, but I'll figure something out."

"Even if you do, the answer is still going to be no."

I sighed. "We'll see."

He shook his head like he couldn't quite believe this was happening to him. Not that I could blame him. It wasn't like I'd ever forced anyone to be my detective mentor before.

"I'm going home now. And can you please just stop? I honestly can't deal with the stress of this case *and* worrying about someone else's safety at the same time. It's too much, okay?" He looked so sincere. So intense, like he was really trying to make me see his point. "It's just too much."

And with that, he headed for the door and walked right out without turning to say goodbye.

Which was so incredibly rude. I mean, I suppose spying on him for several (dozens?) of blocks and all the way into a dark alley could technically be considered rude too, so I probably shouldn't judge him too harshly, but at least I'd been rude behind his back. Of course, I realized with a slight grimace, that might perhaps be a teensy bit worse.

But you know what? He hadn't even acknowledged my remarkably solid arguments. Because I *did* have all my classes behind me. And I *did* have intimate knowledge of the ins and outs of a good crime. Planning crimes was what I did for a living! Which, granted, might not be the greatest argument. But I solved them too, which I thought was an excellent point in my favor.

I'd spent countless hours delving into the minds of bad guys, figuring out exactly what their motivations might be—and not just one motive either; no, I had to run the gamut of every possible motivation so I could pick the one that was best for the book. I had to see the story…er, case… from every potential angle, unraveling the threads that made the most sense depending on that very motivating factor. My god, when I really thought about it, there literally wasn't anyone better equipped to solve a crime than a mystery writer. Just look at Jessica Fletcher! *Murder, She Wrote* had twelve seasons. And that was back in the day when TV shows had like, twenty-four episodes every year!

Okay, even I recognized I was working myself up into a bit of a tizzy over the whole thing, but frankly, I was insulted. What right did Ryan have to tell me I shouldn't be involved in the case? Like it or not, I was *already* involved in the case. Quite personally, if the blood on my favorite shoes had anything to say about it (sidenote to self: clean brown leather wedges).

Not to mention I could already feel the inspiration flowing back toward me, and yeah, maybe it hadn't actually taken up residence in my brain quite yet, but I knew it was there, floating all around me. I just needed a little more time with a mystery to really grasp it.

I shrugged. Fine. If Ryan wanted it this way, he could have it. I'd stay out of his investigation. I'd simply do my own investigation and see who solved the mystery first. And to be honest, I was pretty confident that I could do it just as well—if not better—than he could. Sure, he'd been doing things like this for years, but then again, so had I. Sort of.

Plus, it wasn't like I had a whole lot else on my plate. You know, other than delivering a new book to my publisher. Ugh…which was yet another reason that I needed to do this. I didn't want to plagiarize the story of Ryan's case, obviously, but I also hadn't been this excited about plotting in a

while. Probably because plotting a novel was pretty similar to solving a mystery. All the pieces had to fall into the
right places at the right times. The highs…the lows—they
all had to be there. I mean, if the bad guys only experienced
highs, the crime would never get solved, right? All I had
to do was make sure I had a front-row seat when these bad
guys experienced their lowest of lows.

Of course, I hadn't determined exactly who all the characters in the story were quite yet, but I knew exactly where
to go to find out.

THE NEXT NIGHT—after a productive day binge-reading a
couple of my favorite Nancy books—I went back to the alley
where Ryan had settled on the fire escape to do a little staking out of my own, and frankly, I was much better at getting
the ladder from the balcony down, since I'd thought to bring
a handy-dandy umbrella to hook around it so I didn't have to
jump and make a big kerfuffle. I mean, I might have looked
a little weird carrying an umbrella around when there was
no sight of rain, but whatever—it was dark.

I settled into the same corner where Ryan had been sitting
on the fire escape, quiet as could be, to wait. And it turned
out I didn't even have to wait for long. I couldn't quite believe these guys just had their curtains wide open for all to
see. I mean, I guess it would only be someone in the building across the alley who would see, but still, you'd think if
you were up to something illegal, you'd close the drapes.

Maybe they'd been at it so long they felt invincible or
something. Definitely helpful for me.

Though now that I had a little time to really stake out the
place, it didn't seem like there was a whole lot of illegal stuff

going on in there. It just seemed to be a couple guys milling around. I certainly didn't know what had interested Ryan so much that he'd been taking so many pictures.

But soon, the scene changed. One of the guys brought in a girl, holding her arm like she was a prisoner. Except, the girl appeared content to be there, like she was wanting something from them. Too bad I hadn't brought any listening equipment, though that would have probably cost thousands of dollars and was not the kind of thing I just had lying around. Still, it would have been top-notch to be able to hear what was going on.

Eventually, they took the woman out of the room then brought in another girl and the same type of scenario went down. The girls were obviously desperate for something—they wanted to be involved with these guys.

One of the guys (whom I'd lovingly labeled "dude with the face that looks like he was taking a whiff of his gym bag after leaving it in the trunk for two weeks in August"… I know, I know, wordy, but I was working on it) brought in a brunette. He removed her jacket as two other guys sitting at a small kitchen table—weirdly in the middle of the living room—motioned for her to turn around. In a strange turn of events, at least in the world I lived in, she did one better and gave them a striptease-like dance, crouching, butt out and moving like she was about to start undressing. The men stopped her. Which was maybe the strangest part of it all.

I sighed.

So…fun fact—I was not very good with the whole patience thing. I mean, sure, I could sit and be still if I had to, like last night when I followed Ryan, but it was not my favorite. In fact, it was, by far, the section I'd found the most difficult in my private investigation class. Frankly, I just didn't see the point when there was usually a much more efficient way to find out what you needed to know.

I slipped back down the fire escape, taking my time so no one would be alerted to my presence, then went for a little jaunt around the front of the building. I mean, nothing to see here…la-la-la. Just an inconspicuous lady out for a stroll late at night.

In a not-so-great part of town.

But I wasn't concerned. I was on alert, constantly scanning the vicinity the way I was taught in my classes so no one could sneak up and surprise me.

As I had hoped when I peeked around the building, a couple girls were loitering outside. I leaned my umbrella against the side of the building, flopped the hood of my sweater over my head, stuck my hands in my pockets, slouched and took a deep breath the way I'd been taught in my Intro to Dramatic Performance 101 class. I never thought I'd actually use the class for acting. I'd mostly taken it to help me get into characters' heads when I was writing, but I was excited to put it into practice.

"Hey," I said, walking up to the ladies, fighting the urge to use a fake accent. I'd learned a long time ago they weren't my strongest talent—what might start out as a light Southern lilt could turn into a "your mama done gone and whipped up the best sweet tea evahhhr" in about three seconds flat.

The women looked at me like they weren't very happy someone else had shown up to their scene.

"What's up?" I asked, getting a good look at the three of them.

They were all quite skinny. Dark circles loomed beneath

their eyes and there was a certain glassiness to their gazes, like they'd maybe been down a path of drugs for a while.

I took a chance. "Is this the place you can get the stuff?" I asked.

"Stuff?" one of the girls said innocently.

I tilted my head, hoping the hood was casting shadows over my face so that my face looked as thin as theirs, at least a little bit. "You know what I mean."

Another girl sighed. "Yes, this is the place, but we were here first and if you think you're going to jump ahead, you've got another thing coming." Her hand moved slowly to the waistband of her glittery skirt, bringing my attention to the small, but I'm sure very effective, knife that she had tucked in there.

"Whatever," I said, already turning away, afraid one of the guys would be on his way out to collect another woman at any second. "I'm not really presentable right now anyway. I'm coming back tomorrow though." I glared at her for good measure, my heart pumping.

She sneered right back but looked relieved to see me go.

I walked at as normal a pace as I could muster, but honestly, I couldn't get out of there fast enough. I could faintly hear a man's voice then, talking to the women I had just left, but I didn't dare turn around.

"She was just walking by," one of the girls said, apparently not too excited to let them know I might be back.

The less "competition" the better for them, I supposed.

I turned the corner and was out of sight, taking off into a run as I scooped up my umbrella. Being that close to who knows what kind of a situation had affected me more than I thought it would, and I needed to shed the nervous energy. I felt like I'd just downed a gallon of coffee.

As I neared my building, I slowed. I may not have come up with much evidence on my little nighttime trek, but things had changed.

Now I had a plan.

Chapter Eight

I couldn't sleep.

And when I couldn't sleep my mind could be a bit like a hamster on speed. Did my plan make sense? Would it rain tomorrow? Was the pain in my knee from walking for miles the other night, or was arthritis starting to kick in? Did Liechtenstein have a royal family? How much would it cost to buy the internet? What would magenta taste like?

Of course, I knew I wouldn't be able to write either. Sure, my brain was buzzing, but it was spinning too fast to squeeze anything remotely coherent out of it.

I needed a distraction.

I picked up the mystery I'd been reading, but after going over the same page four times and having absolutely no idea what happened, I set it back down and sighed. I had to find something distracting enough to lull my brain out of its pointless loop, but that was also mindless enough to not require too much thinking power. I needed something to organize or puzzle out.

Ooh! A jigsaw puzzle would be perfect (yup, I could really conjure up a firecrackin' good time when I wanted to). The only problem was I didn't have a puzzle.

Wait. I'd only been to the games room upstairs once since I'd moved in, but I remembered thinking it would be a nice place to relax with friends or do one of the puzzles that resided with the books and games. I didn't necessarily want to sit up there and do a puzzle at three o'clock in the morning in my jammies, but it would probably be okay if I wanted to borrow one, right? I mean, who was even going to know, really? And I could just return it in a few days.

The games room was one floor up, so it didn't take long to get there, which was a good thing since I was hardly looking stellar in my attire of ratty bathrobe, fuzzy unicorn slippers and pajama bottoms that were cut off at the knees—I couldn't stand when the pant bottoms scrunched up when I was trying to sleep so I always just chopped them off.

Unfortunately—as I discovered when I flicked on the light—my theory that I'd be the only one around at that hour was false. Except…why were they sitting in the dark?

I took a step closer. "Hello?" I said, the sound of my voice surprising even me in the silence.

It was a woman, cradling her head in the crook of her elbow, having apparently fallen asleep on top of the puzzle she'd been working on. I was surprised that she didn't wake up when the lights came on. Honestly, I was a little jealous of how deep some people could sleep—I'd jolt awake if a neighbor three floors down discharged a big sneeze. But then I noticed something didn't look quite right. The angle of her body was…off somehow.

I took a few more steps. "Hello?" I said, tentative this time.

She still didn't move. I closed my eyes, gathering all the courage I could find and pushed her ever so slightly on the shoulder to wake her up. At least that's what I was telling myself.

Then I pushed a little harder.

And that's when I knew for sure. The woman was not waking up. She was never going to be waking up again.

It took every ounce of self-control not to scream as I stumbled back out of the room. I braced myself against the wall just outside the door where I couldn't see...oh god... the body anymore.

If I'd thought my mind had been whirling before, it hadn't seen anything yet.

Okay, okay, I told myself. *Calm down.* I had to do something, but in the state I was in, I had absolutely no idea what that something was supposed to be. It's not like I'd ever discovered a dead body before.

I took a moment just to breathe.

Okay, what would a normal person do here? Which made me think of Vic asking me her WWND question. Yes, good. So...what would Nancy do?

With that one moment of focus, it suddenly seemed so simple. Because the answer was clear. I had to tell someone about this. Nancy would likely alert someone in a position of authority, right?

So off I went, down to the ground floor of the building and straight to the security desk, completely forgetting what I was wearing until I was in front of the nighttime security guard and he gave me a bit of a look. It was just my luck he had to be attractive—tall with gorgeous dark skin—and I cursed myself for not spending more time down in the lobby during the night shift. I pulled my ratty robe tighter.

"Um, hi," I said, shooting him an awkward wave. "I'm

Petra from 2201. I was just, um, up in the games room on twenty-three, and uh, well, there's sort of a body in there."

The guard's eyes widened. "What do you mean, a body?" Ozzy—as his name tag stated—asked.

"Um, well, I think it's a dead one?" I said, though it came out more like a question.

I mean, up in the games room I had been completely sure the body was not of the living variety, but now that I was in the bright lights of the lobby, not to mention in the company of another human, I started to second-guess myself. Or maybe it was a last-ditch hope that the poor woman wasn't really gone.

The guard blinked, then moved toward the front doors of the building without saying another word, locking them.

"Follow me," he said, and headed toward the elevators.

When we got in, he pressed the button for the twenty-third floor.

"Oh, um. I don't think I need to go back up there," I said, really, really not wanting to go back up there.

"Well, I'm not going in there by myself!" Ozzy said, looking at me like I'd lost my mind.

Which I thought was a little funny, since Ozzy was one of the biggest, toughest-looking dudes that I'd ever seen. Then again, maybe he hadn't ever discovered a dead body either.

"Couldn't we just call the cops or something?" I asked.

"We could, but the way you said there was a dead body didn't sound all that confident, and I don't want to make myself look like a fool. So I'd like to double-check for myself."

"Right, okay. I mean, I am pretty confident though. I really don't think that lady is getting up anytime soon. Or like, you know. Ever."

And I might have been mistaken, but it looked like Ozzy was trying very hard not to roll his eyes, but I guess I couldn't hold that against him since I was kind of even mistrusting myself. Wait, was it mistrusting or distrusting? Good lord, I was supposed to be a writer.

I really needed some sleep.

The elevator doors opened, and Ozzy stepped out while I sort of just stood there.

"Are you sure you need me to come?" I asked.

"Oh, I am definitely sure," he said, and honestly, I almost felt sorry for him when I saw the look on his face. Like he was trying to be tough, but there was some definite terror behind those eyes.

I sighed. "Fine, but I'm staying in the doorway."

"Just come on," Ozzy said, as he started marching down the hall.

I got the impression he felt like it was his duty to go in there but needed to hurry up and get it over with before he talked himself out of it.

I skulked behind. Why in the hell had I thought it was a good idea to do a stupid puzzle anyway? I stood outside as Ozzy took a deep breath, steeling himself, and marched in. I stayed right where I was.

"Oh no, it's Ms. Lawrence."

"You knew her?"

Ozzy nodded. "Erica Lawrence from 2301. And you're right. There's nothing we can do for her now except call the police and make sure nobody else stumbles on the scene. I'll call in some backup from my security company to stay here in case the police take a while. I can't leave the door downstairs unmanned for too long."

He got on the phone and started making calls.

Erica… I realized then that I knew Erica too. I took another quick peek into the room and had to admit that I hadn't really taken much of a look the first time around. So much for being the excellent witness I thought I'd be. Except, honestly, I think I'd been too scared.

Shit, it was her. She was a friend of Annie's. And well, everyone was a friend of Annie's, but whenever Annie talked about Erica, it gave me the impression that they were quite close.

I suppose I could have gone back to my apartment, but it didn't seem right to leave Ozzy there all alone, so I leaned against the wall in the hallway and slid down to the floor. This was one of the most surreal situations I had ever been in. Even though I wrote about these sorts of things, I had to admit I could have been perfectly content going my whole life without finding a dead body.

When the cavalry arrived, I went back downstairs, thinking I'd try to get some sleep even though I was way more wound up than I was before I'd taken the fateful trek to the games room. When I passed Annie's door just down the hall from mine, I decided to knock on her door. I couldn't bear the thought of Annie finding out from someone who thought it might be good gossip to pass along.

When the door opened, I stood staring at Annie for a good long while before I was able to speak. First, because I thought I'd have to knock several times before she'd even get to the door—it was five in the morning, after all—but she'd opened it as if she was standing there waiting. And second because of her appearance. She wore a long, satiny housecoat in fuchsia, complete with feathery trim that di-

rected the eye down to her pink leopard-print sandal slippers, magnificent sunshine-yellow pedicure and diamond
toe ring. Her robe was hanging slightly ajar, which gave
a pretty good view of her matching nightgown, though it
was really more like a longish teddy. And longish was even
pushing it. It was not lost on me that the woman probably
had better legs than me—not that mine had ever been spectacular or anything—but seriously, Annie was well into her
seventies. I guess what they say is true—the legs really are
the last thing to go.

The look was topped off by a glittering sleeping mask that
would have been right at home at a formal masquerade ball.

And even though it was just Annie and me standing there,
I couldn't help but feel a little underdressed in my plaid flan-
nel cutoffs and ultrathin tank with the hole just under the
armpit. Thank goodness I'd thrown on the terrible housecoat, though I couldn't help but feel a little childish with
my choice of slippers compared to the kitten heel slippers
Annie was wearing.

"Is everything all right, Petra?" Annie asked, starting to
look a bit worried.

"Um…" I tried to formulate my thoughts. "No. No, I'm
afraid everything isn't all right."

"Come in," she said, motioning for me to enter.

And for the second time in a minute, I was rendered
speechless.

I wasn't sure what I was expecting. I suppose I thought
the whole place might be a mishmash of wild colors—a sort
of frenzied boldness to it, much like Annie's outfits often
had. But her place wasn't like that at all. There were certainly bold colors, the most prominent being the lavender

walls, but they weren't exactly just lavender—more like a lavender ombré treatment, that slowly morphed into a plum color near the ceiling. The furniture was tasteful and understated. Mostly antiques, with each piece looking like it had come from a different corner of the globe. The artwork and photographs, the books, the rugs, the layers of pillows on every sitting surface—all of it added worldly flair and I got the impression Annie had collected every piece with love on what must have been decades of travels.

"Your place is amazing, Annie," I said, momentarily forgetting the horrible news I had come to tell her.

"Oh, thank you, dear. That's very kind of you to say." She pointed toward a chair at the heavy wooden table and went to the cupboard to get another cup for the coffee that was already on the table in what looked to be a Royal Albert coffeepot. I realized then that Annie hadn't actually been expecting company and that 5:00 a.m. coffee out of fine china must have been a daily occurrence for her. Annie Whitlock most certainly knew how to live every day to the fullest.

Annie sat and poured coffee into my cup and looked at me expectantly. Now that I was there, I was kind of frozen. I didn't want to just blurt it out, but I didn't know what you were supposed to say to lead up to these things either.

I took a deep breath. "I don't know exactly how to tell you this, but I went upstairs to the games room. I couldn't sleep and thought a puzzle might help calm my mind and make me tired and, well, I found someone."

Annie's head tilted, confused.

"Like someone who had…died." I wasn't sure why I felt the need to whisper the last word, but that's how it came out.

Annie gasped. "You're kidding! Are you all right, dear?" she asked, gently putting her hand on my arm.

"Yeah, yeah, I'm okay, but…it was…it was Erica Lawrence."

Annie's face went pale. "Erica? But I just saw her yesterday afternoon. She seemed perfectly fine."

I nodded. "Yeah, I don't think they really have any information yet, but I saw her myself. The police are up there now."

Annie stood like she was about to march right up there to see for herself.

"I'm not sure you want to go up there," I said. "As her good friend, maybe you want to remember her as she was the last time you saw her?"

Her eyes widened. "Oh no. Is it grisly? My god," she said, putting her hand to her chest, "was she murdered?"

I shook my head. "No, she looks okay, just—" I cleared my throat "—dead." I scrunched my face in a kind of "sorry, was that too harsh?" kind of way.

But Annie just nodded. "You're probably right." She sat back down heavily in her seat, picking up her cup, her hands shaking. "It's just so…terrible. Hasn't the poor woman been through enough? She was widowed already this year."

Right, the widow. That's the other reason I knew her. Shortly after I'd moved in, Annie filled me in on the poor woman, who had been recently widowed for a third time. I guess I hadn't really put two and two together that "the widow" and Erica were the same person.

The weird thing was that she wasn't even old—in her early fifties, maybe. And yeah, as a mystery writer, a youngish woman who'd already had three husbands die on her was basically just a plot waiting to happen, but it wasn't like they'd all happened in a short amount of time or anything. She'd lost her first husband after they'd only been married a year when he was called to duty overseas. Given that he was in the army, this wasn't completely unheard of. According to Annie, the second husband was hurt in an accident at work after almost twenty blissful years of marriage, and this last poor guy—Stan, if I remembered correctly—had simply had a heart attack. I couldn't imagine how much more one woman could take.

Of course, whenever I saw Erica around the building, which, admittedly wasn't very often, she seemed like one of the most optimistic people I knew. It was almost as if having lost so much, she had a greater appreciation of life. For the brief time I'd been acquainted with her, I'd come to admire the stories about her, and it made me doubly sad that the poor woman I'd seen upstairs was Erica.

I sat with Annie for another few minutes, but she was understandably quiet and I had run out of things to say, so we said our goodbyes and promised to keep one another posted if we'd heard any news. I trudged back to my apartment, realizing that even though I hadn't gotten a wink of sleep, morning had arrived.

Chapter Nine

After the 3:00 a.m. shock and subsequent comforting of Annie, the tired was marinating deep into my bones. It had taken a while for the police to deal with everything. I'd captured a few winks at seven and since I worked for myself, I could have technically slept in as late as I wanted, but my body had this fun thing it did where it refused to sleep past nine. I was also, inconveniently, not a napper. Or a great sleeper of any kind, really. Once I tried to stay awake all night before an early-morning flight from Amsterdam to Los Angeles thinking I'd be able to catch some z's on the plane and the eleven hours would pass in no time, but I was sorely mistaken. All I did was create an agitated Petra monster.

Cuppa Joe was my first stop. I needed that caffeine hit like Nancy needed Bess and George. Once I had my apple crisp macchiato double shot in hand, I actually needed a little rest. Or maybe I just didn't want to face that dreaded blinking cursor that awaited me in my apartment. Or, you know, that little matter of a dead body above me and all. Not that Erica's body was still there—at least I hoped it wasn't—but just knowing it had been there a few short hours ago was no small thing. To be honest, it was probably why even the little sleep I'd gotten between seven and nine had been somewhat restless.

I flopped into the nearest chair, ready to veg out until the coffee kicked in. Unfortunately, my gaze landed on the gym next door. The Luxe building was interesting—an apartment/retail combo building with the businesses on the bottom floor while the rest of the floors were apartments. The thing that wasn't so typical was that it housed the Fit Body Factory. Which I thought was an amazing perk when I first moved in—all tenants even received a free gym membership with their rent—but it kind of ended up being a constant source of guilt.

Turns out I was apparently in both a writing and a gym slump. And the gym might not have been so bad if it wasn't sandwiched between Cuppa Joe, where you could pick up all your favorite calorie-laden beverages, and Darkside Doughnuts, which made the most decadent pastry of all time. Seriously, this was not your average doughnut shop—this place was an artisanal sugar factory, churning out creations like the Chocolate Ganache Caramel Custard Toasted Hazelnut Toffee Bit Delight. While the names of their creations may have been a little on the nose, you couldn't really blame them when they sounded as good as that.

My Cuppa and Darkside time might have been a teensy bit more frequent than my time at Fit Body.

The real kicker was that the shops on the ground floor were divided only by glass so you could leisurely watch all those treadmill runners and stationary bikers while you were enjoying your delicious beverage or snack. And while it was aesthetically pleasing, what with all the sunlight the design allowed in, I'm not sure the architects anticipated who, exactly, the business tenants might end up being.

My gaze landed on Eliza, a woman who had moved into the building around the same time as I had. We'd chatted a few times in the elevator and she seemed friendly, but she definitely spent a lot more time at Fit Body than at the Cuppa Joe or Darkside. Watching her on the elliptical, it looked like she was on a mission.

Sadly, the only mission I had was to write my next book and, well…that was best done sitting at my desk. Or lounging in my bed with my laptop.

Of course, there's nothing wrong with being a little softer around the edges, but a person who dedicated that much time to exercise just somehow seemed…more focused. Like she really had her shit together. And yeah, I'd had some wins and lucky breaks in my day, but my motivation seemed to be a little less than optimal lately.

Conversations mingled with the bakery smells as I sat. I'd gotten good at tuning out the chatter, having spent so much time writing in coffee shops, but a few words caught my attention. *Investigation. Body. Suicide.* Clearly the gossip mill had been running on overtime because I had seen Erica and it did not look like a suicide to me. And I mean, I guess I don't really know what every kind of suicide might look like, but the woman looked perfectly fine. You know, except the being-dead part.

I stayed for another twenty minutes or so, kind of zoning out, mostly wondering if I'd ever be able to get another book finished, or if I was going to have to figure out something else to do with my life. I had, after all, written almost the entirety of my first book, *Desperately Seeking Fusion*—a sort of cozy mystery/romance hybrid set mostly in a laboratory—while I was killing time at the old office job. I mean, what did they expect me to do when sorting the mail and filing only took me four hours and the workday was eight? The computer was just sitting there and if I was typing all the time, at least I looked like I was busy.

Honestly, most of my coworkers thought I was the hardest worker they'd ever had in the receptionist position. Hmm… maybe that's where my motivation came from. Did I need to find a way to limit my time so that I'd *have* to write the next book within a certain window? I sat up straighter for a moment, almost ready to start scrolling the want ads when I remembered how much I hated that soul-sucking horror of an office and promptly relaxed back into my seat.

No. I would try absolutely everything else before I would ever go down that road again. On the plus side, that dreaded thought seemed to actually light a fire under my butt. I got up to head straight to my computer, vowing to write something—anything—before the day was done. I was in so much of a hurry, in fact, that as I flew out the coffee shop, I plowed right into a poor unsuspecting person on their way in. A person who was so lightweight that I nearly knocked her right down to the ground.

"Oh my lord, I am so sorry, Eliza," I said, as I grasped on to the Burberry coat of my building-mate.

Being so agile, Eliza was able to steady herself quickly and hadn't really been in any danger of going down. "Whoa there, linebacker," she said, but at least she had a smile on her face.

"Ha-ha, right, linebacker. That's a good one," I said, really hoping she meant because of the tackle and not due to any size discrepancy there might have been between us.

"What's got you all in a tizzy?" Eliza asked.

I tilted my head. Was I in a tizzy? I kind of thought I had been more in a burst of inspiration, but I suppose it may have been coming off a little tizzy-like. Especially considering the woman before me was immaculately put together in her tailored coat, slim-fit pants, hair looking like she had just gotten a salon blowout—how is that even possible when I saw her fifteen minutes ago in a ponytail on that elliptical?—and looking like she just waltzed out of a style blog. I, on the other hand, had all morning to get myself presentable yet I was gracing the coffee shop with my usual leggings and oversize hoodie combo. At least I'd put shoes on instead of slippers this time.

"Oh, um, nothing really. I'm so sorry. I just had a bolt of inspiration about the book I'm writing," I said, not mentioning that I hadn't actually started writing it. "I just wanted to get it down before it flew out of my head."

I also didn't mention that it wasn't really an idea as much as it was a desperate urge not to have to re-enter the corporate world (aka the daily assassination of joy) again, but I'm sure Eliza didn't really care about the details.

"Amazing!" Eliza said, and I wasn't sure if she really thought it was amazing or if she was just humoring me. "It's so great that you have your books. Your confidence is wonderful—you don't feel like you have to impress everybody all the time." She glanced at my outfit then kept right on rolling. "Unfortunately, I chose the professional path. Well, for as long as I have to, anyway," she said, rolling her eyes like she wondered if she had gone the wrong route—

except I could totally tell she didn't actually think she had taken the wrong route. In fact, it sort of seemed like she was thinking that I had taken the wrong route. "Honestly, I envy you. Content with making your own money, such as it is. Right now, I'm dedicating everything to making sure I have enough time to work on myself so I can find the man that will ensure my financial security."

I blinked. "I'm surprised to hear a woman say that sort of thing in this day and age, to be honest."

"I know," she said, "we've really lost our traditional values. Anyway, I better not keep you—you have important writing to do," she said with a smile and a little scrunch of her nose.

"Um," I said. I really wanted to respond with something along the lines of "tradition is pretty much just peer pressure from dead people" but I wasn't sure that would go over well. "Okay, I'll see you arou—"

"Wait," Eliza said, her eyes getting huge. "Did you hear about the death in the building?"

I looked around a little self-consciously, considering the volume of Eliza's inquiry. If anyone in the coffee shop—and probably in Fit Body Factory too—hadn't known about Erica before, they probably did now. Although no one really seemed to pay much attention—most of the patrons of Cuppa Joe had headphones in while they worked…rather productively, I noticed.

"Oh yeah, it's so sad," I said, not particularly wanting to rehash all the details.

"Can you believe anyone would be so selfish? Well, I guess you can hardly blame her, being a widow and all. If I had to suddenly make my own way in this world after being taken care of, I'd want to off myself too. Honestly, I can't wait until I find my forever man and can just sit back and relax."

"Um…" was all I could seem to muster, trying to work out how she could so quickly redirect the topic of a tragic possible suicide straight back to her, before she spoke again.

"Anyway, good luck with the writing." With that she headed to the counter and ordered her skinny hazelnut iced macchiato with an extra shot, light ice, no whip.

When I got back to my floor, Annie and Ryan were talking in the hallway just outside my apartment. Well, just outside Ryan's apartment, I supposed.

"Oh, Petra," Annie said, "I'm still just beside myself with all that has been going on."

I glanced at Ryan, then quickly glanced away. She had no idea.

Annie turned to Ryan, whispering. "It's the strangest thing," she said. "The policemen upstairs, they—I don't know—they seem to have it all wrong."

"What do you mean?" Ryan asked.

"Well," Annie continued, "Ashton from 1805 said he overheard them talking about a suicide note, but there's just no way that Erica would do something like that."

Ryan's eyebrows rose. "Well, unfortunately you can't always tell with these things," he said.

But Annie cut him off right there. "No. I would know. I talked to Erica every day. She was happy."

"Someone looking happy doesn't always mean—"

"I know what you're going to say and I'm going to stop you right there," Annie said, putting a hand up rather close to his face. "She was excited to be starting a new chapter in her life. She had just started a new job and was loving it."

Ryan cleared his throat and rubbed the back of his neck. I could tell he wanted to say something, but probably realized it would be fruitless to argue with Annie. "Well, I'll have to take your word for that."

Annie nodded once like that was the end of the matter. I could tell Ryan wasn't quite as convinced as Annie though.

"Well, I guess I should, uh…" He pointed toward his apartment, taking a step backward toward the safety of it.

"Wait, Ryan. Before you go," Annie said, her tune suddenly changing. "Could I just ask you a teensy favor?"

Ryan swallowed, obviously scared to ask what the favor might be. "Um, sure."

"I know you have connections with the police, and I was just wondering if you could maybe go up there and see what they have to say?" She smiled and batted her eyes. And she didn't look weird doing it either. I mean, what I wouldn't give to be a woman who could literally bat her eyes at someone and not look like she was having some sort of ocular episode.

I glanced at my apartment door, wondering how awkward it would be if I just went inside. Not that I didn't enjoy the way the taut little micromuscles fired all the way up Ryan's shoulders, neck and jaw as he squirmed under Annie's questions.

"Oh, I don't think they'd want me snooping around in their investigation," Ryan said.

But Annie was having none of it. "I just know Erica wouldn't have done anything to hurt herself," she said, her voice starting to shake. "I knew her better than most people did."

If there was anyone Erica might have trusted with her problems, it probably would have been Annie. I mean, I spent at least a few minutes every day with Annie, and I would bet Erica did as well. Ryan must have sensed how much she meant to Annie too. Annie was nothing if not positive at all times—honestly, she was the most optimistic person I had ever met—and to see her upset was frankly, well…upsetting.

He let out an audible and resigned sigh. "Um, I suppose I could see if there's anyone I know up there," he said, looking like it was actually the last thing he wanted to do, but Annie had obviously found a soft spot in his heart too. "Just let me grab my credentials," he said, ducking back into his apartment.

Annie nodded, then turned to me. "I just can't believe they're even suggesting that Erica could do this."

I knew how she felt. I'd had a friend years ago take her own life and no one had seen it coming. It took me a long time to accept the truth. "You knew her a lot better than I did," I said, "but I think we have to at least give this theory some consideration."

Annie looked at me in a way I wouldn't have thought she was capable of. She was so very "live and let live"— accepting and championing everyone's choices, no matter how differently she might have done things—but in that moment she looked…disappointed in me.

But she softened and let out a long sigh. "Look, I know that you can't always tell about these things. That sometimes the people who appear happiest are the ones suffering the most. And given the fact that she's just lost Stan and every-thing, I get why the police think the things they do. But I know Erica. This just doesn't feel like her."

I nodded. I never wanted to be on the receiving end of that look ever again, but still, I had to say something. "Mental health issues don't always look the way we think they should look."

Annie nodded. "Of course, you're right, but I'm still not convinced. I'm not sure anything could convince me."

I nodded back. "Okay then. You knew her the best. I will take your word for it."

"Thank you, dear. Thank you. That means a lot. I just… She was starting that new job and everything. She was excited for the future."

"Of course. Whatever you need from me, just let me know."

Ryan's door opened and he stepped out. "I'll be back shortly, ladies," he said, giving us a nod and heading toward the elevator.

"Do you want some tea or something?" I asked Annie. "We can keep the door open so we can hear when Ryan gets back."

"All right," Annie said, though she looked tired.

But I knew there was no way she was heading back to her apartment before hearing what Ryan had to say. Even then, I was sure poor Annie wasn't getting any sleep anytime soon. I'd just poured the water into the blueberry tea when the elevator dinged. It was Ryan returning.

Annie and I rushed to intercept him as he made his way back.

"Well?" Annie asked, almost breathless.

"I'm sorry, Annie," Ryan said. "It looks like your friend was more troubled than you realized. They're ruling it an open-and-shut case of suicide. She overdosed on her own prescription sleeping pills."

Chapter Ten

Even after the coffee that morning, and the tea with Annie, I still needed to go down to Cuppa Joe for a midafternoon pick-me-up. And after the night I'd had, I figured a lavender sprinkle doughnut from Darkside couldn't hurt either.

On my way back up, I waved at the daytime security person, Hazel—she was kind of my favorite with her coiffed hair and broad shoulders that hinted at a gym regimen rivaling that of a professional bodybuilder even though I had never seen her over at Fit Body Factory. I suspected she had a full gym setup at her house instead, since it seemed like her workouts must have been more like a lifestyle than a hobby.

Hazel waved back with a bored expression, though I didn't take any offense since she was currently being regaled by Lessie Webster, the kid from 412 whose parents apparently thought having security in the building meant a full-time babysitter. The kid was always in the lobby bugging whoever was behind the desk. Frankly, Hazel was a superstar for putting up with it.

I rode the elevator upstairs with a woman who looked a bit like a detective in her trench coat and dead-faced lack of reaction to the smile I gave her as she entered. My suspicions were confirmed as she wheeled around to check the floor buttons with her hand on her hip, efficiently revealing her police badge. I got the feeling she'd mastered the move a long time ago and did it almost without thinking anymore. I assumed she'd be going to the floor above mine, but she didn't press floor twenty-three, and when the elevator arrived on twenty-two, she barged out and made her way down the hall.

I followed slowly behind.

She stopped in front of Ryan's place and knocked, putting more than a little oomph behind it.

Ryan opened the door in jeans and a T-shirt that looked like it was custom designed to fit his generous biceps.

"Hey, Jess," he said. "What's up?"

He glanced my way. After the little run-ins from the previous nights, I expected him to glare at me or something to let me know he was still angry, but strangely, he looked a little uncomfortable, his eyes darting between Jess and me, me and Jess.

I wondered what it meant that he was on a first-name basis with the detective. The way she looked at him—like he was something she'd like to get into her handcuffs, and not in the "you're under arrest" kind of way—made me wonder just how close they were.

I got close to my door and Ryan gave me a little nod. It wasn't a friendly nod, just…neutral. I smiled and raised my hand, almost a wave, but not quite, since I couldn't really do anything that wasn't incredibly awkward around the guy.

Jess, of course, didn't bother to acknowledge my presence as I fished in my hoodie pockets for my keys.

"So we're off," Jess said. "Again, it was open-and-shut so no need to worry, but if there's anything you need…"

I had angled myself so I could just barely see the two of them out of the corner of my eye.

Jess leaned on the door frame provocatively. "You have my number."

Ryan cleared his throat. "That I do," he said, and shifted his door an inch or two, almost as if he wanted to close it.

So. Perhaps things weren't as close between Detective Jess and Ryan as the detective had hoped.

"I guess I'll see you around," she said, turning to leave, though she looked back for several steps as she sauntered down the hall.

I wasn't quite sure how she managed it, to be honest. If I had tried to walk with my head turned that way, there was a ninety-eight percent chance I would have ambled right into a wall.

I put my hand in my pocket to actually find my keys this time and my stomach sank. Where the hell were they? I frantically fumbled in there with both hands, no doubt with a look of panic plastered all over me.

"Uh, they're tucked under your arm."

I'd almost forgotten Ryan was still standing there.

"What?" I said, somewhat distracted by *The Mystery of the Missing Keys*, my mind already whirring over where I could have left them, mentally going through the entire route I had taken down to Cuppa Joe. Had I stopped at the mailbox and set them down?

"Your keys. They're tucked under your elbow there," he said, with that smirk solidly planted on his face.

"Heh-heh," I said, smiling, but not quite able to look him

in the eye. I grabbed the keys and sort of held them in the air. "Forgot I put them there for safekeeping."

I turned and unlocked my door as quickly as I could, diving into my apartment. I'm sure I heard a little chuckle coming from the hallway.

So damned awkward.

I'd just gotten settled in my bed with my laptop on my lap, about to type my first word (JK—I'd been looking up cute outfits on Pinterest for the past half hour) when a knock came at the door. I was happy for the distraction. You know, from my distraction.

"Oh, Petra," Annie said, looking relieved that I opened the door. "I knew you'd be the one I could count on to be home."

I wasn't quite sure how to take that, but Annie kept going so I didn't have to think about it for too long.

"I just can't stop thinking about Erica. She was in the prime of her life and starting this new relationship and everything. I just… I can't stop thinking about how none of this makes any sense."

"Erica was in a new relationship?" I asked. "Didn't her husband just die a few months ago?"

"It was seven months ago, but yes, Erica is one of those relationship people. She really loves sharing her life with a partner."

I nodded. The whole thing seemed to be a bit quick, but who was I to know? Maybe that was her way of grieving, by finding a way to fill that void of despair. It wasn't like the memories of her former husband were going anywhere just because she was dating someone new. It was probably nice to feel something, anything, besides grief.

"So anyway, I want to go have a little look-see in the games room where it all took place. Maybe we can spot something the police have missed."

She said it with such seriousness that I could hardly break it to Annie that the police were professionals, and we were, um, not. As if I had any right to that opinion, given my latest escapades.

"What do you think we might find?"

Annie sighed. "I know it's a long shot, but I want to at least get a feel for the room. See if there are any lingering... vibes or, I don't know, something. But I can't quite bring myself to go up there alone," she finished, her tone becoming more desperate.

"Of course, Annie. Of course I'll go with you."

What else was one supposed to say to a woman beside herself with grief? I tried not to think about the fact that if she truly didn't think Erica had done this, then what did that imply? That someone had done it to her? I glanced up at the ceiling, decidedly uncomfortable with *that* scenario, since it happened right upstairs and everything.

Still, I threw on the first shoes I could find—my unicorn slippers—and followed Annie to the elevator, secretly congratulating myself on being the kind of person who has those little sly smile moments of "oh the things I do for my friends."

As we made our way toward the games room, my stomach began to churn. Whether this was Erica's doing or not, the fact still remained that a body had been in there not so long ago—a visual I'd been working quite diligently to shove into the most secluded cubbyhole of my brain.

For being the one who was most upset, Annie definitely

had more courage than me, squaring her shoulders and striding right in without hesitation. I, on the other hand, stopped at the doorway and peeked before going any farther. I couldn't afford the nightmares if it looked like anything violent had taken place in there. The irony that I was a mystery writer didn't escape me.

I opened one eye slowly, then the other. Because the thing was, the games room looked exactly like it did before. No crime scene tape, no blood, no nothing besides a few random games stacked on the window seat and a half-finished jigsaw puzzle depicting what would have been a clock tower if anyone ever decided to finish it.

"Hey," a perky voice said, nearly vacating my soul from my body.

Annie jumped even more violently as someone stepped out from behind a small alcove.

"Jesus, Eliza, you scared the hell out of us," I said, clutching my chest.

"Good lord, dear. Way to make an entrance," Annie said, closing her eyes and letting out a long whoosh of breath to try to calm her nerves.

"Sorry, didn't mean to scare you," she said. "And technically you were the ones who made the entrance. I was just standing here."

Annie was already having a thorough look around, getting up close and peering at things, bending over the puzzle, then stepping back and peering into the massive bookshelf.

"What are you looking for?" Eliza asked.

"I'm not sure, just something that might be out of place, I suppose," Annie answered.

"Yeah, I guess I'm just being nosy too," Eliza said. "I

wanted to… I don't know. Maybe I thought I could make myself feel better by coming up here. It's a little discombob-ulating having a dead person in the building, you know?"

I nodded, though I couldn't help but think it was a little insensitive of her to essentially be calling us nosy. Annie had been Erica's good friend, after all. We were hoping to find out what had been going on in Erica's mind…trying to figure out what really happened.

"Anyway, the room seems the same as always, I guess." Eliza shrugged as she headed toward the door. "See you guys around."

"Yeah, see ya," I said, glancing at Annie, who didn't say a thing.

In fact, she seemed to be aggressively trying to ignore Eliza altogether, which was very off-brand for Annie. Maybe I wasn't the only one who Eliza rubbed the wrong way.

Unsure what else to do, I started copying Annie. I hadn't really spent any time in the games room, so I had no idea what was normal and what was out of place. Sure, if there had been a gun on the floor or a red handprint like in *The Secret of the Scarlet Hand* or something, I might have picked up on it, but the games room was just a games room, pep-pered with tables and chairs and lined with shelves of books and games. Add the fact that everyone in the building had access and probably moved things around all the time, and I couldn't really see how it was possible to find a clue.

"Hey, ladies." Jamieson, another tenant from the build-ing, popped his head in.

Every time I saw this guy, I tried not to think of the phrase *celibate monkfish*, but dude just gave off vibes. I think Annie had said he was from the twelfth floor—she mostly talked in floors—and that he was lonely, always wandering the building and looking for people to talk to. I got the feeling he was one of those people who had never really found his place in life and now, nearing fifty, he was more socially awkward than ever. I couldn't help but wonder if I was perhaps witnessing my future, which in turn prompted me to leave my body for the briefest of moments, though I recovered quickly, well acquainted with fun little flashes of existential distress.

"Oh, hi, Jamieson," Annie said, still distracted.

But Jamieson was having none of it. He was looking for someone to talk to and we were ripe for the picking. "Wild what happened, hey?"

I nodded solemnly.

In the best of times, I can be a bit socially awkward, but put me in front of another potentially awkward person and it was like I lost all concept of what social interaction was supposed to look like.

It's why I loved Annie so much. She made everything look easy—like it was no big deal. I swear, she could fall down, knock out a tooth, have blood all over the front of her shirt and still be the most confident person in the room. She just had this "life is an incredible adventure" thing going on, no matter what. I'd recently decided I'd like to be Annie when I grew up—if and when that actually happened. Of course, I'd probably have to learn to not feel like a total imposter all the time if I were ever to get myself even remotely close to Annie's realm of existence.

Jamieson sidled up next to me in that way that people who aren't in the know about personal space sometimes do. "You're the writer, right? Petra something?"

He was tall, sort of slouching over me with his questionable amount of deodorant body spray and aura of desperation.

"Yup, Petra Jackson," I said, thinking a handshake would be the most obvious thing to do, but with the way he was standing directly beside me, as if we were watching a play or sporting event or something together, I decided against it.

"Jackson, right," he said, as if he should have known, even though the two of us had never formally met. "Anyway, that's cool—you being a writer and all. We should get together sometime. You *need* to hear my life story— maybe if you're lucky I'll even let you write about it." He winked. Winked!

Sadly, this was something I got all the time. People often thought the hard part about writing was coming up with the ideas. And yeah, given my current bout of writer's block, the ideas weren't exactly flowing, but honestly, ideas were as plentiful as the oxygen in the air. The actual sitting down and writing was the hard part—but no matter how much you tried to tell someone that, they never seemed to believe it. Also, everyone thinks their life is overwhelmingly riveting, and well, let's just say everyone can't be the exception. I stuck with the tried-and-true "um, I'm a fiction writer."

"Well, even fiction writers base their material on living people, right?"

"Maybe," I said, though he didn't seem to be listening to me anymore. His focus was turned to what Annie was doing, which was standing with her hands on her hips and looking frustrated.

"Like I was about to say," Jamieson said, taking a blessed

step toward Annie. "It's just so sad the way Erica lost faith like that."

Annie's expression annoyified (did I mention that, as a writer, I was allowed to make words up when I couldn't find one to fit just right?). But she was still too nice a person to say anything, though I did hear her sigh audibly—something I had never witnessed from her before.

"I guess it just goes to show that when you're doing something as boring as a jigsaw puzzle, you have too much time to think about all the terrible things in life."

Annie's gaze shot up to meet his then, even more annoyified.

I couldn't really blame her. I liked puzzles too. I found them to be the opposite of too much time to think. For me they were a way to relax, almost meditative.

But then Annie said something entirely unexpected. "Erica was definitely not the one doing this puzzle." And it was super weird, because she almost sounded angry about it.

"She most definitely was. I saw it with my own eyes," Jamieson replied, almost as if he couldn't believe anyone would question him.

Annie shook her head. "Erica didn't do puzzles."

Jamieson shrugged. "She was working on this very one just yesterday before…" He trailed off, miraculously reading the room and knowing he didn't have to finish that thought.

"I guess your eyes must have been mistaken," Annie said, standing her ground. "Erica hated puzzles, and solitaire, and anything else that was a one-person activity. She could never see the point in doing something that wasn't a social activity. People were her passion, and she believed connection to be the single most important thing in this world."

"Coulda fooled me last night," Jamieson said, sort of under his breath.

"What's that supposed to mean?" Annie asked.

Jamieson raised his eyebrows. "I tried to come in here last night and talk to her while she was *doing her puzzle*," he said, giving Annie a significant look. "But it was like she couldn't wait to get rid of me," he said.

What a shocker, I thought, though I didn't say it out loud.

"That does not sound like Erica at all," Annie said.

"I know. That's why it was so strange," Jamieson said. "She always had time for me before, but last night was... weird. It was almost like she was afraid to even have me in the room."

"Wait, was there someone else in here with her?"

He shook his head. "Nope, she was just all by herself doing her puzzle. She made it quite clear that she did not want any company."

Annie shook her head like she was dismissing everything Jamieson was saying. The only problem was the one thing I knew about Jamieson—the thing that Annie herself was always saying got him in trouble—was his almost compulsive need to tell the truth.

Annie stormed out of the room, not wanting to hear another word. I rushed after her since the only reason I was even there was to support her—not that I'd done a great job of that. Also, I did not particularly want to be alone with Jamieson.

"Annie, it's okay," I said, rushing to catch up. "Maybe he's mistaking her for someone else or something." I knew better than to argue the point that maybe Erica was, in fact, doing a jigsaw puzzle even if she wasn't fond of them. To be honest, it didn't seem like that big of a deal if someone just decided they wanted to puzzle one day.

She looked at me and stopped just short of rolling her eyes. "You know as well as I do that Jamieson doesn't lie."

"I know but…well, maybe Erica just changed her mind about puzzles or something." I held my breath, waiting for the retaliation, but it never came.

"I honestly don't know what's going on here, Petra, but there is one thing I know for sure."

"What?"

"Something smells fishy in the games room."

Chapter Eleven

When I got back to my apartment that evening, there was a small, beautifully wrapped parcel sitting at my door. Which was weird, since I lived in a secure building. But it was like, really pretty wrapping, so without giving it much thought I tore into it, incredibly curious to see what was inside.

Chocolates. Assorted truffle chocolates, to be exact, which was even more weird, because they were my absolute favorite. But…

…why would someone leave a box of chocolates at my door? Although perhaps *how* might have been the more pertinent question. Unless it was someone from inside the building, of course.

I quickly tore open the card, which said, simply, "From your anonymous admirer."

I swallowed.

Probably it was Annie, I thought. She was the exact kind of thoughtful that would do something like this even when she was clearly hurting more than the rest of us. Of course, it could be…

I glanced at the door across the hall. No, I thought, shaking the idea out of my head. The dude pretty much hated me, and besides, he really didn't seem to be the "I leave snacks surreptitiously at people's doors" sort.

It could be as simple as a fan who'd read my book and wanted to give me something. For all I knew, my publisher could have forwarded it over. Whatever the case, I eased into my apartment already tearing into my first smooth, glorious truffle, not giving it a second thought.

"THANKS FOR COMING," I said, opening the door for Brandt the following day.

He had a rolling suitcase in tow.

"How could I pass up an opportunity to do a full identity makeover?" he said, rather out of character with his giddiness.

Brandt was nothing if not a genius with makeup, and his favorite thing to do with his art was to make a person look entirely different. I didn't exactly call it a disguise when I'd called him—that would have raised too many questions— but I told him I felt like being somebody else for a day and he totally bought it. I mean, who doesn't want to be someone else every now and again? It didn't hurt that I told him he could do whatever he wanted either, within reason, of course. I still wanted to look like a regular woman, but special effects weren't really his thing anyway. He was a more of a "purist" with his craft, as he liked to say.

"I just want to look normal," I explained. "But maybe a little on the seedy or dangerous side. Like maybe I haven't been taking all that great care of myself."

Brandt crinkled his forehead. "What is this for again?" he asked.

Obviously, I hadn't actually told him why I needed the

disguise, uh, makeover. He'd been so excited to come over and get started, he never asked. I'd never met a person so passionate about makeup as my burly co–best friend.

But that was Brandt.

"Um, it's just for this play a writer friend of mine is doing. She wanted to have some extras that looked the part, but she can't really afford to pay a professional makeup artist. And I mean, you're probably too expensive, but if she ends up liking what you do, maybe there would be more in the budget for next time."

He nodded. I knew he didn't care that he wasn't getting paid because it was me, but still, I hoped he'd buy the story.

"What friend is this?"

God, why was he asking so many questions? Usually he couldn't care less about details.

"Becky," I said, quickly pulling a name out of my ass. "You know, from that Portraiture in Oil class I took a while back?"

"Oh yeah, Becky. Right," he said, already digging into his suitcase of goodies.

I suspected he often had to pretend he remembered stuff that he didn't, since he had a habit of not actually paying attention to the conversations he was around for.

Thankfully that was the end of the grilling since once he began, his focus was incredible. An hour later and the magic was complete.

I was an entirely different person, complete with a disturbing nail polish job—light bluish lavender with black tips—that made me look a bit corpsey.

"Wow," I said, as he held a mirror for me to get a look.

"Um, my friend is going to be so impressed and really excited, I think."

"Who, Becky?" Brandt asked.

"Right, yeah. Becky." Cripes, why are names of fake friends so hard to remember?

"Oh, I'm not done yet," he said, turning the suitcase around and unzipping a compartment I didn't even know existed.

He pulled several fake hairpieces out.

"I'm not sure a wig is entirely necessary," I said. "I mean, I'm supposed to look less healthy, not more with some high-shine hair."

He scoffed. "Ye of little faith," he said, pulling a large strand of clip-in extensions from the bunch.

He was already digging into my hair before I could protest, so I just went with it. Thankfully it wasn't a real play, and I wasn't on a time limit, or it might have been a complete disaster. But for the thing I was actually working on, the later I showed up, the better, probably.

He held the mirror up again ten minutes later and I'd been incredibly shortsighted to have questioned him. What he'd done to my hair was an appalling miracle. Usually, my hair was pretty healthy-looking, and a rather generic shade of brown, which I always thought was good since I liked to blend in, but now it had these straggly pieces of slightly lighter and redder throughout, making it not only look like I had a supercheap haircut, but also like I had done some horrible home-color hack job on it too.

It was perfect.

"Brandt, this is really great. Thank you so much."

"You are more than welcome," he said. "Now I just need

to get a picture for my portfolio," he said, whipping out his phone.

I wasn't entirely sure it was a good idea to get this look on record, both because I was supposed to be in disguise, and because it was certainly not the best I had ever looked. Brandt had made me gaunt and pale with darkish circles under my eyes as though I hadn't slept in about three weeks. I was a magnificent disaster.

But I figured helping with his portfolio was the least I could do after he just spent all that time working on me for free.

"Damn, we forgot to get a before picture. Next time I come over, can you put that shirt back on and get one taken? No one will know it was taken on a totally different day."

I laughed. "Yeah, sure."

"Great," he said, packing everything back up.

I loved watching him work. There was a lightness...an excitement to him that wasn't normally there. I couldn't help but wonder, since his work crew got to see him in this giddy state all the time, whether they knew him as a totally different person from the one Vic and I got to see. Mr. Vivacious Effervescence Who Wows You with His Enchanting Charm and Bubbling Personality vs. the He Who Shall React in a Completely Irrational Manner if You Deign to Interrupt His Meal for Any Reason Even If You Are Trying to Save His Life (or Cranky Pants for short) that we got to encounter on the daily.

We never could figure out how he managed to beguile so many women, and I suddenly couldn't wait to tell Vic my theory of *The Strange Case of Dr. Asshole and Mr. Charisma*.

After Brandt left, I read a chapter of *The Whispering*

Statue to help get into the dark space I would need to be in for the character I was about to play. Was it completely ridiculous to think I had any chance of pulling this off? I mean, for a person obsessed with mystery and gore, I was about the most boring person anyone was apt to find. Seriously, for someone who made my living as an artist, whenever I got around real artists—or pretty much anyone with an interesting personality really—I felt about as blah and vanilla as a tub of plain ice cream.

But then I caught another glimpse of myself in the mirror as I searched my closet for something to wear and it gave me an extra boost of confidence. Brandt really was a genius—I was pretty much unrecognizable. If someone who wasn't in my inner circle had seen me walking down the street this morning and then again this evening, they would never in a million years imagine me to be the same person.

I miraculously found something to wear buried deep in my closet. My wardrobe tended to be on the nonflashy side, kind of like the rest of me, so the look I would need wasn't particularly in my wheelhouse. I decided to use my shapewear as a skirt, which was basically a supertight slip designed to hold everything in instead of what it was meant for—underwear. It was black, so you couldn't really tell it wasn't supposed to be a skirt, other than the fact it was skintight and way too damned short.

Once I had the outfit on, the character I was playing came more to life. I was completely and utterly self-conscious due to the skimpy nature of the clothes, but it was certain now; no one in the world, even those closest to me, was ever going to recognize me.

Not that I planned on running into anyone I knew or anything, but still, anonymity was always a good thing when one was about to embark on a dangerous journey into a crime ring. I mean, I assumed it was a crime ring, anyway. It's not like I had a whole lot of experience with these kinds of things.

The realization that this might be a really poor decision charged through my mind again, but I quickly shoved it right back out. I just had to own the character and not even think about my real life. I was a girl who would do anything for her next fix. That's it, that's all.

I grabbed a faux-fur vest from an old Halloween costume...then decided against it. The girls last night had been dressed overtly sexy, but not as ridiculous caricatures. They looked like normal girls out clubbing or something. Other than the slightly unhealthy aura about them, of course.

I was finally ready, and it was time. I put on some highish wedges, but not so high that I was uncomfortable. I didn't want them to hinder my running if the night came to that. Safety first, right? My feet still hurt a bit from walking with Ryan the other night, but I was pretty confident that the adrenaline was going to kick in right about the time I reached the building, so I decided not to worry about it.

I left my apartment puzzling out the details of my character description.

A twentysomething girl, yearning for a taste of something more, leaving her hometown of Channing's Cross (a town brimming with blow-up lawn decorations for every holiday/season/mundane moment) the day after graduation, hungry for all that life had to offer. Joyful and wide-eyed, she wished for a life big enough to match her dreams. But once she had gotten to the big city, something was missing.

A new romance? Career? Lipstick? But in the end, it was the sweet acceptance of the wrong crowd and the floating bliss of drugs that she found. And the never-ending chase for that first taste, that first high, was the only thing that kept her going…

I glanced up, nearing my destination way sooner than I was quite ready for. I figured I'd have the whole walk over to psych myself up, except I got lost in my characterization and, as I neared, I felt very far from ready.

But, like they taught me in the acting class, I took a deep breath and went for it. Three girls loitered outside the building, but none of them were the same ones as the other night, which was good. I didn't think they would recognize me, but I didn't need to be worried about what-ifs either— I had enough chaos and freaking out going on in my mind as it was.

The girls weren't much for chatting and it seemed like none of them really even knew each other so they weren't talking. One by one they were taken inside by the same man I'd seen last night. I'd been worried there was some kind of appointment needed or something, but no one seemed alarmed or even acknowledged that there was an extra girl, so I just stood there and made as little impression as I could.

Some time later, another girl showed up and stood behind me and I marveled that for as weird a situation as this was, it was all very civilized. Everyone was waiting their turn and being very respectful.

I was at the front of the line and nearly peeing myself waiting to see what was going to happen. Twice I almost lost my nerve, ready to take off, but I forced myself to stay, channeling the anxious feeling in my gut into the character I was playing. I imagined that a person in need of a fix would be a little fidgety and whatnot, so that's what I did.

Then the man came. He looked me up and down, his expression completely blank, and took my elbow the way he had done with each of the girls ahead of me. I suddenly realized—too late—that none of the girls who'd gone into the building had come back out. My stomach started to churn. How had I not realized something so significant until the very second it was too late to do anything about it?

Good lord, this detective stuff was a whole different ball game in real life than it was in old-timey sleuth books. Nancy always seemed to have nerves of steel and never got herself into situations she couldn't get out of. Well, she did, but she always found a way out because she was so resourceful.

Surely I was as resourceful as a teenager from the 1930s, given the fact that I had the benefit of having consumed all the mystery books and crime shows, right?

The stairwell was dark but the man at my elbow wasn't rough in the slightest, which put my mind at ease slightly. Maybe these weren't such bad guys after all.

I was led into the room. The same two men sat at the table once again.

"Name?" one of them asked.

"Um…" For some reason I hadn't expected that. How did I not figure that out in my whole character exercise?! "Um, Becky," I answered.

"Okay, Becky, so you're looking to do an exchange of goods and services, correct?"

I couldn't help but think this all seemed rather business-like. Which was somewhat reassuring. "Um, yes."

"Okay, please take off your jacket and turn around for us."

This part didn't feel quite as businesslike. I took off my jacket and turned slowly but didn't do any ridiculous dance moves like the one girl had the other night.

"Okay, fine," he said, in a matter-of-fact way. "You'll do."

I tried to look relieved, only guessing that's what someone in the situation would feel. "Okay," was all I could spit out.

The man asking the questions nodded to the man who had led me in, and he took my elbow again, leading me to another room in the back.

Which turned out to be a bedroom.

My mouth dropped open as I saw other women, the ones I'd been standing with outside, draped around the room, all seemingly passed out.

Before I could register what might be going on, I felt a pinch in my upper arm and the room began to blur.

Chapter Twelve

I knew nothing.

I had no idea where I was. No idea when it was, and only the faintest recollection of how I had gotten the worst head-ache of my life. Fear slithered through me as things started coming back slowly. Brandt doing my makeup. The hair extensions. Standing outside the building.

Ryan's case. I spent a moment savoring the thought of Ryan. I needed to focus my mind on something good for a second…the way he walked, the way he grinned all crooked and adorable. The way he told me to mind my own business.

Damn.

I was beginning to suspect that I maybe should have lis-tened.

The room was dark, with a faint red glow to it. There were red curtains in the room. Was the sun trying to fight its way through the curtains? Could I have been out all night and the sun was already shining?

My mind shot to the worst-case scenario. If something unthinkable happened to me, not a soul in my life had any idea where I was. My god, hadn't I been through this al-ready with the walk the other night? I hadn't left a note, a clue, nothing. Some kind of Nancy fan I was supposed to be. If I never came home, no one would ever know what happened to me. Who would ever imagine I was out investigating some random criminal case? Why would I?

I would just…disappear.

I stayed as still as possible, afraid to make any sudden movements. One, I didn't want to draw attention to myself in case someone was watching, and two, I honestly wasn't sure if I might be injured. And maybe three, because I was afraid it would make my head hurt even worse than it already did. Which seemed impossible, but I wasn't particularly anxious to find out.

It hurt a little to even move my eyes, but I needed to get a sense of what was happening. What I was up against.

Shapes started to form in the blood-colored shadows. A table and one chair in the corner and a bed against the far wall, like a hotel room. It was something of a dump and smelled like it hadn't been cleaned since weekly musical sitcoms had been the hot new thing.

I let out a shaky breath. Two other people shared the room with me—one on the bed and one in the other chair. I could only assume they were the same women I'd seen just before my world went dark. Strange that I would come to first, since they'd obviously been knocked out before I had, but maybe that was because I didn't have any drugs in my system to begin with. I wondered if they were sleeping it off nicely in their haze instead of the excruciating hammering that was gracing me with its presence.

I was somewhat distressed to discover I was duct-taped to a chair. Memories continued slowly sifting back to me. There had been another couple girls behind me in line.

Where were they? Were there other rooms in this place where more women were kept?

I wished I knew how long I'd been out. I just felt so discombobulated. Knowing what time it was might help me find my bearings. Maybe. My head hurt so much, and I was fighting a sort of dull dizziness, one that almost let me focus, but not quite. I took a deep breath, which sent a searing pain into my head, but did clear my mind a little.

I had to admit, I sort of wanted to cry. Sure, I'd gotten myself into this to see what would happen once I got inside, but this was way more than I had bargained for. I don't know what I thought would happen. Maybe they'd give me a thumbs-up and tell me a location to go next, which of course I would have staked out before actually going. I sure as hell never imagined being knocked out and tied to a chair. Blood pulsed in my ears as my panic rose.

I took a breath. *Slow down.*

Go back. Back to the beginning of this whole mess. *What would Nancy do?*

Was Nancy a product of a rampantly sexist society? Yes. Was she stopped at every turn—told she should let the big boys handle it? You bet your tea-length shirtwaist dress she was. Did that stop her from solving every gosh darn mystery in town (and sometimes internationally?). Heck no! If Nancy wanted to solve a mystery, she put on her favorite hat, grabbed her best chums and found those clues—in spite of…nay! *Because* of the raging underestimation that society has always had for teenage girls and women in general!

Okay, yes, this was working. Self-preservation was starting to kick in and I suddenly remembered the great thing about duct tape. Once you got it started it was fairly easy to rip. I glanced around for something to try and gouge it with. Sadly, the criminals had been too smart to just leave a pair of scissors or a razor lying around the room.

Jerks.

There did seem to be a bit of a rough edge to the TV stand, from which a TV was mysteriously absent. I couldn't help but wonder if at some point in the past one of the women had woken up and freaked out, smashing it to try to free herself. A jagged piece of glass would be quite handy at the moment. But that probably would have resulted in slightly more than the maximum threshold of noise to sneak away undetected.

Which was exactly what I was planning on doing.

I shimmied over to the TV stand, trying to be quiet, but every move I made seemed to be ginormous and echoing. My legs were also bound, each taped to a front chair leg, and the maneuvering was not the easiest thing in the world. Especially considering that my head felt like it had a tiny little boxer in there trying to jab his way out.

Eventually I got myself into a position where I could start rubbing the edge of the tape against the rough part. It was a cheap piece of furniture with that faux-veneer coating over particleboard. Luckily for me, a chunk of that laminate had broken off at the corner, thus making for a nice little edge for my escape.

If all went according to plan.

It took longer than I'd hoped, and I was sweating more than my uncle Jack that time he tried to impress his date by entering an impromptu county fair Macarena contest, which was to say, *quite* a fair amount. That stuff was flinging everywhere. But eventually I wore the bottom of the tape until there was a jagged little slice and I began to wriggle, trying to get my wrists to bend so that the tape would rip more and more. As the rip lengthened, it got easier and soon my arms were free. Exhausted, but free.

And that's when I heard the noise. Someone was coming up the hall.

Shit. I wasn't sure if I was making too much noise, getting careless and cocky toward the end of my struggle to get free, but whatever the reason, someone was coming.

I shimmy-hobbled (shobbled?) back to the spot I'd been sitting when I woke up and sat myself and my chair down as quietly as I could, sticking my hands behind my back again the way they'd been before. I could only hope the long strand of tape still hanging from my wrist wasn't obvious. I hung my head as if I was still passed out, which was actually kind of a relief for my neck.

The door opened. I tried to breathe as slowly and quietly as I could, hoping I could fake the relaxed state of someone sleeping, but the way my pulse was racing, and with how badly I wanted to take a peek, it was not the easiest task. But the stakes were too high to fail, so I sat, head flopped like the actress I had been trained to be (thank you, Intro to Dramatic Performance 101).

I guessed the person at the door was a man, both because of the heaviness of the footsteps and the fact that it didn't seem too likely that many women would be involved in this type of crime. When he grabbed me by my hair and lifted my head up, it was confirmed—not only by the size of the hand, but also the stench of way too much cologne. I'd never relaxed into anything more in my life, letting my head flop back down lifelessly when he rudely let my hair go again. I mean, I certainly hoped it looked lifeless. I honestly wasn't sure how to act something like that other than being as floppy as possible. It was all I could do not to contort my face in pain as the tiny boxer in my head decided to switch to kickboxing during all the commotion. The floppy act seemed to do the trick and the man moved to the other girls, giving them the same treatment of making sure they were still passed out. They each passed the test, of course.

The entire time, all I could think about was the tape stuck to my arm and how I was immensely thankful that it was so dark in there, but even still, it seemed impossible that I hadn't been found out.

Soon the door shut again and all I could hear was the heavy breathing coming from the other girls in the room.

I couldn't risk any more noise, but I knew I had to work quickly. I had to get out of that room. I moved to untape my legs, peeling it this time instead of ripping, thinking this might be quieter, but I was very, very mistaken. The sound was somewhat similar to an alley cat brawl. I tried to rip it, but without something to make it jagged, it was totally impossible. I'd seen people use their teeth to get it started before, but that was going to be a bit difficult. I wasn't the least flexible person in the world, but I certainly wasn't the most, either.

So peeling it was. I was forced to go painfully slowly, wondering what my chances were if I were to just rip it fast and loud to still make it out of that room in one piece. Except... I didn't actually have a plan to get out of the room, so I pulled, one painful millimeter at a time, wondering how long it was actually taking and if it was anywhere near what it felt like. After about five hours, or probably a few minutes in real time, I finally got both legs free.

I stood quickly, got a giant head rush (the boxer was really going at it) and sat back down, using all my focus not to make a huge noise when I hit the chair again. I took a few deep breaths and the dizziness passed quickly. In maybe ten seconds I was back up again, searching for a way out.

There were two obvious choices—the door that the man had come through to check on us, and a single window. I quickly peeked out the curtain.

Still night.

I figured darkness was my friend at that point, so that was good—the window, however, was old and looked like it might be hard to open.

But I couldn't think of any other way. I opened the curtains wide to get a better look at what I was dealing with. At this point if someone came in, I was screwed no matter what. I had to chance it and hope I could outrun them if they did come in.

The first thing I noticed was that the window faced the same alley I'd been sitting in just the other night, watching this horrible place so innocently. The second thing I noticed was that there was a balcony—thank goodness, it might have been a deal-breaker if there hadn't been one—and third, I also noticed that I was not the first person who had tried to escape this way; the lock was obviously tampered with. The thing was old and the windows had obviously gotten damp over the years, so the locking mechanism rusted over like it hadn't been maintained at all since it was installed. The real problem though was that it looked like the window itself might be painted shut. Not that I was going to give up.

I pushed up on the wooden crossbar. It didn't budge. Like, at all. I pushed harder, starting to get worried that I was going to have to break the glass. Which would certainly solve my immediate problem, though that pesky little problem of the noise would bring me an even bigger—and more deadly—problem.

I sighed.

I needed something to scrape the creases of the paint. Something thin and sharp. I wished I had worn some sort of a ring or sharp pendant or something, but I had specifically left anything that might allow someone to remember me, and later identify me, at home.

I thought I was being so smart.

I turned and surveyed the room, my hands moving to my hips, which they always seemed to do when I was in thinking mode. Writer friends always looked at me funny when I sat at the table at the coffee shop, super rigid posture with my hands on my hips. I don't know what it was—it just helped me think.

Thankfully, it worked. If I could get another piece of that laminate to break off the TV stand, it would be sharp and hopefully strong enough to get the job done. I moved as stealthily as I could, setting my feet carefully, walking on my toes, back over to the stand.

I couldn't have asked for a better situation. Because of all the rubbing I'd already done, I'd actually ended up loosening one of the broken edges. I grabbed the loose piece and, putting my hand over the spot I wanted it to break to try to dampen the sound, I pulled until I felt the snap.

Then I froze, listening for any movement in the hall and desperately praying to any god who would listen to keep them away just a while longer.

No one came.

I scurried back over to the window and began to scrape as quietly and quickly as I could, stopping to listen every now and again. There wasn't a whole lot I could do if someone came, but I couldn't help myself.

This part didn't actually take as long as I thought it might—that piece of laminate was really quite sharp—and soon I was able to move the window ever so slightly. Remembering back when I'd been at my grandma's old house when I was little, I pressed on either side of the wood frame as hard as I could, with all my weight behind it. I did this a few times in various spots up and down the frame, which loosened it even more.

I wondered how long it had been since this room had felt fresh air. It had to be decades.

Slowly, so slowly, the window started to give a little. Then a little more. Soon I had it open about a foot, maybe a bit more, and decided to risk it, thinking there was a good chance I would fit through.

I squeezed one leg through, then realized I'd have to go both feet first, like I was in some sort of limbo contest or something. The legs went through without much problem, then my butt, although I had to shimmy a little to get that through, then I was out up to my chest and was thankful for the first time in my life to be relatively flat-chested. It got a little awkward trying to balance myself, my abs shaking from the weird angles that I was holding myself at, but soon it was just my head, the window looming above my neck like a guillotine. I turned my head sideways, scraping one ear as I tried to rush through.

But I didn't care.

I was out on the balcony, and I was free.

In an act of utter foolishness, I decided to take one last look back through the window, my gaze landing on a pair of icy blue eyes with a very angry-looking dude attached, charging through the doorway. I turned and pushed the fire escape down as fast as I could, not worrying about noise anymore. Thankfully the window slowed him down too— he was much bigger than me—and my foot touched the ground just as he was making his way out onto the balcony.

I ran.

I didn't really pay too much attention to what direction I was going. My only focus was to get away. I don't know if he even chased me. Maybe they didn't really care about some junkie who'd decided to change her mind and get the hell out of Dodge. Or maybe they did.

I had no idea.

All I knew was that I had to run as fast as I could as far as I could, which I think might have been pretty far considering the adrenaline pulsing through me, until eventually I fell into a heap, somehow ending up down by the river that meandered through the city. I lay there for a while, more than happy to be alone, even if it was in the middle of the night and in a place I didn't particularly know.

I was free. And I was safe, relatively speaking. And I knew that once I regained a little of my strength, I'd be able to follow the walking trails that lined the river until I found something that looked familiar.

I made it back to my apartment just as the sun was peeking over the horizon, more exhausted than I'd ever been in my life. Also starving, given that I couldn't even remember how long it had been since I'd had any vital nutrients like protein or vitamins or Chocolatey Fudge Pop-Tarts.

Chapter Thirteen

After a long shower, made more complicated by the hair extensions, I fell into bed. I was worried the countless disastrous catastrophes that could have taken place during my escape would have sent me straight to my old friend, the Hamster Wheel of Thoughts, but I was asleep the second my head hit the pillow.

I was so dead to the world that I may have never woken up if it hadn't been for the incessant pounding on my apartment door. The noise came to me as if in a dream, but eventually my brain stumbled out of its comatose state long enough to realize I wasn't in my usual recurring dream of stealing an old-timey train (don't ask) and that the knock was real.

I got out of bed slowly—I had never been one to wake up in a jolt—and made my way to the door, forgetting to notice what I was wearing, or to be in any way alarmed that someone had gotten into my building and was now pounding on my door. It would take several more minutes, or at least a cup of coffee, for my recently slumbering brain to arrive at that train (see what I did there?) of thought.

I opened the door.

"What?" I asked, annoyed, with my eyes still half-closed.

"What are you doing?!" Vic asked, seemingly very, very angry, or at least exasperated.

"What?" I managed to get out, trying to melt the frost from the windowpanes of my brain.

"Why haven't you been answering your phone? I've been calling for hours. You've never not answered your phone for that long. Like, ever."

Even for me this was a little ridiculous. Was this what it was like to be drugged? I hadn't noticed it so much last night during my escape, but could there still be traces of something in me? You'd think I would have run it out of me, but I didn't really know about these sorts of things. I made a mental note to look into it—if not for personal interest, then it might be useful for my writing.

"What time is it?" I mumbled, my brain still struggling to catch up.

"It's four in the afternoon," Vic said, apparently noticing my pajamas.

"Obviously you've just woken up, but…were you still sleeping from last night?"

"I had kind of a late night," I said, finding my sofa and sprawling on it, my eyes drooping shut.

"Kind of a late night? I'd say so. Brandt said you were in some sort of play or something. How come I didn't know anything about this?"

As if on cue, the buzzer rang.

"Oh yeah, how did you get into the building?" I asked. "Didn't you have to buzz?"

"Annie let me in. She was down in the lobby like always and knows I'm your friend. She's worried about you too."

"You talked to her about me?" I said, not sure how I felt about that.

"We talk about lots of stuff. But obviously I asked her if she'd seen you today. She could tell that I was frantic. I think I might have worried her."

"Can you get the buzzer? I'm just really sleepy right now," I said, just wanting the thing to shut up.

"It's Brandt," she said, opening the apartment door a crack so he could come on in.

There was something about safety that twigged in my memory, like the door probably shouldn't just be left open like that, but I couldn't quite remember why it was so important. I let my eyes close again.

"I'm going to make some coffee," Vic said. "What the hell is wrong with you, anyway?"

"I don't know. Something. Maybe I'm sick."

"You don't look sick," she said. "Just tired."

I tried to mumble something in reply, but even I didn't know what it was.

When I woke again, Brandt and Vic were whisper-fighting on the other side of the room.

"Well, you were the one who got her all excited about going out to do this stupid play," Vic was saying. She sounded even more angry than she usually did when she talked to Brandt.

"How the hell was I supposed to know she'd go out and get all hammered or whatever this is?"

"Why didn't you go with her?"

"Why would I go with her? She didn't ask me to. It seemed like a private thing. Besides, I had other stuff to do. Why would I go to some stupid play?"

"Um, because your friend was starring in it, apparently."

"She was not starring in it. She said she was like, a bit part or something. I don't know."

"Right. Of course you don't know, because it's not like you actually listen to anything anyone says." Vic was really getting on a roll now.

"Guys," I said.

But they just kept on, like they hadn't heard a thing.

"If she wanted us to be there, she would have told us to be there," Brandt was saying.

"Guys," I said, louder this time.

Vic stopped midword and came over to me.

"Are you okay? Did you like, do drugs or something?" She handed me a cup of coffee, still hot.

"Um, not exactly," I said. "I don't think." I mumbled the last bit into my coffee.

"Wait. Did you just say you don't think?" Vic said, turning to look at me, her expression exasperated.

I nodded, the coffee suddenly very, very interesting. And since it was the first thing I'd put in my body since supper last night, it was also very, very welcome and delicious. *Wait...except... Pop-Tarts? Was there something about Pop-Tarts?*

"What the hell kind of play was this?" Brandt asked.

He must have already known he was going to be in trouble with Vic, but I had a sense that wasn't where his worry actually ended. It was like he almost cared, which made me feel pretty loved, since Brandt did not show that sort of thing easily or often.

But then I felt even more terrible, since, you know, I'd totally put myself into a giant heap of trouble and didn't even let anybody know where I was going or what I was doing.

I sighed.

"I wasn't in a play." I said, staring aggressively at that beautiful cup of coffee.

"Well, what a shocker," Vic said, obviously a little suspicious the whole time.

Brandt, on the other hand, looked downright hurt, like he couldn't quite believe I had used him like that. Which was a totally fair point. I felt like I wanted to puke, and it had nothing to do with any aftereffects of drugs that might still be in my system.

I could tell they both wanted to yell at me, but they just sat staring instead. Which might have been worse. I tried to think of a way to tell them what happened without freaking them out more than they already were, but I couldn't think of a single way to phrase *I voluntarily went to a place known for its shady connections and then got drugged and, you know, held against my will* that sounded adequate. Or smart. Or like I hadn't just announced I had no regard whatsoever for my personal safety.

So I just decided to tell the story from the start, hoping they would at least understand my thought process while I was in the thick of it. Maybe, if I was lucky, they'd be so impressed by my dazzling escape they would completely forget I'd put myself into the horrible situation in the first place.

Unfortunately, that little detail seemed to be stuck in the forefront of both of their minds.

"Are you kidding me, Petra?" Brandt said.

I was fairly certain it was a rhetorical question and there was no right way to answer it, so I kept my mouth shut.

Vic was pacing. Every so often, she'd turn and open her mouth to say something, then change her mind and start pacing again.

I sipped my coffee at a weirdly constant speed until it was gone—way too soon—then wondered if I should just keep pretending there was still coffee in there and fake drink it or what. I certainly couldn't put the cup down; it had become my only shield.

And then, as they tended to do, Brandt and Vic started screaming at each other.

"If you wouldn't have done the makeover, none of this would have happened!" Vic yelled.

"Are you kidding me right now?" Brandt retorted. "Like I'm her damned keeper or something? If Petra wants to lie to us and then go out there and practically get herself killed, that is not on me."

This went on for a while. I wanted to stop them, but my headache was coming back with a vengeance and I could barely concentrate. Then, as they were sort of winding down and looking like maybe they were finally going to get to yelling at me instead of each other, my buzzer went off.

Everybody froze.

Brandt looked sick, clutching at the arms of the chair he was sitting in. "They found you. What if they found you?" To say he looked panicked would be a wee understatement.

"Holy shit," Vic said, her eyes going wide.

"Guys, I'm sure it's not the—" I had no idea what to call the men who'd had me tied up "—um, bad guys."

Brandt snorted. "Bad guys. Jesus." He raked both hands through his hair as he got up and paced.

"But what if it is?" Vic asked, not really making me feel

any better. "If you were drugged, I doubt you would know if someone was following you."

"Look, I was really careful. I took every precaution I've ever learned from all the classes I've taken. You know, the detective course and all the self-defense ones. I remember being very conscious about it. I can't see how they would know where I was."

"Okay, okay. Let's just not answer the buzzer," Vic said. "They won't be able to get into the building. We'll be safe up here."

I smiled.

"What the hell is there to smile about?" she asked.

"It's just that…you said 'we.' Like we're in this together."

She rolled her eyes. "Well, to be honest, I wish right now that I wasn't your friend since you're so determined to put yourself in danger, but you know as well as I do that we're always all in it together."

Brandt looked up at Vic, almost like she'd said something completely profound, which to me it kinda was. I just didn't think Brandt would have felt the same.

It was a lovely moment.

Until a very loud, very urgent knock sounded at the door.

Brandt squealed in a very unmanly way and Vic clutched at my arm. "They found us," she whispered, shaking a little.

Or maybe it was me that was doing the shaking. It was kind of hard to tell.

None of us moved.

"Delivery for Petra Jackson!" a voice came from the other side of the door.

"Are you expecting a package?" Vic asked, still digging

her fingernails into my skin like she was trying to permanently fuse us or something.

I started to pull one claw at a time from my arm. "Not that I can think of, but I'm sure it's no big deal. This is a secure building—people can't get in or out unless they're a delivery guy," I finished as I started toward the door.

"Or masquerading as a delivery guy," Vic said.

My arm froze halfway to the door. I peeked through the peephole instead, only to find a bored-looking dude with a massive arrangement of flowers.

Flowers?

I turned back to my friends and stage-whispered, "He has flowers."

"Behind which he's probably hiding a revolver or something."

I closed my eyes and sighed. My friends really could lean toward the dramatic end of the spectrum when they wanted to. Unfortunately, they were also successful in amping up my paranoia.

"Um," I yelled. "Could you just leave them by the door?"

I peeked through the door again to see the guy roll his eyes and give a little shrug before he set them down and wandered off down the hall, the annoyance showing in his stride. I suppose he had been hoping for a tip, which I gladly would have given him if I hadn't, you know, been afraid for my life. Maybe I could phone the shop and give them one over the phone.

I heard the faint ding of the elevator, then waited a few seconds longer, just to make sure he was gone. When I opened the door, I popped my head out before the rest of me to make sure the coast was clear.

"This girl has absolutely no self-preservation skills," I heard Brandt whisper to Vic, which was annoying since I was totally taking precautions the way they'd taught in my ALERT: Awareness Leads to Evasion of Risks and Trauma training class.

Since the delivery guy had really left—and wasn't hiding around the corner with a deadly weapon as my friends would have me believe—I grabbed the flowers, shutting and locking the door behind me.

"You seriously just brought those in here without a second thought, didn't you?" Brandt said, shaking his head.

"Um, they're flowers," I said, making sure to give the word *flowers* an extra sassy inflection to drive my point home.

"How do you know there's not some kind of poison gas that's going to start leaking out of the paper wrapping or something?" he asked, as if that were the most normal thought in the world.

I sighed, heading to the kitchen for a vase. Of course, I was intercepted by Vic about five steps from my destination. I thought she was going to make me throw them back out in the hall or something, but she simply snatched the card right out from under my nose, ripping the envelope open as if it wasn't a felony to open someone else's mail or, in this case, package.

"'From your anonymous admirer,'" Vic read aloud.

"Anonymous," Brandt said, his eye going comically wide. "What the hell is that supposed to mean?"

"It's nothing," I said, heading for the kitchen again. "I got another one of these—some chocolates—the other day. It's just a fan or something."

Miraculously, the two of them left me in peace for the two minutes it took to climb up on a chair and grab the vase from the top shelf of my cupboard. But I soon discovered they were not about to let me off the hook that easily. As I stepped back into the living room carrying the vase, which I thought would look quite nice on the coffee table, they stopped their frantic whispering to each other and both turned to stare.

Vic cleared her throat. "So, let me get this straight. You've now received two anonymous gifts from a stranger—in your secure building—*and* you are currently wanted by some evil bad guys. And you don't think this is a big deal at all?"

I shrugged. I mean, of course I was a little…jarred by the whole thing, but it was chocolate and flowers… What could be more innocent than chocolate and flowers? After my book had been released, I'd received dozens of gifts like this from fans. Maybe I should have been a little more worried, but frankly, I liked chocolate and flowers, and they both just seemed so…innocuous. "I don't know. I'm guessing my publisher is forwarding them to me or something," I said.

"Okay, so how about you phone them up and see?" Vic said, and the way she set her shoulders I could tell she was not going to let this one go.

I mean, there was a little twig of worry in the back of my mind. But didn't other people sweep those twigs into the back of their minds hoping to never think of them again like I did?

Sadly, the looks on Vic's and Brandt's faces seemed to point to not so much.

I let out a long, annoyed sigh and pulled out my phone.

But as I started scrolling through my contacts, the pounding started again. Since we were already at the most precarious of edges, we all pretty much shot straight out of our skin.

"Oh god, the delivery guy came back to finish us off!" Brandt said.

I gave him a look. "When did he start us off?" Somehow, Brandt didn't seem to find my question funny.

The pounding on the door continued. "Come on, Petra, I know you're in there!"

We all breathed a collective sigh of relief. It was just poor, harmless Johnny. Well, mostly harmless, anyway.

Brandt still clutched at his heart, like there was an invisible string of pearls holding his hand there, and Vic let out a slow, whooshing breath, trying to calm herself from her approximately sixty-foot jump in the air. I moved toward the door.

"Are you sure you want to do that?" Vic asked, flopping onto the couch beside Brandt, looking a little spent.

"Well, I guess I should figure out how he found me," I said, deciding not to add, *So that I can determine how hard that might be, since, you know...bad guys.*

I took a deep breath and opened the door. "Hey, Johnny."

"Petra! I knew you had to be here."

"Indeed," I said, my tone a little chilly.

I couldn't help but notice he had a rather large duffel bag in tow. I made myself a promise then and there that he was absolutely not going to be staying the night. No way, no how. I was over this guy.

Unfortunately, I also knew how hopeless he was and how he probably didn't have anywhere else to go either. But I wasn't going to do it. Johnny was not my problem anymore. And in fact, now that I thought about it, no guy ever should be. If I met someone great… I mean, not that I had anyone specific in mind, and it was pure accident that I glanced across the hall toward a certain neighbor's door, but whoever I dated next was going to be able to take care of his own damned self.

"You going to invite me in, or what?" Johnny asked, flashing that famously Petra-melting smile.

I sighed and moved out of the doorway, motioning for him to come in. *If you have to*, was the general vibe I was trying to project.

Brandt and Vic both stood, giving the place an even more unwelcoming aura.

"Oh, uh. Hey, guys," Johnny said, his smile faltering a little.

He knew as well as I did that Vic and Brandt had been instrumental in helping me find the strength to get away from him in the first place. I mean, I would have been able to do it eventually, but they probably saved me a ton of time and most likely a lot of money too. The guy was a leech. It was just too bad he knew it and I knew it and everybody knew it, and yet he still found a way to get to me.

"How did you find me, Johnny?"

He dropped his huge bag near the entrance to the hallway and came over to sit across from my friends. *Subtle, Johnny, real subtle*, I thought, but was more determined than ever not to let him stay. Wanting to send a clear message, I picked the bag up and hauled it back over near the front door. Johnny made a bit of a pouty face, but then smiled and turned back to Vic and Brandt.

"So, have you guys been good?"

Vic was shooting a death glare that would have made most men faint, but Johnny was well versed in people disliking his presence, so he seemed to shake it right off.

"Johnny, how did you find me?" I asked again, sitting in the other chair, wishing it was farther away from him.

"Oh, you know," he said, waving his hand. "I just did a little asking around."

"Who did you ask?" I demanded.

He looked a little taken aback. "You know, a few people."

"Johnny, you better tell me right now *exactly* how you found me. I am not in any way finding this amusing, or in a mood to be given the runaround."

In a bit of excellent timing that was out of character, Brandt leaned forward and crossed his arms, his giant biceps looking even more menacing.

"Um…" Johnny stuttered, "I, uh, after I saw you guys at brunch, I figured you must still be sorta close to the neighborhood, so I started looking around at some of the classes in the area, 'cause I know how much you like your classes," he said, his voice picking up speed, "and then I just kind of made friends with some of the people who worked at some of the community centers."

I narrowed my gaze. "So you flirted with the poor girls who were on shift until you could scam your way into finding me on one of the registration forms."

"Geez, what did you do, man, hack the computer?" Even Brandt looked scandalized.

Johnny shrugged. "I was just being resourceful."

I sighed. "Well, I guess that's good."

Johnny's face lit up and he started to smile.

"No," I said, putting my hand up. "Not good for you—

you're still in my bad books—but at least the other bad guys probably won't be able to find me the same way," I said, turning to Brandt and Vic. "It's not like they know my name or anything."

"Bad guys?" Johnny asked. "What bad guys?"

"Never mind," Brandt said, standing. "It's time to go now."

"Well, it sure was great to see you," Johnny said, leaning back and putting his hands behind his head, settling in and getting comfy.

"Oh no, you don't—you're the one who's leaving," Vic said, grabbing him a bit more forcefully than was absolutely necessary, dragging him up out of the chair.

"But I haven't even gotten to talk to Petra yet," he whined.

"We have nothing to talk about, Johnny," I said. "I just wanted to know how you found me. And now you can forget that you did."

"Don't even think of coming back," Brandt added. "Ever."

"But, Petra…" Johnny turned to me, looking like he was in shock.

It was totally an act, but I could feel myself starting to falter. He was just so helpless and I always had so much trouble watching someone in distress.

"Come on," Vic said, draping the duffel bag handle over Johnny's shoulder, nearly knocking him over.

"Do not let him back in," Brandt mumbled as he passed me.

"Of course I won't," I said. And I meant it. If he was out of my sight, that puppy-dog pout gone, I knew I'd be okay. Johnny was toxic and I was not interested in living in that environment again—and it had been toxic, very toxic, even before I found out he cheated on me.

I was actually starting to get a little annoyed that he'd even tried to knock on my door again. I mean, who did he think he was? More importantly, who did he think I was? Someone who was part of whatever world he thought owed him a favor.

No.

I was finished.

And thankfully, I had a couple of great friends to back me up. I didn't even wince as Brandt gave Johnny an earnest little shove out the door before he closed it with a firmness that wasn't quite a slam, but definitely sent a message. "That should stop him from sending the stupid little gifts," he said, wiping his hands, as if ridding himself of the entire situation.

"Oh my god, you're right," Vic said. "It probably was that little weasel that sent them."

"Oh probably," I said, though as hard as I tried, I couldn't stop a little shivery twinge from shuddering through my stomach, because I was fairly sure if the flowers had been from Johnny, there'd be no way he'd leave without making sure he'd been given full credit for his generosity.

Chapter Fourteen

I was going stir-crazy. We're talking straight-up cabin fever. Fidgety. Antsy. Fantsy, as it were. I hadn't left the house in two days and couldn't stand being stuck for even one day. I needed excitement, I needed people… I needed the hell out.

But Vic would have my head if she found out I was out and about on the streets. Brandt and I tried to convince her that my disguise had been a good one and that none of the thugs (what Brandt had taken to calling them) would ever recognize me, but Vic was adamant. The stupid investigation class had taught us to stay indoors with the curtains shut for at least a week if you thought your cover was blown or if you were in any sort of danger, so that's what I had foolishly promised her I would do. She vowed to de-friend me due to her high stress levels if I didn't "at the very least" (her words) do this for her.

So I promised. And I was totally keeping my promise too, even though I was sure she wouldn't have approved of the fact that I was sitting in the lobby chatting it up with Annie.

"You've been around here a lot lately," Annie mused.

Fair, since I'd been sitting with her practically every waking minute and she'd probably had it up to her peacock-feather fascinator hat with me intruding on her space.

"I know, sorry. Just let me know if I'm bugging you too much. I'm just, um, laying low. Ex-boyfriend issues. You know how it is."

"Boy, do I," she said, chuckling and shaking her head. "I have been there. And you are certainly not bugging me. I like the company."

Truth be told, even with the literal feather in her cap, Annie was still not herself. She wasn't as chatty, spending much of her time sort of staring into space, no doubt thinking about Erica and how unfair the whole situation was. Especially since I knew she was still skeptical about the police's suicide theory.

"Okay, good," I said. "You're like an icon in this city—people want to come through and visit with you, not me."

"An icon!" Annie said, delighted. "Well, that would be something, wouldn't it?" She was laughing, but still looked pretty pleased.

"You are," I insisted. "It's an honor to even live in the same building as you do."

She swatted my hand. "Well, you're exaggerating," she said, "but thank you. You do know how to make an old woman feel good about herself."

"If there is anything you are not, it's old," I assured her.

She smiled again. "You flatter me too much."

I shrugged. "Just saying what's true."

"I guess age is just a number," she said. "Honestly, I don't feel any older than I did when I was thirty."

"And why should you?"

"True enough," she said. "True enough."

We settled into a comfortable silence. Since I was down visiting so much, we'd pretty much covered every topic imaginable, but found we were pretty comfortable with each other just sitting and chilling too. It was a kind of lovely relief not to have to constantly worry about what to say next (someone tell my nonexistent manuscript, please).

After a while though, Annie announced she had an idea.

"I feel like I need to do something. Maybe we can plan a little get-together? Something to celebrate Erica." She perked up at the idea. "We should do it this weekend."

"I'm not sure I should leave the building for a little while longer."

"That's what I mean—you won't have to leave the building. We'll do it on the roof."

"We have a roof?" I shook my head. "I mean, obviously we have a roof—every building has a roof—but we have a roof that you can have a party on?"

"Have you really never been up there?" Annie asked, shocked. "Oh, it's beautiful. You can see half the city up there. Didn't you get a tour of the building when you viewed it?"

I shrugged. "I just sent the deposit in without even seeing the place. I was kind of desperate to get out of my old place."

She nodded. "The guy, right?"

"How did you guess?" I said, shooting her a crooked smile.

Annie stood. "Well, let's go," she said, already headed for the elevator. "You are in for a treat."

It turned out Annie was not exaggerating. I couldn't believe I hadn't discovered this wonderful sanctum before. It was gorgeous. There were outdoor couches and rugs and tables and everything you'd ever need to relax. And the view was unbelievable. You could see half the city and all the way down the river.

"And don't worry about the cold," Annie said. "All those tall metal things are heaters and this place really gets quite comfortable, even when it's chilly out."

"It's amazing," I said.

I was already having all sorts of gatherings in my mind, especially summer ones. The barbecues were especially intriguing. I'd always wanted to take the Learn to Grill Like a Pit Boss class down at the community center, and now I had the perfect excuse to go ahead and sign up.

Of course, thinking about classes made me think of Johnny, which was super irritating, but what was I going to do? Not go to any more classes? Inconceivable.

"So, let's do it tomorrow," Annie said, excited.

"Tomorrow? Isn't that kind of short notice?"

Annie shrugged. "We live in an apartment building with over a hundred units. I realize people love to make plans these days, but surely we could find a handful of people to come out. It doesn't have to be big. The smaller the better, actually. More intimate. More opportunities to get to know a few of the neighbors."

"I thought you already knew all the neighbors."

Annie grinned. "Most of them. I'm sure there are a few newcomers I haven't met yet," she said with a wink.

And if there was anyone who could pull off a wink without looking ridiculous, it was Annie. In fact, it made her even more charming somehow.

"It's so great of you to do this, Annie," I said, already excited for tomorrow night. "I hope it's not a lot of work."

She shrugged. "No work at all. I'll put up a poster in each of the elevators, we'll make it bring your own booze. I'll whip up a few appetizers, and voilà! Party on the roof!"

Honestly, the woman was incredible. I had never left a conversation with Annie where I hadn't felt better when I walked away than when I'd said hello.

THE NEXT DAY was taking longer than a sloth's dive into Ativan, so I decided to make a bit of food for the party too. I couldn't go out for ingredients, so I had to make do with what I had in the pantry. That meant a no-go on a fancy appetizer, but I was able to whip up a pan of my favorite puffed wheat cake. I mean, I know puffed wheat cake is more of a kiddie snack, but I swear, it was impossible to pass up, probably because the chocolatey, sticky goodness took me straight back to my childhood.

I decided to head up to the roof a little early with my puffed wheat cake and a bottle of wine in tow, trying to decide if I was the world's most juvenile party guest ever, or if I had just discovered the world's best new breakup ritual. I almost wanted to get dumped just to see.

In the elevator, I admired Annie's poster, which was adorned with glitter glue and colorful stickers. I should have known Annie was not one to half-ass anything—not even a simple poster. And it certainly got the point across. If I hadn't known about the party already, there was no way I would have wanted to miss it.

As I pushed through the roof door, I was not surprised that Annie had absolutely outdone herself again. She'd somehow made a flurry of streamers look less graduation circa 1993 and more classy chic, and had bouquets of tasteful balloons in the corners, making the space seem even more intimate than before. It was a little chilly, so I spent about ten minutes mulling over the idea of turning the heaters on. This required quite a lengthy assessment since I felt like any adultlike person should be able to do that sort of thing, but also machines that spewed gas generally shot waves of terror through me. I considered the approximately 3,683 catastrophic scenarios that could happen with a misfire. But after visualizing the entire building imploding, I put my scaredy pants away and gave it a shot. Turned out they were easy to run, really, just a simple dial to turn them to the appropriate temperature, and a button to light them. I set them all fairly low, figuring I could always turn up the temperature later if it wasn't warm enough.

I relocated my puffed wheat cake from a chair to a more sensible empty table, which looked like the perfect place for a food area, and sneaked behind the bar in search of a corkscrew. There wasn't a ton of stuff back there, but it had all the basics a good bar should have, and I quickly opened my wine, realizing I hadn't thought to bring up a glass. Fortunately, the bar had glasses and even a dishwasher for easy cleanup at the end of the night.

I settled under one of the heat lamps, wine in hand, feeling more relaxed than I had in days. A few other folks decided to come up a little early too, and I had a nice chat with a couple from the twelfth floor whose guacamole-and-salsa platter made my puffed wheat cake look like it belonged at a toddler's bouncy castle birthday. But the woman, Ella, squealed when she saw it.

"It has been so long since I've had this," she said, digging out a piece. "I used to love it so much."

"Me too!" I smiled.

Soon Annie arrived, bringing the largest platter of puff pastry appetizers I had ever seen.

"Have you been cooking all day?" I asked.

"Oh goodness, no," she said. "The only cooking I do is the shortcut way. I made these with ready-to-bake pastry and a few other simple ingredients. Took me twenty minutes."

I couldn't help but feel a little like my twenty minutes of cooking was a bit uninspired compared to Annie's. Although I supposed she did have several decades of entertaining experience on me. I vowed that the best thing I could do for myself was try to learn from the master. Maybe in forty years I would be the charming older lady that people made a point to stop and visit, though at that moment I felt more like a wobbly baby platypus. Parties, amirite?

Luckily, everyone in the building was so nice and quite a few people made the trek up. The food table was full, with some dishes even overflowing onto the bar. It had been a while since I'd eaten anything other than takeout, so I indulged way more than was necessary.

I couldn't help but think we should try to make this a monthly affair. Maybe I'd even find someone in the building to go to a class with, or maybe just coffee. How had I not thought of this before? Of course, no building I'd ever lived in had a handy-dandy entertaining space ready to go like that, which was a pretty big part of what made it so easy to put together.

"I'm so glad we decided to do this," a voice came from behind me.

I turned to see Eliza, sipping on a complicated-looking drink with both a maraschino cherry and what looked like a dried hot pepper of some sort sticking out of it. I wasn't quite sure what she meant by *we*, but I supposed she just wanted to be a part of a community, which, after all, was the whole point of the gathering.

"Oh, hi, Eliza," I said, sipping my wine.

She was, as always, very put together in her jeans/blazer combo with all the right accessories and hair looking like she had just left the salon.

"So how is the book coming along?" she said, glancing around behind me.

This was a move I was familiar with. I tended to be approachable or nonthreatening or something, because people would often use me as their "conversation buddy" until someone more interesting came along.

"Um, yeah, it's good," I lied. I certainly wasn't going to confide in Eliza of all people that I had absolutely no mystery for my heroine to stumble into.

"That's great," she said, suddenly spotting someone superior behind me. "Oh, there's Axel," she said, already stepping away. "Great chatting with you."

She was off before I could say, *Yeah, you too.* Not that I was complaining. After the weird conversation about her wildly traditional values earlier, I honestly wasn't sure we had a single thing in common.

Annie made her rounds across the rooftop, eyes sparkling more with each new person she talked to. She put everyone at ease, making them all feel like the most special person in the room. She flitted over to a couple leaning on the railing close to the entrance to the roof, where the door was opening.

My breath caught. I hadn't imagined that he'd come. Although, by the way Annie beelined straight for him, I had the sneaking suspicion she'd invited him personally. I also couldn't help but notice how she sneaked a quick glance my way before motioning him toward the food and the bar.

Ryan's glance followed hers and our eyes met for the briefest of moments, making my heart do a kind of whirligig sort of thing. Which was ridiculous. What was I, some love-struck teenager in the eighth grade? My first instinct was to find somewhere to hide—my nerves cracking like a glass case in the climax of a heist mystery. Instead, I found a place to sit alone, you know, just to see if he might stop over to say hi.

Immediately after I sat, I silently scolded myself over how passive-aggressive I was being with such a loser move, but it was too late to stand back up without looking ridiculous. And so I sat, nursing my glass of wine as if it were my lifeline, which, in the moment, I kind of felt like it was. Unfortunately, all the situation did was make me drink faster than normal and before I knew it my glass was half-gone. And since I did not particularly want to make a drunken-schoolgirl impression on all my new neighbors in a building I was beginning to adore more each day, the next sip I took was a very, very small one.

But then I started getting quite bored. And when I was bored, my thoughts usually leaped around wildly like an unattended toddler after scarfing a family-sized bag of cotton candy. Soon those thoughts were bounding into Ryan's case, spinning through ideas of what might have happened to the poor girls that had been in the room with me.

"Something troubling you?" a sexy voice asked.

My stomach tensed and I set my wine down reflexively

on the nearest surface, a rustic tiled coffee table in front of me. By some miracle it just wobbled a bit on the edge of the grout and didn't come crashing down.

"Uh, no, not really," I said. "Just daydreaming, I guess." Somehow, I managed a smile.

He sat down. Which was good, but I instantly felt bad that I hadn't invited him to sit, which probably would have been the polite thing to do, right? Ruminating about that, then wondering if it had been the rudest thing he'd ever witnessed, I made an even bigger idiot of myself by not paying attention to what he was saying.

I blinked. "Sorry, what?"

He laughed. "I just said that must be a hazard of the job."

I tilted my head, confused.

"You know, the daydreaming. Being a writer, I imagine you're probably always dreaming new stuff up." He paused. "For your stories?"

Leave it to me to transform a nice normal situation into its most awkward possible iteration. "Um, right! The daydreaming. Ha-ha. Yes, definitely part of the job," I said, pretty much sputtering the whole thing out.

Why was it so incredibly hard to impress the people you wanted to most? I mean, not that I needed to impress anyone, but if there *was* one person I'd hoped to dazzle, he was sitting directly beside me. So close, in fact, that it suddenly felt a lot warmer since he'd sat down. Although that totally might have been because of the mortifiery (aka flaming-hot blushing) over how ridiculous I was.

My mind spun with things that might be good conversation starters, but every thought seemed to be more ludicrous than the last. My classes? No, he already knew about those.

My job? No, we'd covered that, lord help me. His job? Hell no! Way too volatile.

I cleared my throat, successfully bringing even more attention to the awkward silence we had been experiencing for way too long already.

Finally, I gave up and just grabbed my glass of wine.

"Jesus!" he yelled.

I froze. "What?"

He grabbed my hand, pulling it closer to him. If I hadn't been so taken off guard, I might have even been excited by the sudden physical contact, but by the look on his face, it was not something I should get too excited over. He looked downright…angry?

"What?" I asked again.

"You're her."

I squinted. "Her who?"

"The girl from the other night. In the apartment."

Oh. Shit.

Chapter Fifteen

I tried to think of the best way to pretend I didn't know what he was talking about, but the guy was trained to spot a lie. He was searching me now, his eyes roaming over my hair…my face.

"Christ, I knew there was something…off about that girl," he said. "Something I wasn't putting my finger on." He squinted. "You were in disguise."

"I, um, don't know what you're talking about."

He shook my hand, not violently, but in a way that certainly got my attention.

"The nail polish," he said. "It's not like there are a hundred women out there walking around with this particular manicure," he said, finally dropping my hand.

It flopped to my lap.

"I'm sure there must be other women who like to do their nails like this," I said, trying to sound as innocent as possible, though knowing damned well I wasn't going to get away with it.

Ryan put his head in his hands. "How did I not figure it out?" He looked up then, straight into my eyes. "I guess I thought you wouldn't be that foolhardy. Or, you know, you might listen to me or something." He shook his head.

After I tried—and I'm pretty sure, failed—to process the fact that he'd just used the word *foolhardy* with absolutely no hint of irony, shame washed over me. I mean, as if I didn't already know how dangerous the whole night had been, I really didn't need him treating me like some kid that he caught stealing cookies or something.

Suddenly, Ryan seemed to remember something. He looked around, frantic. "Shit, we've got to get you out of the open." He grabbed my arm and pulled me up from the couch. He was gentle but firm, a sense of urgency fueling him. He led me off the roof and in a moment we were in the elevator on our way back down to our floor.

"I was kind of having a good time up there," I said, knocking him back into the present moment.

"Do you have a death wish?"

I figured he wouldn't believe me even if I told him I didn't, so I just shrugged.

"Because pulling a stunt like you pulled the other night is a really good way to get that accomplished. Hell, you practically did get yourself killed. Or maybe worse."

I didn't really know what might be worse than getting killed and couldn't help but think he was being a little bit dramatic.

"I wasn't going to get killed."

His mouth dropped open like he couldn't believe I was going to argue with him about it. "You were knocked out and tied to a chair."

I shrugged again. I mean, the jig was obviously up, but I still didn't particularly want to admit to everything that had gone down.

"I wouldn't have been killed." I said. "I'm sure those other girls are just fine."

He balked. "Okay, maybe they're not dead, but I can guarantee you they are far from fine."

"I can take care of myself," I insisted. "I'm trained in self-defense. You saw what I could do the other night." I unlocked the door to my apartment and went in.

I was both excited and a little freaked out that he followed.

"And that's all well and fine…when you're conscious," he said, staring me down, knowing I wasn't going to come up with some great argument about that.

"I was fine. I got out. I think pretty well on my feet."

"And now they're going to be after you. They know what you look like."

I tilted my head. "Obviously they don't. Even you didn't recognize me."

He narrowed his eyes, his jaw clenching and unclenching like he didn't quite know what to do with all the angry energy coursing through him.

I was starting to calm a little though. If there was anything I was sure of, it was that he would never hurt me. Or anyone else, for that matter. You know, unless it was a bad guy and he had no choice in the matter. He was the kind of guy who saved lives. Like mine, for instance.

"You need to get that nail polish off," he said, then stared at me until I got up to get the polish remover.

I came back into the room where he was pacing.

"Look, this case is a lot bigger than I thought. It's drugs and forced prostitution and runs way deeper than I ever imagined when I started. These guys work like well-oiled machines. It's going to be a while before I have enough to be able to bring them down."

"Um, okay," I said, not really sure where he was going with all that.

I started to wipe the polish off.

"Look, you can't stay here. It's too dangerous. Especially with me being in this building too. Any one of them could be onto me at any moment and could easily follow me here. And my god, if they found you here too, the whole building could be in danger."

"Well, I obviously don't want to put anyone in danger, but it's not like I have anywhere to go."

"Go to one of your friend's houses. That girl. Or that big guy, whatever."

"Um, Ryan? I'm not going anywhere. This is my house. This is where I feel safe."

"You have to go," he insisted.

"Um, no. Actually I don't. Besides, you're putting every-one at way more risk than I am."

"This is my home base. My office is here. All my stuff."

"Yeah, well, same."

"But I'm actually trying to solve a case."

"Well, duh, so am I. What the hell do you think I was doing that night? Just out having a little fun?"

He started to pace. "I can't believe this is happening. I have never in my life ever had anyone stick their nose into my life like this."

"I'm not sticking my nose in your life," I said, insulted that he still thought this was all about him. "Obviously this is at least as much about me as it is about you at this point."

His eyes opened wide. "Because you followed me!" His voice was getting louder, more disbelieving.

I sighed. "Okay. I get it. I got involved with something that wasn't really my business. But it wasn't like I thought in a million years that I would stumble upon something like this."

"Yeah, well. I guess you never know, right?" he said calmly, then his voice got louder again. "Which is why you don't just go around following people!"

He sat down, exasperated, like he seriously didn't know what the hell he was going to do with me. Which may have been a valid point, since no matter how much he might have wanted me to stay out of it, I definitely wasn't going to stay out of it. But I also didn't need him worrying about me.

"Look, it's nobody's fault," I said, even though it was maybe a little my fault—which was exactly why I had to help fix it. "It's not even a problem."

"Not a problem? How can you say that? You were *abducted* the other night. You don't think that's a problem?"

I shrugged again. "No. Now we know more about how they work than we did before, right?"

"Not really. I'd seen them drug the women before."

"Well, now we know more about how secure they are and stuff. And—" I hesitated to say it, but I knew we'd have to get to the real issue eventually "—now we know how to get back inside."

His eyes looked like they were ready to pop right out of his skull. "Get back in?!" His voice cracked and sort of squealed at the end, which I'd kind of anticipated, but nonetheless it made my nether regions do a little flip.

I nodded. "You said yourself that this case was taking

longer than you'd expected." I figured it was best not to mention that I was actually doing him a favor. "But with me helping, we can get in there and get what you need and get out. And hopefully with a bunch of arrests and stuff."

He was much calmer than I expected, sitting there just looking at me with those gorgeous eyes of his. Staring, I might add, just a little longer than I was particularly comfortable with.

It was starting to get a little uncomfortable, actually.

After an eternity of infinitude, he spoke. "You have got to be out of your mind if you think I'm going to be on board with you helping me on this case. Especially considering you're self-destructive enough to be doing things like you were doing the other night."

"Why does everybody keep saying that? I am not self-destructive. I mean, maybe my tolerance for danger is slightly higher than an average person's, but that's only because I am confident in my abilities. I'm trained."

"Yeah, yeah. The self-defense. The spying," he said pointedly, looking me in the eye.

I could see again why he made such a good detective. In one stare, he had a way of making me want to disclose all my secrets…and I didn't even really have secrets. Though the way he was looking at me, I kinda wished I did so I could spill my guts like a guilt-ridden six-year-old. Except I suddenly realized I had a lot more gumption when I was six. Right…gumption. I just went ahead and did stuff for the hell of it even when I knew it wasn't "allowed." People seemed to think it was cute, actually. And you know what? It *was* cute. It was goddamned adorable. I decided then and there to adopt the mindset of my past cute self and be the Emperor of My Own Domain. Who the hell was this guy (no matter how exquisite he was) to tell me what I could and couldn't do, anyway?

"Look, I know you don't think I'm capable or whatever, and that's fine. I'm used to being underestimated, and people always make fun of my classes, but at the end of the day, I've spent hundreds of hours gathering knowledge and gaining practical experience."

"Not in detective work," he retorted, though I could see I was starting to wear him down a little.

Or maybe just exhaust him.

I tilted my head. "A lot of it is, actually. It helps with my work as a writer so I've taken a lot in exactly that sort of thing... Elemental Weapons Design for Dummies, my Kickass Combat workouts, this one class called The Authentic Art of Disguise, although Brandt is much more of an expert at that."

"But...why would you want to risk your life like that?"

I shrugged. "Why do you do it?"

"Money, for one," he said, exasperated. "And you haven't mentioned one word about getting in on that."

"I don't want your money," I said. "I just want experience."

"I thought you already had all the experience you need," he challenged.

I sighed. "Fine, whatever. You're obviously not interested in doing this together, but like it or not, I'm in this now. Do you think I can sleep at night knowing those guys are still out there? And that maybe some of them might even be looking for me?"

"That's exactly why you should have never gotten involved."

"Maybe, but it doesn't change the fact that I am involved

and that's not changing until these guys are found and hopefully arrested."

"And that's precisely what I'm trying to do."

I nodded. "And we could probably do it twice as fast if we helped each other out, but if you're not up for that, just try not to get in my way, okay?"

He nearly choked on his own spit. "Petra, you *cannot* keep trying to catch these guys. What will you even do if you do get back in there, which, by the way, is about the stupidest thing anyone could do? Even if you can get inside, what's going to happen then? Do you have a plan? Someone you're going to call?"

I bit my lip. "Honestly, I was hoping that person would be you or that you would, I don't know, be on the other end of the secret wire I would be wearing or whatever, but I can see that's not going to be the case, so I'll have to find someone else to help me."

"Oh my god, drag some other poor innocent soul into this already out-of-control situation? You really have no sense of who these people are."

"So fill me in."

He sighed and ran his hands through his hair again roughly. I couldn't remember a time when I had gotten someone so worked up before. I was a little disappointed in myself that it felt kind of…powerful. How awful was it to be gratified that I was making someone else miserable?

"Look, by now you probably already know almost as much as I do. There are bad guys, and from what I can gather, they have this ingenious and well-organized prostitution ring."

I nodded, things clicking into place.

"They find the girls by preying on their drug addiction so they don't even have to kidnap them or do anything against their will," he continued. "The girls just willingly waltz right on into the madness. I've heard rumblings around town that the girls get bid on at some sort of horrible auction for rich dudes."

"So why don't the cops just find out where the auction is and take it down?"

"The police," he said with a despondent look of doom. "The police don't know anything. They just have a bunch of missing girls. And frankly, probably only half of them have even been reported missing. Most of them are assumed runaways by their families. In a lot of neighborhoods, it's often a relief to have one less mouth to feed, you know?"

The thought made my stomach turn. "So what's your plan?" I asked.

"I'm still working on that. Surveilling. Trying to figure out who all the players are and how all the pieces fit together."

"And then what? Take down the bad guys?"

"We don't really use the term *bad guys*."

"Well, I do," I said. "I'm not about to run around calling them perps or something. I seriously cannot get away with that kind of lingo."

He actually chuckled.

"Run this by me one more time. Exactly what kind of training and experience do you have?"

And with that I knew I had him.

Chapter Sixteen

I'd love to say he agreed to let me help right then and there, but it took another hour and a half of convincing (I wouldn't call it hounding, exactly). Eventually I wore Ryan down, deciding not to tell him about the True Visionaries in Negotiating and the How to Debate Like a Genius classes I'd taken.

But I knew the idea of a dazzling and crafty sidekick was beginning to grow on him when he finally filled me in on the specific details of his case.

"I was hired by this woman…the mother of a missing girl. It has taken me a while, but I've tracked down this group, the one you oh so gracefully stumbled upon the other night. They're pretty bad guys," he said, shooting me a "why the hell did you have to go and do that?" look, even though we were so past that already. "Like *bad* bad. As bad as it gets. They run a prostitution ring where they take girls off the streets…the fresh, younger ones, like Kathleen, my client's daughter, and give them the drugs they want."

"Jesus," I said.

He nodded. "The thing about these guys though is they give the girls a life that isn't half-bad. I mean, it's not good. It's forced prostitution, the girls are totally coerced. But word on the street is that it's kind of like the luxurious spa version of prostitution and drugs. They apparently get to live in this big mansion and get treated pretty well. The catch is that they have to sleep with old rich guys, but they get their fix and a safe place to stay."

"Huh," was about all I could muster. I mean, sleeping with random guys who were paying for it was not number one on my "fun things to do on the weekend" list, but for someone who'd been living on the streets, it kinda sounded like a rescue of sorts.

"The other catch," Ryan continued, "is that no one seems to know what happens to the girls once they are no longer useful. Once they get older or too far into the drugs and lose their looks or what have you. They just…disappear." He said the last word ominously. I could only assume he meant that they get dead.

"That…doesn't sound good," I stupidly said.

"Exactly. So we can't half-ass any of this," he finished.

And even though he didn't say *like you've been doing so far* at the end of his sentence, I felt the sting of the implied words anyway.

"Look," I said, "I'm really sorry about all of this. I know how stupid it was to be following you in the first place. I don't want you to think that I just go around following people all the time. I just… I've had this writer's block for a while now and I guess I was curious about you."

"Curious?" he asked, raising an eyebrow.

Of course that would be the word he focused on. "But mostly," I said, shooting him a look that I hoped would suggest we were just casually going to skip over that part, "I was desperate. Desperate to find anything even remotely interesting for my heroine to get into."

Ryan looked weirdly thoughtful for a moment. "You're putting a lot of pressure on yourself for this next book."

I sighed. "I know you think it's just silly fiction, or whatever, but it's important to me."

He shook his head. "That's not what I meant. I just… I think it's nice that you're worried about what people will think of the next book."

"Not just any people. The fans. The ones who spent their hard-earned money on my first book. It's like… I'm so grateful to them for making it the success that it was. There are so many choices out there and the fact that even a single person picked up my book and thought it looked interesting is a huge deal. I just—" I swallowed "—I just don't want to let them down, you know?"

Ryan nodded. "I read it, you know." The words were quiet, barely audible.

A viselike knot gripped my stomach. "What do you mean?"

"Your book," he said casually, as if it were the most normal thing in the world.

My god, I had a hard enough time when complete strangers came up to me and said they read my book, but someone I knew? Someone I was hoping to get to know better? That was too much. It was funny, when I was writing my first book, I guess I hadn't really thought the whole thing through. I hadn't imagined what it would feel like for people to read it…and then come up to me and want to talk about it. For as cool as I thought it might be, it ended up being an exercise in that whole "leaning in to discomfort" thing that people were always talking about. I wasn't sure how to describe the feeling really, other than maybe overexposed? Like someone had waltzed in and taken a leisurely stroll through my brain. And does one really want a bunch of people loitering around in there? I still didn't know if the answer was yes or no, but either way, it was something that I still found…disconcerting.

As I was trying to come to terms with the fact that Ryan was now one of my brain-loiterers, he continued. "You know, *Desperately Seeking Fusion*? It was…good."

I distinctly did not like the little pause near the end of his sentence.

"Good?" I said, crossing my arms over my chest.

He nodded. "At first I was just going to look up the blurb, but the premise was original—it piqued my interest, actually." To say he sounded reluctant to say the words was an understatement. "I guess I never imagined a cozy mystery set in a science lab. I was very impressed with your research. It must have been quite a challenge to make sure all the tech and terminology, not to mention the science, was correct. I bet there are people out there just waiting to tell authors they've screwed up some tiny detail that doesn't matter the slightest for the plot."

"There definitely are," was all I could say, my mind still reeling.

"So I started reading a bit in the store, you know, for my own research," he said, shooting me a sheepish grin, "and I guess I kind of got sucked in."

"Your own research?"

Ryan shrugged one shoulder. "I needed to see what kind of a person I'd gotten myself tangled up with," he said. "And

I figured, what better way to get a read on a person than to actually, you know, *read* a person."

I rolled my eyes. "Wait. You said you read it. Like, the whole thing?"

"I…did," he said, still weirdly pausing between words.

I wasn't sure whether he was trying to go slow to spare my feelings, or if he was trying his hardest not to compliment my book.

"When did you have time? We just met the other day."

"Yesterday."

"You read the whole thing yesterday?"

"Yes."

"In one day."

"In one sitting, actually. Well, besides the first few pages I read in the store."

"And you just couldn't stop?" I said, still not sure if he was messing with me or not.

He let out a low growl of sorts then and looked like he was regretting life at the moment. "I was just so sure I knew what was going to happen and wanted to see if I was right."

"Huh," I said, not quite sure how to respond to that little tidbit.

He'd just explained the exact thing I'd been trying to do with the book. Have the reader sure they were going to guess what had happened, what was going to happen and why it all came together that way. Of course, the better mysteries are the ones that the reader is sure they know the ending to, but in the end, is utterly wrong.

He fidgeted with the collar of his shirt.

"Well…?" I asked.

"Well what?"

"Were you right?"

He broke out in a crooked grin then, like he was conceding something. "I have to say, I absolutely did not see the ending coming. I was so damned sure too." He looked down and shook his head, still smiling. "It's pretty rare when I don't see the twist coming."

A feeling washed over me—a shot of energy filling up my torso and spreading to my limbs like a burst of white light. Was this...pride?

"You thought Reggie was the one that did it, right?"

"One hundred percent, and I was feeling pretty confident about it too," he said. "And then when Monique, oh my god, it was like she came out of nowhere, except then—when I thought back over the whole thing—it almost seemed inevitable. I don't know how I didn't catch it."

I was smiling like I'd just been handed an Academy Award. Except, you know, not for acting or whatever. "That was exactly what I was going for."

"It was great. A damned good mystery, really," he said, his smile growing.

I sighed a big, happy sigh, the goofy smile still plastered all over my face. "So...does that mean we're ready then? You have a newfound trust in my wit and ability to be involved in a damned good mystery?"

"Oh, hell no," he said, his smile fading fast. "I mean, I have no doubt you can craft a good mystery, but I'm not really sure it translates into real-world skill."

My smile faded even faster than his. "So, being a mystery reader doesn't help in solving real mysteries, and neither does being a mystery writer?"

He shook his head. "The bad guys in novels are usually clever, outsmarting the detective time and time again."

"Until they don't," I piped in.

"Right. But that's not the way it is with real criminals. Real criminals get emotional, often doing stupid things. Real criminals also get lucky way more than those of us in law enforcement would like to admit. Real criminals don't have a neat and tidy motive all the time—hell, sometimes I don't think they even know why they do the things they do."

"So, we have to be smarter than them," I said.

"Sometimes, yeah, we have to be smarter than them. But sometimes we have to also try to be as emotional or out of control as them. Or at least think that way. We have to be irrational, angry, scared…all the things real people are."

I had to admit, this was a fascinating trek into the mind of criminals, and I couldn't help but think this whole conversation was going to come in very handy if I ever got the motivation to sit down and write my next novel. A task, I suddenly found, that didn't feel quite as daunting as it had yesterday. I mean, it still felt like I was trapped on a set of railroad tracks just down the line from an oncoming train that I had to somehow stop before it ran over me. But honestly, it was an improvement from where my mindset *had* been—which was somewhere in the vicinity of stopping a world-ending asteroid streaking toward Earth with my bare hands.

THE NEXT DAY, Annie and I decided we should have a debriefing tea session after yesterday's party—though mostly I think she wanted to talk about the part where Ryan dragged me out of there. So when I opened my door and was instead greeted by a construction worker in full gear—tool belt, orange vest and, most oddly, a hard hat—I was somewhat taken aback.

I glanced at the ceiling, thinking my friends really had been unfair when they claimed I didn't have any self-preservation skills. I mean, seriously, one glance at a hard hat and immediately I was surveying my surroundings for any and all potential threats. I took a step back as I tried to wrap my head around this unexpected caller.

And that's when things really careened toward the weird.

The guy set down what looked like a speaker, pushed a button on his phone, calmly placed it into his tool belt and proceeded to start dancing to the music emanating from the speaker at his feet.

Just as my thoughts started going *I'm sorry, what?* the elevator doors opened. Out of the corner of my eye (I mean, obviously I wasn't about to take the fronts of my eyes off this, I now realized, quite attractive stranger in front of me), I saw Annie begin to stroll toward my door.

But my mind was so occupied with the situation in front of me that I couldn't even figure out whether I should be relieved that I was no longer alone with this stranger, or weirded out that she was witnessing this…spectacle of human strangeness that was unfolding.

But that's when the weirdness began to multiply. Tenfold.

Because as Mr. Construction Worker Man began a slow spin, gyrating the whole way, inch by inch he started removing his brightly colored vest. Which was so unanticipated, it even stopped Annie in her tracks. The man did not seem to mind the additional audience.

Maybe I was in shock or something, because I kind of

just stood there watching this guy twirl the vest in the air, eventually flinging it off to the side. This was followed by a similar production with his shirt.

I realized I should probably try to find out what in the wits of Nancy D. was going on, but to be honest, I was a little caught off guard by the chisel-y-ness of his abs and couldn't quite find the fortitude to speak.

Just as the gentleman's tear-away pants were being whisked off in a flourish—which, I might add, showcased an impressive bulge beneath a vibrant orange G-string, complete with caution symbol on the front—Ryan decided it was the perfect time to mosey on out of his apartment to see what the hell was going on.

To the stranger's credit, his performance didn't falter as he finished with a couple more spins and a move that perhaps might best be described as a full-body shimmy-shimmy.

The dude cocked one eyebrow and spoke for the first time. "If you want this to go any further, I'm afraid we'll have to take this inside your apartment."

"Um…" Clearly, I was still searching for my coherence. "I think we're good?" I said, not sure why my voice rose at the end like it was a question.

He shrugged in a sort of "suit yourself" way and fished a card out of his tool belt. I couldn't help but think it was an awfully handy accessory, and briefly wondered why the fashion world hadn't figured out something similar for everyday wear.

"From your anonymous admirer," he said as he handed me his card, gathered his clothes and speaker in a bundle, then simply walked away, waiting patiently for the elevator in his G-string and work boots as the three of us stood frozen, still not quite sure what we had just witnessed.

Not surprisingly, it was Annie who finally broke the silence once the elevator had whooshed our new friend away and we all continued to stare at its doors a few moments longer.

"Well," she said, pulling an accordion-style hand fan from somewhere in the depths of her complicated multipatterned, pocket-heavy pantsuit, which she proceeded to flick open like a pro, fluttering it lightly at her face, "that was certainly invigorating!"

Finally, I glanced at the card, which simply said, Jack P.'s Strip-O-Grams with his number listed neatly below, and honestly, I had to admire the no-fuss, no-muss attitude of both his performance and his marketing materials.

"Anonymous admirer?" Ryan said.

Of course that was the part he would latch on to.

"It's nothing," I said, kind of waving the thought away. "Ready for tea?" I added, turning to Annie, hoping Ryan would just drop it.

Unfortunately, as I headed into my apartment, both Annie and Ryan followed.

"It's not nothing," he said, his tone amplified with a bit of a growl as he said each word. Which should have been frustrating but was honestly damned sexy. "Someone just sent a complete stranger to your place of residence to do a strip show and you think that's nothing? Is this the sort of thing that happens to you a lot?"

I gave him a look. "No, I can honestly say I've never had a strip-o-gram delivered to me before, and frankly I thought the whole notion of a strip-o-gram was one of those urban legend things, but I have to say, Jack *was* kind of entertaining."

"And how!" Annie piped in, fan still in hand, fluttering away.

"Whether your—" Ryan seemed to be mustering up the fortitude to say the words "—strip-o-gram was entertaining or not, is not really the point here. The point is that someone sent an anonymous—"

The poor man seemed to be at a loss for words again.

"Gift?" I said, helpfully.

He took a slow breath, closing his eyes. "Fine," he growled, "an anonymous *gift*—" he spit out the word like it pained him "—which means we have a very big problem."

"Gifts, actually," I said.

His eyebrows rose and I swore I detected a hint of a tremble in his body, which kind of made me regret saying anything.

"I'm sorry?" he asked.

"Not to interrupt, lovelies, but I think tea might be better some other time," Annie said, moving toward the door.

"Annie, you don't have to go."

She looked from me to Ryan, then back to me, then again to Ryan. "I really think I do," she said, her fan becoming a little less fluttery and moving more into the manic oscillation category as she eased herself out the door.

I watched her go for as long as I could get away with, then turned my attention back to Ryan, who was waiting with alarming patience for me to explain.

"I don't know, I got some chocolates and some flowers," I finally said, my entire insides cringing in wait for his reaction.

"Show me."

I scrunched up my face. "Well obviously I ate the chocolates, but the flowers are over here," I said, pointing to the coffee table.

"You ate…the chocolates," he said, all stuttery, like he couldn't quite believe it.

"What? They were really good chocolates."

He stood blinking for what seemed like a lifetime, his mouth hanging open a little like he was trying to figure out what to say.

But I held fast to the belief that anyone with a pulse and some taste buds would have absolutely eaten the chocolates.

"Didn't you ever go like, trick-or-treating or whatever as a kid? Didn't we all learn about candy safety?"

I shrugged. And honestly, all this talk about chocolates was kind of making me wish I still had some of the sketchy chocolates because I really could have used a hit of sugar right then.

He gave me a look out of the side of his eyes that told me he once again thought I could use some work in the self-preservation department. He marched over to the flowers and whipped the card from the stems with a flourish.

"'From your anonymous admirer,'" he said, and seriously, that growl was really starting to get to the bottom of things. The bottom of my nether regions, that was.

I shrugged again. "It's just a fan or whatever."

"Or whatever," he deadpanned.

"Yeah," I said, crossing my arms.

"I don't even know what to say to you. Your recklessness is going to get us all in trouble."

"Or," I said, raising my eyebrows, "maybe it just might solve this mystery."

He closed his eyes and shook his head ever so slightly, taking a little pause for composure. "I'm taking this," he said, lifting the card he held in his hand. He moved toward me and plucked Jack P.'s card from my grip as well, then headed for the door.

"In need of a gift for someone special?" I asked. I mean, how could I resist, right?

But he just let out a final, low growl and headed on his decidedly unmerry way, which of course made me smile all the more.

THE NEXT DAY, Ryan insisted on testing some of my battle skills, and quite frankly, I was not going to argue. Mostly, because I might get to see some of his skills too, but more importantly, observe him in his workout gear, which, lord willing, would be shirtless.

Sadly, he showed up to our rooftop workout in a full tracksuit. I mean, sure it was cold out and everything, but way to let a girl down, dude.

Still, the exercise was far from a loss considering the three milliseconds it took for a shivery heat to build down my spine when his gaze met mine as we lined up for sparring. The way he stared…so intense, searing…almost like… lust? But the moment broke too soon, and he was rushing me, my mind jumping into fight mode as he charged.

Muscle memory kicked in as I sidestepped the blow, but he was so fast, and before I could get my bearings, he had me in a choke hold with one arm, his other hand planting itself around my waist—a move that felt so familiar, the graze of his thumb across the bare skin under the hem of my hoodie igniting a turbulent fire deep in my belly.

Fortunately, one of the first moves they taught in my Always Be Aware self-defense class was how to get out of the exact situation I'd found myself in. I grabbed the arm he had around my neck with both hands and took a step forward, launching my leg back to kick out his knee. As he started to buckle, I used the momentum to flip him over my head, quickly straddling him while he was still stunned, readying my arm for a blow in case he wanted to continue.

He let out a low groan, causing my thighs to tingle in response.

"Nice move," he said, panting and rubbing the back of his neck, then relaxing back into the floor, his hands coming down to rest on my legs with that same, familiar touch, like we'd done this a hundred times before. The smirk that accompanied his words nearly undid me.

And maybe that's why I just sat there, straddling him (dear god) and gazing into his eyes. And for a while, he gazed right back. Suddenly, I had a hard time catching my breath.

Of course, Ryan seemed to come to his senses before I did, since I felt him tense up in that way you do when you're not sure what the hell to do. Like he was frozen, not wanting to disturb the moment, or perhaps, more likely, not wanting to embarrass me by asking if I was ever going to, you know, stop straddling him (to which the obvious answer should have been absolutely not). But, being a gentlewoman—or, at least, as gentlewomanly as someone who just upended a grown-ass man over her shoulder then straddled him like he was her prize can be—I eventually heaved myself off the poor man.

"Again," Ryan said as we climbed to our feet, and he shed his light jacket.

Sadly, he was still not shirtless, but what I wouldn't give to be a piece of that T-shirt clinging to him in all the right places like it was custom-made. Honestly, even with the chill of the wind, it really was getting rather hot up on that rooftop. I peeled my own hoodie off, a moment of self-consciousness flowing over me and my exercise bra. But I didn't have much time to think about it, since Ryan was already headed my way.

I quickly moved into a defensive stance, stepping out to give myself a wide base, both front to back and left to right with my legs diagonal from each other. It didn't stop Ryan's momentum though, and before I knew what was happening, he'd taken us both down.

There were plenty of maneuvers I could try to gain control of the situation, but there was one little problem. The weight of him on me felt more like it was always meant to be there instead of something akin to an attack. With the distraction of this thought, it only took a moment for him to pin both my hands above my head, holding them with one hand while the other rested gently close to my neck in a sort of gentle mock-strangle as proof that he'd bested me, but without being too threatening.

Frankly, it was one hell of a turn-on.

His face was inches from mine, our breath heavy with the exertion...and maybe something else.

"I guess we might have to work a little more on this one," I said, not meaning for it to sound as suggestive as it did.

Perhaps because I'd said it as I stared directly at his delectable lips.

I quickly snapped my eyes back to his, but he'd definitely caught me staring.

He cleared his throat and lifted himself off me, holding out his hand to help me up, which I accepted only after I took a moment to catch my breath and try to pretend the last minute or so hadn't actually happened.

Way too soon—and with great sorrow—the hand-to-hand portion of the day was complete as he pulled out a few of his Tasers and hand combat weapons to show me how to use them—as if I didn't already know (you'd be surprised at how many licensed weaponry classes were out there). I think I may have impressed him, which only annoyed me slightly. Most of the time I was more than happy to be underestimated—frankly it usually gave me the advantage—but one doesn't really want the guy she's crushing on to underestimate her.

I didn't want to get into a real fight or anything, but I couldn't help but think that that might be the only way to show Ryan what I could really do. Although, it would probably say more for my acting and improvisation skills if I were to be able to avoid a fight altogether. Either way, I hoped to shimmy further toward the "impressed" side of the old sliding scale by the time this operation was complete. I tried not to think about the whole "I could also end up on the dead end of the scale" possibility, but unfortunately, the notion did manage to wiggle into my mind once or twice.

Chapter Seventeen

Ryan had pointed out, quite correctly, that I couldn't very well go back to the apartment looking even remotely like I had looked the last time I had, you know, escaped and whatever. We were both pretty sure the bad guys weren't going to look all that kindly on my waltzing back in again.

So we called in Brandt for a consultation.

At first, he wanted to go full-on living dead, but Ryan countered that they only took the girls who still looked half-decent, so I'd have to pass their initial attractiveness test just to get back into the scary room, tied up like I had been the other night. They'd had plenty of time to look me over and knew very well what I looked like—at least what I'd looked like in that first disguise. And while it was a good one, we all agreed this one had to be even better, making me look completely different from both myself and the, er, less put together version of myself.

"We've got to go complete opposite then," Brandt said. "Brown contacts. Dark hair. I can maybe do something with makeup to change the shape of your eyes."

A strange wave of calm washed over me. I'd seen Brandt perform miracles with his skills. He used to work with a photographer who specialized in temporarily altering regular people to look like their favorite celebrities, and I felt oddly secure in his hands.

As we made final preparations, Ryan tested the listening device he'd gotten, which would allow him to hear everything I heard. It was a cheap-looking pin, like a promotional button, but he assured me it was top-of-the-line. Totally wireless and no one would ever suspect it was a bug.

Brandt thought it was ridiculous at first, but in the end, he ended up designing the entire look around it. Kind of like an old-school Madonna look, but his plan was to make a more modern look, like an on-purpose '90s retro thing. He even found a few more of the old-school buttons to make a nice little cluster out of them, which I thought was kind of ingenious, but Ryan just rolled his eyes. It didn't seem like he was having as much fun as the rest of us at the makeover party.

"I cannot believe you are calling this a makeover party," he said, his jaw clenched.

"What? The situation has enough tension and drama as it is. Is it really so bad to try to have a little fun with it?"

He sighed and went back to his apartment to "double-check his supplies," whatever that meant. For a steely private eye, he sure seemed to have a lot of nervous jitters.

Brandt got to work on my face while Vic poured us each a glass of wine.

"Make sure to hide mine," I said, taking a quick sip. "Somehow I doubt Ryan would approve of me going in drunk."

Vic quickly grabbed the glass away. "Shit. I never even thought of that."

I rolled my eyes. "Vic, I'm not going to get drunk. I am, however, going to have a single glass of this lovely wine you brought to calm my nerves a little. No more, I promise."

"Okay," she said, handing it back over, "but this is it."

I nodded. "Thanks, Mom."

She gave me a look. If there was ever anything Vic always said she wasn't interested in, it was being anybody's mom.

As Brandt worked his magic, Ryan popped in every few minutes to see how the "disguise," as he insisted on calling it, was going—apparently, in his mind, makeovers were for teenagers and divorcées. The whole thing was making it rather hard to enjoy my wine, since I had to quickly ditch it every time the door opened, though in truth, I was somewhat torn—I really did enjoy watching the guy enter a room. I don't know if Brandt could feel my heart speed up or what, but he sighed and shook his head every time I spotted Ryan.

"Okay, I'm almost done. Just your lips are left," Brandt said. "If you want to finish that wine you better chug it, because you can't be drinking until they are set, and it's gonna take a little time."

I shrugged and downed the rest of the glass. Not that there was much left anyway. Vic whisked the glass away and put it directly in the dishwasher in case Ryan got all detective-y and decided to count how many used glasses were hanging around. I could just see him canceling the whole thing based on something super insignificant, just to have an excuse not to do it.

"Okay, guys," Brandt said, "I think we're done."

As he was talking, Ryan came in for an update.

"Wow," Vic said, glancing over at Brandt. "You are actually really good at this." Her mouth hung open for a second as she looked at him.

"Um, yeah," Brandt said, acting offended, though I knew he got it all the time. Nobody expected his big ol' self to be a genius artist with a makeup brush.

"My god," Ryan said. "That is amazing."

He sat staring at me for a moment and I gladly stared back, but it got uncomfortable pretty quickly. And it's not like he was staring at me, like Petra me; he was staring at whatever concoction Brandt had come up with.

"Do I get to see or are you all going to sit there and make me feel like a freak?" I asked.

"Right. Sorry," Brandt said, sneaking a glance over at Vic.

Which was so entirely weird it almost made me forget that I was about to embark on a dangerous mission. Ooh, I liked the idea of calling it a dangerous mission. Maybe I could use that in my book.

Brandt held a mirror up and I gasped. "Holy crap," I said, although the words were not coming out of my mouth.

I mean, they were, obviously, but it was certainly not the mouth I was used to seeing when I looked in the mirror. My lips were suddenly fuller, but somehow also seemed smaller, more delicate. Almost heart shaped.

And the rest of me was not any more recognizable than the lips. My face was pale with hints of dark circles under my eyes and a bit of a sunken look to my cheeks. I wore a straight black wig with long bangs, covering even my eyebrows, which were normally one of my more distinctive features.

But perhaps it was my eyes that were the most changed.

Somehow Brandt had lined them to look completely different, more almond shaped, but only slightly—nothing over-the-top that would have anyone guessing this had not been my look since birth.

"Wow," was honestly all I could say to the reflection in the mirror, my voice completely weird coming out of the face of a stranger.

"Shit," I said. "My voice. What am I supposed to do about my voice?"

"Did you speak to them before?" Ryan asked, suddenly looking concerned all over again.

Sigh. Those ten seconds without that look had been nice.

"Well, yeah," I said. "They asked me a few questions. Had me agree to work with them, you know, before they knocked me out."

"Damn," Ryan said. "I don't suppose..."

"What?"

"Well, your acting classes? Was there ever any accent work or anything like that?"

I raised my eyebrows. "There was. The only problem was I was really kind of bad at it."

He looked worried. And suddenly I felt worried. I couldn't believe I hadn't thought of this before that moment, which was very close to when we had to get going.

Vic piped in, "Maybe you could just pretend to be kind of meek or whatever and just nod and use gestures as much as you can. And if you have to answer something, just do it really quiet, like you're scared and just want to get the hell out of there."

I raised one eyebrow. "That shouldn't be too hard. I mean,

not that I'm scared, but I'm sure it wouldn't be too far of a reach, at least."

Ryan was nodding. "Yeah, that's not bad. Change your demeanor, your personality. The voice isn't as big a part as the way you present yourself. Just speak softly if you have to speak." He nodded a kind of kudos at Vic.

I couldn't help but feel pretty proud of my friends at that moment. Without Brandt, none of this would be possible, and Vic just ended up solving a major problem in about five seconds.

Someone knocked on the door, making me jump. All eyes turned to me, but I had as much of an idea about who it might be as they did.

"Come on, Petra, open up!" a very familiar, and irritatingly whiny voice came from the other side of the door.

"Again with this bloody guy?" Brandt said, as he finished packing up his gear.

"What bloody guy?" Ryan asked.

Vic sighed. "Petra's idiotic ex," she said, then turned to me. "Sorry, no offense."

"Oh, don't worry, none taken."

"Well, he can't see you like that," Ryan said, looking more and more stressed out by the second.

"Actually," Brandt said, puffing his chest a little, "I wouldn't mind testing out my work."

"What do you mean?" I asked.

"I want to see if he recognizes you." He grinned. "This guy lived with you for months. I know he's an idiot, but still. Let's see if he figures it out."

"This isn't a game, you guys," Ryan said.

"Actually, I kind of want to see too," I jumped in. "If we

can fool him, I'll know we can fool anybody, and I think it will help me feel a little more confident about the situation. Besides, I should probably practice my new personality."

Ryan shook his head in defeat and sat, leaving Vic to open the door.

"She's not here," Vic said in the "I hate your guts and everything you stand for" voice she reserved for Johnny.

Johnny immediately barged in and looked everybody over, quickly deciding Vic was right. "Well, where the hell is she? Like in the bathroom or something?"

"She went out," Brandt said, crossing his arms and looking altogether menacing.

"Why are all you guys here then?" he asked, unable to keep that whine from creeping into his voice. It was like he was a petulant five-year-old that never grew up.

What had I ever seen in him?

"And who's the new girl?" he asked with a couple of eyebrow pumps.

Ugh.

"And I don't even know this guy," he went on, gesturing at Ryan, as if it was impossible that someone he didn't know could be in my house. "Who is this guy?"

It was more than a little obvious that Johnny had taken an immediate dislike to Ryan, which was basically how he felt about any good-looking guy. The competition sent his tiny ego reeling.

"Why are you here?" Brandt said, his voice slightly lower and a little more booming than usual.

"I just… I need to talk to Petra." He was slowly inching toward the couch that I was sitting on, and I did not want him to get any closer.

"Like we said," Vic said, blocking him from the path of the couch. "She's not here. And how in the hell do you keep getting into the building, anyhow?"

He shrugged. "People are nice. They let me in."

"Christ," Ryan whispered under his breath, obviously less than pleased at the security in the building.

I threw Vic a pleading look.

She jumped into action. "Okay, well, we'll tell her you stopped by." She grabbed his shoulders and pivoted him around toward the door, pushing him slightly toward it, and then a few moments later the pushing intensified.

"I can just wait for her," he said.

"No," Brandt boomed. "You can't."

"But you guys all get to be here when she's not." The whining had reached high-level patheticism.

"Yup, we sure do," Vic said, just to add a little salt to the wound.

She opened the door and gave him one last good shove.

"You know what?" Ryan said, suddenly getting up from his chair and walking at a somewhat alarming pace toward Johnny.

The look on Johnny's face was a fairly hilarious mash-up of stunned and afraid.

"I wouldn't bother coming back to this building if I were you," he said, stopping just inside my apartment as Johnny backed out. "I'm going to make sure no one lets you in again." And with that he slammed the door in his face.

I wasn't sure if I should be pleased or insulted. I mean, Ryan didn't even know if I wanted to see Johnny again or not. But I couldn't help but feel a lovely warmth radiating through my stomach.

And you know what? I did have a feeling it would be the last time I'd see Johnny, at least for a very long time. More importantly, I realized I was pretty pleased about that and couldn't help the tiny smile that crept across my face.

Ryan stood facing the door for a moment, then slowly turned. "Sorry about that." He cleared his throat. "But we really do need to be going."

I nodded and took a deep breath.

"Okay. Let's do this."

Chapter Eighteen

I waited in the alley until Ryan was in position on the fire escape across from the apartment where I'd previously been held. He signaled me with a quick wave and I was off, around to the front of the building.

I stood in line again, but this time there was only one person in front of me. I didn't speak at all and didn't even get a strange look.

Things were going perfectly.

I stood in front of the table just like I had last time, although this time I may have been slightly sweatier. Not my face, thank goodness—Brandt had powdered the whistling Dixie out of that so the makeup would all stay in place—but under my armpits had that tingling, moist feeling when your body is about to pull a *Case of the Disappearing Deodorant*.

It also took everything in me not to look out the window into the back alley. Knowing Ryan was there this time made me ten times as nervous—although that may have helped as I was being questioned, because I was sure I was way more nervous this time, which naturally made my mannerisms different. The fact that I knew what was coming this time might have been a wee bit of a factor too. I kept thinking they were so dense for not figuring out who I was, but then I'd remember how amazing Brandt was at his job and I relaxed into my weird little performance.

In a flash, they scooted me past the first hurdle and led me down the hallway toward the same room I'd been kept in previously. The door swung open, and like before, a couple girls were already there, passed out and tied up.

I quickly remembered I was supposed to be taking the scene in for the first time (actually, this wasn't so quick—I'd one hundred percent been focused on my acting and had forgotten what I was really there for...you know, just for a second though). I gasped a teeny gasp—subtlety was the main thing they grilled into you in acting class, and did my best to look startled and confused, my gaze quickly moving from one girl to the other, then I made a move like I was going to try to get away. And before I could even feel relief that I didn't even really have to act that part—I was out cold, flopping to the floor in a lifeless heap.

Except, of course I wasn't.

I played dead while the guy picked me up off the floor and pretty much threw me on the bed, putting one half of a pair of handcuffs around my wrist and the other around one of the metal headboard rails. I thanked my lucky stars this hadn't been my fate the other night.

Our plan worked. Ryan had found a prosthetic sleeve thing that went over my arm and worked like a "dummy" limb. It was extremely realistic, fitting snugly over my real arm, the inside of it anatomically accurate enough to fool someone into thinking they were giving you a needle, when really the drug emptied harmlessly into the prosthetic. Don't even ask me where he found it. In fact, I didn't really want to know because I was picturing a supersecret spy store that only proper spies were allowed access to, like some kind of Spies R Us situation with retinal scans and everything. I would have been breathtakingly disappointed if it was just like, Amazon or whatever.

Both the girls in the room were out, although one was moaning softly as if she was in some sort of blissful haze. My gaze shot to the window, and I couldn't help but smile, knowing we were already getting one over on these assholes, and that this time I wasn't alone.

Unfortunately, things got real boring real fast and I wished the mic in the button was a two-way deal where Ryan and I could have a conversation. But while that definitely would have made the time go faster, talking was probably not the safest thing for me to do.

If only I knew he was out there. I mean, I knew he was, and was fairly certain that he wouldn't leave me, but still, it would be nice to have some sort of confirmation. Being in that room, even if it was with two other girls, was as lonely as the poor Ténéré Tree—famous for being the only landmark in two hundred fifty miles of Sahara Desert, and also famously knocked over by a drunk driver (which is honestly pretty impressive—what are the odds?). Unrelated, but did I mention that my mind tended to wander when confronted with boredom?

Time crawled to a resounding halt. I tried not to think about what came next. I'd been so worried about getting to this point, I hadn't really thought much past it, and now that I had all the time in the world, I was seriously starting to get a little anxious.

I thought about Ryan out there, wondering if the wait was

worse for him or me. Knowing the way he was taking on all the responsibility for my safety, a good gambler might have bet on him. Of course, wondering how he was feeling got me thinking about all kinds of Ryan-related things. I couldn't help but remember the moments we'd touched when we were sparring. The tension. The spark. What the moment might be like just before he kissed me, you know, if that ever happened. What other…things might be like with Ryan. And honestly, I had a *lot* of time to kill so things got a little R-rated. And yeah, I knew he'd barely given any indication that he might possibly be interested, other than a certain…tension whenever we were in a room together, or maybe that was only on my end. A thought that catapulted me back to the time Annie said Ryan tended to have more sophisticated girlfriends.

Sigh. Daydreaming was frustrating business.

Finally, there was shuffling outside the door. I kept my head down as if I were passed out like the other girls.

Two guys came in and grabbed the first girl from a chair against the wall where her hands were tied up over her head around a sconce. I felt a little sorry for her. The way her arms were, it seemed like it must be terrible on the shoulders for any length of time, but then again, she wasn't fake passed out like I was. She probably wasn't feeling a thing. They hauled her out of the room, then came back for me. I did my best to play dead, though it took everything I had not to flinch when one of the guys whipped something out of his pocket. I'm sure I tensed, but they didn't seem to notice and thankfully all it ended up being was the key to release the handcuffs.

I stayed as limp as I could as they hauled me down a different set of stairs, which led out into the alley. I fought the urge to look up at Ryan's balcony, hoping he was invisible up there. Thank Nancy for people who had too much stuff and used their balconies for extra storage.

Propped up on a bench seat, they duct-taped our legs. Seriously, these guys loved that stuff. Ryan's car was at the other end of the alley. I hoped he'd be able to get to it quickly enough to follow. I had the tracker on me, of course, but I'd seen more than a few spy movies in my day and right before the big climax, the technology always seemed to crap out.

The men left the back of the truck, and I sneaked a quick peek at my surroundings. The other girls were propped up on the opposite side. We were in a tall vehicle, more like a box truck than a van, which would hopefully make it easier for Ryan to follow. I quickly shut my eyes as one of the men got back into the vehicle.

There was very little else about the truck that gave me any clues to what might happen next. No windows, not even a smell besides a bit of stale dust.

This was when I was reminded, yet again, how difficult it was to play the part of someone passed out. Every instinct in my body screamed to open my eyes, which would have been a disaster. I tried to focus on relaxing my face, since every movement and noise around me made me want to flinch.

I hadn't anticipated how exhausting it would be. I wondered if I could get away with a catnap, then realized that this was probably the part where I should pay attention. Try to get a handle on which direction we were going and how far we drove—just like they'd taught in my online class. Sure, Ryan would be taking care of that, but then I started thinking about trust. God, my mind could have some terri-

ble timing. Because when I really thought about it, I didn't
know that much about Ryan. I mean, my instinct was that
he was exceptional, but now that I had a merciless eternity
to think about it, I had no actual basis for this conclusion.
Could I really trust myself to be impartial considering how
attracted I was to him? Because, let's face it, my track record in the trusting-men department was not spectacular.

And honest to god, did one of these guys really have to
sit in the back with us? Because I had a huge crick in my
neck. Keeping my head flopped to my chest was no joke,
but that was the position of the other girls, so that's what I
went with. The other guy went up front with the driver. Or
maybe he *was* the driver. I supposed it didn't really take an
army to haul around three passed-out chicks.

The truck finally moved, and I caught myself holding my
breath. I let it out slowly, super freaked at the guy sitting beside me, but he didn't seem to notice. I tried to relax and not
think about the kink in my neck, which was obviously impossible. It was the only thing I could think of. Well, except
Ryan and whether or not I could trust him and, more importantly, if I'd ever get to see him without his shirt on. And I
guess I kind of had this anticipatory worry thing going on
about what might await me once the truck stopped. Also,
why did I have "Super Freak" in my head all of a sudden?

What felt like an hour later, we finally stopped, but then
again, time had done that thing where it lollygags for days,
then rushes, then lollygags again until time means nothing, so it may have been much less. Or more. I really had
no idea. From what I could tell, the road changed about
halfway through the drive, like we were on gravel instead
of pavement, and I wondered how Ryan was supposed to

follow on some remote road without being noticed. In my private investigation course, they'd taught us to drive without any headlights on, but I wasn't even sure cars could do that anymore. Seemed like anything from this century had automatic running lights. Although, I supposed that was something that could probably be doctored. Still, if he was driving without headlights, it would have been pretty dangerous considering the speed that we seemed to be going.

Ugh, I needed to relax and trust Ryan to be there for me. He was a professional. I was pretty sure.

As they dragged me out of the truck, I risked a quick peek, acting as if I was groggily fighting to wake up, and caught a tiny glimpse of our destination—a huge mansion, apparently in the middle of nowhere. From the bit I was able to see, it wasn't some creepy old place either—it was new, as if it had been built in the past few years.

I wondered if it had been built specifically for this horrible purpose.

Chapter Nineteen

The other girls and I were put into a bright room where they continued to sleep off whatever drugs were pumping through their system. One girl was a bit more conscious than the other, which I figured was a good thing. I could probably get away with being slightly more awake if I needed to.

I started stirring. Several additional girls were in the room with us, though they were more alert. Oddly, a few of them were in full-on evening gowns—the kind I'd always wanted to wear, but unless you were a movie star or millionaire, you'd never really have the occasion. I mean, the fanciest events I ever went to were weddings, and sparkly evening gowns were certainly not a thing with the crowd I hung out with. Was it bad that I was a little excited that I might get to wear one of them?

And then...things got super boring again. And yes, all the classes I had taken had pointed out that surveillance was more sitting and waiting than it was rushing around the countryside finding clues every five minutes—Nancy had mismanaged my expectations on that one—but still, I couldn't have imagined the absolute atrophy of my will to endure. I really thought fear and danger would be the hard part, but a bit of jeopardy would have been absolute life candy right about then. I honestly didn't know what the hell was up with my personality—a massive disaster could strike and I'd flutter like a delicate butterfly into problem-solving mode, all graceful and elegant…then the one time my zipper gets stuck on my coat, I'm thrashing around like certain death is nigh.

Perhaps the whole situation was giving me too much time to think. Maybe I could get into a comfortable position and indulge in a little catnap. I mean, it wasn't like I was getting any good surveillance in anyway—I was stuck in another damned room, and I'd already taken mental pictures of all the girls in there with me. Besides, I was a superlight sleeper, so if anyone came in or went out, I'd be able to catch it.

Approximately twelve years later, I blinked my eyes open. Apparently, the adrenaline of the day made me more tired than I realized. Wiping the drool from the corner of my mouth, I realized a few of the girls were missing from the room, and even more disturbing, an emerald green evening gown was laid out on the couch five inches away. I'd missed someone setting it down RIGHT BESIDE ME. The gown was definitely meant for me, since the other girls who'd arrived with me had gowns beside them too. The girl who'd started coming out of her trance before my nap had already started undressing.

"Are we supposed to put these on?" I asked, hoping my words came out sounding kind of slurred. Was that what drugs were supposed to do to a person? I mean, I knew alcohol did, but I wasn't sure about drugs. I hadn't been around them much.

The girl just nodded kind of lazily. "That's what some-one said."

I started to undress as quickly as possible, hiding myself like I was in a high school locker room. It had been years since I'd been forced to change in front of strangers and the experience wasn't one I missed. I scrambled into the dress and struggled with the zipper. Eventually, I got it up, but my neck was not a particularly willing participant after all the head hanging (way to go me that my head flopped the same way during my li'l nap). Also, the dress was a little tight. At least I wouldn't have to act uncomfortable, since I was, in fact, aggressively uncomfortable. I could barely sit in the thing but managed to sort of lounge-lean into the couch without the dress digging into my guts too much.

I kept my eyes and ears open for any clues, then suddenly realized now that I'd changed, I was no longer wearing my wire tracker thing.

Damn. Who would have thought we'd have to change clothes? I grabbed my shirt, pretending to start folding it, seeing if I could find a way to somehow get the wire off and back on me somewhere, but a man came into the room and told us we needed to be ready in two minutes. The fact that a man had barged in was to be expected, I supposed, but I couldn't help but be surprised at the women who were still changing and half-naked. They barely flinched at the sight of him. Good thing I was already changed since I probably would have reacted quite differently, like screamed or flailed to cover myself or something equally discreet.

Note to self. Do not react to anything.

I could not figure a way to get the wire off the shirt, par-ticularly without wrecking it. What looked like a simple button had wires out the back that continued down into the shirt, sewn in place. With the short amount of time I had, not to mention all the people milling about, I'd never be able to pull it off.

I needed to let Ryan know that I didn't have it anymore, and the only thing I could think of was to try and destroy it so that maybe it would go dead. I hoped it would be obvious if it went out of service, like a warning signal would come up or something, but there was a very real chance that the thing could just go dead and Ryan would think I was just being really quiet. Or like, napping.

Still, what choice did I have? I started picking at the button, pretending like it was a nervous habit I was doing to help try to calm my nerves. One of the other girls was pacing around anxiously, so I figured it wasn't a huge stretch. Soon, I had the front of the button nearly yanked right off, along with a good portion of my nail polish.

I only hoped it was enough to make the thing go black.

A few minutes later most of the girls were ready to go, although I wasn't sure where. A man (I'd have been shocked if his name wasn't Igor) herded us into a line and led us through a series of hallways. I made a mental note of which directions we turned the way I was taught in Everyday Surveillance, even though I wasn't sure why I'd want to go back to that dressing room. Except that my clothes were still there—not that they were likely clothes I'd ever wear again. Still, out of habit, or maybe just to help keep my mind occupied, I marked our steps in my mind and tried not to panic. Things were already starting to go wrong, and I wondered if I should be planning an escape route, just in case. I glanced around, making sure not to look too alert though no one seemed to be paying attention to me anyway, and compiled mental notes.

The mansion was set up as a house would be, not an institution, so there weren't clearly marked exits. Still, there were windows on the south walls of a grand room we were being herded through, so there was a good chance any doors on that wall led outside.

They herded us into a smaller room, this one dimly lit. The shadowy atmosphere lent an even creepier vibe to the place, and since I already knew I was in the middle of nowhere with a bunch of criminals, that was saying something.

My nerves began to twitch, and my heart beat a little faster. I took a few deep breaths to calm myself. The other girls started looking a little uneasy as well, which did not help deter my brain from performing its favorite little catastrophe disco.

A door opened on the opposite side of the room and an elegant woman in her own evening gown—much more tasteful than the rest of ours with a high neck and long sleeves—made the rest of us look like a bunch of prostitutes. Which was probably the point.

The man who'd led us into the room put his hand around the arm of the first girl and guided her toward the door where the woman stood. She gave the girl a once-over, nodded and went back out the door. The man and rather terrified-looking girl followed behind.

Soon the man and woman returned, the two of them leading the next girl out, and then the next. I tried to breathe, feeling more alone than I'd ever remembered feeling in my whole life.

Maybe half an hour later, I was at the front of the line,

quaking like Jell-O on a roller coaster, trying to balance in my heels. It was bad enough I felt like I was going to topple over in the tight dress, but heels too? I mean, seriously, what was the point of all this? I desperately wanted the woman to hurry up and get back so I could just get whatever this was over with, but at the same time, I willed that damned door to stay closed forever.

Unfortunately, it didn't.

And then I was being pushed through the door and almost immediately toward a flight of stairs. The space was completely black except for a couple of dim lights on the stairs, like in a movie theater to guide you in the dark. I could hear voices, like the murmur of a small crowd somewhere nearby.

My pulse jackhammered as the woman gripped my arm, forcing me up the stairs. She was much less gentle than the man had been, almost as if she was angry with me, although I couldn't fathom what on earth I might have done to her.

She shoved me through a black curtain and into an explosion of floodlights. I blinked and raised my arm to block the searing glare, trying desperately to see something, anything.

I was on some kind of a stage—the murmuring I'd heard loud now. I blinked again, my eyes adjusting a little. Below the stage was a small crowd, though I still couldn't see much. I got the sense they were sitting, but my eyes had begun to water from the abrupt change in light.

I had absolutely no idea what I was supposed to do.

A voice came from my left, maybe twenty feet away. "Okay, gentlemen, we'll start the bidding at one thousand."

Bidding?

I'd been to a few charity bachelor auctions, so I knew

right away what must be going on. I was being auctioned off. *Jesus.* Somehow, I didn't think the winning bidder was just going to expect a nice dinner out of the deal. I guess the whole prostitution ring theory was confirmed. And I was the current item up for bids.

In the depth of my guts, my inner anatomy decided to hold a twerking contest. *What the hell had I gotten myself into?*

And I had no way of knowing if Ryan was anywhere that he could help. Without my wire, he probably didn't even know what was going on. Had no idea there might be a limit to how much time we had before I was "sold" and taken who knows where.

My mind started whirling with possible ways to escape. I couldn't shake the deep sense of dread telling me I had waited too long.

I put my arm up again, trying to see something, anything. An exit, preferably—although in the heels I wasn't really sure how far I could make it even if I was able to find a way out.

The audience was all men, all dressed in expensive suits and tuxes. The only women I'd seen since I'd left my apartment were the drugged ones and the horrible lady outside the stage. I wondered how she could justify being a part of all this. Money, I supposed. People did some really terrible things in the name of good ol' cash. Still, this was pretty extreme. Of course, I had to remind myself that I was supposedly here of my own accord. Perhaps not for money, but for what it could buy. Drugs. The twerking amped up to a full-blown dance party.

The bidding continued and the unwelcome question of

how much I was worth took a wander through my mind. Ugh. No matter what the bid came to, I reminded myself, I was worth more than all of this. All these girls were.

I tried to look at some of the faces in the crowd. Especially the ones raising their paddles to bid. Could I take them in a fight? Would I be able to slip away without anyone knowing?

My eyes had more time to adjust, and I started to see much better. A man at the back lifted his paddle to place a bid. He caught my eye, and my heart skipped a beat.

Ryan.

I let a huge whoosh of air out, my whole body relaxing with relief.

I wasn't alone! And honest to goodness, that was the only thing that mattered in that moment. Except for the little issue of the tux he was wearing—and might I add, looking hotter than a foot-long row of flame emojis. The attire was an interesting surprise, and a bit of a puzzle—somehow I doubted they handed out tuxes at the door—but who cared! Ryan would simply bid on me, take me to wherever the people who won these things went and we'd simply slip away.

I was so relieved that I forgot what we were trying to accomplish and almost smiled at him, catching myself just in time. I quickly looked away and made sure not to look in his direction again. I mean, it wasn't likely these people would ever realize we were in this together, but then again, I had absolutely no idea how Ryan had even gotten in there.

But none of that mattered. Everything was going to be okay now.

Except, something weird was happening. The bidding was starting to slow down and now that I thought about it,

Ryan seemed to have stopped raising his paddle. I stole a glance his way, but his face was unreadable. Staring straight ahead and not catching my eye, his jawline was set as if it were made of stone.

"Sold!" the auctioneer said loudly, banging the gavel onto his podium hard, knocking me back into the bleak reality of the present.

What in the actual bloody hell, was all I could think.

I took a deep breath. Okay. Ryan must have a good reason for doing what he was doing. Maybe he didn't have the kind of money these other guys were playing with. Come to think of it, I had absolutely no idea what I had even sold for. Which was probably a good thing.

What wasn't as good was when my stomach whirled out one last grievous tango as, out of the corner of my eye, I spotted Ryan being led away by two guys that were so immense and neckless they could have only been one thing.

Security.

Chapter Twenty

I stood in a luxurious bedroom, complete with a very creepy-looking older gentleman smoking a cigar. And honestly, I don't usually get angry (unless you beat me at Monopoly), but the fumes were enough to make my already churning stomach want to relieve itself of its contents.

But I had to keep it together. Not only did I have to figure a way out of this room, but now I needed to figure out what was happening with Ryan and possibly even rescue him too.

And I had no idea how I was going to do it.

Especially in the damned heels.

The man had risen from his perch on the end of the bed as I was ushered in, then nodded to the guy who'd led me in. The jerk had the nerve to friggin' leave, making it just me and Cigar Man.

I cleared my throat and tried a smile, though I was pretty sure it didn't come out like I was super happy to be there. I choked back the excess saliva that invaded my mouth, both because of the churning stomach and the sickly sweet scent of the cigar.

He, however, was able to give me a full smile. And if I thought he looked creepy before, it was ten times worse now that he was looking me up and down and licking his lips. I fought the urge to shiver.

He set down his cigar and moved over to me, running his hands down the length of my arms. It took every ounce of self-control I had not to run screaming out of there. I couldn't quite bring myself to look him in the face, hoping the "too shy to talk" thing had a bit more mileage.

Not that he seemed very interested in talking.

As he circled behind me, I fully understood that I was on my own. Who knew what had happened to Ryan after he was escorted out?

I closed my eyes. *Okay*, I told myself. *First, I need to get out of here, then I can figure out what to do about the rescuing Ryan situation.*

I had to hatch a plan, and ideally it would happen in a somewhat brisk manner.

So, WWND?

As the carcinogen of a human continued his circle around me, I forced a smile, catching his eye for half a second and giving him the best knowing look that I could muster. He stopped in front of me, and I unbuttoned his suit jacket, pretending I was concentrating very hard on the task at hand. He looked like he had just swallowed a goddamned canary.

I held on to the lapel and began to walk around him, as if I was about to peel off his coat, then in as swift a move as I could manage, I reached around and pulled the other side of the jacket around his back as well, jerking both sides hard so that his arms were forced backward, still tangled in the jacket. I held the jacket in place with my left hand and curled my right arm around his neck, putting him in the sleeper hold I'd learned at Marge in Charge: A Woman's Guide to Self-Defense.

And people made fun of my classes. Honestly.

Everyone should take more classes. They really did come quite in handy.

Cigar Man struggled, but he wasn't a very big dude, and it didn't take long before he passed out from the lack of oxygen. I didn't want to hold the move for too long because I didn't want to truly hurt him, but unfortunately, my expertise on the matter was a tad flimsy, so I had to hope that instinct would come through. He flopped into my arms, and I held him for a few seconds longer, quickly realizing that he likely wouldn't be out for more than a minute, so my best bet would be to tie him up and maybe find a way to gag him.

I gently set him on the floor, which was more than the bastard deserved, but I couldn't bring myself to just drop him.

My eyes darted around the room searching for something to tie him with. Sadly, there didn't seem to be a rope conveniently nearby. In my fave amateur sleuth books, there was always a handy-dandy implement for whatever the situation called for.

Sigh. Why did real life have to be so hard?

I went back to the guy and undid his belt then wrangled the jacket off his arms. I cinched the belt around his wrists as best as I could, heaving him over to the bed. I raised his arms over his head and lifted a corner of the bed, dragging it just enough to hook his arms underneath so his arms were essentially above his head and looped around the bed leg. It wouldn't be impossible to get out of my makeshift trap, but hopefully by the time he woke, he'd be in too much pain and fatigue to fight his way out easily.

But I needed to keep him quiet too.

I ripped a pillowcase off one of the pillows and tried ripping it apart, wanting to make a strip of material to shove in his mouth and another to tie tightly around it so he couldn't just spit it out. Sadly, the bedding was really good quality, proving impossible to rip.

I let out a groan and glanced around one more time, looking for something sharp. Then it hit me. The heels.

I ripped off one shoe and held the fabric taut, shoving the stiletto through the material and ripping as hard as I could. Once I got the hole started, I was able to tear the material easily and soon had a fairly large chunk along with one strip. I shoved the chunk into his mouth and tied the strip around his head as tight as possible, then listened to make sure he was still breathing. I didn't particularly want a death on my hands, to be honest.

Kicking off the other shoe, I made a beeline for the door, pausing to listen. When I didn't hear anything, I cracked it open a sliver and peeked out. The hallway seemed deserted.

Easing it open a bit more, I stuck my head out and peered around, but the coast was clear. I darted through the door and headed to the right, hoping my sense of direction wouldn't fail me. The house was a maze of hallways and I was probably completely turned around, but I ran anyway.

My mind swirled.

Now that I'd gotten out, I had no idea whether I should just find a way to get the hell out or sneak around to try to find Ryan. Ryan could take care of himself, but his situation had looked slightly dire the last time I'd seen him. Still,

I knew that he'd kick my ass if he found out I had a chance to escape and didn't take it.

Okay, first, find an exit. Someplace that would lead me outside…then, once I had an escape route planned, I'd reassess the situation and see if it was safe for me to go back in. Or maybe I could actually get all the way outside and start peeking in windows. *I wonder what the chances were that they'd have Ryan in a room with a window?* But as I was thinking it, I realized I had yet to see a window that wasn't covered by heavy, impenetrable drapes.

I sighed. I swear, Nancy never had such troublesome dilemmas.

I slowed a bit as I approached a corner, my ears straining, but I was met with silence. I turned the corner at a fairly good clip, thinking I was close to the outside perimeter of the house. Maybe one more hallway and an exit door would appear.

Unfortunately, something very tall and very solid and dressed in a very alluring tux clotheslined me around my waist, stopping me mid-stride. I bounced back from the momentum I had going and stumbled, though my captor pulled me close.

"What are you doing?" the voice whisper-yelled at me.

My breath hitched. Up close, the man smelled even better than I imagined.

"Um, hi, Ryan."

He stared into my eyes. I held tight to his arms, which felt even more muscular than they looked. That same feeling of familiarity rushed through me—like tea and a good mystery, like the sun on your face on a perfect spring day, like curling up under the covers and starting a favorite movie.

It felt like home.

He blinked, startled, but much to my disappointment, he took a step back, keeping his arms out to steady me, which was probably a good thing, since I was suddenly feeling a bit woozy.

"You can't just go running around like that. There are security guys everywhere," he whispered, looking rather angry.

"I was listening for noise," I whispered back harshly, annoyed that he still didn't think I could do anything by myself.

"And how'd that go for you?" he asked, raising an eyebrow.

I narrowed my eyes. "Whatever. You're very quiet."

He closed his eyes and sighed, then took my hand. I'd like to say that the skin-to-skin contact didn't affect me, but my mind did go somewhat foggy, I was embarrassed to admit.

"How did you get out, anyway?" he asked.

"I have skills," I said, and gave him a look that hopefully conveyed that he really needed to stop underestimating me. I put my hand on my hip. "Besides, I could ask you the same thing."

He shot me a little smirk that sort of made my heart melt, then dragged me down the hall. Unlike me, he stopped to peek around the next corner.

Show-off.

We made it to what seemed to be the foyer, a huge room with a grand staircase and, blessedly, a set of large double doors on the other side.

"We're going to have to make a run for it," Ryan said.

"We've been lucky so far but I'm going to assume they have cameras on this area."

"Okay," I said, supposing I could just follow his lead.

"Go!" he said and shot off in a sprint.

Which took me by surprise to say the least, but I was off in an instant, headed straight for the front door. He grabbed the doorknob and flung the door wide, turning to guide me out ahead of him, which made my heart do a little stutter flutter. I thought he'd been thinking it was every man for himself, but now I realized he wanted to get a head start to get the door open for me. What a gentleman.

The only unfortunate part was that instead of flying gracefully through that door, I spluttered to a dead stop.

Mostly due to the three guns pointed directly at my head, a circumstance that was becoming kind of an alarming pattern.

Chapter Twenty-One

My hands flew above my head without even having to think about it and I'm sure my eyes were as big as the barrels of those guns. Seriously, they looked really friggin' huge from my vantage point.

"Ryan Kent," Ryan's voice uttered calmly beside me. "Private investigator. I'm the one who called this in."

I nearly gasped. Ryan was his first name. And holy mother-of-pearl, there was just something about a guy with two first names. Or two last names. Or, whatever...two great names in any case.

"Someone take these two out for questioning," one of the men holding a gun said.

My mind seemed to start working again, at least a little, and I finally registered that the gun-pointing dudes had uniforms on. SWAT and police uniforms to be exact.

For being the good guys, the police certainly weren't overly gentle with us. I wasn't sure if they thought we were lying about who we were, although I wasn't quite sure why else we'd be making an escape, but in any case, we were soon led to a "safe zone," where ambulances were arriving and official-looking people—some in uniforms and some in crumpled suits—waited for the police to do their job inside the mansion.

Additional police surrounded the perimeter of the building, which was a good thing, since several people in various stages of undress were trying to make their escape. If it hadn't been such a terrible situation, the whole thing might have been kind of funny, considering how obvious it was that some of the men had never run more than three steps in their lives.

Emergency vehicles continued to show up. Some of the men were secured in the backs of large trucks, several at a time. There was a chorus of "Don't you know who I am?" and "My lawyer is going to have your badge."

I shook my head. It always amazed me how certain people honestly thought they were entitled to get away with anything no matter who they hurt or what laws they broke. I suddenly got a sick feeling some of them probably *would* get off with a slap on the wrist at best.

I sighed. I liked money as much as the next person, but when too much of it was put in the hands of people like these guys, it became dangerous.

Girls were being led to the ambulances to be checked over.

"I hope they get the help that they need," I said.

Ryan nodded. "I'm sure they will for tonight. Hopefully at least some of them will be able to stay off the streets." He held the picture of his client's daughter in his hand, scrutinizing each girl as they were led past us.

I couldn't get over the sheer size of the operation going on around us. All because of Ryan and me. Well, okay, mostly Ryan—I may have been the bait, but knowing how to get this many people to come out into the middle of nowhere in the middle of the night was not one of my skills.

Eventually, the girl in the picture, Kathleen, made an appearance. A female emergency medical technician was leading her down the lawn toward our group. Ryan went to her, rechecking the picture several times.

"Kathleen?" he asked.

She glared at him. I supposed it had been a while since she'd had someone come up to her who wanted to help. I expected her to smile. To be relieved. Instead she glared even harder.

Ryan turned to me. "Can you give us a minute? I need to talk to Kathleen about a private issue."

"Uh, sure," I said, stumbling away in the too-tight dress and trying to understand what kind of issue would be too private for one of her rescuers to hear. I'd thought I'd kind of earned my way into the circle of trust or whatever, but then when Kathleen let out a wail, yelling at Ryan about being a bastard and a liar, I was embarrassingly relieved that I hadn't been there.

"Is she okay?" was all I could say as he wandered back over to me.

"Um," he said, clearly searching for what to say, "unfortunately, it's not the first time I found someone who didn't want to be found."

I shook my head. Being a private investigator in real life did not seem to have the warm fuzzy feelings that usually came at the end of my Nancy novels.

"Her mother will be relieved though," I said.

But Ryan just nodded absently, staring after Kathleen.

He pulled out his phone and dialed, walking a few paces away for privacy.

A few minutes later he came over. "Come on," he said, hanging up. "Let's grab your clothes and get out of here. We've given them all they need."

I nodded, wondering why no one needed to question me. But it didn't really seem like the time to ask—Ryan just looked so...sad or something—so I just followed him back into the mansion where I retrieved my clothes and quickly changed in one of the many powder rooms, ditching the wig and wiping off as much of the makeup as I could.

We drove in silence for a while until eventually, I couldn't take it anymore. "So uh, I'm sorry that Kathleen was kind of...well, not happy, but you did a really good thing, you know."

He nodded. Then it was his turn to clear his throat. "Yeah, and um, I want to thank you for your help. I couldn't have done it without you." I could tell it was a little difficult to spit the words out.

I smiled. "You're welcome. It was fun."

He shot me a look that conveyed that I should definitely have *not* thought any of the past few days had been fun.

"So, why didn't any of the cops need to question me?" I asked.

In every movie and TV show I'd ever seen, every witness was thoroughly questioned, especially the ones that had played a major part in the takedown.

"I told them you worked with me." He said it quick and terse, like he was not exactly keen to add anything to that little tidbit.

So I just smiled.

When we got back to our building, things got quiet again. The old tension was back, especially in the elevator. What was it with elevators that turned you into a beacon of dumbassery with absolutely nothing to say? I stared at the numbers as we slowly rose to our floor.

Ryan cleared his throat. "So, uh, I know we've had kind of a long night, but I was just thinking… I could really use a drink and I'm wondering if maybe you do, too?"

I tilted my head, then nodded. "Yeah, actually I could but I don't have anything at my place right now." I couldn't imagine there was any of the wine left from earlier. Brandt and Vic liked their wine as much as I did.

"I've got a few things if you want to stop in for a bit," he said, actively avoiding eye contact.

"Um, yeah. That sounds nice," I said, trying my best not to let on that my stomach was suddenly hosting a gymnastics floor routine competition.

It was strange following Ryan to his door instead of heading to mine. I wondered if Brandt and Vic had stayed, waiting for me to get back. It wasn't like they hadn't slept over before if they'd had a bit much to drink or whatever, but I was sure that wasn't the case tonight. I'd texted them both to let them know it was over and that everything was okay, so it wasn't like they'd be worried or anything.

Strange. Come to think of it, neither of them had texted me back. Oh well, they'd probably fallen asleep. Either way, I wanted to have a drink with Ryan way more than I wanted to debrief my friends.

For being in the same building, Ryan's apartment was very different from mine. While mine was mostly white with pops of color in the artwork, rugs and cushions, his was sleek, polished wood and plenty of smoky gray and metal. So much more moody and dark than mine was, but I loved it anyway.

The walls had some black-and-white photography, but just architecture-type pieces. No personal or family photos to be seen anywhere.

"So, what do you feel like?" Ryan asked, taking off his coat.

"Whatever you're having. I'm not picky."

He went to the fridge and grabbed a couple bottles of import beer.

"Perfect, thanks," I said as he handed one to me.

I wandered the apartment a bit, stopping in front of a gleaming metal bookcase.

"Shit," he whispered.

For a second, I didn't know why he'd said it, but then I saw. A huge collection—maybe the entire series—of Hardy Boys books.

As a writer, I knew the English language had a word for pretty much everything. A *snollygoster*, for example, was a dishonest and corrupt person. Then there was the word *tessellate*, which was to form or arrange in a checkerboard pattern. Specific, right? But in that moment, I could contest that there were still words we hadn't suitably invented yet, such as a collective term for nieces and nephews, or a monumental-enough word to describe the feeling that was enveloping me.

I turned toward him, letting loose my best "seriously, you were heckling me about my Nancy books?" look.

He rolled his eyes, looking rather sheepish. "Okay, okay. I'm sorry. I get it."

"I am never going to let you live this down," I said, running my finger along the spines.

"I have no doubt," he said, laughing a little.

I studied the titles, marveling at how similar some of them were to my treasured Nancy books. *The Clue of the Broken Blade* was so similar to Nancy's *The Clue of the Broken Locket* and *While the Clock Ticked* made me instantly think of the very first Nancy book, *The Secret of the Old Clock*.

A strange feeling twigged in my mind. A flash of...something. I felt like I had noticed clocks more than average lately, like there was something I should be remembering.

Of course, the thought didn't have much chance to take hold considering I was occupying space with Ryan. I shook my head again, still a bit stunned with the whole Hardy Boys discovery and flopped onto the couch. Ryan quickly took a spot close to me. I'd expected him to sit in one of the chairs but was absolutely not going to complain that he wasn't.

"So, listen," he said, sitting upright and looking slightly uncomfortable. "I just wanted to officially say thank you for all your help with the case."

I smiled. "No problem."

"Seriously, Petra. I don't think I could have finished this one without you on the inside. And I'm still sick about how much danger you were in, but I also get that you can handle yourself. You're pretty great, actually."

My heart flip-flopped. "That might be the best compliment anyone has ever given me," I said.

He sort of smiled shyly, quickly taking a sip of his beer.

I'm not sure if it was the adrenaline of the day or finally being safe and sound in my own building, but suddenly I was very, very tired. I tried to sip my beer and just relax. Ryan finally leaned back too. We were sitting so close our arms were nearly touching and I could feel the warmth of him.

"I don't know about you," I finally said, "but that was one exhausting day."

"One for the books," he said, and let out a yawn.

I took a big gulp of my beer and sat up, setting it down on the coffee table. "I should probably get out of your hair."

He sat up too, and suddenly his face was inches from mine. He reached out to set his beer down beside mine.

His lips. Those gorgeous lips were so close. I couldn't take my eyes off them, hypnotized. He smelled so good, and I wanted nothing more than for this moment to never end.

Then he leaned in and…promptly leaned back again. I wasn't sure my heart could take it—one second it looked like he was about to kiss me, and the next he seemed almost disgusted.

"I'm sorry, I can't do this," he said.

There were absolutely no words. What in the hell was someone supposed to say when something like that happened?

He ran his hands through his hair, some sort of internal struggle clearly taking place behind those hazel eyes.

"Ryan, what's going on?"

He sighed. "There's something I haven't told you."

"Oh god, are you married or something?"

Honestly, it was the exact sort of thing I would have written into one of my novels to send the tension through the roof.

"No," he said, though by the look on his face it almost

seemed like he wished it was as simple as that. Which was to say, not simple at all.

"I… I haven't exactly told you everything about Kathleen's case," he started.

"Okay," I said, drawing the word out.

"I haven't told you who hired me to find her."

"You said it was her mother."

"Right, but I haven't told you who her mother was."

I tilted my head, questioning.

He swallowed. "It was Erica."

Chapter Twenty-Two

To say that I was shocked would be to say that my pal Nancy fancied a little mystery every now and then. "Erica from upstairs?"

He nodded.

"The woman who hired you to find her daughter is the same woman who died by suicide a week ago in this very building?"

"That's right."

My mind raced as I tried to breathe. "The one that Annie is completely positive did not actually die by suicide, but potentially by something else altogether. Maybe even by some*one* else altogether."

He nodded.

"And you're only now getting around to telling me this?"

"I know. It was stupid, and I'm sorry. I was just so freaked out about how deep you had already gotten involved in this whole thing and I thought I could protect you by keeping your part as small as possible." He shook his head. "Not that it was at all small, mind you, but I would have liked it to have been."

"Why are you telling me now?"

"Because…" He dropped his gaze, unable to look me in the eye. "Because when I sat down beside you just now, I wanted to kiss you, but I couldn't do that knowing I had this huge secret I was keeping from you."

And it was so stupid, and it probably happened mostly because I was so damned tired, but my eyes welled up. Or maybe it was because I was feeling so unworthy lately—unable to write, unable to do anything productive with my life—certain that this man in front of me was so far out of my league with his "put together" dates…except here he was telling me he wanted to kiss me and it just felt…well, nice, I guess.

Or maybe I was processing the fact that Kathleen, this poor girl who had just been freed from a drug and prostitution crime ring, had to be told that her mother was gone too. Oh, that's probably exactly what Ryan was doing when Kathleen screamed.

"That poor girl," I sort of whispered, my mind wandering over the cruelty of it all.

Ryan nodded.

"Obviously Erica's death has to be connected to the whole thing. I mean, I suppose a parent could conceivably want to end everything if their child is gone, but there was always hope that Kathleen would be found, right?"

Ryan nodded. "Yes, I think they're probably connected."

"Why haven't you talked to the police about any of this?"

"I have." He shrugged. "They know about Kathleen being missing and they believe—just like you said—that's the very reason that Erica decided to end things. That she'd given up hope on ever finding Kathleen alive. They're rationalizing that she just couldn't deal with it anymore."

"But Erica hadn't given up on Kathleen. She hired you, for crying out loud."

"I agree, but the police said the evidence of suicide is just too overwhelming. There was a note."

I rolled my eyes. "That's the oldest trick in the book. Suicide notes are easy to fake or coerce—anyone who's ever read a mystery knows that."

Ryan nodded. "I agree."

I could feel my anxiety starting to rise. "So what? Now Kathleen just comes back, and we're all supposed to say, *So sorry, but your mom's gone, here, have a little life insurance money to make it all better*?"

Ryan let out a breath, almost like a humorless chuckle. "We can't even do that much," he said, the pained expression returning to his eyes. "I talked to a friend at the police department. Shortly before her death, Erica rewrote her will and left everything to her new boyfriend."

My mouth dropped open. "That doesn't make any sense."

"The cops think it does, since their theory is that Erica thought Kathleen was gone forever."

"Except you knew that wasn't true."

"I *suspected* it wasn't true. That's a long way from knowing."

"Jesus. That is so messed up. And who is this boyfriend, anyway? Her husband just died, but all of a sudden, she's so close to this guy that she leaves everything she owns to him?"

Ryan shrugged. "After Kathleen, I don't think there was anyone else to leave anything to."

"But Kathleen is alive."

"Yeah," was all he said.

He didn't have to explain how awful the whole situation was. That much was more than clear. I could not stop thinking about how Kathleen was supposed to take this news. Being trapped inside the crime ring, she would have had no way of knowing her mom was even gone, let alone that she'd changed her will. Kathleen was essentially going to have to restart her whole life all alone and without any money to even get herself back together.

"Who was this guy, anyway?"

Ryan shook his head. "I don't know."

"But do you think he's legit? Was Erica really in love with him?"

"I don't know, Petra. I never saw the guy. I didn't know about any of this until after they found Erica."

"It's just…it's just not right. We have to tell Annie."

"I'm not sure that's a good idea. I'd like to close the case on my own and then break the news to her once we know exactly what went down."

"Ryan, you know how much Annie cared about Erica."

"I know," he said. "I just don't want anyone else more mixed up in this than they have to be."

"But Annie might know something we don't."

"Petra," he said. "It's over. There's nothing we can do other than hope Kathleen can bounce back from this."

"Well, isn't that just…bullshit!"

I stood, not knowing what to do with myself. I had to move.

He nodded. "I know. I'm sorry."

I started toward the door.

"Petra, you don't look okay."

"That's because I'm not okay. This can't be it. This can't be the end of Erica's story."

Ryan sighed. "What are you going to do?"

"I don't know. I just need some time to think."

"There really isn't anything to think about. Is it terrible? Absolutely," he said, answering his own question. "But there's a lot of shitty things in this world that we can't do anything about, and unfortunately, this is one of them."

I let out a breath. "Fine. Then I guess I just need time to process. Time to try to get my head on straight again. I need some air."

I opened the door and stepped into the hallway, half expecting Ryan to try to stop me. But he didn't, which I took as a good sign. A sign that he trusted me enough not to do something stupid. Which was quite nice considering I didn't even trust myself not to do something stupid.

I headed to the roof. I really did need some air. Even though Ryan's apartment was minimalist and spacious, it was starting to feel like the walls were closing in on me. And I knew my apartment would be no better.

As I flung the door open, the air hit me like an ocean wave. The night was chilly, and I didn't have my coat, but something about it felt right. Like I wasn't supposed to be too comfortable in that moment. The breeze was strong and blew my hair back from my face, taking my breath away for a moment, but at the same time, it felt good. Like an invigorating freedom after being stagnant too long.

I walked to the edge of the roof, leaning on the rail, looking out onto the city.

Lights twinkled as far as the eye could see. It really was the most spectacular view of the cityscape I'd ever seen. So much life going on out there. It seemed perverse, that the world could just go on like nothing happened, even though someone's life had just utterly fallen apart. I suppose that was how it always worked. One person thrived while the next got kicked in the groin.

And then the cycle continued.

But thinking about that made me wonder why some people hardly ever got kicked, while the rest could barely get up before getting slammed right back down again.

I thought about Kathleen. The world was not a fair place.

A tear crept into my eye, quickly getting whisked across my temple by the wind. I wiped at the coolness of it, then laid my head on my arms as I leaned into the railing.

Somewhere a clock began to strike the hour.

I'd loved that sound as a kid. It was always strange to me to have a clock on the outside of a building. It was kind of an old-fashioned thing from a world before the time of digital watches and smartphones. I supposed there was probably a time when the average person couldn't even afford a pocket watch and depended on those sorts of public clocks to let them know when they needed to be somewhere.

I glanced around to find the source of the chimes. Several blocks away stood a tall building with an even taller tower. Probably a municipal building of sorts, something that taxpayer dollars kept maintained. It was a beautiful stone building, and I couldn't help but think I had seen something similar recently.

The puzzle.

There had been a clock tower like the one I was looking at on the puzzle that Erica had been working on right before her death.

Except Annie swore Erica would never be doing a puzzle. And didn't it seem strange that someone would feel the urge to do something they had never shown any interest in right before they were about to end everything? Especially something as mundane as a jigsaw puzzle? I tried to run through Erica's thought process of deciding things were so terrible that she just couldn't take it anymore, but then heading to the games room. Why didn't she just stay in her apartment to do what she needed to do? And why the puzzle?

Something didn't add up.

I forced myself to think about something I really did not want to think about. The way Erica looked that night, with her head slumped on the table, one arm above her head. One finger sticking out, almost…pointing.

I shook my head. I was sure that must have been a coincidence, had just been the way she had fallen. The police said that Erica had overdosed on her own sleeping pills. But again, why not just go to sleep in your own bed? The whole thing was just strange.

So strange that I decided I wanted another look at the puzzle. If it was even still there. I doubted the police had spent precious time cleaning it up, but maybe they needed it as evidence. Of course, if there was no suspicion of foul play, what kind of evidence did they really need though?

I moved quickly, on a mission now, heading to the games room, taking a moment to pause outside the doorway to take a deep breath and compose myself before stepping inside. I flicked on the light and my heart soared. I don't know why I thought it was so important that the puzzle still be there, but something wouldn't stop niggling at my brain.

The puzzle was only partially done, and if the box hadn't

been sitting off to the side, I might not have known what it was supposed to be a picture of. The full outer edge of the puzzle had been completed, but there was only one other section started.

The clock.

Again, I tried to picture how Erica had been lying. Maybe it was just my imagination, but now that I was picturing her again, I could almost swear that she had been pointing directly at that clock.

I started to pace.

This had to be nothing, right? But something about the whole situation didn't quite add up. I mean, maybe it was Annie getting into my head, but the thing was, Annie was not someone who spoke willy-nilly. She was thoughtful. She was careful. People didn't always take her seriously with the way she dressed, but that was only until they knew her. And that's what was bothering me so much.

I trusted Annie. Which also meant I was very much leaning toward believing her when she said she knew Erica well enough to know she wasn't in a place where she'd be willing to do what the police were saying she'd done. And that meant that Annie must be right about Erica hating puzzles too.

I paced some more. What would have brought Erica to the games room in the first place? Was it possible she was meeting someone? No, Jamieson had seen Erica in there alone. But then, if she was alone, why would Erica treat Jamieson the way she did? I mean, a lot of people would try to get rid of Jamieson—he was a bit of a dung beetle, honestly, but Jamieson himself said that Erica had always been good to him and it was out of character to act the way she did. Of course, if the police were to be believed, she wouldn't have been in a normal state of mind, but still. Wouldn't she have seemed sad, or upset, or something? But Jamieson said she just seemed like she wanted to be alone.

So...what if she had good reason to want him out of there? Like maybe because he might be in danger. Because the long and the short of it was that if Erica hadn't taken her own life, then absolutely there was danger lurking around very close. But...where?

I stopped pacing and turned to the table. Then glanced beyond it.

The alcove.

That day that Annie and I had come in here, Eliza had scared the absolute shiznit out of us because she'd been hiding in that alcove. And she hadn't even been hiding on purpose—there was just a lot of space back there. A person could easily have been hiding, waiting for Jamieson to leave.

Of course, then the question became, why would Erica stay?

I needed more to go on. I needed a damned clue.

It took me a moment to work up the nerve to sit in the chair Erica had been sitting in when I found her that night, but I wanted to get a sense of what things looked like from her perspective. Maybe if I could see what she saw, something would stand out. I sat and peered around the room. The alcove was almost a natural place for someone to be sitting, or maybe standing, if they were talking to Erica. Especially if they had an idea about what they were about to do.

I took a deep breath, letting the idea wash over me. Was I really sitting here by myself thinking murder? I swallowed.

Okay, this was fine. This was the kind of stuff I had an

interest in. Although if I was being honest, it was more the puzzling things out that got me going than the actual catching of criminals. I always thought that sort of thing was best left to the professionals. Except in this case, the professionals had given up.

And hadn't I proved to myself over the past few days that I was more capable than I ever thought?

I nodded, having sufficiently talked myself into pushing the potential danger out of my mind and focusing on the one thing I could focus on. Finding clues and figuring out what really happened to Erica.

Unfortunately, sitting where Erica had been sitting wasn't really making any giant clues jump out at me. I got up and went to the alcove, searching the floor to see if there were any shoe prints or, even better, seeing if anything had been dropped. Of course, if there had been anything obvious, the police would have noticed it and I wouldn't be the only one still searching for the truth.

I sat back down.

The puzzle was literally the only thing I had to go on, and it wasn't much. I mean, what did Erica doing a puzzle even mean? Maybe she was just trying to distract her mind from the danger in front of her. Or maybe, in some desperate long shot, she was trying to leave a message behind.

And if I had any chance at deciphering it, I needed to enlist some help.

Chapter Twenty-Three

"I'm sorry to show up so late," I said, as a concerned-looking Annie opened the door. The woman was truly a miracle. Here it was, two in the morning and she was the picture of radiance. Unfortunately, I was pretty sure the same could not be said for me considering I was still in my disguise clothes, my hair was likely inexplicable and I had no makeup on. You know, except for the dark and probably smeared eyeliner that I couldn't quite get off completely back at the mansion.

"What's going on, dear?" she asked, ushering me inside.

Bless the woman's soul, she didn't even ask why I was knocking on her door so late.

"Annie, have you been inside Erica's apartment?"

Annie tilted her head in question. "Of course, why?"

"Does she have a clock?"

"That's a strange question. Doesn't everybody have a clock? I believe I have about seven of them myself."

I nodded. "Of course, yeah. I was just wondering if there was ever anything significant about Erica and a clock."

Annie crinkled her brows together. "I don't really think

so. I mean, she did have that gorgeous antique on her mantel, but she never told me how she got it or anything like that."

I nodded. "I suppose it would be bad form to break into the apartment of someone who had just died, hey?" I said, joking.

Annie raised her eyebrows. "Well, we wouldn't really have to break in, dear. I do have a key."

My eyes went wide. "Have you been in there since she's been gone? Is anything out of place?"

Annie's eyes glistened over. "I… I know I should go in there and make sure everything is in order. Her plants are probably way overdue to be watered but…"

"I'm so sorry, Annie. This must be incredibly difficult for you."

She nodded. "Maybe it wouldn't be so difficult if I had someone with me when I go. Would you be willing to go in there with me?"

"Of course," I said quickly, hoping I didn't sound too eager.

We made our way to Erica's apartment and the silence that met Annie's knock at Erica's door was absolute.

"I'm not sure why I'm even knocking. It doesn't seem right to just walk in, I guess," she said, sadness filling her voice.

As Annie turned the key, the excitement I'd had about possibly finding more clues had waned and the realization that Erica would never step foot in her apartment again hit me in the guts. Whether Erica was responsible for her own death or not, the whole thing was just so unfair.

Annie paused in the doorway, taking a moment before she could continue inside. Eventually she flicked on a switch and the apartment was instantly bathed in muted light. The place was decorated elegantly, stark but cozy, and the scent of spiced fruit and cedar subtly filled the air. I mean, I wasn't one for fancy fragrances (for me, essential oils were what dripped down your chin whilst eating saucy ribs), but this was nice, not too chokey.

"It's strange that the curtains are all closed. Erica always had everything wide open, though I suppose that night she'd probably already closed them for the evening."

I nodded, not sure what to say. "Maybe we should leave everything the way it is," I said.

"I'm not sure that really matters anymore," Annie said, implying what both of us already knew. That there would be no further investigation.

I glanced around, admiring Erica's taste. The place was minimally decorated, and the few pieces she did have on display were obviously well taken care of and loved. I couldn't help but notice the antique clock sitting on the fireplace mantel and it took everything in me not to run over to examine it.

"I'm surprised Michael hasn't been around yet to collect his things," Annie said.

"Michael?"

"Erica's new beau, Michael Turner. They made such a beautiful couple. So different, yet both so attractive in their own ways."

"Erica was beautiful," I said. "So put together. She always seemed so full of life…" I trailed off, cursing myself for choosing those words.

But Annie nodded. "She was. That's why none of this makes any sense," she said, her voice cracking on the last word. She cleared her throat. "And Michael, he was a real looker with those striking blue eyes."

"Striking blue eyes?" I asked, wondering if maybe I'd seen him around the building with Erica. I felt like I had seen eyes that matched that description recently...

"They're quite marvelous, really. He has this dark hair, which is such a contrast to those eyes. The kind of look that's not easy to forget."

I furrowed my brow trying to place where I'd seen someone exactly like that.

Annie moved down the hall and into what I assumed was Erica's bedroom, and my attention moved back to the clock, but as the light flicked on down the hall, Annie let out a little scream. "Oh my lord, Michael, you nearly scared me half to death."

Michael? My mind spun as I followed Annie's voice. Why was Michael here? More importantly, why hadn't he answered the door when we knocked?

Dread crawled up my insides, taking hold of my heart as a heavy clunk sounded from the bedroom.

I rushed in to find a man standing over Annie, who was, oddly, lying on the ground. In the moment it took me to process what had happened, the man turned, meeting my gaze. His eyes. Those steely, ice-blue eyes.

The same eyes that my gaze had locked with during my escape from the apartment Ryan had been staking out.

"You're Michael?" The words fell out of my mouth before I could catch them.

But Michael didn't say anything. He did, however, begin moving toward me—slightly less stunned about the whole situation than I was. Still, I was able to turn and take a few steps, moving toward the front door, but Michael was too fast, his viselike grip clamping around my arm, flinging me back hard. I stumbled but stayed on my feet.

"Okay, okay," I said, putting my hands up to show I wasn't going to run.

He pointed to the sofa. "Sit."

I hated that I followed his command, but I wasn't especially in control of my reactions in that moment, fear having apparently moved into my brain and evicted everything else.

Finally, I got myself together enough to speak. "What did you do to Annie?" I asked, fearing the worst.

I hadn't seen any blood, but it wasn't like I'd had a whole lot of time to process the scene.

He shrugged. "I'm sure she'll be fine. Might have a bit of a headache later though," he said, kind of sneering like he was proud of himself.

"Shouldn't you be skipping town or something after the big roundup of your buddies?" I asked.

It was nice to see it was his turn to be surprised. Given the disguise that day I'd escaped the apartment, it was clear that he didn't recognize me.

He blinked a few times, then said, "I don't know what you're talking about. I was just gathering a few of my things before building maintenance cleans out Erica's things."

"Right," I said, nodding. "That's why you're lurking around in the dark and knocking out harmless ladies in the bedroom." Honestly, the moron didn't even deserve one of my signature eye rolls.

He shrugged, then went to a drawer in the kitchen. I guess since he'd been dating Erica he knew exactly where she kept the duct tape. Or maybe it was his—lord knew the dude loved the stuff.

Michael sat me in a kitchen chair, wrapping my wrists with the tape, then moved to my ankles. He really did have a knack for it.

Once I was secured, he resumed rummaging around, this time in the kitchen.

"What are you looking for?" I asked. "Don't you already know where everything is?"

He shot me an exasperated glare.

"No, seriously. I mean, you already have everything you want, right? Except…why wouldn't you have left town by now? Being here is a pretty big risk. Anyone could walk in on you at any time, and we can certainly assume you've got a warrant for your arrest out there."

He shook his head. "They probably have an arrest warrant for Michael Turner."

"Exactly," I said.

"The only thing is, my name isn't Michael Turner."

My stomach dropped. "But… Erica called you Michael. She would have named Michael Turner when she changed her will."

"Nope. She put my real name."

"Which is?"

He grinned. "Nice try," he said, then continued searching.

"Okay, so if you have this will with your real name on it, and I presume since you belong to what seems to be a long-standing crime ring, you probably already have a way of getting the money into some offshore bank account or something, which you'll be able to access once you've skipped town." Honestly, I wasn't sure I was pulling off all the lingo like *skipped town* and *crime ring*—I mean, I didn't even know if people used those phrases in real life, but Michael didn't seem to think anything of it. Or maybe he was just trying to ignore me.

Michael continued searching while I did a little searching of my own. Searching of my brain, that is, to try to come up with some idea of how to get someone from outside that apartment to figure out Annie and I were in there and that we were in danger.

I thought of my favorite girl detective again. She would have probably come up with at least three different solutions for alerting someone to our situation, and she didn't even have cell phones to rely on back then. Unfortunately, my brain had become too dependent on my damned phone, and it was literally the only thing I could think of to use. And yeah, I could think of about seven ways to use it—text someone, have it make loud noises, send out a tweet or, you know, dial emergency services. The only problem was the small matter of my hands tied behind my back.

Okay, channel Nancy, I thought. Back in the days before cell phones she always found a way to alert people to danger. Maybe I could start a fire and get the smoke alarms to go off. Of course, that would be somewhat challenging without the use of my hands. *Come on, think.* Then I had it. I stood, super awkward and crouched over with the chair attached to my ankles and everything, but thanks to my yoga classes, I was pretty well versed in chair pose. *Okay, here goes,* I said in my head, as I sat down as hard and as loud as I could. I did it again. Stand. Sit. Stand. Sit. The chair clanged as the legs met the floor. I knew it was a long shot—everyone in the building was probably asleep—but I couldn't sit there and do nothing.

Unfortunately, Michael didn't love my little performance and abruptly came over and smacked me right in the face. In the face! I mean, how much ruder could you get than smacking someone open-handed right across the cheek? What a jackwagon.

Once I straightened back up, I gave him my best glare to let him know I did not appreciate his reaction. I mean, I guess he hadn't appreciated my reaction to what he was doing either, but I don't think there was any question as to who was in the wrong.

Michael started pacing, doing less searching and more… I don't know, getting worked up like a hyena in heat (absolutely no idea if hyenas go into heat, but it paints a picture, yeah?) and part of that was probably my fault, but I think it also had to do with the fact that he was not finding what he was looking for.

And then it hit me.

Another will.

That had to be the piece of the puzzle that I'd been missing. If he already had it all worked out with the offshore account and all that, the only thing that would have been holding him there was the possibility of another—perhaps more recent—will.

My mouth dropped open. "She told you there was another one, didn't she?"

Michael's head whipped around to face me. "What do you know?" he asked, breathing hard through his nose like an angry bull.

"Hey, man, don't look at me. I'm just figuring this out as

we go. And the only thing I can think of that would explain you still hanging around is that there must be another will stashed somewhere." I let out a humorless chuckle. "And it seems like you might be having a little trouble locating it." I shook my head like he was pathetic. And yeah, it wasn't like I had any idea where another will might be either, but I barely knew the woman.

"Oh, shut up, would you?"

I shrugged as best as I could with my hands tied behind my back. "Erica must have been pretty smart. Planting that seed of doubt, probably right when you were about to murder her. Or maybe after you had already poisoned her with her own sleeping pills. How did you get her to take them anyway? I mean, I assume you crushed them up in her tea, but how did you get her to write out the note and drink it?"

"You're so damned smart, why don't you tell me?"

I had to say, I was getting really tired of this asshat.

"It had to be Kathleen, didn't it? Erica knew you had her. She was willing to give up her own life to save her child. The child that you no doubt lulled into that life with the drugs and the rest of it."

He tilted his head. "You'd be surprised how easy it is to get troubled young women to go down the wrong path. There's a lot of pressure on kids these days. Pressure to be perfect. Pressure to perform. When you grow up on social media, your whole life is about what people think. How many views and likes you get. And when nobody is paying attention to you, it's easy to believe that you're not worthy of people's time. That you're not interesting. That, in fact, you're not worthwhile at all."

"And that's where you come in. How very predatory of you. So…how do you do it?"

Michael sighed. "Once someone is already feeling like they're worthless—which, to be honest, is most of the younger generation these days—all you have to do is pay them a tiny bit of attention."

"But why would any young woman care about attention from some old guy like you? No offense," I added—I mean, I wasn't a monster.

"They wouldn't. We have recruiters for that. Gorgeous young people. Men and women who spend time on social media getting attractive young women to meet with them. Eventually most of them do, they're so desperate for attention. By the time they get to them, they're primed to do almost anything to impress the one person who really gets them." He chuckled. "So frail. So gullible. All it takes then is a little push to try the drugs—just a little convincing that it's no big deal, and voilà, after a time or two they're hooked."

I shook my head, bitterness flooding my mouth. To use people's insecurities against them was a special kind of evil, and these bastards had made a whole damned industry out of it.

"So what then?" I asked. "Why mess with Erica too? Wasn't destroying her daughter enough?"

"For years we didn't bother with the parents. But then we acquired some contacts in the police force and found out how desperate these people were to get their kids back. They would do almost anything."

"Really? It took you having an insider to figure out

that parents love their children? Some personal life you must have."

"Actually, it was *not* having a personal life that made the idea come to me. You see, the thing about beautiful young women is that often the mothers are beautiful too. And some of them are single," he said, pumping his eyebrows.

Honestly, what a skeev.

"And the thing with the older generation of single women is that sometimes they have a whole lot of cash to part with—you know, in case something tragic were to ever happen to them."

The bile rose in my throat. "You're disgusting."

He turned to me. "You know, that's something that I am perfectly fine being. I like the company of women and I like money. Besides, I've been told they quite like my company as well," he said, those icy blues twinkling.

"Gross."

He tilted his head in a "perhaps, but it works for me" kind of way.

"Too bad Erica was a little too smart for you." I grinned.

He shook his head, clearly annoyed that I kept interrupting his progress. He looked around some more, which gave me time to think about what my next plan of action would be since clearly the banging the chair against the floor hadn't done much. Although, now that I was thinking about it again, the tape around my ankles had gotten somewhat looser above my right foot. I wiggled my ankle around, realizing that the tape had stuck more to my sock than it had to my jeans on that side. If I could just keep wiggling until my sock came off, I might be able to get my foot free.

With one eye on Michael, I wiggled that foot like my life

depended on it, which, I was beginning to think, it probably did.

I wiggled and twisted until it felt like my ankle was about to pop out of place, and then suddenly the hem of my jeans came loose from the tape completely, my sock pulling down around my heel. A few more wiggles and my foot was free.

I glanced around, twisting a bit and shimmying my chair as quietly as I could. Thankfully, Michael had other things on his mind as he began throwing items out of the kitchen drawers, seemingly more desperate by the second.

I was about five feet from the window, so I shimmied a bit closer then stopped to double-check if Michael was paying attention. I mean, if I was being completely honest, the wiggling might have worn me out more than I cared to admit, and I might have enjoyed the tiny break it gave me to catch my breath.

I took a deep breath and shimmied even closer. Four feet now. Another glance over my shoulder, then another shimmy. Three feet. A couple more feet and I could… Well, I wasn't sure, but I hoped something would miraculously come to me in the next few seconds.

Two feet away.

"Hey, what are you doing?"

Without thinking, I kicked my foot out, smashing through the window, the glass scraping my bare foot as it broke through, pain jolting up my leg.

And then the chair I was in was being whipped around and the last thing I saw before everything went black was a look of absolute contempt on Michael's face.

Chapter Twenty-Four

Shuffling noises were the first thing I noticed. The pain behind my right eye was the second. There was no third, since the pain was pretty much all that was on my immediate radar after I'd discovered its existence.

I slowly tried to blink my eyes open, squinting at the light.

"She's coming to," a voice said. And goddamn, it was a sexy voice. "Petra, are you okay?"

I tried to nod, but that made me close my eyes again, trying to fight off the angry jolt that blazed through my head. After a careful, shallow breath—I'd tried a deep one, but that was no good for the head either—I opened my eyes once more.

"Hey," I said, though it was more of a croak.

"Hey," Ryan said, tucking a piece of my hair behind my ear.

And it was so gentle, his fingers grazing my jawline, his eyes filled with concern.

It was only then I remembered where I was. Against my better judgment, my eyes darted around the room, trying to figure out what had happened.

Annie was sitting on the couch. She was holding an ice pack to her head, but besides that she looked as good as ever. I breathed a sigh of relief.

"Michael?" I asked, worried.

"We have him, Petra. Thanks to you, we have him."

Another layer of stress left my body.

I tried to sit, Ryan helping me. "Watch your foot," he said.

My foot. I'd forgotten all about my foot, which seemed to be oozing quite a lot of blood. The chair I'd been taped to sat—still upended—a few feet away. Ryan must have cut me free.

"How long was I out?"

"Just a few minutes," Ryan said. "The paramedics aren't even here yet. Don't move too much, okay?"

I nodded, which sent another wave of pain through my head. I raised my hand to my head, feeling for the goose egg I already knew was there.

"What happened?"

"I heard a smash and rushed out to my balcony to see what was up, and there were still a few pieces of glass raining down to the street. Which got me thinking about the thumping sounds I'd heard earlier. It hadn't occurred to me that they were coming from Erica's apartment. But somehow the falling glass made me realize."

My eyes widened. "Was Michael still in here?"

"He was racing down the hall, trying to get away."

I smiled. "But you stopped him."

"No," he said, shifting a little. "I just kept wondering about the glass and the thumping and I thought Annie, or maybe you," he said, meeting my eyes, letting me know how worried he'd been, "had been in here."

"You risked letting him get away to help me?"

He nodded. "And I would do it again."

My smile widened, then fell away. "But you said you had him."

Ryan nodded. "Hazel from security came to the rescue. She was just coming on shift and saw the glass too. She headed for the stairs to see what was going on and since Michael had seen me coming off the elevator, he took the stairs instead." He shrugged. "Poor choice on his part. Hazel knew right away that he was up to no good and detained him."

"I always liked that girl," I said, moving my jaw a little, testing how far the pain went.

The paramedics came in then and pulled Ryan away so they could shine lights in my eyes and press a bit on my goose egg—basically doing everything that would make me hurt just a bit more. In the end though, they said I would be okay and that I didn't need to go to the hospital.

They checked out Annie and gave her the same prognosis.

By then the cops had arrived and were taking everyone's statement, sitting us one by one on the couch to do so.

I was oh so lucky enough to be questioned by Jess, the detective who clearly had a history with Ryan, but I relayed everything that went down without letting it affect me. Much. I told them all about how he'd hurt Annie and then started rummaging through the place.

"I think I was kind of annoying him," I said. "I was doing it on purpose, trying to distract him from what he was doing."

Detective Jess glanced up from her notepad. "And what was he doing?"

"Just rummaging around in everything looking for the…"

And I'm not sure why my eyes chose that second to land on Erica's fancy clock on the mantel above her fireplace at the exact time I was saying those words, but they did. And that made it all click. The way Erica's hand had been pointing to that clock in the puzzle. I always knew my Nancy love would be the thing that saved me.

Well, okay, I had already technically been saved, but the full mystery had yet to be solved.

Detective Jess stared at me, no doubt wondering if I was having some sort of medical issue, but in that moment, I couldn't think about her. All I could think about was the very first Nancy novel—*The Secret of the Old Clock*—because the clock in that book had a secret compartment.

I held my breath and fought through the pain as I got up and limped over to the clock, pulling it from the mantel. It was heavier than I thought it would be.

I turned it around so the back was facing me but couldn't see any obvious openings or compartments. Which I suppose was good or else Michael may have found it, but I did encounter my first niggle of doubt.

I flipped it upside down. Same thing.

Then I shook it, and I was sure Annie was about to tell me to put the poor thing down—it probably wasn't super constructive to shake an antique clock after all—but then she heard the same thing I heard.

A distinct rustle of paper.

"Is there something in there?" she asked, moving closer.

I nodded. "I think so. I just have to figure out how to get—"

I'd been fiddling with the face of the clock, wondering if perhaps it might somehow flip open when...it did! The entire face hinged open to reveal the compartment that I had hoped beyond hope existed.

I reached in and withdrew the few sheets of paper hidden inside, unfolding them to see perhaps the most beautiful words in the English language.

"Last Will and Testament."

"We need to get this to whoever is dealing with Erica's estate," I said.

Annie nodded, speechless since the clock had revealed its secret. Finally, she spoke. "I'll call Kathleen."

I relayed the rest of my story to the police, including my suspicion about the double wills, and how Erica had been coerced into the first one, but had been smart enough to write a second, hiding it.

"There's just one thing I can't figure out," I said. "I don't understand why she would tell Michael about the second will."

"She must not have had time to tell anyone else about it before Michael got to her," Ryan said. "Maybe she thought if her apartment was ransacked from his searching, someone might clue in as to what he was looking for. It might have been the only way anyone would know they should even be looking for something."

"Right, that makes sense," I said. "Still, that was a risky move."

He nodded. "It must have been the only move she had left."

A moment of silence fell over the room then, until Detective Jess cleared her throat. "Well, I guess we're about done here," she said. "Ryan, can I walk you back to your apartment?"

I had to admit, I did not love the way her eyebrow rose in a sort of "come hither" way.

Ryan looked from Jess to me, then back to Jess. "Actually, yeah," he said, and I hated to admit how much my heart sank in that moment. "In fact," he continued, gently grabbing hold of my elbow, "you and I are both going to make sure Petra gets back to her place safe and sound."

It was all I could do not to jump up and down and squeal. Which probably would have hurt quite a lot, so I just did it in my mind instead. I wish I could say the look of disappointment on Jess's face didn't affect me, but honestly, I was feeling extraordinarily gloaty. Of course, then I started wondering why, exactly, he wanted her there when he walked me back to my place.

"You guys go ahead. I'll make sure everything's locked up tight," Hazel—who'd been up there observing since the cops showed up—chimed in.

"Thanks, Hazel," Ryan said.

I was so aware of his hand on my lower back, gently guiding me out of the apartment, I don't even remember how we got to the elevator, but as we stepped in, he let go and I regained my ability to think.

"Are you sure you're okay?" he asked.

"Yeah, I think so," I said. "I think I just need some sleep."

"Did the paramedics say that was okay? No risk of concussion or anything?"

I nodded. "I asked. They said sleep would probably do me good."

"Okay, good," he said as the elevator doors opened on our floor.

We headed down the hall, a little twinge of disappointment zipping through me that he didn't put his hand on my back again.

And way too fast we were at my door, me fiddling to find my key, as was my way.

"Before you go in," Ryan said, "there's something we all need to discuss."

"I really don't know, outside of what just happened upstairs, what the three of us would have to discuss," Jess said.

And as much as I didn't want to be, I was definitely on the same page as Detective Jess about that.

But Ryan continued. "Normally I would agree, and this certainly isn't a conversation I ever envisioned myself having to have, but there is the little issue of a certain anonymous admirer."

"Ugh," I groaned. "Do we really have to file a report? Or can we at least do it some other time? My head is still killing me and honestly, I'd just like to relax," I said.

But then I noticed the tension in the hallway had increased about a millionfold and that Jess had gone unnervingly still. Ryan hadn't taken his eyes off her.

And I couldn't, for the life of Nancy, figure out what the hell was going on.

But something definitely was.

"Shit," Jess finally said, sort of under her breath.

"No kidding," Ryan said. "What the hell were you thinking?"

My eyeballs bounced between Ryan and Jess like they were playing Ping-Pong. "Um, not to get in the middle of something, but can someone tell me what's going on?"

"Oh, you're definitely in the middle of it whether you like

it or not," Ryan said, though from his tone, he was decidedly not happy to have me in the middle of…whatever this was.

"I've been doing some research on your 'anonymous admirer,'" he said, using air quotes and everything.

"Okay…" I said, the word trailing off like a question.

Ryan turned to Jess and stared. "Are you going to tell her or am I?" he asked. As hard as I tried, I was absolutely not catching on.

And then Jess opened her mouth and I thought she was about to, I don't know, do something police-y, but then she said, "I'll stop, I promise. Just don't go to the captain with this."

Wait. What?

"That will be up to Petra," Ryan said, and it seemed like this whole conversation was starting to mean that Jess was the one who had been sending the gifts, which made absolutely no sense at all. Still searching the ground for an answer that clearly wasn't going to be found there, my body spit out the word "Why?" before I could even stop it.

Jess let out a long sigh and scratched her forehead. She looked like she would be much happier if the building would just go ahead and crumble all around us.

"I don't know. I just, ugh…" She winced as if she were in pain. "I guess I didn't like the attention you were getting. I wanted it to seem like maybe you were unavailable, and… I don't know, make things a bit uncomfortable for you in the process." She glanced at Ryan.

And that was the moment he started looking like he was kind of in pain too. Or maybe it was more like that awful secondhand embarrassment you get when you're watching the auditions of a singing reality TV show and the person thinks they're amazing when they're clearly not.

"Look," Ryan said, "we've been over this, Jess. I'm sorry about that one night, but I've told you, I'm not looking to get into anything."

"With me, anyway," she said, turning to stare daggers into me, which seemed kind of uncalled-for.

He sighed. "Yeah, I guess with you, Jess. Are you happy? Is that what you wanted to hear?"

And then the hardened detective's eyes welled up, and I really, really don't do well when someone else's eyes well up because it always makes my eyes want to well up and then I start thinking about what it must be like to be in their situation and lord knows I'd had my fair share of dating rejection all the way back to Jacob Corby in seventh grade when he made me think he was into me, except what he was really into was someone else doing his English essay for him.

But then she covered her tears by getting even angrier, this time aiming her resentment at me. "Are you going to press charges, or not?"

"I… I…" I stuttered, still in shock that my anonymous admirer was a woman who was, what? Jealous of…me? That was definitely something I needed a minute with. But now that the identity of said admirer was out in the open, I was fairly certain the gifts would stop. Which, to be honest, was kind of a shame. I mean, this woman knew how to send a gift, I thought, wistfully wondering how Jack P. was doing. But then I pulled my shoulders back. "No. I'm not going to press charges."

"Okay then," Detective Jess said with a nod. She turned and walked away, unable to even glance at Ryan again.

And then she was at the elevator, and it took forever for it to get there, and Jess stared so hard at those doors I was afraid she might burn a hole through them, until finally the doors opened and she got on. As the doors were closing, I couldn't stop myself from yelling, "They were really good chocolates!"

And then she was gone.

I turned slowly to Ryan.

"Um, that was unexpected."

"It was," Ryan agreed. "I, uh, I'm sorry for being mad at you about the anonymous-admirer thing."

"Because…" I let the word trail off.

I knew he felt responsible, and after all the grief he'd given me, I couldn't help but make him squirm a little.

He ran a hand through his hair. "Because I slept with her, okay? And it was a long time ago and it was just one stupid night when I was on a stakeout with her since we were working the same case. We ended up catching the bad guys and went for drinks to celebrate and one thing led to another, and well, it was stupid. Because she got attached. And didn't seem to want to let it go. But mostly, I could avoid her. Until this thing in our building. Which I guess… set her off again."

I nodded, trying my best to process that little bout of word vomit.

"I thought you said you didn't use the term *bad guys*."

"That's what you got out of all that?"

I shrugged. "I'm still processing."

"How long do you think you're going to need for that?" he asked.

I tilted my head one way, and then the other, my head

feeling surprisingly better. "I think I'm good. There's just one thing I don't entirely get. Why did she fixate on me?"

"It was because..." he started to say, then paused.

That look of uncomfortable pain came over him again and I decided the poor guy had been tortured enough for one day.

"Well, thanks for everything," I said, finally moving my key toward the lock.

"Thank you," he said. "Without you, I'm not sure anyone ever would have found the other will and Kathleen would have been out of luck. Maybe even out on the street."

I shrugged one shoulder. "I didn't really do anything."

Ryan gave me kind of a stern look then, like he was going to lay into me about not giving myself enough credit or something, but then, he apparently decided to do something different.

He moved in close. "It was because she was always able to tell when I was into someone else."

And then he leaned down and kissed me.

And I nearly fell to the floor.

But somehow, I remained upright and even found a way to ease into the kiss as if it had been expected all along. His lips were warm and soft, energy flowing through them straight into me, swirling to my toes. He put his hand on the back of my neck and pulled me closer—gentle but somehow also urgent.

I'm embarrassed to say I may have moaned a little.

But the moan only seemed to get him more fired up as he pulled me tighter, then put his hands under my butt, hiking me onto his hips.

Funny how certain things—adrenaline, a shock of surprise, a concentrated shot of longing straight to the nether regions—can make the exhaustion of an impossible day completely disappear.

Ryan pulled back and looked at me, though all I wanted was to feel his lips again, for them to never leave mine. He moved toward his apartment door and had it open in three seconds flat.

Show-off.

"I'd really love to take this to the bedroom," he said in a gravelly voice. "But I don't want to rush if you don't want to."

My head nodded rapidly and of its own accord, like some kind of bobblehead, hopefully a sexy one (ooh, sexy bobblehead. New Halloween costume?). "Bedroom, yes, please. Rushing can be good sometimes," I said, even though I'd imagined the moment so many times it hardly felt like rushing.

My limbs were heavy, wholly relaxed, as he eased me onto the bed, then stood to tear off his shirt and holy moly, was *that* worth the wait. I scrabbled with my own shirt, arms flailing like I'd grown an extra set and all they wanted to do was tangle. Finally free, his hand found my waist and he closed the gap between us, the heat of our skin threatening to ignite a fire as my legs wrapped around him. He pressed against me, crushing his hips to mine, easing the exquisite pressure, but only for a moment before it built again, tenfold.

He kissed my neck, and up under my ear, then began to work his way down, tasting his way—an explorer mapping new worlds—my breath catching as he moved to my breast, lips grazing over the lacy fabric of my bra, my body reacting immediately and intensely. I fought to release myself from the cloth prison, flinging the offending annoyance across the room, running my hand through his hair as he took my breast into his mouth, an epicenter of pleasure pulsing shock waves through me.

My hands uncovered all the mysteries of his body— I couldn't get enough of his arms, his strong back—and then as he rose, his chest…his zipper. All the clothes had to go, a frantic flurry of rushing, hurrying, racing…then everything slowing as our bodies came together again, tumbling onto the bed, taking a moment just to look at each other and breathe.

Ryan tucked a strand of hair behind my ear and kissed me again, gently this time, though the gentleness didn't last long as I wrapped around him, rising to him, a wave of need. His weight, his mouth, his hands. I wanted him more than I wanted to breathe. And then he was inside me and everything blurred, fell away. That feeling of home again.

His mouth found mine and we lost ourselves to each other in a haze of movement—hips, hands, legs. Time somehow moved both too fast and too slow as the desire, the demand, the hunger built until finally, I cried out in release. He tensed, his own release crashing through him.

He collapsed onto me as we both trembled, my arms weak and falling away as we tried to catch our breath, my mind taking its time coming back to my body, having vacated to another plane of existence somewhere along the way.

Eventually he managed to roll off me and pulled me close.

"Sorry, I'm a little dazed," he said, his signature smirk playing at his lips.

I nodded. "I know the feeling. Dazed but utterly satisfied."

"Yeah," he said, breathing hard.

He leaned up on one elbow, running his hand across my stomach. "I think I'm going to enjoy being right across the hall from you."

"It really is lucky," I said, raising an eyebrow. "You'll be able to consult with me on all your cases now."

His smirk tugged the corner of his lip a little farther up. "Not exactly what I meant," he said, leaning in for a long, slow kiss as he slid his hand up my side.

IT TOOK ANOTHER round for the exhaustion to finally catch up with us. I wasn't quite ready to spend the night—it seemed like too much too soon, and I wanted to savor every moment of whatever this Ryan and me thing was going to be—so, half-dressed, we found ourselves at his door.

He looked at me and smiled.

I smiled back.

"I'll see you tomorrow?"

"Absolutely." He leaned down and gave me one last, sweet kiss.

"Mmm…good night," I said, eventually tearing myself away.

It took everything in me to wait until I made it safely into my own apartment before I jumped up with a fist pump and let out a little squeal.

But then, when I glanced up and noticed the state of my apartment, all thoughts of Ryan shot straight out of my head.

Because there was something much, much more shocking happening on my floor.

Two entangled bodies, naked and barely covered with my tiny couch blanket, were sprawled in the middle of my living room.

What was even more shocking was that those two bodies belonged to very familiar people.

Brandt and Vic.

I nearly dropped my keys.

After a moment or two of utter astoundment—opening and closing my mouth like a fish—I blinked, and then smiled. Man, was I going to heckle them when they woke up.

Stepping over my two best friends and into my room, I crawled into bed.

But instead of dropping into the longest sleep of my life, I found I suddenly wasn't tired.

I had also suddenly come to a realization. The character I wanted to write—the Amelia Jones in my head—was so complete already, so kick-ass in every way, that there was nowhere interesting for her to go. No room to grow.

Maybe I needed her to be…a little flawed. A little unsure. A little more real.

A little more like me.

And suddenly my mind filled with ideas. With potential. With stories.

I pulled out my laptop and began to write.

* * * * *

COMING SOON!

We really hope you enjoyed reading this book.
If you're looking for more romance
be sure to head to the shops when
new books are available on

Thursday 14th March

To see which titles are coming soon, please visit
millsandboon.co.uk/nextmonth

MILLS & BOON

afterglow BOOKS

Introducing our newest series, Afterglow.

From showing up to glowing up, Afterglow characters are on the path to leading their best lives and finding romance along the way – with a dash of sizzling spice!

Follow characters from all walks of life as they chase their dreams and find that true love is only the beginning...

OUT NOW

millsandboon.co.uk

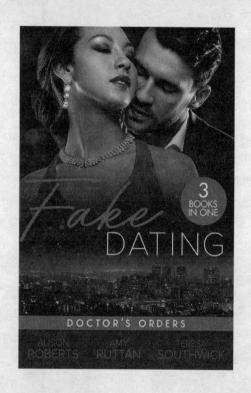